Under the Apple Tree . . .

Half way down the hill, almost hidden from their view by the canopy of the tree under which they stood, two blue figures watched another in a sports-coat crouching over something covered with a white sheet.

An unmistakeable shape lying under a white sheet. Martin stared at it, feeling suddenly a bit sick. He noticed a booted toe poking out at one end, some brown, shrivelled apple cores huddling in a fold of linen.

"What's doing?" said Toby, almost casually.
Without a word one of the uniformed police who had been standing guard bent down and whisked the white cloth away. A faint whiff of camphor and the sour smell of sickness rose into the air. Damien Treloar, glazed eyes staring, mouth twisted into a horror, looked up at them. He was very, very dead.

GRIM PICKINGS

Jennifer Rowe

BANTAM BOOKS
NEW YORK · TORONTO · LONDON · SYDNEY · AUCKLAND

GRIM PICKINGS
A Bantam Crime Line Book/September 1991

*Bantam Books are published by Bantam Books, a division of
Bantam Doubleday Dell Publishing Group, Inc. Its trademark,
consisting of the words "Bantam Books" and the portrayal of a
rooster, is Registered in U.S. Patent and Trademark Office and
in other countries. Marca Registrada. Bantam Books, 666 Fifth
Avenue, New York, New York 10103.*

PRINTED IN THE UNITED STATES OF AMERICA

RAD   0 9 8 7 6 5 4 3 2 1

For Ruth, Mim and Roz, with thanks

Cast of Characters

☙☙☙

The owner of the apple orchard
Alice Allcott

The Tender family
Betsy Tender, Alice Allcott's niece, a housewife
Wilf Tender, Betsy's husband, a real estate salesman
Chris Tender, their son, a schoolteacher
Susan (Sonsy) Tender, his wife, a nursing sister
Anna Treloar, Betsy and Wilf's daughter, a model
Damien Treloar, Anna's estranged husband, an antique
   dealer
Rodney Tender, Betsy and Wilf's youngest child, a high
   school student

The other house party guests
Jeremy Darcy, a friend of Chris Tender, a journalist
Kate Delaney, his wife, a book editor
Zoe Darcy, their 7-year-old daughter
Verity (Birdie) Birdwood, friend of Kate, a research
   assistant
Nick Bedford, friend of Chris and Jeremy, an academic
Jill Mission, Nick's defacto wife, a book editor

The neighbours
Theresa Sullivan, craft shop owner
Nel Sullivan, her baby daughter

The police
Simon Toby, Detective-sergeant
Martin McGlinchy, Detective-constable

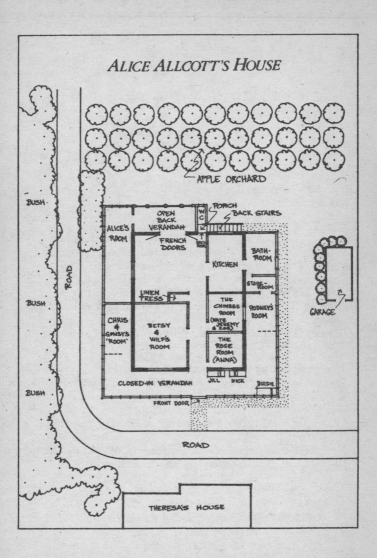

ALICE ALLCOTT'S HOUSE

APPLE ORCHARD

BUSH

BUSH

BUSH

ROAD

ALICE'S ROOM

OPEN BACK VERANDAH

FRENCH DOORS

WC

PORCH

BACK STAIRS

KITCHEN

BATH-ROOM

LINEN PRESS

STORE-ROOM

THE CHINESE ROOM (KATE, JEREMY & ZOE)

RODNEY'S ROOM

CHRIS & GINGY'S 'ROOM'

BETSY & WILF'S ROOM

THE ROSE ROOM (ANNA)

CLOSED-IN VERANDAH

JILL NICK

BIRDIE

FRONT DOOR

GARAGE

ROAD

THERESA'S HOUSE

Contents

1

Into Apple Country

₷₷₷

'I suppose the whole bunch'll be up there again this year,'
Jeremy groaned. 'The Tender family en masse . . . I think
I'm getting too old to cope with it, Kate.'

Kate laughed at her husband as he hunched over
the wheel.

'You said that last year, *and* the year before that!
You always end up enjoying yourself. I don't know
why you have to go through this ritualised complaint!
Chris is one of your oldest friends, after all.'

'Maybe he is. That doesn't mean I have to live in
his loopy family's pocket, does it? Or trek up the
mountains to break my back over his great aunt's apple trees every year for that matter.'

'Oh go on—poor old Alice—once a year! Anyway, you used to love the apple-picking. In the old
days . . .'

'Yeah . . . well . . .' Jeremy sighed. 'It's not the
same anymore, is it? Even Chris isn't the same. We
have less in common every time we see each other
these days. He wouldn't have minded if we'd said we
couldn't make it this year.'

'Betsy would've. She was terribly keen to have all
the same old crowd, as she put it, together again. You
know,' said Kate, smiling to herself, 'on the phone she

got quite sentimental. She told me that you were like a brother to Chris, and that made you, sort of, her son as well.'

'Oh, perish the thought!'

'Think of my position. It makes her my mother-in-law, which is infinitely worse.' Kate shook her head. 'Poor old Betsy. Zoe loves her, anyway.'

'You love everyone when you're seven.'

'Oh no you don't. Zoe's quite capable of hating people to the death. But Betsy's good with kids.'

Kate twisted round to check the back seat. Zoe rocked in her seat-belt, eyes closed, *The Folk of the Faraway Tree* still clutched in one hand.

'She's still asleep. No wonder. She was still awake at eleven last night, she was so excited about today. She adores Alice's place. And come on, Jeremy, it won't be that bad. Nick and Jill will be there like always. Betsy wasn't going to let them off the hook, either. And think of the pastoral bliss—the crisp Blue Mountains mornings, the apples winking through the mist, the green grass caressing your gumboots . . .'

'The leeches screaming for blood.'

'Oh, yes, I'd forgotten about them. Heavens, I must remind Zoe before tomorrow.'

'Yeah.'

Kate fell silent. She looked out at the valleys falling away from the road in misty blue folds and shivered a little. It was getting cold.

The car sped on through the lengthening shadows, following the twists and turns of a road that climbed higher and higher, into apple country.

Anna lugged her bag into the Rose room and put it down on the chair in the corner. The late afternoon sun leaked secondhand through the dusty window pane that looked out onto the closed-in front verandah. The smell of the old room, just the same as ever, made her feel like a child again. She always had the

Rose room when the family came to Auntie Alice's place for the annual apple-picking. Except for last year—well, she wouldn't think of that. She sat on the bed with its flounced, faded chintz cover, and looked around her. Roses still showed pink on the thin carpet square. Roses, beautiful art-deco roses, twined along the thin wallpaper frieze below the picture rail: pink roses, green leaves, pink, green, pink, green, all around the room. She used to lie in bed in the chilly mountain mornings, cosy, half-asleep, counting the roses. It was hard to keep count. You kept losing your place, and having to start again. There were thirty-six. She'd finally established that when she was twelve.

She looked at her reflection in the wardrobe mirror. Not twelve anymore, but twice twelve. No more little girl, with fringe and ponytail. Now the old mirror showed a young woman with a smooth cap of dark hair, a fine-boned model's face, big brown eyes. It was a very beautiful face. She accepted that quite easily. After all, she made her living by it. Being beautiful was her job. Had been, she thought ruefully, long before she started earning money at it.

'Darling!'

It was her mother's voice. Anna jumped guiltily off the bed.

'When you've finished there could you come and help me? In Christopher's room?'

'Yes, Mum, sorry . . . I'll be just a sec.'

She quickly stripped off the flimsy bedspread and the thin grey blankets that lay beneath. She began making up the bed with the pink sheets her mother had laid out. How typical of Mum: pink sheets for Anna, for the Rose room.

She stretched over to tuck the sheets in against the wall. It wasn't a long stretch. The bed was very narrow—a real maiden's couch, she thought grimly. Last year, for once, she hadn't slept in this bed, but on a mattress on the closed-in side verandah—with Damien. A married couple had to have a double bed, even on holiday, by her mother's lights, however much she might disapprove of the match.

Well, that was last year. Now Damien was gone and she—she was back in the Rose room.

She left the room, and walked out the old front door on to the closed-in verandah that ran around three sides of the house. Round to the right, at the side, where the verandah was sectioned off with a rough masonite partition, Betsy was struggling to spread a pale blue striped sheet over the double mattress on the floor. The old wardrobe stood ready to be pulled into its place at the foot of the mattress, to provide a fourth wall. Anna smiled wryly. This year her brother Chris and his new wife were to share the connubial couch. Ah well, life went on.

'Come on, darling, I'm dying for a cup of tea.'

'Mum, why don't you just leave it to them to do?'

'Oh, I like to have everything nice when they arrive. And, honestly, Anna, the way Christopher's living with poor little Sue I think he'll be thrilled to have a nicely made bed and some good clean sheets to snuggle into for a change. Really, she has no idea!'

They tucked, pulled up the second sheet, tucked again and began arranging the blankets. Betsy went on:

'The house is always in chaos—clothes everywhere, dirty dishes in the sink. You know how fastidious Christopher is. It must be distressing for him. I'm nearly sick with worry about it all.'

'If Chris finds it so upsetting there's nothing to stop him cleaning it up, is there?' said Anna irritably. She paused. 'Damien always did half the housework.' It cost her an effort even to say his name.

Her mother straightened up and looked at her. 'Surely you aren't holding up Damien as some sort of example, darling, after what he put you through?'

'No, no I didn't mean to bring him up, God knows. I just meant that Sonsy works all day at the hospital.

In fact, she's often on night shift, isn't she? She works just as hard as Chris does.'

'Well, I don't know about that, Anna. She works with her hands, certainly, and there's nothing wrong with that. But Christopher works with his mind. That's infinitely more tiring. He admits that himself. He can't be expected to slave away at housework after teaching all day. I know he does a fair bit, because he's let that much slip, poor old boy. It's not that he ever complains. He's very loyal to poor little Sue.' She sighed.

'Mum, Sonsy's not too bright, but she's . . . she adores Chris. She'd . . .'

'Oh, darling, I'm not criticising Sue, please don't think that. For goodness sake, it's none of my business! And I'm really very fond of Sue in a way. I think she tries hard. But she hasn't had the advantages of a good home—and it's not as if she's terribly willing to learn differently—to fit in with the sort of life Christopher has always planned for himself. Marriage should be a partnership, Anna—give and take on both sides, and I'm just sorry that . . .'

'Yes, Mum, yes I know,' Anna interrupted. She couldn't bear to go on talking about it. Couldn't go on resisting her mother's eloquence for the dubious honour of carrying her little sister-in-law's tattered banner. Betsy was right—Chris must be repenting his marriage; certainly was, in fact, because despite her mother's disclaimers, it was obvious she had talked the whole thing over with him.

They pulled up the gay crocheted rug that served as a bedspread and smoothed it down, then between them dragged the wardrobe into position, leaving room for a doorway. A tea chest with another rug over it stood against the wall beside the mattress, and a small vase of wildflowers had been placed upon it. Another little touch of welcome for Chris and Sonsy. Anna had a similar offering in her room. Really, Mum was indefatigable.

'Well, that looks rather cosy, doesn't it?' said Betsy, looking round the little makeshift bedroom with satisfaction.

Suddenly Anna felt a warm rush of affection for her mother. She tried so hard and did so much—and they took it all for granted. And she worried so much about them all—poor old Dad, the business just dwindling away, she and the mess with Damien, Rodney, helplessly adolescent, and now Chris and silly little Sonsy—heavens, even her nickname was childish. Betsy looked elegant and well-groomed as ever, but now, in her softened mood, Anna saw that there were fine lines of strain around her mother's eyes and mouth; that she looked suddenly a little older, a little tireder. No wonder, being the pillar on which such a rocky family temple rested.

She went over and put her arm around her mother's shoulders.

'Poor old Mum, your kids aren't very good pickers, are they? Look, come on, I'll make us a cup of tea, and then I'll do Kate and Jeremy's room.'

Betsy looked up at her daughter gratefully. 'A cup of tea would be marvellous.'

They walked together around the corner of the verandah and towards the door into the hallway.

'Shame the verandah was ever closed in, really, wasn't it?' said Anna. 'The house'd look much better if it was open.'

'Yes, I suppose so, Anna. Poor old Auntie Alice certainly doesn't need the space, up here all alone. But when we're here for the apple-picking it comes in handy. How would we ever fit in if we didn't have the verandah? Christopher and Sue are there, Rodney's on the other side, and there's room along here at the front for Nick and Jill.'

Anna looked at the camp stretchers sitting primly nose to tail along the verandah wall. No honeymoon suite for Nick and Jill. They may have been living together for as long as Kate and Jeremy had been married—twelve or thirteen years, it must be now. But in Betsy's eyes they were single people and accordingly slept apart. This might be Alice Allcott's house, but the annual apple-picking was a Betsy Tender production, played with her cast and by her rules.

They entered the house proper and walked down the dim corridor, past bedrooms opening on either side of them. Betsy and Wilf always had the big room on the left. It had been Auntie Alice's parents' room. Her mother had told her that it had always seemed very grand to her as a child and Anna could remember being slightly awed by it, too, not least by the tale that after Alice's father died, his will and a cache of sovereigns had been found in a tin box under a loose floorboard beneath the bed. Now the room just seemed over-furnished and depressing. Dim, dominated by the huge oak bedstead at one end and a massive carved wardrobe at the other, it ran the whole length of the corridor, except for the small slit that was the linen cupboard, next to the living room door. Piles of linen sheets, embroidered tablecloths and pillowcases with lace and covered buttons rose in there, in a haze of camphor.

Two bedrooms lay on the right—her own and the little room into which Kate, Jeremy and Zoe would somehow squeeze for the week. It was always called the Chinese room because of the lanterns that decorated the frieze below the picture rail. Auntie Alice used to sleep there, but a few years ago she'd had a partition put up, blocking off part of the closed-in verandah to create a bedroom for herself at the back of the house.

'I wonder why Auntie Alice moved out of her room, Mum? It would've been much warmer for her here than out on the verandah,' said Anna, looking curiously in at the doorway.

'Oh, Anna, heaven knows!' sighed Betsy. 'She said something about wanting to watch the trees. That's why she had the windows put in at the back and everything. She's really getting very . . . peculiar, you know, darling. I worry about her all alone up here. This holiday I'm really going to try to get her to agree to come down to Sydney to live, where I can keep an eye on her.'

They walked into the cluttered living room, and through a door on the right, into the kitchen. Anna filled the kettle and looked around her at the collected trivia of generations. A calendar dating from the Queen's Coronation hung on the wall next to an ancient railway timetable. A great black iron pot hung from a hook beside the old fuel stove. That at least would be worth having, thought Anna. It must date from the very early days. She suddenly felt depressed on Alice's behalf.

'Mum, she's always lived here. She'll never move.'

'She'll *have* to move, Anna. There's just no other solution. The house is too much for her—heavens, *look* at this kitchen, and that horrible old bathroom in there, all smelly from the lino, and that storeroom place next door. She'll just have to see reason. She'll be happy enough in a little unit in Sydney, as long as there's a view. She can take her favourite things with her. As it is she doesn't know where to find anything. You ask her about this or that and she just shrugs, or sends you on a wild goose chase. And your father and I can keep this place up—get rid of some of the clutter and turn it into a really nice holiday place for all of us. Poor Rodney—his friends at school are always having him to their beach houses, or ski lodges or whatever, and he really feels it that he can't return invitations like that. So it would really suit everyone. The best thing all round.'

Betsy stood for a moment, thinking, a small smile on her lips. You could almost hear the wheels going round in her head, Anna thought. Betsy was a great one for plans. And once a plan was made, in Betsy's view, that was that. She just expected that people would fall into line. The funny thing was, people usually did. But Anna suspected her mother may have met her match in Alice Allcott. She was a tough old bird, Auntie Alice.

Alice Allcott sat on her verandah, and let her mind drift. For how many years had she sat here, in the late afternoon, with the paper or a book, and watched the apple trees grow? For how many years? A lifetime. She had been born in this house, eighty years ago. She had learned to walk on the bare boards of the old corridor and the living room that was the house's centre and heart.

She had grown up with the apple trees, warmed by the mountain sun, braced by the mountain chill. She had lived her life by the seasons—the cold winters, when leafless boughs clattered together in the orchard; the chilly, exciting springs that brought the frail blossoms, and the bees; the warm, green summers and the autumns when the apples hung heavy on the trees, glistening red through the morning and evening mists.

The trees were old and gnarled now, like she was. She hadn't planted any new ones—not for a long time. She'd sold the back sections to some new people five years ago, because money was getting scarce, and it was hard keeping up the work. But she'd held on to the home trees. She'd always keep them, till she dropped. Then—well . . . then Betsy could have her way.

She heard voices behind her in the living room and instinctively lowered her head till her chin touched her chest. She breathed evenly.

The French doors behind her opened. 'She's asleep, Mum,' whispered Anna's voice. 'Leave her then, poor old thing.' That was Betsy. 'She's really getting very . . .' The door clicked shut.

Alice Allcott kept her head down. 'Poor old thing',

was it? Her jaw tightened. How was she going to stand
this week? Betsy was really getting to be a menace.
She'd never really been fond of Betsy, she thought
suddenly. Even as a girl she'd been a bossy, managing
little thing. A real goody two-shoes, too. So sure she
knew the best, even then. And now! Oh, Lord!

She shifted irritably in her chair, and leaned her
head back, letting her hooded eyes open until the trees
swam through her eyelashes in a golden mist. But still,
poor Bet was all the family she had, now. Her sister
Lily's girl, and Lily long gone. Nice of her to bother
with an old aunt, really. Popping up every month or
so, tidying up and everything. But then, Bet had always been one for doing the right thing, oh yes. Even
if she got no thanks for it.

Alice smiled slightly. Well, the week wouldn't last
forever. The picking would get done, and as usual she
wouldn't have to pay the pickers. She could hardly
have let her beauties drop and rot, after all, even if
they were all going to end up at the juice factory. The
old trees would be relieved of their load, and another
year's round would be complete. And as for this bee
Bet had in her bonnet, about moving to Sydney—well,
she'd just have to make Bet understand once and for
all that there was nothing doing! She'd just have to
lump it.

Alice leaned back in her chair, and watched her
trees grow.

In the kitchen Anna and her mother poured the tea
into mugs. Anna looked out the window above the
sink.

'Oh look, here's Dad,' she exclaimed, sighting the
familiar figure rounding the corner of the house.

She went into the living room to open the back door
for him. 'Hello, Dad, are you OK?' she said solicitously, taking the loaded shopping basket.

'Oh, fine, honey,' said her father, with a smile. 'I had a good walk.'

He looked tired, though, thought Anna. The walk had put some colour in his cheeks, but his hands were cold.

'Come into the kitchen. We're having a cup of tea,' she said, and putting an arm through his led him through to where her mother was waiting, smiling over three steaming mugs and a plate of rock cakes.

'Wilfie, you look frozen. Have a cup of tea. Did you get the milk?'

'Yes, got everything,' said Wilfred Tender, wrapping his hands around the warm mug and lowering himself cautiously on to a stool. 'It's a bit nippy out there. My word! Where's Alice?'

'Having a little snooze on the back verandah. It wasn't worth waking her for tea,' his wife answered. 'Looking very old, Wilf, isn't she?' she added in a lower voice.

'Yes, I suppose she is. Lost a bit of spark since I last saw her.' He smiled sadly. 'I s'pose we all have, Bet. The years will tell.'

Anna and Betsy exchanged glances. This was a common theme with Wilf lately.

'You know the old bloke opposite? The old bloke with the goat?' Wilf went on drearily.

'Oh, vaguely,' said Anna. 'Mr . . . Simpson or something . . . a little man, very skinny.'

'Yes, that's the one. Cranky old chap. Simkiss, not Simpson.' He waited.

'Yes,' said Betsy patiently. 'What about him, Wilf? Did you see him? Is that it? Perky as ever, I suppose.'

'No,' said Wilf. 'He's dead.'

Anna gave a snort of laughter.

'*Anna!*' said her mother disapprovingly. 'What's the matter with you?'

'It's no laughing matter, Anna,' said Wilf seriously. 'He just dropped, apparently. Heart.' He shook his head. 'I'd have thought Alice would have mentioned it, Bet.'

'No . . . she never . . . oh, wait a minute, of course she did. Oh, it was a good six months ago. I remember now. She didn't say that much about it. Seemed more glad than sorry—you know how she can be. The house was sold eventually. The sign was up for a long time. I wonder who bought it?'

'Oh, I met the lady on the way home,' said Wilf, cheering up at having some news to tell. 'Had a bit of a chat. Seems like a nice woman—a bit arty looking, but quite a pleasant person, really. Mrs. Sullivan her name is. She's a widow.'

'What's she look like, Wilfie?' Betsy asked. 'I've never seen hide nor hair of her when I've been up.'

'Oh, well, she's a big sort of woman—must be as tall as me, and big with it, you know the sort of thing. Don't know what Alice would make of her. She runs some sort of souvenir shop in town. Must be hard to make ends meet. She's got quite a young baby—no other kids, though.'

'Dear dear,' Betsy tutted. 'Her husband couldn't have died all that long ago then. What happened to him, Wilf?'

'For goodness sake, I could hardly ask the woman that, could I? Just talking over the front fence!'

'Well, I suppose not. I just thought it might have come up.' Betsy paused. 'Well, anyway, Wilfie, why don't you go and have a little lie down,' she went on briskly. 'The bed's all made up.'

'Why aren't all the others coming up tonight?' asked Anna, as she slowly gathered the remains of afternoon tea and carried them to the sink.

'Oh, Nick's got some university thing. Drama society or something. Dear old Nick. Christopher will be so pleased to see him, and Jeremy. He loves to get together with his mates. Always has. It takes him out of himself. They're nice boys. Old friends are golden: it's an old saying, but there's a lot of truth in it, Anna.'

'Yes,' said Anna drily. 'Of course, they're hardly boys anymore, Mum. And they're all married now— or as good as, in Nick's case.'

'Oh, well!' Betsy dismissed the wives with a shrug. 'The girls are welcome too, of course. Anyway, Nick and Jill will be up tomorrow morning. And I actually asked Kate's friend, what's her name, Verity, for to-morrow instead of tonight. I thought it would be eas-ier . . .' She broke off to usher Wilfred tenderly out of the kitchen and up the hall into the bedroom.

Anna finished clearing the table and wiped up the crumbs. She looked around. Heavens, this house was full of junk! Every available surface was cluttered. Every drawer was full. Old doorknobs, vases, hooks, tea-cosies, old bolts levered off doors and never thrown away, nails, packets of playing cards, and a thousand more objects without meaning or purpose tumbled to-gether in a mad miscellany in every crevice. Obvi-ously Auntie Alice never threw anything away. If she did decide to move to Sydney the clean-up would be fantastic!

Her mother reappeared. 'Here, darling, I'll do that. You get on to the Chinese room. The sheet are in there.'

'Where's this Verity going to sleep?'

'She'll just have to make do with the divan in the corner of the verandah, near Rodney. She's bringing a sleeping-bag, apparently. Actually, Anna, it's really a bit of a curse having a stranger pushed on us this year, with poor old Alice the way she is. But when Katie asked me I couldn't say no, really. You'd think Katie would have more sense.'

'Oh well, I suppose she thought you'd say no if it was inconvenient.'

'Darling, of course she didn't think any such thing. I'd never say no, you know that . . . Can't even think of the girl's last name . . . Verity . . . Verity . . . oh! Verity Birdwood, that's it! Verity Birdwood. Funny name, isn't it?'

'Oh! Birdie! That must be Birdie!' exclaimed Anna. Her mother turned to her. 'Do you know her, Anna?'

'Oh, no, I've never met her. But I've heard Jeremy mention her. She's something in the ABC. A research assistant, I think. A bit of a character, from what Jeremy said. She and Kate went to school together.'

'Oh well, I hope she fits in. I really want everything to go smoothly. Look, Anna, are you going to do that room or not? Well, just give Rodney a call on your way will you? He's out the back checking the ladders and things for tomorrow.'

Anna wandered off to do her appointed tasks. Betsy began washing up the tea things. Wilfred Tender lay staring at the ceiling in the bedroom. And Alice Allcott watched her trees grow as the shadows lengthened.

Sonsy stared out the window. Black shapes loomed and vanished at the side of the road. Every now and then a depressed-looking horse raised its head and stared as the car passed. Lighted windows shone in the old cottages that hunched among ranks of loaded trees, silvery in the moonlight, mist billowing around their knees.

The houses looked small, the lighted windows friendly. She wished she and Chris were going to one of them—going anywhere except to Aunt Alice's old rambling weatherboard, full of childhood memories for her husband, full of his family, his clever, joking friends, his elegant, concerned mother. She folded her hands, one over the other, in her lap, and tucked her chin into her chest.

'Spark up, Sonsy!' Chris turned to glance at her, the small line she dreaded creasing the space between his eyebrows.

'Oh, I'm OK. I'm just, you know, relaxing. I had a hard day,' she gabbled. Oh, she was hopeless, she thought in despair. Why couldn't she just be cool. Take things in her stride. God knows, she spent all day every day keeping the old dears calm at the hospital. Everyone there thought she was permanently happy and unflappable. Communist plots, kidnappers, poison in the tea—there was no fear, practically, that she hadn't met with in her patients, and she could always settle them down. Why couldn't she get control of her own stupid terrors? She had to. Now, especially. Nurse, heal thyself, she thought sternly, and smiled at her own joke.

'That's better!' Chris said approvingly, glancing at her again. Then his voice softened. 'Darling, I know you're not looking forward to this. I know Mum's sometimes a bit of a trial, but she loves these family things. The apple-picking's really fun. And Kate'll be there, don't forget. You like Kate, don't you?'

'Oh yes, Kate's nice,' said Sonsy. 'And Jeremy's interesting—but I don't think he likes me.'

'Of course he does, dingbat. How could he help it?' Chris reached over and took her warm, rough little hand. 'How about turning on the news?'

Suddenly everything was all right again. She'd been silly to get in a stew. What could Betsy do to her, anyway? Sonsy turned on the radio. They moved on through the dark.

2

The Old Crowd

☙

They sat in the living room, after dinner. A big fire crackled; drawn curtains shut out the cold, misty night.

Zoe had retired to her camp stretcher in the Chinese room with enormous anticipation and delight, and had quickly fallen asleep, despite her doze in the car. She remembered the house from last year, and the year before—remembered it better than Kate did, actually. Everything about the rambling old place was exotic and fascinating to Zoe, from the mantelpiece clock that chimed every quarter hour to the mossy stones by the old water tank.

Usually Kate felt enormously relaxed once Zoe was safely asleep in a strange place, as though a hurdle long looming had been successfully jumped. But tonight, though she lounged back with every appearance of contentment in her comfortable chair, her stomach full of Betsy's good soup and apple pie, the embroidery that only seemed to get done on holidays waiting on her lap, a feeling of tension kept her mind nervy and active. The situation felt strange—ridiculous, though, that it should, she told herself. This was their seventh year apple-picking. She knew all these people very well.

Old Alice sat by the fire as she always did, in the

same wicker chair with the same pale, soft cushions padding the seat and the back. She didn't look any older, but she did look tireder, and she had been strangely silent when they arrived. She'd just smiled and nodded at them, leaving all the welcome and bustle to Betsy. That wasn't like her, not at all.

Kate sighed. Well, she was getting on a bit, old Alice. Maybe all this was a bit overwhelming. Maybe she was losing her grip a little. She'd talked to Zoe, while Betsy was settling Chris and Sonsy in, but even that was a bit—disturbing. Kate had come in from the bedroom and found them, heads together, over an old book—a *Pilgrim's Progress* with lithographs. Zoe was tracing with a fascinated finger the lovingly detailed miniature burdens, scaly and horrible, carried by some junior seekers after truth in one particularly gruesome plate, when her mother appeared.

'We couldn't find *Elves and Fairies*, but Auntie Alice found this and it's even better. She's going to find me her old train, and her Noah's Ark, soon, too. Look, Mum, see, I told you! Children do have sins. Mr Blakely said so, and here's a picture of it!' she'd said challengingly.

'Zoe, I never said . . . there are lots of ways of looking at . . .' Kate had begun lamely, with a sense of the impossibility of impressing her daughter with a complicated view of life, death and infinity at this hour of the night, given the more attractively simple evidence offered by Mr Blakely, who gave jellybeans for correct answers in Scripture, and the unknown *Pilgrim's Progress* lithographer.

'I bet Jamie Nettsby would have the biggest burden of all our class,' Zoe had said seriously. 'He punches girls, you know, Mum.'

'Oh, he mightn't have the biggest one, you never know,' Kate had said, half delighted, half appalled by this religious discussion.

'No,' Alice had turned back to the fire, 'it depends on what you call sins, like I said. You might find that the biggest, ugliest lump turns up on the person you'd least expect. The one who seems to be a perfect specimen might be black and rotten to the core. You never know.'

Kate had led the highly stimulated Zoe away to change into her pyjamas with some misgivings. Alice was a fascinating character, but maybe rather rich fare for a 7-year-old of Zoe's imagination.

But no dreams of hideous sin-burdens or rotten apples seemed to be disturbing her daughter's slumbers now, anyway, and Kate found herself musing on the elemental nature of the old lady sitting so unmoving by the fire. What a bizarre contrast to her guests she seemed, with her craggy old face, long grey plait and shapeless, almost tattered garments.

There was Betsy, with her glossy, professionally set hair, her discreet but immaculate make-up over a still fine pink and white complexion, her bright brown darting eyes and trim, even elegant, figure. Tailored beige slacks, expensive polo-necked cashmere pullover in shades of pink, little suede boots: the perfect figure of an attractive matron on holiday. She was talking vivaciously to Chris and Jeremy at present—about their university days, and how she, Betsy, hoped that young Rodney would have as good a time as they had had when his turn came.

Behind her, in the shadows, sat Wilfred Tender—Wilf, as negative as Betsy was positive. If Betsy reminded Kate of a wren, busy, smart, head ever-cocked for the sound of a juicy worm within reach of her sharp little beak, Wilf was like a mopoke: grey, tousled and mournful. He was a short, plumpish man with a rather hesitating voice. His eyes were very pale blue, his hair sparse. What an unlikely pair, thought Kate, as so often before. And yet they seemed to rub along together all right.

Certainly the children of the marriage had got their looks from their mother. Beautiful Anna sat under the standard lamp on the other side of the room, her long

legs in boots and faded jeans tucked under her, a wine-
red jumper with a wide rolled neck throwing pink
shadows up to her soft, lovely face. The jumper had
been a present from her mother, she'd told Kate.
Lucky Anna—it must have cost a fortune. For all her
beauty she looked abstracted and nervy, Kate thought.
Her slender fingers rolled and fiddled with two dried
grass stalks while she stared out into the room without
appearing to notice what was going on around her.

Chris sat next to his mother, his arm around the
back of the couch behind her, laughing as he and Jeremy swapped reminiscences. He was thirty-four now,
and in Kate's view far better looking than he'd been
in his twenties, when his dark, brooding features, the
heavy eyebrows over deep-set eyes, strong nose and
soft, wide mouth, had been rather too great a burden
for his thin young face to carry, so that sometimes he
looked quite clownish—an effect that his ready wit
had encouraged him to exploit. Now he was heavier,
thicker set, and those strong features had come into
their own. What a shame, thought Kate, that with
that physical maturity the quixotic sense of fun that
had enlivened so many parties in the old days seemed
to have departed. Chris took himself more seriously
now, and it showed. Too many years as a teacher,
maybe. Too many years of being the boss frog in a
small pond.

Almost without thinking she moved her arm so that
it rested against Jeremy's knee. That hadn't happened
to Jeremy. He was still the same quick-tempered,
clever, funny man she'd married twelve years ago.

Just now he was laughing good-humouredly at a
rather weak sally offered by Rodney, whose adolescent gawkiness seemed to call up a protective urge in
Jeremy, when he was feeling generous. Rodney's un-
formed, slightly chubby face was creased with delight.
He was revelling in this loud, cosy chat with the fel-
las. The unexpected acceptance into the camaraderie
of adult male reminiscence and humour brought a

flush to his cheeks and an increasingly raucous tone to his voice.

On the other side of the room sat Sonsy, Chris's wife, well and truly excluded from this magic circle of light and fair laughter. She knew it, too. Kate looked at her and felt vaguely irritated. She'd been her usual bouncy, kittenish self when she and Chris had arrived just after Kate, Jeremy and Zoe. But she'd grown progressively quieter as the evening wore on and Betsy claimed more and more of Chris's attention. Good heavens, the child was obviously jealous of her husband's mother. How pathetic, thought Kate. If it mattered to her, why didn't she put up a bit of a fight instead of moping away like a puppy on a doorstep.

As if Sonsy felt her gaze she looked up, and Kate was shocked at the real unhappiness that deepened the blue eyes that met hers. Her feelings underwent a somersault. Oh, how could a little thing like this fight an old campaigner like Betsy, mistress of the velvet-muffled jibe, the sideways thrust? And why didn't Chris pull himself together and look after his bride of less than a year, whom he must expect to feel a bit strange in this atmosphere.

Betsy's voice rose to a squeak, disturbing Kate's pleasurably mounting ire.

'Ah, Roddy, they were naughty boys in those days! Christopher, Jeremy and Nick. The terrible trio! Oh dear, when I think of the nights I spent waiting for Christopher to come home—I was honestly in fear and trembling every time, waiting for the car to come in. Wasn't I Wilf?'

Wilfred Tender jumped a little at being so suddenly appealed to, and everyone else in the room seemed to blink, as though surprised to remember that he existed at all. He was dressed in shades of grey, and his clothes might almost have been chosen for camouflage, so successfully had he merged with the faded curtains in the shadowy corner he had chosen.

'Pardon? I didn't catch . . .'

'I was just saying to the boys, darling,' Betsy repeated, patiently lively, 'how I used to be frantic with worry when Christopher was late home, in the old days.'

'Oh . . . yes,' murmured Wilf. 'Nothing ever happened, though. There was no need.'

'Well, be that as it may,' Betsy said sharply, 'someone had to be aware of the comings and goings.' Suddenly she recovered her temper. 'Still,' she said, smiling indulgently around the room, 'boys will be boys! What could a poor old Mum do?'

'Plenty, in my case, Mum,' said Anna, with a rueful smile.

'You weren't a boy, darling. Girls have to be protected, for their own good. Now, Kate, surely you'll agree with that . . . now that you've got a little girl of your own?'

'Oh, yes,' Kate said. 'Yes. I think girls still need more protection than boys.'

'There you are then, you see, Anna?' nodded Betsy. 'Kate knows.'

'Still, though,' said Kate, following a line of thought, 'I hope—Jeremy and I hope—that at least we won't have to protect Zoe from herself. I mean, protection can go too far.' She became aware of a certain tension in the room. Betsy waited, smiling indulgently, her head on one side. Kate floundered on. 'I mean, you know, I hope she'll be self-assured enough for us to be able to look after her reasonably unobtrusively—without treating her like some halfwitted innocent who needs constant guarding.'

There was a little silence. Kate realised that her tongue had moved faster than her brain—yet again.

Betsy gave a tight little smile. 'Don't make the mistake of thinking that Wilf and I didn't respect Anna's intelligence, Katie,' she said.

'Oh, oh yes, no, of course, I didn't mean . . .' Kate burbled, cursing herself for a fool.

'Oh, Kate, of course you did!' snapped Anna, un-curling her slender legs and stretching them out in front of her. 'It's true!' She stared at her shining brown boot tops, with her strong eyebrows knitted.

'Anna, that is simply ridiculous darling. Your father and I . . .'

'It doesn't matter anymore, Mum. It mattered then, but I didn't know it then. The fact was that I didn't have any idea what life was all about. At twenty-one I was still a baby. It got me into all sorts of trouble.'

'You're still a baby I reckon,' Rodney broke in in-dignantly, his face flushed and his hands clenched. 'You can't blame Mum for you getting yourself mar-ried to a nurd like Damien.'

'Roddy, please!'

'Oh, shut up, Rodney. You wouldn't know.' Anna stood up and walked to the door. She dragged her parka from the pile waiting on the table and slipped it on. 'I'm going for a walk,' she said. The door closed behind her, and they heard her booted steps tap down the back stairs.

'Betsy, I'm sorry,' said Kate. 'I really didn't mean anything personal when I said . . .'

'That's all right, Katie.' Betsy smiled at her gently, regretfully. It was the smile of a woman who had suffered much. 'You weren't to know. Anna hasn't been herself since that unfortunate business with Da-mien. That man has a lot to answer for.'

'Don't worry, Kate,' Chris added. 'Anna's on a hair trigger these days. Still has a yen for the old Damien, if you ask me.'

'Oh, rubbish, Christopher!' his mother interrupted sharply. 'She's seen through him completely.' She turned back to Kate. 'What Anna doesn't understand is that if her father and I did seem . . . over-protective at times—and I can see that you might think that, dear—there was good reason. She is a very, very beautiful and sensitive girl, you know, and for that reason has always been under pressures that more . . .

that young women more in the mainstream couldn't possibly understand.'

Kate could do nothing but nod and smile bravely on. She'd transgressed, and now she was paying the penalty.

'Well,' said Betsy, with an air of moving away from unpleasant ground, 'we mustn't bicker on our first evening, must we?' She raised her voice slightly. 'The annual invasion, Auntie Alice. Except for Nick and Jill, who'll be up tomorrow, the old crowd's all present and correct, ready for the fray. Aren't we, everyone?' Her smiling gaze raked the room, drawing nods and smiles from all sides and little murmurs of enthusiastic agreement from the more susceptible.

'Ah, well, Bet, you wanted to come up, and it's nice to see you, but like I said I wish you hadn't bothered this year,' said Alice. The flickering glare of the fire lit up the lower half of the weathered old face with its strong nose and thin-lipped mouth, leaving the hooded eyes, deeply set, in shadow. 'The crop's not much good. Hardly worth picking. Trees are too old. Like me. Not worth a crumpet.'

'You say that every single year, Auntie Alice,' said Chris, laughing. 'Go on—the trees are OK, and the juice place will take the apples like always, won't they?'

'Oh, they say so, matey.' The lips tightened and tilted a bit at the corners. 'Anyhow, like it or not, I s'pose the trees'll be picked like every year, while I'm here anyway, the blooming things. You can't just leave the fruit to rot after spending all year fiddling and spraying and carrying on to get it going.'

'Of course you can't, darling,' said Betsy tactfully. 'Don't you worry about anything. We'll organise ourselves. Let us do the worrying for a while.' She paused. 'And while we're here,' she added lightly, 'you and I will have a good talk about things. It's really time to make a few decisions about the future, don't you think?'

The old figure in the chair hunched a bit, but didn't speak. Alice gazed at the fire.

Betsy's face registered the rebuff for a fleeting moment. Then she shook her head gently and smiled sadly.

There was an uncomfortable silence, broken only by the striking of the clock on the mantelpiece. Nine o'clock. Surely it was later than that! Kate could feel Jeremy's eyes on her. She stared carefully down at her hands.

Across the room Sonsy wriggled, darting a glance at Chris who was looking protectively at his mother. He was feeling for her discomfort, feeling sorry for her. Sonsy wasn't. She was on old Alice's side. Why couldn't Betsy just leave her alone? Why couldn't she leave *anyone* alone? Always managing, so tactfully, so 'Sue, dear, I noticed Christopher's shirts were getting a bit frayed. Men are so *hopeless* with these things, and you're so busy. I found these on special and I couldn't resist . . . Sue, dear, I copied out that lamb recipe for you. It's very quick and nourishing, and Christopher's so particular . . . the other day I thought he was looking a bit . . . Well, Chris, what *I'd* do is put the sideboard against the back wall and . . . look, I'll draw you a plan . . . of course, Susan might have another . . . but what I'd do is . . .' The worst of it was, Sonsy thought drearily, that somehow to object to anything put *you* in the wrong. It was always so *nice* of her, so tactfully done. It made you so childish, so stubborn, to refuse to fall in with her—like poor old Alice hunched up there, her very resistance proof that she was indeed losing her grip, getting past it, needing help, *needing* to move into a nice little apartment down in Sydney, in a retirement village, under Betsy's eye. She shivered.

'Sue, do you need another jumper, dear? Come closer to the fire.' Betsy's bird-like eye was on her. Sonsy flushed, smiled, shook her head.

'My new cashmere's so cosy—dear, I love it. Such

an extravagance, but still,' said Betsy complacently, stroking the pink softness of her sleeve. 'Sue, I'm sure I saw you shiver, and I thought you must be . . . Christopher, I think Sue's cold. Make her move closer to the fire . . . It's always as well to say straight out up here, Sue, isn't it Chris? Up here we're very rough and ready. Once these boys get up into their old stamping grounds we women just have to look after ourselves.' She giggled.

Kate felt desperate. She stood up, stumbling a little against the rickety arm of the old chair.

'Come on, Sonsy,' she said. 'Let's get the washing-up out of the way.'

Sonsy sprang to her feet. Oh, a thousand thanks to Kate. Anything to get out from under Betsy's eye.

'Righto,' groaned Chris, heaving himself up. 'I knew this was too good to last. Come on, Jeremy.'

'Now you boys stay where you are,' cried Betsy playfully. 'I'll help the girls.' She quickly rose and gently pushed her son back to his seat. 'You've had a hard day, and you need your rest. This is women's work.' She turned to Kate and smiled beguilingly, her arm round Chris's shoulder. 'Oh dear, aren't I awful? These liberated girls will be cross with me . . . Now, don't be cross, Katie. We old women are used to looking after our menfolk. We spoil them, I suppose.' She gave Chris's shoulder a little squeeze.

'Good thing too, Mum,' Chris smiled up at her from the couch, oh, so smugly, Sonsy thought, her cheeks burning. Somehow, it had happened again. Chris and his mother on one side, and she on the other. He was like a different person when Betsy was around.

Kate stared at Chris for a minute. He grinned back, challenging her to say something.

She smiled sweetly at Betsy. 'Oh, well, Betsy. You know your way to your son's heart, anyway. But Sonsy and I can manage. You stay here with Alice and have a good rest by the fire. We'll organise ourselves. We'll keep the door shut so you can stay nice and snug.'

She ushered Sonsy into the kitchen and shut the door behind them. The room was cold, and mist swirled against the cracked window pane. Kate turned on the hot tap over the sink, and mist rose from inside, frosting the window completely. She looked at Sonsy and smiled through the steam.

'That makes her so mad,' she smirked. 'If there's one thing Betsy hates, it's being organised. I'll wash, you wipe.'

Sonsy felt a wave of relief wash over her, relaxing the tension that had held her whole body rigid all evening. She leant against the sink, a tea-towel in her hand, and watched the detergent bubbles fluffing in the bowl.

They heard the back door open and close, and after a pause someone walked down the back steps. Sonsy leaned forward and rubbed at the steamy window.

'Someone going out?' Kate looked over her shoulder.

'Betsy. She's going into the orchard,' said Sonsy. 'What can she be doing?'

Kate clicked her tongue. 'Oh, it's because I said that about staying nice and snug, I suppose. And she's probably still upset about that thing with Anna. She's going down to sit in the orchard for a while, to calm down. She always does that. I forgot—you haven't been up here before, have you? She's got a special place down there—look, see? A big old tree with overhanging branches, and a log put under it for a seat. It was her cubby, when she visited here as a little girl. Look, there she is—you can just see her parka shining in the mist—just sitting there and having a commune with nature. Poor old Betsy. Mind you, she really does like sitting there, but it fulfils a dual purpose—lets everyone know she's been upset, see? So they feel guilty, and watch their tongues next time.'

Sonsy looked at her curiously. 'Kate, you've know Betsy—all of them—a long time, haven't you?'

'Oh, ages. A good fifteen years. Chris and Jeremy have been friends since their first year at university.'

'Yes, I know. I don't seem to get on with Betsy very well,' said Sonsy hesitantly.

'Oh,' said Kate, smiling encouragingly, 'you've taken her darling boy away from her, haven't you? She'll get used to it.'

'If I last that long,' said Sonsy grimly.

'Look, Sonsy,' said Kate earnestly, 'I know she can be awful—but I'm always, just as she gets me the most irritated, so sorry for her. I'm sure you will be too, once you . . .'

'*Sorry* for her?'

'Yeah, well, it's sad, really, Sonsy, when you think about it. She's got all this push, and need to run things, and there she is hitched to poor old Wilf— hardly real estate agent of the year, is he? And her kids are all growing up and leaving home—getting married . . .'

'Yes, but Kate, she gets them back! Look at Anna. Home again with Mum, after only a year and a half!' Sonsy frowned down at the fork in her hand and began polishing it, quite unnecessarily, with the tea- towel. 'You don't know how bad she is, Kate, you've got no idea! She didn't want Anna to marry Damien, and she didn't want Chris to marry me.'

'Sonsy, that's silly . . .' Kate began automatically. And then she stopped, and looked up from the dishes. Sonsy was trembling. Her pretty, heart-shaped face with its childish fringe was burning, and her big blue eyes were full of tears.

'Sonsy, you don't *really* think there's a danger that Chris . . .'

'You *saw* him in there, Kate. You *saw* how he . . .'

'Oh yes, yes, but that was just a little . . .'

'Of course it was only a little thing, Kate. I know that. Oh, it must seem mad to you. It's just she gets me so rattled. It's as though she's saying to Chris, "Look, see, she's not up to it. She's not good enough for you. She's silly, she's unsophisticated, she's not our class." '

Kate was filled with remorse. Underneath her own basic, unthinking goodwill towards pretty Sonsy she had always herself wondered why Chris, so self-important these days, had chosen to marry such an apparently empty-headed clinging vine.

'Oh, Sonsy, I'm sure—if that's true—I'm sure Chris doesn't take any . . .' she said, ridiculously lifting a froth-covered, rubber-gloved paw from the sink, and clasping Sonsy's hand, only to snatch it, dripping, back. 'Oh, sorry.'

'But that's the thing, Kate, he does take notice. You can see it. Every time they get together it's worse. And afterwards, when we're by ourselves again, it takes ages to bring him round again. She's spoiling everything. And now . . . I just don't know what to do, Kate.' Tears fell down Sonsy's cheeks and she rubbed at them with the tea-towel.

'Sonsy, I'll get Jeremy to talk to Chris and find out . . .'

'No, no, oh please Kate! Oh, I shouldn't have said anything, I knew I shouldn't,' cried Sonsy in fright. 'Oh, please! Chris would be so angry . . . I couldn't bear it, really, please don't . . .'

'OK, OK, Sonsy, OK, don't worry, I won't say anything to anyone if you don't want me to.' Kate hastily put her arm around the smaller girl's shoulders, heedless, this time, of her wet hand. Gosh, she thought. This is terrible. She felt the soft body trembling against her, and was filled with rage against smug Chris. What business had he taking a child like this, inviting her to cling to him and then coldly withdrawing and jeering at her for being unable to stand alone.

'Chris should have more sense . . .' she began, but Sonsy cut her off.

'No, no, it's not Chris's fault. It's me. It's my fault. If only his mother—if only she'd leave us alone! She's in and out of the house all the time now . . . She even

drops in when I'm on night duty, and tidies the
house . . . Oh, I wish she'd go away somewhere. I
wish she'd die!'

They stood looking at one another side by side over
the cooling dishwater. The window frame creaked as
the wind outside swirled the mist and buffeted the
loaded apple trees.

The kitchen door opened and Jeremy's head appeared. 'Need any help? Or will I make a cup of tea?'
he enquired, staring at them curiously. He came into
the room and shut the door behind him.

Kate looked at Sonsy. The soft little face had gone
blank. Then the eyes dropped and, mechanically, silently, the girl began to dry the dishes.

'What's up with Tootsie?' whispered Jeremy, as he
and Kate struggled to undress in the dark bedroom,
dodging the camp stretcher sagging with Zoe, encased
in a sleeping bag like a pink caterpillar in a cocoon,
and profoundly asleep. 'She was bending your ear out
there, wasn't she?'

'She's very upset, Jeremy. Poor little thing . . .
she's . . .'

'Oh, bunk! Have you gone soft in the centre or
something? That little dill . . : Ouch!'

'Serves you right. Careful, you'll wake Zoe.'

'Oh, God, that hurt. What a bloody stupid place to
put the stretcher, Kate! It's impossible to . . .'

'There was nowhere else for it to go. She's not a
dill . . . She's just young, and Chris is giving her an
awful time—aided and abetted by mother-of-the-
year.'

'Oh, that woman's a case, I've always said that. But
why Chris married poor Sonsy I don't know. She's a
good-natured little thing, and she's very pretty, but
what a bunny!'

The bed creaked as Jeremy climbed in. 'Oh, God,
this bed is worse than it was last year, Katie. Look,

this is the last time I'm going to do this. It's no fun any-more.'

'Yes, this was a mistake,' said Kate, crawling awk-wardly in beside him. 'The whole thing's giving me the creeps. Poor little Sonsy . . . Betsy's making her life a misery. She's got her jumpy as a cat. You know what she said to me . . . ?'

'Oh Sonsy . . . Betsy. What about old Alice? She's looking mad as a meat-axe. All she talks about is apple trees and spray. She's obsessed. And Anna's a bundle of nerves. She nearly bit my head off when I asked her if she'd seen Damien lately.'

'Well, they've only been separated a few months, for goodness sake.'

'It was Betsy who finally broke them up, you know. Even Chris could see that. He never had much time for Damien—what a beauty like Anna saw in a pho-ney like that I'll never understand—anyhow, even Chris said that Betsy had worked on Anna till she left him.'

'That's what Sonsy said. But how could Betsy . . . ?'

'Oh, use your imagination, sweetie. Anna's not ex-actly Mrs Tough, is she? She's always run to Mummy—they all have—look at young Rodney. He's going the same way. And Betsy works on it. Encour-ages them all to think they're badly done by, then helps them maintain their rage, to coin a phrase. She's a case, that woman.'

'You said that. Do you want your apple, by the way? She's left us one each, like always.'

'No. Couldn't face it. And please, for God's sake, don't eat yours. I can't stand the crunching.'

'I don't want it, anyway.'

They lay in silence a moment.

'I wonder what Wilf thinks about it all? He's so quiet. He's even quieter than he used to be. And when you think he's a real estate agent . . . he's not very salesmanlike, is he?' said Kate.

'No. And I don't think he sells much either, from what

Chris says. Just enough to get by, I think. Chris mentioned it because Betsy's having the house done up again, and he's been wanting to borrow a bit from them himself. God, imagine being married to Betsy . . .'

Just before she dropped off to sleep, Kate remembered she hadn't got round to telling Jeremy about Sonsy's outburst over the soapsuds. Maybe it was just as well. Yes, she'd keep it to herself. It wasn't the kind of thing that was going to come up again, anyway.

3

Bitter Rot

'My God it's cold. It's freezing.' Jeremy struggled into his jeans. A sly, ice little hand plumped onto the small of his back.

'Aagh! Zoe, don't do that. It's not funny, it's silly.'

'Ha ha, Daddy is a scaredy cat. Daddy is an scaredy cat,' shrieked Zoe, dancing around in high delight at having poked the tiger to such good effect.

'Be quiet Zoe! Calm down. Be a grown-up girl, please,' begged Kate.

'You haven't got your shoes on,' Zoe pointed out.

'No, I'm going to stay in my socks for breakfast, because then we'll all be putting on gumboots for the apple picking.'

'You've got mine. They did get packed, didn't they?' Zoe worried.

'Yes, of course they did. You remember. Now look, darling, don't forget what I said about the leeches last night, and never go out without your gumboots. OK?'

'Yes. But Mum?'

'Yes.'

'Where are my gumboots now?'

'Oh, darling—they're somewhere. I'll find them after breakfast.'

Zoe's lip quivered. 'I need them now.'

'Why on earth?'

'I need to go to the toilet.'

'But Zoe, there aren't any leeches there, darling. The toilet's just outside the back door. Leeches live . . .'

'I *know* that, but one might be hiding there. I don't want it to bite me.' Tears started to gather in Zoe's brown eyes.

'Oh, for heaven's sake!' groaned Jeremy. 'Look, here they are, Zoe darling. Put them on and let's get out of this ice-box. Kate, you've got feathers or something in your hair.'

Their breath showing white in the chilly air they made their crowded final preparations for respectable entry into the house-party breakfast jollities.

At the big table in the living room the Tender clan, and Sonsy, sat eating porridge with brown sugar. Alice, who must have eaten earlier, was back in her chair by the fire, which popped and flamed with early morning energy, but as yet threw out little heat.

'Don't wait on us, Betsy,' protested Kate feebly, as a steaming plate appeared in front of her. 'I can . . .'

'Of course, Katie. But I'll just spoil you all this morning. After today everyone can fend for themselves,' said Betsy. 'Oh, doesn't that big girl love her porridge? Don't you have porridge at home, darling?'

'Yes,' said Zoe, raising her head from her bowl briefly. 'But not nice like this. Just ordinary, lumpy porridge. Without cream . . .'

Disloyal little wretch, thought Kate savagely. She tasted her own breakfast. Still, it was very nice. She took another spoonful.

'Oh,' said Betsy, laughing delightedly. 'My big boys, and my big girl, grew up on their old Mum's porridge. It's just a matter of hovering over it a bit, Katie, to get that creaminess. People just tend to bung it on and leave it, that's the trouble.'

'Yeah,' said Chris. 'There's nothing worse. You

watch Mum making it tomorrow, Sonsy, and see if you can pick up the knack.'

Sonsy reddened and looked confused.

'Oh, it's terribly fattening, anyway,' said Anna languidly, pushing her plate away half-finished. 'We shouldn't eat it at all, really.'

Rodney looked at her scornfully. 'You're practically a skeleton already, Anna,' he said. 'I bet you've got that aner-whatsis disease.'

'Don't tease your sister, Roddy,' said Betsy. 'It's part of her job to be slim, you know that. People with anorexia starve themselves. They don't just watch their weight.'

'The daughter of one of the fellows at bowls had it,' said Wilf suddenly. Everyone jumped a little.

"She had it,' Wilf went on mournfully. 'Died of it in the end. They were feeding her with a tube. Bert said her bones stuck out so you'd think her skin would split. It killed his wife. Just after that she dropped dead. Heart attack.' He went back to his porridge.

There was a short silence.

'Well! What an awful subject for breakfast,' shrilled Betsy, recovering. 'Let's get on and finish up here, then we can have a go at those apples. We're picking as usual from the bottom of the orchard, working up towards the house. Auntie Alice has had the slasher through, so we shouldn't have trouble with leeches this year, but remember, if you do get one on you I always have the salt and the iodine on hand, and . . .'

'We know, Mum!' said Anna.

'Well, that's all very well, Anna, but remember last year . . . um . . .' Betsy trailed off uncertainly, and looked for once as though she could have bitten her tongue.

'Yeah, Damien nearly peed himself,' guffawed Rodney, raucously disgusted. 'It was only a little one, too.'

'*Roddy!*' Betsy was pink and sharp.

'He just sat there, I remember, on the grass waiting for you to come with the salt to get it off, and he was *white.* Just *white.* And he kept asking for more iodine on this tiny little spot. I've never seen anyone so frightened of a little . . .'

'Rodney, that's *enough.*'

'Mum, you don't have to be scared of Damien's name being mentioned, you know,' said Anna coldly. 'He's not the devil, or something.' She looked at her brother, sitting smirking opposite. 'And you don't have to be so smug, either,' she said to him. 'So Damien hated creepy crawlies. So what. Lots of people do.'

'Oh, yes, I do,' chattered Kate, acutely aware of Zoe's flesh creeping.

'It's one thing for girls,' said Rodney tolerantly. 'But not for men. Only poofters go on like that.'

'*Roddy!*' cried Betsy. 'Remember where you are and who is present, please.' She cast her eyes in Zoe's direction.

Anna looked at her brother's plump, red face with dislike. 'You wouldn't know a real man if you fell over one, Rodney. Real men have brains. They're not just overweight bully boys, whatever that ridiculous school you go to teaches you.'

'Rodney,' said Betsy, desperately forestalling her son's passionate reply. 'Rodney, you've finished; you get togged up and go and get the bags from the garage. Go on, now.'

Rodney grimaced but obeyed. He grabbed an apple from the big bowl in the middle of the table and made for the back door, where his gumboots and parka stood waiting.

'Young Rodney!' It was Alice. She craned forward in her chair, her beaky nose red and her eyebrows knitted. 'Don't you forget the spray, matey, will you? There's poison on them apples out there. Don't you go eating off the trees. Hear me?'

'Yes, Auntie Alice,' mumbled Rodney, flushing. He held up the apple he'd taken from the bowl. 'This is OK, isn't it?'

'Of course it is, you know that!' snapped Alice. 'Any

fruit inside this house, I've picked, see? I know which trees've been sprayed. I'm the only one that knows. You just eat from the big bowl and you'll be all right. Eat off the trees and you might get a fright.' She turned back to the fire, chuckling to herself. Chris and Anna exchanged grins as Rodney disappeared through the doorway.

'Mum,' Zoe whispered urgently. 'Mum, what did she say?'

'Auntie Alice said don't eat the apples off the trees, because they might be poisonous. I'll explain it to you outside,' said Kate distractedly.

'Yes,' said Betsy loudly. 'Off we go everyone. I'll get you started, then come back to the washing-up. Come on.'

She bustled the group to the door and slipped on her own smart, pale-blue parka and shiny, black gumboots. Everyone else followed suit, and stepped out onto the wooden porch and down the concrete stairs to the path, where mist billowed like dry ice in a play, shrouding the nearby garage and the apple trees across the lawn in a white cloud. They huddled together, blinking and blowing in the sudden cold.

'Rodney's got the ladders down there waiting, and he'll give you each a bag down there. We've put the hopper between the first and second bottom rows, so you won't have to walk far every time. Oh dear, I hope the weather clears up.'

'It'll be OK later on.' said Chris cheerfully. 'Well, let's get going, eh?'

'Um, Betsy, would there really be much spray on the apples at this time of the year?' Kate asked nervously. 'I mean, enough to actually hurt you? Alice seemed very . . .'

'Katie—and listen everyone! I really think it might be better to not eat the apples off the trees this year. Now I know we always make a joke of poor old Auntie Alice saying that . . .'

'She just doesn't want us to eat her profits, Mum,'

said Chris, grinning. 'You know that. She thinks we'll eat more than we pick. There'd be no reason to spray at this time of year. And if you really think she's sprayed we can hardly cart the hoppers to the juicer, can we?'

Betsy looked distracted. 'I'm going to ring and ask them,' she said. 'I'm sure they've got some sort of checking system. They'll tell me what's best. Let's just get the things picked. Look, I know, Chris, it sounds mad but this time I'm not . . . I just think she might have done a bit of spraying recently . . . she's very keen on it at the moment. The storeroom's packed with bottles and tins of it—all different sorts. I don't want anyone getting sick. So let's just eat the apples in the big bowl this year, like Auntie Alice says. All right?'

Everyone murmured agreement, and the group split up.

'Now, Zoe, you remember that, won't you?' said Kate, as they trudged through the bright green grass behind the house.

'Yes, but it isn't fair,' said Zoe crossly. 'It's no fun when you can't eat the apples. They're better on the trees than in the big bowl.'

'I'm with you there, Zoe,' said Jeremy. 'God—cold, leeches, poisonous apples, batty old personages. What a holiday!'

'What's a batty . . . ?'

'Nothing. Come on, I'll race you to the trees.'

They took off for the magic treeline fifty metres away, where round red balls hung, glinting luminously through the mist, polished and wet in the damp air. Kate wandered slowly after them. Things were very peculiar this year. The apple-picking seemed peripheral to all sorts of other matters. She and Jeremy had joined the Tenders for this annual festival for years now. It had always been fun, notwithstanding Betsy's rather ruthlessly dominating sweetness and light, to get together and tackle a job so satisfying amid surroundings so beautiful.

But this year . . . instead of being part of the team now straggling towards the waiting trees she, Jeremy and Zoe seemed outsiders, despite Betsy's protestations and cheer-leading. The Tenders seemed to be grappling with all sorts of problems of their own, and the last thing they needed, thought Kate, was an audience. And Nick and Jill would be arriving soon. And Birdie. Oh, what an idiot she'd been to ask Birdie to come! What would she make of all this? Then Kate smiled to herself—oh, Birdie would manage. She always did.

'Come on, Mum!' Zoe jumped up and down among the trees, her red parka glimmering in the mist. 'It's lovely here.'

Kate hurried, and as she caught up with Jeremy and Zoe she found herself, as every year, drawn into the spell of the orchard: the stillness, the smell of damp earth and old bark, of wet leaves and ripe apples. Their boots shone slippery black as they strode through the grass, raw between the trees where the slasher had been put through, lush and dark green round the trunks and under the low boughs.

Down at the bottom of the orchard Rodney was waiting with yellow cloth bags. The ladders stood in place, the empty hopper yawned in the middle of the second row.

'Right,' said Rodney officiously as they reached him, 'you're first so you start down at the beginning of this row.' He pointed to a distant tree, where two ladders stood waiting.

They accepted their bags, and trudged off towards their appointed task.

Kate and Jeremy climbed their ladders, and began picking from opposite sides of the tree. Zoe scuffled around the lower branches. Twist, pull, twist, pull. The yellow bags filled and grew heavy, the rhythm settled in. They didn't talk. Around them they could hear the others climbing their ladders and settling into the task at hand: Sonsy's little shrieks as she leaned too far for safety, Rodney's guffaws of laughter. But the mist muffled the sounds, as though they were listening to them through a velvet curtain. Only the whistling of the magpies pierced the misty barrier and came rippling to their ears throaty and cold.

Jeremy collected Kate's bag and went off to empty the apples into the hopper. He came back to report that Nick and Jill had arrived, and gone straight to work.

'Mum, Mum, can I go and see Jill? Can I?' pleaded Zoe.

'OK, darling, but don't stop them working and come back quickly,' said Kate. 'We'll see them at morning tea.'

Zoe slipped her head out of her bag strap and ran unsteadily towards the hopper, slipping a little in the rough grass. She adored Nick and Jill.

By the time Betsy's call for morning tea came the mist had lifted and the sun was out. The apple-pickers converged on the grass behind the house where Betsy had put out rugs, plates of rock cakes and mugs of tea.

'G'day, mate!'

Nick grinned at Jeremy, shielding his eyes against the sun. His light brown hair and beard glittered in the watery light. He was a plain man, with a plump, freckled face, a bumpy nose and clever hazel eyes, now lit with genuine pleasure. The feeling of genial goodwill he always radiated made things seem suddenly as ordinary and pleasant as they had ever been, Kate thought. Nick had a real talent for that. Jill knelt beside him—tall, brightly plumaged as a parrot, with her wiry red hair standing out in a bush, ineffectively controlled by two fantastic combs in the shape of dragonflies. Where did she find these things? She must be a striking addition to the sober offices of Pinkie and Sons, 'publishers to the gentry', as Kate's own, more commercially oriented employer called them.

Kate bent to give her a kiss. 'How's things, Jillie?'

'Oh, frantic as ever. I was so glad to get away. And my big book is . . . um . . . anyway . . .' Jill looked disconcerted for a minute and then went on, 'how about you?'

'Everything late as usual. I shouldn't be here. My authors are all having fits. It's the same every year. What about your big book? What—?'

'Oh, forget it, for God's sake, Katie,' drawled Jeremy. 'You're supposed to be on holidays. Relax for once.'

'Don't say Kate's getting as neurotic about work as Jill is, Jeremy?' said Nick, turning to him and only half joking.

'Don't be ridiculous, Nick,' snapped Jill. 'You think anyone who does a good day's work for their pay's neurotic. Just because you can swan around with a lecture here and a seminar there . . .'

'Jeremy can't talk, anyway,' Kate broke in. 'When he's with his work people he talks about nothing else but work. And when he's on a big story I hear about nothing else day in, day out. Talk about the pot calling the kettle black!'

'OK, OK, don't get all excited,' grinned Jeremy. 'Work yourselves to death if you want to. Just spare us the details—and the cliches.'

They laughed and relaxed, and sat silent for a while, sipping their tea, unconsciously lifting their chins a little to absorb the light and warmth filtering so palely through the cool, blue air.

'Well, how are the workers?' said Betsy brightly, kneeling down on the rug beside them.

'Going fine,' said Kate, smiling at her. 'It's a beautiful morning now, Betsy.'

'Yes, aren't we lucky?'

Alice turned towards the sound of voices and

squinted at Betsy, 'Bet!' she barked. 'Have you told the new ones about the apples?'

'The . . .' Betsy looked bewildered.

'About the spray, girl!'

'Oh . . . oh, yes, Auntie Alice. They know all about it.' Betsy looked in embarrassed fashion at Nick and Jill, who nodded and smiled at the old lady.

'Good-oh, then,' said Alice, and flashed her teeth at them.

'D'you do all your own spraying, Alice?' called Nick genially. 'Big job.'

'Ah . . . I do some of it, like, when I have to. But I have some boys come in with a tractor through the year. They've got all the equipment—masks and that. You can't get it on you, you know. That's as bad as swallowing it—for some of them. I'd never do it on me own, now.'

'Alice, I didn't realise the sprays they used now were really that dangerous,' said Jill. 'To eat on the fruit, I mean.'

'Oh, my word they're dangerous. When they're new, that is, like for the first few weeks after spraying. I've got a storeroom full of bottles that'd put you out of the way quick smart if you had a sip out of them.' She sniggered.

'The storeroom—you mean that partitioned bit off the bathroom?' said Jill, fascinated.

'Yeah. Right next to the kitchen. Handy, eh? For unwelcome visitors.' This time Alice laughed outright and Jill laughed with her, though a trifle uncertainly.

'You're teasing Jillie, Auntie Alice, aren't you?' said Betsy, smiling rather wanly.

'I don't think she's teasing at all,' said Nick, grinning. 'Go on, Alice, tell us poor laypeople what you've got, and what it's all for.'

Alice regarded him tolerantly. 'We'd be here all day, matey; we've got apples to pick. You have, anyhow. The names wouldn't mean much to you—oh, maybe a few would—like, there's Codling Moth—

heard about that I s'pose? Grubs eat holes into the fruit and you find the blighters inside it. You spray with Azinphos-methyl for that at petal fall, then every two weeks or so right through to harvest.'

'Good Lord, Alice—that often?' said Jeremy, interested despite himself. 'Is this Azinphos stuff poisonous?'

'I tell you they're all poisonous. You wouldn't want to drink any of them, matey. Another proper pest round here's Bitter Rot—it's a disease, like. A fungus thing. Apple gets a brown spot and under that the flesh rots. Horrible thing to see, it is. You spray at greentip for that, and then all through the hot weather. Then there's Scab . . .'

Nick held up his hands. 'Alice! Codling Moth, Bitter Rot, Scab—they sound like low characters in a Jacobean play . . . And the cures and preventatives for all these are in your storeroom?'

'Course they are—well no, I'm a liar, I s'pose. Most stuff I buy in just before I need it. But I got bits and pieces in there, leftovers mainly, with the metho and that. Waste not, want not, eh?' Alice grinned around. She was enjoying herself. 'A little brown bottle of Parathion on the top shelf, there. A great invention that—great pesticide. Teaspoon in your tea or on the palm of your hand, and you're done. And I got some Fenthion, and some of that Azinphos-methyl I told you about—that's a powder, and DDT, and then there's the weedkillers . . .'

Kate stared at her tea. Suddenly it tasted bitter. She caught Betsy's eye and flushed.

'Auntie Alice, this is an awful subject,' said Betsy nervously. 'Maybe we should all finish up and get back to work.'

'Ah yes, well . . .' Alice stretched and looked amused.

'It's a lot of work for you, Alice,' said Jill earnestly. 'How do you manage on your own?'

'I'm always saying that to Auntie Alice, Jill,' said

Betsy eagerly. 'I'm terrified she'll break her hip or something in the house, and no one will know.'

'Oh, like I said, I get people in when I have to,' said Alice, speaking to Jill and ignoring Betsy, 'I don't mind being by myself. And Theresa Sullivan's popping in and out, like . . .' she stopped and looked shifty.

'The lady across the road?' asked Anna curiously. 'Dad met her yesterday.'

'Did he?' Alice sniffed. 'Yeah—well, I see a bit of Theresa. And she'd notice,' she raised her voice slightly, but still didn't look at Betsy, 'if I wasn't getting round. I've given her a key, so she can get in if she's worried.'

'*Auntie Alice!* You gave this . . . Theresa a *key?* Was that wise, darling? You hardly know her,' shrilled Betsy, very put out.

'Know her as well as I know anybody round here,' retorted Alice. 'All the old ones've died or moved away. Whole street's deserted now, most of the time. City people've bought the houses up for holiday places, and hardly come near them. Anyhow, she's given me *her* key too—key to her side door, hanging right now on a nail beside the phone. So we can burgle each other's houses, or murder each other in our beds, can't we Bet? If we feel inclined.' She turned her back.

Betsy sighed. 'I didn't mean . . .' she said helplessly and gave up with a brief shrug of her shoulders.

'Auntie Betsy!'

Betsy gave a slight start. 'Oh, Zoe, I didn't see you there. What is it, dear?'

'Could I go and sit in your special place?'

Betsy's face softened. 'Of course you can, Zoe. Thank you for asking. You're a dear, polite girl. Here look . . . take another rock cake and have your own private picnic. You can sit there any time you like while you're up here. Remember I said that last year?'

'Yes,' said Zoe, taking the cake gravely. 'Thank you.'

She sped off into the orchard. They watched her veer off to the right and duck her head to creep under the overhanging branches of Betsy's tree.

'Oh, many's the time I did that as a child,' said Betsy quietly. 'It's very still and green in there. You feel quite alone. Makes you realise things aren't as bad as they seem, if you've got worries.'

Kate looked at her. The sad, tired little lines at the corners of Betsy's mouth were suddenly very noticeable in the bright sunlight, and her eyes, usually snapping with bright energy, were soft.

'You still often sit there, Betsy, don't you?' she said gently.

'Oh yes.' Betsy smiled sadly. 'Old habits die hard, Katie. Especially when they're nice ones. Well . . .' the organising light reappeared in her eyes. 'I'd better get on—you too.' She began collecting mugs and plates and stacking them neatly.

'Righto, Mum. We'll get back to it in a sec. Just give us five minutes,' said Chris lazily. 'Don't worry.'

She looked at him indulgently. 'Five minutes then, Christopher.' She smiled and trotted back to the house with her laden tray.

Kate lay back on the rug and closed her eyes. The light swam pink against her eyelids. She tried to re-capture the lazy, contented feeling she'd had before Betsy's arrival, but it eluded her. Something was wrong here—she could feel it. Last year Damien had been with them, and that had been a strain, certainly. But this year something was gnawing away underneath the surface of things—like Alice's Bitter Rot. Pale brown spots on the rosy surface, concealing real spoiling underneath. Maybe you could spray for it . . . at greentip? . . . at spurburst? . . . at pink? Oh, those names were great . . . Kate smiled in spite of herself, drifting in a pink haze . . .

"Well, look who I found!' Betsy's voice cut through the pink haze and brought Kate to a sitting position, feeling vaguely guilty. She focused on the two figures

coming towards them. Betsy looked infinitely tall and
elegant beside the small, rather scruffy woman am-
bling beside her, glasses winking in the sun.

'So now,' said Betsy gaily, 'the party's complete.
Kate, will you do the honours?'

For all her bright hospitality, Betsy was looking a
trifle disconcerted by the new arrival. She was definitely not out of the top drawer. A bush of brown,
frizzy hair stood out around her small, pointed face.
Strange, hazel, almost golden eyes peered through
huge tortoiseshell-rimmed spectacles. Her hands were
stuck firmly into the pockets of a duffle coat that had
seen better days. The group on the grass looked up at
her, and she smiled and blinked, waiting.

'Hello, Birdie,' said Kate.

4

Betsy Means Well

The sun was setting and the mist beginning to rise in the valleys when the day's work ended.

The bottom rows of trees were picked bare, standing up a little straighter already, the hopper full to the brim with apples that for some reason looked ordinary now, robbed of the glamour they had had among the trees.

The lights of the house shone golden through the dusk as the apple-pickers trudged in little groups up the slope.

'Oh, my arms! They're paralysed,' groaned Jill. 'And my knees are all wobbly.'

'You're getting old, Jillie,' hooted Rodney. 'Can't take it! You'll feel worse in the morning.'

'Thanks, Rodney, you're a great comfort,' answered Jill tolerantly.

They crossed the lawn and filed wearily up the back steps. The door snapped open and Betsy's face appeared.

'Boots on the porch, everyone. Cup of tea waiting.'

'Oh, thank God,' muttered Kate, and struggling out of her gumboots followed the others inside, blinking in the warm light, dazzled by the leaping flames in the fireplace. Zoe, pink and warm in dressing gown

and slippers, sat in state with Alice on the sofa. The
old face and the young one turned up from the snakes
and ladders board to regard the dishevelled invaders
of their peace.

Kate hauled off her parka and went over to her
daughter. 'You look cosy, darling.'

'Yes,' agreed Zoe complacently. 'I am. I've had my
shower, and a glass of lemonade, and Auntie Alice
showed me all her deadly poisons like she said about
this morning. Later she's going to find her train, and
her Noah's Ark for me. And Mum, I've won two games
out of three. Auntie Alice keeps meeting snakes.'

'Yes, I'm out of luck tonight,' agreed Alice. 'Can't
take a trick.'

'Zoe, you know not to touch the storeroom bottles,
don't you,' said Kate anxiously. 'I don't really like
you . . .'

'Mum!'

'The little one was interested,' said Alice defensively. 'She knows not to touch, don't you, love?'

Zoe nodded. 'Only with rubber gloves on, like you
said,' she said solemnly. 'You said, when you were my
age . . .'

'Yeah, well, that was then,' said Alice hastily, darting a guilty look at Kate. 'Things are different now.'

Zoe looked at her mother. 'You look funny, Mum,'
she said, rather obviously changing the subject. 'Your
nose is all red.'

'You can't put me off like that, madam! Anyway,
so my nose might be red. I've been out slaving in the
cold while you've been having hot showers and toast-
ing your toes.'

'You *said* to come in!' cried Zoe indignantly. 'You
said to come in when Auntie Alice did. And Auntie
Betsy had *her* shower before afternoon tea, even. And
she said . . .'

'Oh, of course, darling, I was only teasing. But listen, you remember what I said, and stay out of that

storeroom. OK? Well, look, I'm going to get in line for the bathroom. I'll see you later.'

The Betsy shower system after apple-picking was a masterpiece of organisation designed to make the scanty hot water system last the distance, and at the same time let everyone shower before dinner. It meant there were always two or three people in the bathroom at one time. While each person showered for three minutes by the kitchen clock, the next in line took off their clothes and waited shivering for their turn, shifting from foot to foot on the cold bathroom linoleum. At a call from Betsy next door in the kitchen, the person in the shower would reluctantly emerge from the luxurious flood in a cloud of steam and the next person would take their place. As mixed bathing was not part of Betsy's life view, a strict order had to be maintained—'girls' first, 'boys' second, with a married couple to bridge the hiatus between the sexes.

Jeremy would have no part of the 'ludicrous business', as he called it, and to Kate's chagrin always remained unconcernedly unwashed for his entire stay. Betsy had no idea that he objected to the system, and probably believed that Jeremy never washed at home either. She never said anything about his failure to indulge, anyway. She'd learned long ago to leave Jeremy alone.

Kate collected her things from the bedroom and wandered back to the kitchen. Betsy fussed over the dinner. She looked fresh and pink, and smelled faintly of jasmine. She took her shower in mid-afternoon privacy, 'so there'll be enough hot water for the workers later,' she always said. Anna was leaning against the door to the bathroom, staring into space.

The water was running now. Birdie had gone in first—the privilege of the stranger. Jill must be in there too, waiting her turn. Kate lined up beside Anna.

'Isn't this the end?' muttered Anna. 'I don't think

Mum's come to terms with the fact we aren't kids any-more.'

'Oh, well, it's the hot water, isn't it?' said Kate soothingly. 'And the timing.'

'Oh, that's the excuse, anyway. We could just as well have quick showers in turns without all this business. Mum just loves the bloody system. Treating us like kids,' muttered Anna.

Kate looked at her. She was frowning, with her lower lip stuck out: a pouting, weak, sulky sort of frown. She looked very like Rodney, at that moment—and Chris, too, thought Kate. She'd seen both the boys look like that when things weren't going their way. The spoilt kid look, she always called it to herself. She'd never seen Anna look like that before, though. It wasn't pleasant.

'Anna!' the voice cut into her thoughts. 'Anna, quick, it's your turn to get ready. Hurry darling, didn't you hear me call out? The water won't last if everyone doesn't . . .' Betsy's voice was rising.

The sulky look disappeared and a guilty obedience took its place. 'OK, OK, Mum,' Anna murmured, and disappeared into the bathroom. A little gasp of steam escaped as the old door clicked shut behind her. Betsy smiled brightly at Kate and moved off, her eyes flicking automatically to the clock on the fridge. It wouldn't do to give Jill more than her due time.

Kate took Anna's place against the door, feeling a fool. Sonsy sidled up to her, clutching a flowered plastic sponge bag, a red dressing gown and a pink towel.

'I'm after you,' she said. 'Who's in there now?'

'To my knowledge, Birdie, Jill and Anna,' said Kate wearily. 'Birdie getting dressed, Jill in the shower, Anna getting undressed. It's a packed house.'

They stood uneasily together, backs to the wall.

'That's a pretty dressing gown, Sonsy,' said Kate desperately. 'Lovely colour. Pretty buttons aren't they? Like little red cups.'

'Yes, it was . . .' Sonsy began, and was abruptly cut

off by a sudden tumult from the bathroom. A terrified scream split the air, and Kate sprang back from the door as it was thumped violently from the other side. There was a burst of shouting and banging, and then silence. The door opened and Birdie's head peeped out. Her face looked small and naked without her glasses, and she blinked short sightedly at the gaping crowd drawn from all corners of the house by the furore.

'It's OK. Anna found a leech on her leg and got a bit of a fright. She's all right now.'

'Is that *all*,' roared Rodney. 'I thought you had an axe-murderer in there, or something. God, what a noise!'

Betsy rushed forward. 'Annie, don't touch it, don't touch it! I'm coming with the salt. Someone turn off the shower.'

The door opened wide emitting a burst of warm air and steam, and Birdie, wearing an exotic striped wrapper, appeared with Anna in tow. Anna looked as pale as her cream bathrobe. She was limping, and holding her leg just under the knee.

'It was there, eating me right through my sock. It was huge. Must have been there for ages. Oh, horrible!' She shuddered and looked sick. 'I ripped it off. I didn't think. Now the stupid thing won't stop bleeding.'

'Oh, you silly girl,' snapped Betsy. 'I don't know what's the matter with you! Let me see. Look out! Don't get blood on your gown.'

'It's *OK*, Mum, It's *OK*. Just let me sit down a minute.' Anna's eyes were huge in her pale face, and she started to move rather shakily towards the living room.

Betsy stepped forward, 'Anna!' she cried sharply. 'Stay here on the lino, while I get the iodine. Don't go bleeding . . .'

But someone moved in front of her and took Anna's arm.

'Come on, Anna, get into the warm.' It was Wilf. With care he guided Anna through the crowd and into the living room, and sat her down on the couch, propping the injured leg up on a footstool.

'Get the iodine, Rodney,' he said. 'And some cotton wool, or a tissue or something.'

Rodney glanced at his mother and, finding her face closed, ducked his head and fetched a small bottle and some cotton wool from the kitchen sideboard. Without a word he passed the things to his father, and retreated.

Kate stood with the silent onlookers and watched as Wilf clumsily dabbed at the leech-bite. She felt someone ought to do something to break the tension that gripped the group. It was strange and worrying. She was aware of Zoe and Alice staring from their place by the fire. Zoe's eyes were wide with interest, Alice was—Alice was smiling! Not a very pleasant smile, either. Without thinking any further Kate stepped forward.

'Anna, would you like a cup of tea?'

Jeremy laughed. 'Kate Delaney's universal remedy.'

The tension abruptly relaxed. Chris went to put the kettle on. Anna took the cotton wool pad from her father and held it to her leg, and people began to move and speak freely again, clustering around Anna, reminiscing loudly to each other about leech-bites they had heard about or experienced. Zoe and Alice disappeared together into the front of the house.

'Thanks, Dad. I'm OK now,' Anna said, smiling at him gently. 'It gave me a fright. What an idiot.'

Wilf gave her a little pat and, muttering something about things to do, pottered off in the direction of his bedroom.

Kate watched him go, and found herself smiling. She turned to say something to Jeremy and saw Betsy standing at the kitchen door, watching Wilf's retreating back. Her face was totally unguarded, and the expression was a curious mixture of anger, concern and something else. Fear? Kate stared at her and suddenly Betsy moved and caught her eye. Instantly the expression disappeared and a smile took its place. But the bird-like eyes didn't smile, and the top lip caught a little on the teeth as it lifted, giving the smile a fixed and artificial air. Then Betsy turned and went over to the stove.

'Kate, what are you looking like that for?' whispered Jeremy, digging her in the ribs. 'Standing there dreaming with your mouth open. You look half-witted.'

Kate turned to him blankly. Birdie was beside him, towel and sponge bag over one arm, and neatly folded clothes on the other. She had her glasses back on. Her amber eyes were alive, her mouth twitching at the corners. 'Very curious, Laney, wasn't it?' she said, 'I realised when the smile appeared that she'd caught someone looking.'

Kate leaned towards her. 'You saw too?' she whispered.

'Oh yes,' said Birdie calmly. 'She's a fascinating person. I've hardly been able to take my eyes off her.'

'Who are you talking about?' hissed Jeremy.

'Shh, I'll tell you later.' Kate hissed back. The whole incident had given her the creeps. In retrospect, even Wilf's tender concern for his daughter, which had seemed so touching, had something excessive and highly charged about it that was rather repellant. And what had Betsy's strange expression meant? What was she afraid of? Was she jealous of Wilf's attachment to his daughter? Put out because he'd been the centre of attention, not she, in this time of crisis?

'Mum? Mum!' Zoe was tugging at her arm. 'Look what we found.'

'The Noah's Ark?' said Kate, looking vaguely at a conglomeration of what looked like junk, in a beautiful old cane clothes basket.

'No,' said Zoe scornfully. 'You know what an *Ark* looks like, Mummy. We couldn't find the Ark *but* we

found some tennis rackets, and a net, and these . . .
these what? . . .' She looked at Alice for a prompt.
'Quoits, yes . . . and look at this!' She held up a beautiful black lace shawl, and some black lace mittens.
'That I can play being old-fashioned with, and use
this fan. See? The gloves have no fingers.'

'That's lovely, darling. If Alice's sure you can.
That's a beautiful shawl, Alice. And the mittens!
They're exquisite. They're probably valuable. Do you
think Zoe . . .'

'Mum!' Zoe's voice rose protestingly.

'She'll be careful, won't you, love?' said Alice gruffly
and nodded to Zoe who scuttled to the fireside with
her booty without a backward glance. Alice grinned.
'It's a miracle the moths haven't got them, out in that
old cupboard,' she said. 'The little lass may as well
get some fun out of them. I think they must have been
Aunt Jemima's. Somewhere there's another lovely
shawl of hers—black again, with great big red roses
on it and a fringe going right down to your feet. A
beauty. I'll look for it directly. She was a gay old dog,
Aunt Jemima. Ah well. "Golden girls and youths all
must as chimney sweepers come to dust." Dad used to
say that over and over. Time and again he'd say it.'
She wandered over to her chair by the fire.

Depressing old Dad, thought Kate, and rose to help
set the table.

'And two servings spoons, if you would, Katie,' said
Betsy. 'And that's right, I think. We're nearly ready.
You can put the dressing on the salad.' She rapped on
the bathroom door. 'Roddy!' she called. 'Out, now.
Dinner.'

'You didn't get your shower, dear, or change,' she
said to Kate concernedly.

'No . . . no, it doesn't matter, Betsy. I'll just skip
it. Or have one just before bed. The hot water ought
to be recovered by then, oughtn't it?'

'Oh, yes,' said Betsy vaguely. 'It's just nice to feel comfortable before dinner, I always think. Anyway . . . Verity and Jill had theirs, so I'm glad about that. I mean, they're the real visitors, if you know what I mean. Jill has been up before, of course, but she doesn't always bother, and I never feel she's one of the family like Nick—or like you and Jeremy, dear.'

Kate made a non-committal noise and bent to her task.

'Verity . . .' Betsy hesitated and lowered her voice. 'Did you say you went to school together, Katie?'

'Yes, we did.'

Betsy nodded thoughtfully. You could almost hear her thought processes. Kate smiled to herself and tossed the salad.

'A very intelligent girl, I can see that . . . scholarship, I suppose . . . to school?'

'Yes. She did win a scholarship, but . . .'

'Oh, I'm not asking any questions, dear. Heavens, I don't want to pry into anyone's background. I mean, you are what you make yourself, aren't you, these days? It's just that, heavens, I know what fees are at those schools—I mean, Roddy's are *appalling*. Nothing to some people, but really . . .'

Betsy chattered on, and Kate listened with half an ear, faintly amused. She'd been going to say that Birdie had won the scholarship to their very expensive school, but her father hadn't taken it up, preferring it to go to a girl whose family needed the help. Uncharacteristically unbusinesslike of him—but he was an unpredictable man. On the whole, she was glad she hadn't said it. If Betsy once found out that Birdie wasn't the poor working girl she took her for, but the daughter of a very rich man whose name was a household word, in financial circles at least, she'd be all over her like a rash, and Birdie would hate that. She went to a lot of trouble to keep that relationship quiet, and if she chose to work for a living, as a research assistant, too, instead of as the solicitor she was qualified to be, and dress like an impoverished student, and give away a substantial part of her family income, that was her business.

It wasn't that Birdie disliked her father, or anything. She loved him, as far as Kate could see, and he adored her. He was a short, plain man, and she looked very like him. But her eyes, her huge amber eyes, had come from her mother. She had died while Birdie was still at school, but Kate remembered her well—a very beautiful, an extraordinarily beautiful, woman. Perhaps Birdie had always thought that she could never compete with her, and that was why she'd chosen to make no effort to 'make the most of herself', as they say in women's magazines. She was a strange girl. And, in many ways, it must have been a difficult childhood.

'Katie, Katie, you're daydreaming.' Chris snapped his fingers in front of her nose, and she blinked. 'Give me the salad, and let's get into dinner. We're all starving.'

At dinner Betsy was bright, Rodney raucous, Nick genial, but the rest of the party was somewhat subdued. Zoe, resplendent in black shawl and fingerless mittens, tucked away the first half of her spaghetti bolognese with gusto, slowed down noticeably over the remainder, picked at her salad, and uncomplainingly allowed herself to be taken to bed without asking for dessert. The miracle of fresh air, thought Kate.

'There's only fruit cake for dessert tonight anyway,' said Betsy. 'I was going to do a pudding, but with all the excitement . . .' She smiled around the table.

Anna got up. 'Well, since I've done everyone out of their rightful desserts—ha ha—I'll get the cake, and coffee?'

'Thank you, darling,' said Betsy. 'That would be lovely.' She leaned back in her chair and closed her eyes—just for a moment, but long enough for everyone to register that she was feeling weary, and to become aware of how tirelessly she had worked all day to ensure things went smoothly.

Anna felt the usual stab of guilt. Chris looked worried. Wilf sat as still as a stick insect on a tree. Nick, Jill, Kate and Jeremy exchanged glances.

Sonsy watched them reacting and was aware of rising irritation mixed, as always, with self-disgust. What a mean and petty person she must be, to resent this woman so much. She pushed her chair back from the table and stood up, stumbling a little, and blushing. 'I'll give you a hand, Anna,' she murmured, and walked to the kitchen without looking at anyone.

'Funny little thing!' She heard Betsy's voice superior, tolerant, maddening, as the door closed behind her.

Kate sipped her coffee and bent to get out her embroidery.

'Are you still going on your lovely wildflower sampler, Katie?' asked Betsy.

'Yes,' said Kate ruefully. 'I don't think I'll ever finish it.'

'I don't know how you have the patience,' Jill said. 'Let's see how far you've got—oh yes—that's new, and that. Oh, you've done quite a bit since I saw it last.'

'Actually, *I've* got some embroidery too, this year,' said Betsy brightly. She opened a natty little cane basket and displayed a partly finished tapestry. 'Isn't it going to be pretty?'

'Oh, that's *very* nice, yes,' said Kate, getting up to look at the printed canvas picture—a conventional tight bouquet of pastel spring flowers.

'The dearest little oval frame came with the kit. It'll look lovely in the hall, I think. I'm really tickled with it. I'm only a beginner of course, but still . . .'

'Oh, Betsy, what's this? Oh, isn't that a lovely old tin! Where did you get it?' Kate lifted a rather battered tin box from the sewing basket. On its lid three koalas sat in a gum tree, staring ruminatively, as koalas do, into the far distance.

'That's my old treasure box,' said Betsy, surprised and rather discomfitted, Kate realised, kicking herself, that polite praise of her embroidery had suddenly turned into enthusiasm over its accoutrements. 'I'm keeping my silks in it.' She sighed and smiled. 'I've had this box,' she said sentimentally, 'since I was a little girl.'

'You used to keep photos and things in it, didn't you, Mum?' said Rodney encouragingly.

'That's right, Roddy, I did. Dear old box. I used to take it on trips away and everything. Oh, many's the time I sat in my cubby in the orchard here—you know, the overhanging apple tree—sat on the old log, you know, going through my treasures. I was telling Zoe about it today. Bless her heart, she's taken an old shoe box to start her own collection of treasures, hasn't she, Alice?'

Alice muttered into the fire.

'Poor little soul,' said Betsy. 'Life's so complicated for the young ones now, isn't it? Simple pleasures like cubbies and treasure boxes and things—I mean, they miss out on all that, don't they? Now that mums are working, and there are all these child care centres, and so many people are living in the inner city, I mean, there's no space or time left for all that, is there?'

'Well, I don't know about that . . .' Kate felt her hackles rising, though she knew this was Betsy's payback and should be ignored.

'No, look, Katie. It's not that I blame the *parents*. Heavens, they've got to think of themselves, do what they want to do, live where they want to live. I mean, that's what we're all told we've got to do now, isn't it? Why *should* they sacrifice everything for their children, like we did? It's just not the way people think, these days. No.' Betsy sighed and opened her box of embroidery silks. 'That's all gone, and probably very rightly. It's hard for old traditionalists like me to get used to, that's all. In my day the kiddies came first, and that was that.' She smiled to herself. 'I just hope Chris and Sue don't think they're going to put any grandchild of mine in a creche,' she said playfully. 'I won't let them, and that's that! I'm perfectly capable of looking after a baby, old as I am.'

Kate straightened, filled with speechless rage, and looked over Betsy's glossy bent head at Jeremy who winked at her, and grinned. She stole a look at Sonsy, who was pulling at the hem of her jumper, head down, face in shadow.

Betsy selected some pink cotton and threaded the needle composedly. 'You don't do any fancywork, do you Jill?' she said, black eyes darting.

'Oh, no,' drawled Jill, in her husky voice. 'I'm hopeless. Not like Kate.'

'It's a shame, dear—it's so relaxing. And it's not hard at all, I've found. Watching Kate struggling away, I used to be quite terrified of the idea. But really it's quite simple—I mean, well, you know what I mean, Kate.'

Kate nodded and smiled, boiling.

'Sonsy, why don't you show Kate your stuff,' said Chris encouragingly.

'Oh, it's nothing.' Sonsy looked up with anxious, almost pleading eyes.

'You brought it didn't you, like I said? Where is it?'

'Chris . . . it's in our room somewhere, it doesn't matter . . . I'll get it later,' Sonsy said in a low voice.

'Don't be shy, dear. *I* wasn't,' cried Betsy. 'I didn't know you'd started embroidery. Isn't this lovely?' She looked around, beaming. 'All the women, stitching away. You can see who the domestic creatures in this room are, boys.'

Rodney groaned.

Chris got up and left the room, ignoring Sonsy's urgently restraining hand. He returned with a large mauve-flowered sewing basket with plastic handles.

'Oh,' said Betsy, with raised eyebrows. 'What an
. . . unusual basket, Sue dear. It's . . . very sweet.
Where on earth did you get it?'

Sonsy looked her in the eye for the first time that
night. 'My mother made it for me,' she said softly.
'When I first went nursing.'

Betsy was reduced to silence for once. Being caught
sneering at someone's dead mother tended to put even
Betsy on the back foot.

Sonsy opened the basket and took out a round embroidery frame over which a square of linen had been
stretched. Kate moved closer, to see, and caught her
breath. She'd been expecting . . . well, she didn't
know what she'd been expecting . . . but she hadn't
expected this. Exquisitely fine, detailed work—an old
gardener, a woman in a straw hat, sitting in a late
afternoon garden where every shade of green, and
touches of brown and gold, melted one into the other
creating shadows, strands and pools of light, and an
impression of total peace and silence.

She looked at Sonsy. 'It's exquisite. It's just fantastic, Sonsy. I had no idea you did this kind of thing,'
she said. Sonsy coloured and smiled faintly.

Chris beamed. 'She never shows anyone,' he said,
'she's so shy about it. I tell her she's crazy. The bloody
things take her six months—a year—to make and she
just puts them away—or gives them away, to that
place where she works. They've got a couple already,
from before we were married. This one's for us,
though. She promised.'

'You never said, Chris!' Betsy craned forward, a line
between her eyebrows. 'I never knew Sue did fancywork.'

'No, well . . .' Chris looked hesitant. 'Sonsy's quite
. . . private about it, you know?'

Betsy eyes widened and hardened. She bent forward and put an elegant hand out for the frame.

For a moment Sonsy hesitated, and Kate understood in that moment her 'shyness'. She'd wanted one

thing that was her own, uncontrolled, untainted by Betsy's little smears and stabs. Now she was going to have to hand it over and have Betsy touch, patronise, spoil.

'Oh,' Kate cried, as spontaneously as she could, and almost snatched the frame from Sonsy's had, clearing Betsy's by a whisker. 'Look at this, Jeremy!' She faced the picture in his direction, and he, Nick and Jill took it in. Their admiring silence was eloquent.

'Sue, where on earth did you get that kit?' said Betsy, brow furrowed. 'I've never seen it in the shops. Could I see the colour chart, please? It looks very complicated, but I daresay . . .'

'No, no, mum,' laughed Chris, 'there's no kit. Sonsy makes up her own patterns and colours and things.'

'Oh I *see*,' said Betsy. 'I thought there was something different about it. All that green and those mixed stitches. Still, it's very individual, Sue, even if . . .'

'It's brilliant, Sonsy,' said Kate sincerely. 'I've never seen anything like it.'

'Kate's a dear, generous girl,' said Betsy warmly, her eyes like flint. 'Always has been. I love enthusiastic people.' She cast down her eyes and brushed at her tapestry regretfully. 'Well . . . I suppose I'd better put my poor little effort away, and get about the dishes. This is obviously no place for a beginner to be fiddling about.' She bundled her work back into her basket and put the treasure box on top of it, biting her lip.

Chris's smile faded and for a moment he looked confused.

Poor dope, thought Kate, as she returned Sonsy's embroidery to her eager hands, and watched her packing it away in the hideous mauve sewing basket. He's got no idea of the ego he's dealing with. Still, he won't be called to account. It'll be poor old Sonsy who'll pay for this. Suddenly unable to stand the tension any longer, she walked over to Jeremy and grabbed him by the hand.

'We'll wash up, Betsy,' she said. 'I insist. Come on, Jeremy.'

Jeremy and Kate muttered together over the kitchen sink.

'Look, Kate, it's simple. Just say you're getting one of your sore throats, and we'll . . .'

'Jeremy, we can't! No one would believe it. Betsy'd feel terrible. She'd know . . .'

'Well, for God's sake, what does it matter? Anyone with any brains'd expect it. This whole thing's turning into a nightmare. It always was a crazy family . . . now they all seem to be going completely off the air.'

'Jeremy, we can't. The apples . . . Birdie . . .'

Jeremy flapped his soaking tea-towel on the stove in disgust. 'Let Birdie look after herself. You didn't make her come. Anyway, she seems to be enjoying it. She would! She thrives on other people's scenes, that woman. She's inhuman.'

'No, she's not. She's not at all. You always . . .'

'Well, I'm not interested in Birdie. Where's another tea-towel?'

'There, in that cupboard. On the bottom shelf.'

'There's everything *but* tea-towels in here.' Jeremy began feeling blindly around in the cupboard among the mounds of tea-cosies, milk jug covers, doilies and tray cloths, cherished, no doubt, by Alice's mother and never used since her death. A collection of tarnished napkin rings bounced onto the cracked green linoleum and rolled off in all directions. 'Hell!'

'You messer, Jeremy. You messer. Why don't you look!' Kate dived for the escaping napkin rings just as Jeremy did the same. They bumped foreheads, hard, Jeremy yelled and sat on the floor, his head in his hands.

Kate straightened up feeling that surge of unreasoning fury a bumped head always creates.

The door from the living room opened and Jill's face

with its wild frizz of red hair peeped around at them. 'Oh, sorry,' she said, her eyes wide, eyebrows shooting up.

'Oh, come in, Jillie, it's all right. We've just been trying to knock each other out,' said Kate, good humour suddenly restored. She held out her hand and hauled Jeremy to his feet.

'More brain cells bite the dust,' he groaned, rubbing his forehead. 'As if it isn't bad enough . . .'

'I came in to see if I could help,' said Jill. 'Well, actually, I couldn't stand the tension, to be strictly honest. It's appalling in there. What's going on?'

'Beats me,' said Jeremy. 'Anyway, we might be going tomorrow. Kate's feeling a bit sick.'

'Don't you *dare*, Jeremy Darcy. And leave Nick and me stuck here with the Tenderhearteds!' whispered Jill furiously.

'We're not going, Jill. Of course we're not,' said Kate calmly. 'We can't. Oh, damn—these rubber gloves are leaking. They're useless things—too thin. Jillie, I saw a packet of them on the table there, at the back. A four-pack. There are three pairs left in it. See? Could you get me another pair? Thanks.'

'Of *course* we can go, if you're sick, Katie . . .' Jeremy wasn't going to give up. But before he could go on the living room door opened again and Nick slid through.

'Godfather, what do you think you're doing leaving me in there like a shag on a rock, Jill?'

He turned to Jeremy. 'Betsy's had a go at Sonsy and Alice so far and now she's on to Anna. They're all like cats on hot bricks.'

'Oh, I *know*,' said Kate. 'We went through it last night. Isn't it awful?'

'That woman'll get herself murdered one day,' said Jeremy grimly. 'And no one'd be surprised except her. She'd be astonished.'

'Yes, poor Betsy,' said Kate. 'She really means well . . .'

'Oh, Katie, you're incorrigible.' Jeremy regarded his wife indulgently. 'She doesn't mean well . . . use your head! She doesn't know what she means. She just knows what she wants. And what she wants is to have everyone jumping when she says jump.'

'I think she's got something on her mind, though, Jeremy, really,' said Kate earnestly. 'The way she looked at Wilf tonight . . . she looked scared, I told you . . .'

'Yeah, well, he's a funny character, that's for sure,' said Nick, stroking his beard thoughtfully. 'Those stories of his . . . talk about lugubrious.'

'And what about Alice? Honestly!' said Jill. 'But still, I wish Betsy'd leave her alone. She obviously doesn't want to leave this house. I mean, what does it matter if it's messy and old. She doesn't mind. She likes to have all her junk around her. Even if she doesn't know where anything is, she knows it's here somewhere, and that's all she cares about. Who wants to play Mah Jong, anyway? Scrabbles's more my level and she knows where *that* is. I wouldn't mind a game, actually. How about . . .'

'But, look, Nick, what's she getting at Anna about now?' Kate broke in, impatient for once with Jill's stream-of-consciousness vivacity. 'Not the leech thing again, surely.'

'No.'

'Well, what?'

'Oh, we were getting a lecture on the evils of Damien Treloar when I left,' Nick said carelessly, studying his thumbnail. 'His cruelty to poor little Annie, his conceit, pomposity and general moral turpitude.'

'Oh, for goodness sake!' Kate exploded. 'It's so stupid. The man's not that bad.'

'He's a little twirp,' said Jeremy. 'What Anna ever married him for, I don't . . .'

'He's in fact an extremely intelligent and attractive man,' interrupted Jill in a high voice. Kate and Jeremy looked at her in surprise. She looked back rather aggressively, her pale skin with its dusting of freckles flushed pink right down to the neck of her striped jumper.

'Oh, Jill's a great fan of Damien's these days.' Nick smiled without humour. He was as pale as Jill was pink. 'Won't hear a word against him. They're working together on a book, you know. Closely. Intimately, you might say.'

'Shut up, Nick, you're talking drivel,' snapped Jill. She turned to Kate. 'Damien has in fact written a very good book on Australian antiques, with his own photographs, which are *also* very good, and he's doing it with Pinkies and I'm his editor. That's all. It's an important book so I'm spending a bit of time on it, and he's a perfectionist, so I've had to see a bit of him along the way. Nothing special or intimate about it.' She held her head right up and spoke harshly and rather defiantly, a manner which didn't suit her and which made her words less convincing than they ought to be. Plainly, Damien was an issue between her and Nick.

'Well, if all your authors get the loving treatment you ladle out to that smarmy little creep, it's a wonder Pinkies isn't raided,' sneered Nick.

Kate stared at him in amazement. Gone was the genial, easy-going Nick, always her ally in spreading oil on troubled waters between their more unpredictable partners. His face was white, his eyes cold, his lips drawn back from his teeth. A jealous mask. Nick *jealous*. It seemed like a contradiction in terms. Distantly she heard the sound of a knock at the front door, and someone going to answer it. She hoped Zoe wouldn't wake.

'Nick, you're very offensive and stupid,' said Jill, still in that hard, repellent voice. 'If you can't tell by now . . .'

'Oh, I can tell all right. You're transparent. What's so laughable is your disgusting taste. God! Damien bloody Treloar!'

The four stood staring at one another, shocked by the raw feelings so suddenly exposed between them. They'd been friends for a very long time, but somehow, though both couples had had their ups and downs, the proprieties had always been observed between the four of them, whatever Kate may have confided to Jill, serious-faced, over lunchtime coffee, or Nick had complained about to Jeremy, embarrassed and distressed, over a beer after work.

Kate put out her hand and laid it on Nick's arm. 'Nick, don't . . .'

The door opened. Chris looked in at them, his dark, good-looking face tense. 'Ah, sorry, ah . . . Jill, someone's here to see you.'

'To see *me?* Who on earth?' Jill's surprise was almost comical.

'Ah . . . it's Damien. Damien Treloar.'

5

Good Wives

666

To Anna the next half hour was a nightmare. Damien
smiling, charming, only the tone of his voice and the
self-consciousness of his gestures betraying, to her at
least, his high state of tension. When the knock had
come at the door and Rodney had rushed to answer
it, she'd been relieved. Anything to deflect her mother's attention, to be released from her father's silent,
concentrated concern, Rodney's smirking. Chris's su-
periority, stupid little Sonsy's distress, the obvious embarrassment of Nick and Jill, who had separately
escaped to the kitchen.

Then Rodney had come back into the room with his
eyebrows up and his face tomato red. He had looked
at Betsy.

'It . . . it's Damien. He's in the hall.'

'God, speak of the devil!' exploded Chris.

Anna's heart gave a sickening jolt. She felt the blood
rush to her cheeks and tingle to her very finger ends.
Damien here. Come to take her away. Take her back
to independence, the grown-up world she'd experienced so briefly. She half hated him. But he was her
lifeline. She struggled to keep her face expressionless,
to stay sitting in her chair.

Rodney looked at her and on his lips an involuntary smile trembled. He raised his hand to disguise it.

'He says he's here to see Jill.'

Jill! The shock was like a blow to the stomach. What did Damien have to do with Jill? She looked quickly at Betsy, whose face was a brittle mask, caught a glimpse of Sonsy looking irritatingly white and tragic, noted Alice sitting forward in her chair eyes alert, brow deeply furrowed, looking like an old witch.

And then Damien was in the room, a folder under his arm, apologising for the intrusion, greeting them all, smiling at her like an old friend, asking for Jill.

'She mentioned she'd be staying here, and when I found I'd be up here myself this weekend I thought you wouldn't mind if I dropped a few photographs in to her. I suppose she's told you about the book.'

No, no, Jill hadn't told us, thought Anna. She wouldn't, of course. So Damien's book was to be published—and by Pinkies. Very prestigious. Had he approached them using his 'contacts'—Jill, in this case? Or had Jill approached him? Well, what did it matter! The excitement that had filled her body had drained away, leaving only a nervous irritability.

Jill came in—tall, exotic, gaudy in scarlet and green. Her magnificent hair stood out round her face like red wires. Her chin was up, her cheeks flushed, her nipples standing out through the fine wool of her skimpy pullover. Damien greeted her with exactly the right mixture of friendliness and professional interest, but his eyes flicked up and down her body in a way that was more intimate than merely admiring.

Kate and Jeremy had followed Jill in. Nick was with them, his face tense.

Anna was filled with rage and frustration. How dare Damien do this? How dare he come in here and parade his pathetic flirtations in front of her. Shaming her in front of everyone.

'Well, Damien. Will you have a drink?' Betsy said coolly, the perfect lady, civilised to the last. Anna willed him to refuse, to go as suddenly as he'd come. At the same time she knew that his going would leave her flat and empty with nothing, nothing to fear or to hope for. And so with another part of her mind she willed him to stay, and she watched with hopelessly jangled feelings as he smiled and accepted. He sat down beside Sonsy, casually laying his arm along the back of the couch. She looked at him like a petrified rabbit, silly little fool. He murmured something to her and she shrank away from him—hopelessly gauche, absurdly fearful, looking around for Chris to protect her from this new danger.

Anna's lip curled. She'd show them she was made from the proper stuff, show him that she didn't care. Show him that she couldn't be manipulated and played with—not anymore.

Jill sat on a high stool by the table, leaning back against it. Her long, well-shaped legs stretched in front of her, crossed at the ankles. She radiated energy and defiance, superbly ignoring Nick who scowled over a drink behind her.

'What brings you up here, Damien?' she said, in her distinctive, husky voice, when he'd accepted his drink from Chris, complimented the unsmiling Alice on the pretty little wine glass, lifted his drink in a general toast and settled back, looking amused.

'Well, other than your bright eyes, sweetie, I had a few dealers to see, and the weather looked good—so I came on up.' He leaned back and turned towards Sonsy.

'Little Sonsy,' he said, inclining his head towards her, and trying unsuccessfully to catch her eye. 'Your first year up here—and how are you liking it?'

Sonsy flushed, smiled and murmured.

'That's good,' he said. 'I guess you fit in better than I did, eh?' He looked around at the assembled Tenders, winked at Kate, and grinned. 'Can't say I really excelled in the healthy outdoor life stakes—or the parlour games. Played Mah Jong yet?'

'No,' said Chris evenly. 'We can't find the set.'

'Oh, bad luck! It was a lovely old thing, too. Still, it'll probably turn up, and then you can all get together around the table and have a really good go like always—without me to slow things up—or maybe Sonsy'll fill that role this year.' He smiled at her and her flush deepened.

'Anna had a huge leech on her leg, earlier,' said Rodney loudly, suddenly pushing himself forward from his place by the wall to deliver this shot.

Damien looked at him coldly. 'Very nasty,' he said, but his mouth tightened, and he paled slightly.

'They're horrible things, aren't they?' chattered Kate. 'Zoe's so scared of them. I tell her they don't really hurt you, but . . .'

'Fellow at bowls . . .' Wilf came out of camouflage, his slightly querulous voice raised. 'Fellow at bowls told me you shouldn't ever underestimate the leech.'

There was a paralysed silence.

'The silent killers, he called them,' said Wilf. 'He was in Malaya for years. He said ninety-nine out of a hundred blokes'd have a dozen on them at once, and no ill effects. Then the hundredth bloke'd get one, and he'd just keel over. Allergic, see. Shock. Heart failure. He'd fall over and never get up.' He nodded solemnly around the room. 'You can't be too careful,' he said, and sank back in his chair.

Damien licked his top lip, under his sandy moustache. 'Well, there you are,' he said. He looked sick.

'I had no idea . . .' began Kate.

'Where are you staying, Damien?' said Jill determinedly, at the same time.

'Oh, I'll lay my lonely head down in some motel or other,' said Damien, obviously relieved by the change of subject. Colour began to seep back into his face. 'Can anyone recommend a place?' He bent towards Sonsy and his voice softened. 'How about you, little sister-in-law?'

Sonsy shook her head wordlessly, her eyes wide. She

seemed fascinated by him. Now she'd met his gaze she couldn't shake it. She was pale, and breathing fast.

A relatively normal conversation about accommodation started. Damien continued to ask Sonsy's opinion. A couple of times he shifted in his seat and his fingers brushed her shoulder. Anna concentrated on keeping her expression pleasantly interested. Oh, couldn't he leave any woman alone?

· She noticed with satisfaction that Jill was looking a bit put out. Now she was getting a taste of what life with Damien Treloar was all about. No doubt this display with Sonsy was all for her benefit. Anna knew him so well. He loved to torment people—especially women, for whom he had a special game. He would devote himself to winning them, using every gram of his not inconsiderable charm. He would flatter, smoulder, be beside himself with unstated longing for them. And then, when they were expanding, softening to him, he would turn the spotlight onto someone else, leaving them shaken, wrong-footed, half fearing they'd made fools of themselves, misinterpreted his interest, thrown themselves at him. It gave him a feeling of power, and the more beautiful and confident the woman, the better. She'd seen it often, suffered it herself. It was despicable. But then, how easily, easily, no matter how enraged and humiliated one had felt, could he win confidence back again when he was ready. Hadn't he convinced her, time and again, that it was her, her only, that he loved, and that all the other was just a game, a diversion, a weakness. And, even after all that had happened, she still really believed that.

He would laugh about the other women afterwards—make jokes about their physical imperfections—a nose a bit too big, bony knees, hairy legs, anything. How they would have writhed to hear him, those confident beauties, those clever, wisecracking blue-stockings! How it paid them back for those smug, patronising, pitying looks at parties, when they thought they were taking him from her so effortlessly.

For a while Anna had played his game. Oh yes. But in the end she had left. One night, in some fit of desperate rage she'd told her mother all about it. And that was, simply, that. Betsy had made it so clear, the path she had to take. Anna knew she was right. No good blaming poor old Mum because she'd fallen for an unreliable bastard. Of course she had to leave him.

He'd tried to woo her back a few times, but by then she was back at home, and she couldn't, *couldn't* go back on all she'd said, go back to that, that degradation, as Betsy had called it. If only she hadn't confessed quite so much—hadn't told her mother, in her misery and wish to discredit Damien, instinctively knowing how, about the—other games he liked to play when they were alone, in bed. Betsy had been so shocked, though she'd tried to hide it. If Anna went back, Betsy would know she was going back to all that, too. She'd know that every night . . . and maybe she'd told Dad. It was possible, even probable. She could feel her father's protective eye on her now. How would he feel if she returned to a man whom he must think depraved? What would he think of her?

But she found herself looking at Damien's long slender fingers as they caressed the wine glass, the skin of his leg above his sock as he crossed his knee, the fine white smoothness of his throat above his open-necked shirt. He looked up, and their eyes met. His heavy-lidded grey eyes . . . full of meaning and warm longing.

She felt a passionate stirring, a yearning to touch him, and suddenly the two halves of her mind clicked together. She was free of indecision and doubt. She knew what she wanted. She wanted him, whatever the cost, and now she knew that he wanted her too. He *had* come for her. The whole thing with Jill and the photographs had been a blind to get him under Betsy's guard. She leaned back and dropped her eyes.

The message had been exchanged. Later he'd find a way of speaking to her alone. They'd wait till the family was asleep. She'd pack a few things. And then . . . they'd just go.

In a dream she heard him start up a flirtatious conversation with Jill, as a second round of drinks was poured. Good . . . good, no one could guess what had passed between them. It had happened too quickly, surely. Her eyes flicked around the room. Auntie Alice looked as sour as a lemon, staring at Damien as if he was some noxious pest on an apple tree. Chris was leafing through an old *Reader's Digest*, elaborately ignoring the whole thing. Wilf was abstracted, staring into space. Betsy's face was unreadable, but it seemed to Anna that she had relaxed slightly, Damien's act with Jill, however distasteful it might be, having no doubt reassured her that he wasn't trying to worm his way back into her daughter's life, anyway.

Sonsy looked sick, probably disconcerted to find that the naughty man didn't have designs on her after all. Transparent as usual, Kate was concernedly watching Jill, darting nervous little glances at Nick's thunderous face and Jeremy's furrowed brow. Rodney loomed in the background, hands deep in his pockets. He too was looking at Jill, his plump face pouted in a rather comical expression of adolescent prudery. And beside Kate, that woman Birdie—Verity what's-her-name—was sitting as still as an animal scenting the air. Her amber eyes, unblinking behind the glasses, were turned to Anna, watching her survey of the room. Anna smiled at her, her best brave, little-girl-lost smile, and was reassured by a vague, answering curve of the lips. No, Birdie was no threat. Butch, scruffy little thing. She was a born wallflower, a watcher-on-the-sidelines all her life. Even if she'd noticed anything she wouldn't understand it, and anyway, who would she tell if she did? No, all was well. It was just a matter of waiting till Damien made his move. She'd know how to play along, when the time came.

• • •

Sonsy sat rigidly, her hands clasped in her lap. She looked down at them, and noticed almost with surprise that the knuckles were white, and her nails were cutting into her palms. She was acutely aware of Damien's arm carelessly stretched across the couch back, behind her head. Chris was pretending to read, but every now and then she felt his eyes on her. He must think she'd been silly, being so overawed by Damien. He must compare her to Jill, laughing, talking, tossing a clever answer back for every clever question Damien could throw at her.

She stole a glance at Chris and found he was looking at her. He frowned, the line between his eyebrows deepening until he was almost scowling. She looked at him, fascinated, for a moment, then dropped her eyes to her hands again. Her cheeks felt fiery. Another thought struck her. Maybe Chris thought *she* had flirted with Damien, encouraging him to be familiar. Maybe he thought that she was quiet now because Jill had regained Damien's attention, and she was jealous. Oh, that's probably what he did think. Her heart began to beat too fast. She swallowed, willing herself to be calm.

'Sue,' Betsy's voice cut through her thoughts. 'You're very quiet. Is anything wrong, dear?'

Everyone stopped talking and looked at her.

Sonsy jumped. 'Oh, nothing, Betsy . . . I was just thinking . . .'

'Private little thoughts? Oh, I can see Christopher will have to look to his laurels. You seem to have made a conquest here, Damien!' She giggled, but her bright brown eyes darted round the room, coming to rest on Chris who sat silent in his chair, the magazine still open on his lap.

Sonsy blushed and gasped. 'Oh, no . . .' she began, and stopped. Her face was hot, the blood throbbing in her ears. She was in a trap. She couldn't make it right. Suddenly it all became too much for her. Her eyes filling with tears she jumped up and bolted from the room.

'Honestly, Betsy,' drawled Damien Treloar. 'You shouldn't tease poor Sonsy like that. She isn't up to it.'

'Oh, I feel dreadful,' said Betsy, eyes wide. 'I had no idea I'd be touching on a sore spot. I'm so sorry, Christopher. I'll apologise to her in the morning.'

Oh, you old hypocrite, thought Kate savagely.

Chris, grim-faced, shut his magazine. 'Don't worry, Mum,' he said coldly. 'Sonsy's a bit nervy. Please don't apologise to her. She's the one who should be apologising to you, and everyone else, not the other way around.'

There was an embarrassed silence, into which the sharp tap on the front door exploded like a shot. Rodney escaped to answer it. They heard voices and he returned with a tall, intense-looking woman with a broad, intelligent face, short-sighted grey eyes and a mass of grey-streaked black hair which was tied at the back with a scarf and hung heavily almost to her waist. She looked about forty, and was extremely handsome in her way. In a bright canvas sling, against her chest, was a tiny baby, fast asleep. Its little hands clutched the soft material of its mother's jacket, a soft mass of gingery hair stood up like a bird's crest on its head. One blue-clad foot stuck negligently from the sling. The woman, sensing their interest, instinctively curved a protective arm around the little body and seeing Alice by the fire, stepped forward.

'Um . . . I'm sorry to barge in on you like this, Alice, with your family here and everything,' she said, 'but I've absolutely got to make a phone call, and I was wondering . . .'

'Course. Help yourself, Theresa,' muttered Alice. 'You know the way, love. Off you go.'

'Thank you. Oh, hello, Mr Tender. Sorry, I didn't see you there. Not wearing my glasses,' said the woman, now revealed as the 'arty type' from across the road. She smiled at Wilf, who had risen to greet her.

'See you've got the young chappie with you to-night,' said Wilf.

She looked down and again curved her arm around her little burden. 'Oh . . . yes . . . she's—it's a girl, actually, Mr Tender. She's only three months. I can't leave her in the house by herself. She likes the sling. It makes her sleep.'

'Well, Wilf, we're going to have to introduce our-selves if you won't do it for us.' Betsy's voice sounded immature, squeaky almost, after the quiet, measured depth of Theresa's few words.

'Oh, sorry Bet,' mumbled Wilf, and stood uncer-tainly, at a loss as to what to do next.

'She doesn't want to be bothered with all that, Bet,' snapped Alice. 'Just go through, love,' she said to The-resa, and there was something urgently protective in the voice. Theresa ducked her head and began to move. But Betsy smiled and took charge.

'I'm Betsy Tender, Auntie Alice's niece,' she said brightly, taking Theresa's arm and turning her to face the others. 'And this is my daughter Anna, my son Christopher, and of course you met my little boy, Rodney, when you came in. My . . . um . . . Damien Treloar . . . Jill Mission . . . Christopher's friend, Jer-emy Darcy . . .'

Kate kept her head down until it came to her turn to nod and smile. Obviously the poor woman didn't want to know all these people. What were they to her? She just wanted to make a phone call, and get back home with her baby. Kate remembered that feeling, that feeling of intense, almost agonising bond-ing with a tiny child, so recently growing and moving inside you. It was as if you were still part of one an-other. The feeling wore off after a while, and other, more complex emotions took its place. But while it remained . . .

'Kate Delaney . . .'

Kate raised her head and smiled at Theresa. 'Hello,' she said. Theresa looked white and strained. The calm she had brought into the room had disappeared. The baby turned and wriggled, making little whimpering noises.

'Kate is actually Jeremy's lawful wedded wife, Mrs Sullivan,' Betsy went on archly. 'She kept her maiden name. She's one of those liberated ladies. But she and Jeremy are safely married, all the same. They've got a dear little girl of their own, you know. Quite legitimate, I'm happy to say!' She gave a tinkling laugh.

Kate could have kicked her.

'Look, if you don't mind I think I'll just . . .' said Theresa, turning abruptly and making for the kitchen.

They heard her lift the receiver and begin to dial.

'Well, that was a bit . . .' Betsy began.

'I think I better be making tracks,' said Damien, standing up. 'I've got a busy day tomorrow. Thanks for the drink.'

Anna looked up. He was going! She stared at him, not caring if anyone saw her this time. And again their eyes met, and she felt certainty flood through her. He was planning something. He looked mischievous, excited, triumphant almost. *I have a secret and I won't tell—yet*, said his eyes. *You'll see, Anna.*

'Oh, of course, Damien. Well . . .' said Betsy stiffly.

'Goodbye, Auntie Alice. Nice to see you again,' said Damien smoothly, smiling at the old woman's scowling face. Her lip curled slightly and she grunted, settling back into her chair and deliberately lowering her eyes.

He grinned on, unabashed, and stood looking round without haste. 'See you later,' he said. 'Bye, Jillie my sweet. Be good.'

The phone tinkled and Theresa came back into the room. 'Thanks, Alice, I'll be off now . . . I'll let myself out.'

'I'm just going, too. I'll walk out with you,' said Damien.

She tucked her head down and made for the door without acknowledging him or anyone else. He shrugged, lifted a hand in silent farewell, and left them. They heard the two pairs of footsteps go down the corridor and through to the verandah. The front door opened and closed with a bang.

Unconsciously everyone relaxed. Anna felt the scrutiny of several pairs of eyes, and kept her head down.

'Well, I might make a cup of tea, I think,' said Kate. 'Everyone want one?'

'Coffee, please, Katie,' said Betsy absently. '*What* an extraordinary woman. Terribly abrupt, wasn't she? Is she always like that, Auntie Alice?'

'She's not a great talker,' said Alice sullenly. 'Keeps pretty much to herself. Suits me.'

'Almost rude, really,' Betsy persisted. 'There's never any need for that, however shy you are.'

'She seemed to be put off when you started talking about Kate's name, Mum,' Rodney said. 'Didn't she, Kate?'

'I didn't notice,' Kate lied.

'Well, she did, and when you said about Zoe not being a bastard.'

'Roddy!'

'Well, you know, illegitimate. I was thinking maybe . . .'

'Oh!' cried Betsy, eyes bright, nose, thought Kate, positively twitching. 'Oh! Of course! You mean her baby might be . . . she mightn't be . . . Oh how *awful* . . . I had no . . .'

'That's *enough*, Bet!'

Betsy jumped like a guilty child. Alice was half up from her chair, her bony hands gripping the arm rests, knuckles white.

'Leave the poor girl alone. You don't know a thing about her and no need for you to know. Leave her alone. Concentrate on your own problems. Peck the life out of your own family if you like, but leave my neighbours out of it.'

Betsy was crimson. 'Auntie Alice, I was just . . .'

'Well just *don't*,' thundered Alice. 'I don't know what you think you're doing, Bet, coming up here, poking and prying everywhere, trying to run everything and telling me what to do, when it's plain as the nose on your face that you can't manage your own affairs. How you could invite that worm of a son-in-law of yours to sit down in my lounge as if you owned the place's beyond me. You should have sent him packing!'

'Now, look, Auntie Alice . . .'

'Don't you now look me. I'm telling you. That man's not fit to breathe the same air as Theresa Sullivan, who you're so keen on running down. Smarmy little grub he is, smiling and cavorting around the place. I always said it, and I'll say it now, it was a black day when poor Anna took up with him. He's a rotter and a spoiler. And you as good as welcome him with open arms!'

She heaved herself into a standing position and looked at them all, her hooded eyes glittering feverishly under thick bows. Then she turned and pushed past Wilf doing his disappearing trick against the curtains, and banged through the French doors leading out to the back verandah. They heard a slam as she shut herself into her bedroom.

There was a silence, then Anna started to laugh.

'Well, Mum, you've got two people locked in their rooms so far,' she gasped. 'D'you want to try for three and win the jackpot?'

Barely ten minutes later, when Betsy's tears were still being mopped up and Kate was pouring the coffee and tea into mugs with a feverish haste, there was an apologetic knock at the back door.

'Oh, what next?' groaned Chris.

The door opened and Damien sidled in sheepishly. Somehow his reappearance, so totally unexpected to everyone but Anna, was quite anticlimactic after the upheavals of the evening. He was like a speaker at a dinner who'd done his turn, been thanked and got his applause, and then insisted on popping back to add a few more things he'd forgotten to say. Even Jill barely stirred at his entrance. He had put on a parka, and tiny droplets of water shone on its pale-blue surface like scales. His hair flopped over his forehead in damp curls, and his moustache glistened.

'Look, ah, I'm very sorry . . .' he began, and blinked in the light. 'I don't know how to tell you this, but I'm a bit stuck. Two tyres flat as tacks. I think kids have been at them. I've only got one spare.'

'Well, look, mate, that's bad luck, but . . .' Chris began.

'I thought maybe . . .' Damien spoke directly to Betsy, ignoring his brother-in-law. 'I thought you might let me doss down in the garage. I've got a sleeping-bag with me, by a stroke of good luck, and I'd be . . . out of everyone's way there.'

'Oh, Damien . . . it's not terribly convenient, actually,' said Betsy hesitantly. 'Is it Wilf?' She turned to her husband.

Wilf, stunned by this unexpected appeal, took a few moments to pull himself together and murmur the required agreement.

'Oh, I see.' Damien looked uncharacteristically downcast. 'Well, sure, I understand.' Then he regained his normal manner, and smiled at Betsy. 'Bit of a problem, eh? I can see your point. But it's bloody dark and cold out there, and tonight I can't sleep in the van. It's loaded up with things I bought today, you see. Kingsvale, Miss Pym's in Candlebark, Honeywell's—God, I had a spree! And sharing the van with a bunch of hand-carved picture frames bristling with nasty, lumpy little gumnuts and things, and a box of huge, old books, not to mention table linen from the year dot stinking of mothballs, doesn't exactly fill me with delighted anticipation.' He spread out his hands and grinned beguilingly. 'Look, Betsy, I've done a hard day's work, and I've got a van full of stuff and receipts to prove it. I'm hungry, I'm bushed. I need a night's sleep. Can't we bury the hatchet just for this one last time? I'm holding out the olive branch, Betsy.' He laughed, and his eyes twinkled at her. 'Betsy, the dove of peace is hovering meaningfully above my head. How about it?'

'Well, Damien . . .' said Betsy slowly. Kate watched her, fascinated. She tried to follow the thought processes which must be warring within Betsy's fertile brain: the wish to be civilised . . . not to be seen to be cowed by Alice . . . or to be unsure of Anna . . . the urge to annoy Nick . . . and a conflicting urge to disappoint Jill . . . a tempting chance to taunt Sonsy with Damien's presence tomorrow morning, perhaps . . . a strong urge to get rid of the menace altogether, and throw his charm back in his face. Which way would the scales tilt?

Several people in the room held their breath, waiting for Betsy's decision.

Finally she put her shoulders back, and smiled—a rather brittle smile, without warmth. She looked straight into Damien's eyes, as if she was warning him off.

'Well, under the circumstances I don't see I can really refuse, Damien. But the garage it will have to be, I'm afraid. And one of the boys will drive you into the village in the morning, before breakfast. The petrol station there has a workshop. It reopens at seven, so you'll be able to get away early.'

'That's very kind of you, Betsy. I appreciate it,' said Damien formally. 'After all, there's no reason in the world why you should help me out.'

'No, there isn't,' said Betsy coldly. 'But there you are.' She had taken control of the situation again. The tension in the room relaxed. She stood up and walked towards the kitchen.

'There's no light in the garage. I'll get you a kerosene lamp.'

'I'll do it, Mum,' said Rodney, pushing himself away from the wall against which he'd been affectedly slouching like a gangster in a film since Damien's reappearance.

'No,' she said sharply, 'I'll do it,' and she strode on. It was as if she wanted to bear the whole responsibility of Damien Treloar herself, unaided. As though her precious Roddy might be contaminated by having anything to do with him, thought Anna amusedly.

Even Damien's insouciance was affected by this indirect snub. He stared at her, and as she moved past him to go into the kitchen he put his hand on her arm. She stopped short.

'Betsy,' he said regretfully. 'Betsy this is no good. We've . . . we used to be part of the same family. I hate all these bad feelings between us.'

'Oh, spare us,' muttered Jeremy in disgust. Kate dug her elbow into his ribs.

Damien went on as if there had been no interruption.

'You know what I think? I think we ought to straighten out a few things. Not now, when we're all tired, but first thing tomorrow morning. I think we should have a good talk, all of us, the old crowd. I've learned a lot of things in the last few months . . .' He glanced briefly at Anna, and then at Jill, and then looked back to Betsy. 'I've been thinking hard, all the time I've been alone and working on the book, finishing the photographs, and everything. I've learned quite a bit about—selfishness, and dishonesty, and manipulation, and the effects they can have.' Again his eyes flickered to the calm face of Anna, the intent figure of Jill. 'I've woken up to a few things, about myself and other people. I think it's time it was all discussed, and brought out into the open, thrashed out, so that I at least can start off fresh, with nothing on my conscience or my mind.'

Kate heard Birdie draw a little, sharp breath beside her.

Betsy stood looking at Damien, and over her face a shadow of uncertainty passed like a wisp of a cloud dimming the sun on a windy afternoon.

Kate forced herself to look at Jill. She was smiling slightly to herself, looking at the toes of her flat, green shoes and turning them in and out. *Was* there something going on between Jill and Damien? It seemed so . . . unlikely. Jill and Damien Treloar? Damien after Nick? Was it possible? Well, it seemed so. Damien seemed to be about to clear the decks, and his conscience, in typical self-indulgent style, so as to be free to pursue other, more rewarding, goals.

But Anna . . . she didn't seem at all put out by all this. She was calm, almost abstracted, as though her mind was on something else entirely, or she was treasuring a secret no one else knew about. Strange. Maybe Jill was just a red herring. Maybe Damien's little talk was going to be about him and Anna getting back together.

'I don't know that all these dramatics are necessary. We'll see in the morning, Damien,' Betsy said, still in a formal tone but with an edge Kate couldn't quite place. 'I'll get you the lamp.' She went into the kitchen.

'Well, I think I'll be off, then,' said Nick, rising from his chair. His face was pale.

'What do you mean, off?' asked Jill crossly.

'I'm going. Leaving you to get on with it, Jillie. Hope you'll both be very happy.'

'Nick! Don't be ridiculous!' she exclaimed, turning to him and glancing nervously behind her at the slight figure lounging by the door.

But Nick pulled away from her, pushed roughly past the smiling Damien and, grabbing his parka from the table, disappeared before anyone else had a chance to react.

Jill tightened her lips and flopped down in her chair again. Her fists were clenched.

The could hear Betsy clattering and talking to herself in the kitchen. Kate shivered in the draught from the back door, hanging slightly ajar after Nick's abrupt departure. It was freezing.

'For God's sake, shut the door!' exclaimed Jeremy. He stared icily at Damien as he moved to do so.

'Jeremy, go and get Nick back,' Kate said. 'This is ridiculous. It's awful.'

Jill swung round in her chair, with angry eyes. 'Oh, let him stew in his own juice! He's acting like a child. He'll get over it.'

'Mum . . .'

The door into the hall swung open to reveal Zoe, rumpled and ruffled, shivering in her pyjamas and bare feet. She blinked at them, her eyes dark with sleep.

'Why is everyone shouting for? I woke up.' She stared at Jill hunched in her chair.

'Well, it's Zoe. Hello, honey,' said Damien softly. Zoe stared at him and didn't answer.

'Zoe, darling, I'm sorry. Come on.' Kate hurried over to her daughter and began to usher her back to bed. Zoe struggled a little and stopped at the bedroom door.

'What's wrong with Jill, Mum?' she whispered. 'Why is she crying? Why is Damien here? Did Damien hurt Jill?'

'No, no, of course not, darling . . . Jill's OK,' murmured Kate. Out of the corner of her eye she saw a movement and turned quickly. Nothing. Just a bare corridor and the dim doorway of Betsy and Wilf's room, the big double bed looming in shadow. This place is getting me down, she thought. I'm seeing spooks now. She ushered Zoe back to bed.

'I hate Damien. Auntie Alice says he's a leech and a rotter. He always makes people cry. He did last year, too.'

'That's enough, Zoe. Now snuggle down and go back to sleep, like a good girl.' Kate gave the sleeping-bag a final pat and froze. In the mirror of the old wardrobe in the corner, the doorway to Betsy's room showed like a frame of a picture. And through the frame crept a little figure in a red dressing gown with a hood, eyes huge and shadowed in the half-light. Sonsy. As Kate watched she looked up and down the corridor and then slipped out of the frame towards the front of the house.

Kate straightened up and frowned. What was Sonsy doing in Betsy and Wilf's room? Funny, creeping little thing. She sighed, looked around the cluttered room and suddenly longed for home. The old house seemed filled with secrets and malice, the wind that swirled the clutching mist outside made the boards creak and the tin roof flap. It was not pleasant. It was getting on her nerves. Suddenly she made up her mind. Jeremy was right. Life was too short for this sort of thing. Tomorrow they'd make their excuses and go. How marvellous! She felt inexpressibly relieved, and was surprised. She hadn't realised just how much the atmosphere had been weighing her down until this moment. Well, she'd made a sensible decision at last. She'd explain to Birdie. Jeremy would be pleased. Zoe wouldn't, but maybe a waffle at the Paragon—or a horseride somewhere on the way back—or a couple of days in a hotel—why not? They had the whole week. Planning happily, Kate wandered back to the living room.

The party was breaking up. Damien had taken himself off to his hard bed in the garage at last. Chris and Jeremy had their heads together—talking about Nick, probably. Jill had gone for a walk, apparently. Birdie was in the bathroom cleaning her teeth. Rodney had gone into his room through the storeroom ('to save waking Zoe again, dear', said Betsy, infinitely thoughtful. 'She's such a nervy little thing, isn't she?'). Anna sat still in her chair, cheeks pink, eyes glowing.

'I hope he's careful of that lamp, Anna,' said Betsy, darting a sharp glance at her. 'They're dangerous things . . .' She began clearing the table of mugs, glasses and plates, clattering the dishes to attract attention to the fact that she was doing it alone. Then she clicked her tongue in annoyance. 'Oh, look at that, that . . . Damien didn't take the bally thermos and cake after all that!'

'Oh, for goodness sake, don't fuss, Mum,' said Anna. 'What does it matter? I don't know why you bothered. You don't even like him.'

'Oh, don't start on me now, darling.' Betsy suddenly looked at her with real appeal in her eyes. 'I'm so tired.'

And indeed she did look exhausted. There were little pouches under her eyes and deeper lines beside her mouth. The strain of the evening had told on her, thought Kate sympathetically. How ironic, since most of the ruckus had been her own doing. Still, poor old Betsy. Awful to be your own worst enemy.

Anna seemed to have the same thought. 'Oh, sorry, sorry, poor old Mum.' She stood up and stretched, her body arching magnificently as she yawned and shook her hair back. 'I'm off to bed. Leave those things, Mum. We'll do them in the morning.' She stood over her mother, tall and beautiful, and then impulsively put her arms around her and gave her a hug. Betsy looked surprised and touched, and hugged her back. Kate caught the twinkle of tears in her eyes.

Later, in bed, Kate listened to the clock in the living room strike eleven. It was early, really, but she felt exhausted. Thank God they'd be going in the morning. She turned over and, in the delicious moments before sleep came, thought happily of the next few days, free of tension and responsibility for other people's troubles. Later, much later, when she could think of the days that followed without a horrified shudder, she would remember those rosy plans and wryly smile at how little one could ever imagine what the future had in store.

By midnight the house was silent. Anna, lying staring at the ceiling in the Rose room, heard the clock strike with rising excitment. Now, surely, she had waited long enough. There hadn't been a sound for over half an hour. Only the wind, pulling at the roof and pushing at the windows. She slipped cautiously from under the covers and sat on the edge of the bed, listening for a moment before she got up. She pulled the blankets up and bunched them to look as if the bed was occupied, then picked up her boots, tiptoed to the door, and slipped like a shadow down the corridor, and into the living room. Compressing her lips she twisted the old brass knob of the back door. It was unlocked! Left for Nick and Jill, of course. Maybe they were on their way in right now. Well, she'd have to risk it. Nick and Jill weren't her worry. Mum and Dad were all that mattered now. She had to get to Damien before Betsy found out, armour herself with his need for her against Betsy's tears, sweet reasonableness, and finally, anger.

She slipped out the door and down the stairs. On the path she began putting on her boots. She could see part of the garage from where she stood, the soft flicker of the lamp showing at the high windows. Damien was waiting. She started forward, treading on the wet grass instead of the concrete path, almost without thinking consciously that this way her boots would make no noise. Her heart beat fast, her whole attention was fixed on the garage, and that warm light, flickering in the dark.

So she didn't hear the faint click as the back door opened behind her, and was unaware that a shadow slipped down the stairs and followed her, keeping near the shrubs that lined the path.

The garage was before her now. She crept up to its dark side and towards the door, hesitating, now that the moment had come, half afraid, almost shy, of taking the last, irrevocable step. And then she heard Damien's laugh—a low teasing laugh, and a movement, and an answering murmur. He was not alone.

'Don't make problems, old girl. I know what I'm doing. It's out of your hands.' Damien's clear, confident voice floated out into the fog from the window above her head.

Again there was a low murmur. Anna strained to catch the words, but could distinguish nothing.

Damien's voice responded—crooning, gentle. 'Oh, yes, honey, my beautiful girl. My beautiful, red-headed girl. You're my darling, aren't you? My own sweet darling . . .' The crooning went on. Anna felt cold and sick. So it had been Jill all the time.

There was another low murmur, and this time Anna caught her own name. Damien's voice sharpened. 'Look, Anna's not an issue,' he said. 'Anna and I are finished. We have been for a long time.'

'Whatever I may have thought, there's no future with a mummy's little girl like that for me.' The voice dropped again, and Anna, eyes screwed tightly shut, fists clenched, could almost see his hand stretch out to stroke, caress. 'Not with you around, anyway, bright-eyes.' He laughed softly, delightedly. 'Oh, God, poor old Anna, mummy's little girl, daddy's little sweetheart . . . too much! No!' His voice grew firm. 'No—don't say anything. Please. Look, you mightn't have planned for this—you mightn't want it, even—but you've got it, old girl. Come on—accept the inevitable. It's fate, as far as I'm concerned. There's no turning back.' And again, as if moved by his own words, he began to purr and croon, and his voice trembled with an aching sweetness that made Anna writhe. Never, never, had he sounded like that for her. 'Now I've found you—oh, I'm not going to lose you, am I?

No one can take you away from me, ever again. My dear heart . . .'

You *bastard.* You *bastard.* That *bitch!* The words thundered in Anna's head. For a moment she thought she'd screamed them aloud. But Damien spoke on, calm now, and firm.

'Look, we've got the rest of our lives before us. We've already produced something really special together. We're a great team. And tomorrow I'm going to tell those Tenders where to get off. A few home truths'll shake them up!' He laughed and went on, almost as though he was talking to himself. 'Who'd have thought my little idea would grow into such a winner? The experience of a lifetime bearing fruit at last. And what an irony . . .'

Anna could stay no longer. Blindly she felt her way along the garage wall, and began to stumble back towards the house. Her mind spun and jangled . . . 'Anna's not an issue . . . poor old Anna . . . daddy's little sweetheart . . . we're a great team . . . irony'. Irony! The book she'd lived with all their married life, a winner for Damien and Jill! She wasn't to share in its success, be thanked for her support, revel in the optimism and security of Damien on the crest of a wave. She was to be given back to her family, a reject, a poor sick thing.

She reached her bedroom and sat on the bed. And felt, with relief, the shame and hurt overtaken and overwhelmed by a tidal wave of rage.

6

The Morning After

ϾϾϾ

Detective-constable Martin McGlinchy yawned
hugely, picked up his mug of tea and leaned back in
his chair, eyes closed. He was dimly aware of the
phone ringing in the front of the house, but made no
move to answer it. Mum would get it—it was bound
to be Auntie Val anyway. No one else'd have the nerve
to ring this early. Yap, yap, yap. That woman spent
her life with a phone attached to her ear. She'd even
been on talk-back radio, gas-bagging away. God, the
things people listened to, Constable McGlinchy
thought, shaking his woolly head. Still, some people
had nothing else to do, apparently. And in this out-
of-the-way hole it was no wonder. Nothing ever happened in the mountains, except the odd lost hiker, the
usual domestics and, now and then, a bushfire. He
took a sip of tea and tried to wake up. He'd have to
get going. Didn't do to be too late. You never knew
when you'd be wanted to investigate some matter of
life or death—like a stolen wheelbarrow or something.

'Mart! Mart!' his mother's voice shrilled down the
hall. 'Mart, phone. Quick!'

Groaning, Martin unfolded himself and trailed to
the phone. His mother was hissing at him and point-

ing to the receiver. What now? He put the phone to his ear and yawned before speaking.

'Hello . . .' His eyes fluttered closed.

'McGlinchy!'

Martin's eyes snapped open. 'Yes sir.' He had almost squeaked in his surprise. Simon Toby ringing him at home. This was unprecedented. His mind raced frantically. What had he done wrong? What had he forgotten?

'McGlinchy, I want you to come to the station as quickly as you can.'

'What's up, sir?'

'Some trouble down in the old part of Atherton. I'll tell you when you get here. Get a move on.'

'Yes, sir!'

Martin hung up and started tearing at his pyjama jacket. This sounded more like it. It must be really big if old Simon Toby wouldn't even talk about it on the phone. Marijuana in someone's backyard, maybe. Or a big burglary. Some of those old houses were packed with valuables, and no locks to speak of, either. He hurried to his room and began to throw on his clothes.

Three-quarters of an hour later Martin was not feeling so enthusiastic.

'Sounds like a pretty straightforward accident to me, sir,' he said glumly, as he swung the car down to the turn-off. He glanced at his superior, sitting stolidly beside him.

'Yes, well . . . you're probably right, Martin. But Roberts and Chan thought we ought to take a look before the body was moved—just in case. Now, slow down, let's see . . . there's the place . . . that old weatherboard last in the row—on the corner. Nice spot, eh? Park behind Roberts. Oh good, the doc's here too.'

Martin pulled the car into the kerb directly opposite

the old house. It looked almost derelict. The fence sagged under the weight of a scrambling climbing rose, the paint had peeled from the old weatherboards, and rust spotted the iron roof. The verandah that surrounded the house had been closed in with fibro and opaque, bubbly glass, giving the house a blind, secret look. Over to the right side of the house, surrounded by bushes, stood a rickety garage, the door wide open.

'Come on, Martin. Let's get going.'

Martin scrambled from the car, and as he turned to lock the door glanced at the house outside which they were parked. It was trim enough, anyway. His eye caught a movement at a window, as if a curtain had been quickly twitched back.

He straightened his shoulders and adopted his formal look as he and Simon Toby crossed the narrow road and walked down the short path to the front door of the house. He didn't want to make a muck of this. If it turned out to be a real case, a case he could get his teeth into, it might lead to a transfer— Lithgow, Penrith—or even Sydney. He fingered the notebook in his pocket as Toby knocked.

The door opened and a tall, scared-looking, rather soft-faced boy stood looking at them.

'Detective-sergeant Toby, son,' Martin's superior said gently. 'I understand you've had some trouble here this morning.'

The boy turned without letting go of the door.

'Mum!' he bawled.

They heard the tap of approaching footsteps.

'Mum, it's the . . .' the boy began.

'It's all right, darling, I'm here.' A tall, dark woman joined the boy at the door, put her arm around him, and looked at the newcomers enquiringly. She was pale and showed signs of stress, but radiated a protective energy. The boy relaxed within the safety of her force field.

Simon Toby smiled pleasantly. 'I'm Detective-sergeant Toby and this is Detective-constable Mc-Glinchy. You would be Mrs Elizabeth Tender?'

He waited for her nod.

'We're just going to have a look at a few things, Mrs Tender, and talk to a few people in the house. Just a matter of routine.'

The woman opened the door wide and they stepped in. The atmosphere of the house was cool and stuffy. There were camp stretchers ranged along the verandah wall, and suitcases and carry bags littered the floor. Weak, dusty sunlight seeped through the bubbly glass windows.

'Ah . . . we have a lot of people staying . . . please excuse the mess,' the woman said. 'This is my younger son, Rodney. Um . . . I suppose you want to see the . . . outside first. The doctor . . . arrived. He's out there with your people.'

She led them down the hall, through a cluttered sitting room where a group of people stopped talking to watch them pass, and out the back door.

'Thank you, Mrs Tender. We'll be right from here,' said Toby quietly, and nodded to the woman as she muttered something and turned back to the house, shutting the door behind her. They walked down the back steps and began to cross a broad strip of wet grass. Martin shaded his eyes and looked down into the orchard.

About half way down the hill, almost hidden from their view by the canopy of the tree under which they stood, two blue figures watched another in a sports-coat crouching over something covered with a white sheet. As they drew closer the crouching figure stood up and, catching sight of the two detectives, lifted an arm in salute.

'G'day,' called Toby and hitched at his belt.

Martin followed him down the hill and with him pushed through the hanging leafy canopy to join the others in the green shade of the old apple tree—one of the biggest Martin had ever seen. There was an old sawn log lying on the grass by its trunk. Put there years ago as a seat, probably. The overhanging branches dipped down on all sides, making a little round room of the space within. And on the damp floor of the little room was the reason for their presence. An unmistakeable shape lying under a white sheet. Martin stared at it, feeling suddenly a bit sick. He noticed a booted toe poking out at one end, some brown, shrivelled apple cores huddling in a fold of linen.

'What's doing?' said Toby, almost casually.

Without a word one of the uniformed police who had been standing guard bent down and whisked the white cloth away. A faint whiff of camphor and the sour smell of sickness rose into the air. Damien Treloar, glazed eyes staring, mouth twisted into a horror, looked up at them. He was very, very dead.

Kate watched from the kitchen window as the white-shrouded body was carefully buckled to a stretcher and carried away. She turned to Jeremy.

'Gosh, I'll be glad to get out of here. I never want to see this house again. I'm going right now to start . . .'

Jeremy put his arm around her shoulders.

'Look, darling, I think you'd better hold off a bit. I don't think the cops'll let us buzz off just like that.'

'But why not? It's obvious what happened. He was hungry, and he came out and ate the apples. They found four cores near the body. Alice told everyone not to eat them, the apples on the trees. Oh, when I think . . . I didn't really believe she'd sprayed. I mean, why would she, just before picking? Jeremy, do you realise Zoe could easily have . . .'

'Yes, I know. Any of us could've. And think of the bloody juice factory! But still, you know, Kate, I wouldn't have thought a few apples sprayed like that could kill someone. Would you?'

'No . . .' said Kate slowly. 'I would have thought
you might get sick, but not actually *die*. Still, it happened, didn't it?' She thought a moment. 'I suppose
it might depend on the person. I mean, Damien could
have had an allergy to the stuff, or anything.'

'That's an idea,' said Jeremy. 'Maybe that's just how
it was. Poor bastard. Anyway, they'll soon know.
They'll do a post-mortem now.'

'A post-mortem. An autopsy? Will they?'

'A post-mortem?' Kate and Jeremy turned as the
words crackled behind them.

Anna had entered the room, her mother hovering
anxiously at her heels. They were both pale, but Anna
spoke through stiff lips and looked as though she had
been stricken by some illness that had left her weak,
listless and defeated, whereas Betsy was shimmering
and vibrating with energy.

Betsy came in sharply. 'Oh, surely not. Anna, don't
worry about that. It's obvious what happened. The
doctor would have seen it straight away.' She caught
a movement by the back door and hurried out. They
heard her high voice enquiring and the bass rumble
of reply. Then there was silence, and another burst of
speech. They waited, and in a moment Betsy reappeared. She was subdued, but calm, and even smiled
as she faced them.

'It seems you're right, Jeremy.' She turned to Anna
and spoke reassuringly.

'Apparently a post-mortem is always done in cases
like this, Annie.' She paused. 'Actually, Mr . . . Sergeant Toby would like to talk to everyone about, you
know, Damien, and what happened last night and
everything. Could you come in and join us? Kate?
Jeremy?'

Kate involuntarily glanced at Jeremy. He was looking very serious. What did all this mean? Surely the
idiot policeman didn't think Damien had killed himself purposely? What a ludicrous method to choose.
Eating one poisoned apple after another until you fell

over! No, he couldn't think that. But what other reason could he have? She sighed. No doubt it was, as he said, just routine. Well, they obviously weren't going to be leaving apple country this morning. Maybe they could get off after lunch.

'It's a shocking thing. Shocking,' said Betsy in a high 'formal' voice, similar to the one she used on the telephone. 'I can't tell you how shocked we all are. A terrible accident.'

They were all sitting around the living room—all but Zoe, who had been sent across the road 'to help Theresa with the baby' for an hour or two. They were sitting, thought Kate, in strained imitation of their usual gatherings. Alice by the fire, Betsy on the couch with her boys, Wilf disappearing into the curtains and the others distributed awkwardly about. But this time their attention was riveted not on Betsy but on a big, balding man with a quizzically wrinkled forehead and large freckled hands pressed on his knees: Detective-sergeant Simon Toby, untidy in a pale grey suit wrinkled at the thighs, a button missing from his drip-dry shirt. His tall, skinny assistant, whose name Kate hadn't caught, sat behind him with a notebook. He was very young and looked pleasant, but not too bright—not like a detective at all, with his bushy brown hair and clumsy, langorous manner.

'Yes,' Toby paused and looked around him, letting his eyes come to rest on the white-faced Anna. 'It must be upsetting for all of you, and that's why I'd like to clear this up and get out of your way as quickly as possible, Mrs Tender. Now, I understand the deceased, Mr Treloar, your daughter's husband, was sleeping in the garage. Is that right?'

Betsy looked harried and embarrassed. 'Yes . . . my daughter's estranged husband, Mr . . . Detective-sergeant. He had called in to see . . . us all and . . .'

'He hadn't called for any special reason, then?' Toby enquired.

'Yes. He did, actually,' Jill was pink but determined. 'He called to drop some transparencies off to me. I'm a book editor at Pinkie and Sons. I'm working on a book of his, and he . . .'

'Oh, I see,' said Toby smoothly. 'Have you got the photographs here, Miss ah . . . it was Miss Mission wasn't it? Yes. Have you got the photographs handy?'

'Oh yes,' said Jill, surprised. She walked over to the sideboard and picked up a folder which she handed to him.

'I see.' Toby held the sheet of transparencies to the light. 'Furniture and vases and things, eh?'

'It's a book on Australian antiques,' said Jill and even in this strange setting her enthusiasm was obvious. 'Damien is . . . was, a real expert. Knew what all these things were worth, and how to do them up, and look after them. This was all going into the book.' She paused.

'And you were urgently waiting on these slides, Miss Mission?' Toby asked quietly.

Jill looked at him, and her treacherous red-head's skin stained an even deeper pink.

'Oh, no, not really. I mean, I wasn't going back to work for a week. But . . . but Damien is . . . was, like that. It was his first book, too, and first authors tend to be . . . you know. He got terribly enthusiastic about everything. Once he had some stuff he couldn't wait to show it to me. He'd really got into his stride in the last few months. He'd found some marvellous examples of the sorts of things he talked about in the book. He lived—alone, and I think he needed someone to share his enthusiasm. So he'd ring me up, almost every week, saying, you know, I've found some things that are really great, and prove a point I've been trying to prove for ages, or something. He'd chat like that. Just very enthusiastic and full of it all. He was like that, wasn't he Anna?'

Anna looked at her unsmiling. 'You'd know more about it than I would, Jill, these days, I think.'

Kate glanced at Betsy. She was pale as chalk.

There was a nasty little silence. Toby cleared his throat.

'Well. He dropped off his photos and what happened then, Mrs Tender?'

'Oh, well, um, we had a drink, and then . . .'

'Mrs Sullivan came to ring up,' Rodney chipped in importantly.

'Oh yes, a neighbour of my aunt's came to ring up. The lady across the road. She only stayed a couple of minutes and Damien left when she did. Left the first time, I mean.'

'What time would that have been?'

'Oh, I've no idea,' said Betsy, looking around helplessly.

'It was exactly 9.45. Quarter to ten, exactly,' said Wilf from his corner. 'I know, because I looked at my watch and then at the clock, because I was thinking of going to bed. And the clock struck the quarter hour.'

Toby cleared his throat again. 'Thank you, sir. So when did Mr Treloar return to the house? Straight away, I suppose?'

'Well, practically . . . he must have,' said Betsy doubtfully.

'No, but wait a minute,' said Kate slowly. 'Not that it matters, I suppose, the time, but actually it couldn't have been straight away because I remember I had time to make a cup of tea and start pouring it . . . and, before that . . .' She hesitated and flushed. 'Oh, well it's not important.'

'Please go on, Miss . . . it's Miss Delaney, isn't it?' Toby leaned forward. 'I've got to get the whole evening mapped out, and everything helps.'

'Oh,' said Kate, looking confused. 'Oh, I was just going to say that we'd had a bit of a talk, you know, even before I started making tea, and that means . . .'

'Bit of a talk,' growled Alice, turning round in her chair. 'Say what you mean, missie.' She grinned maliciously at Toby. 'We had a rip-roaring fight, that's what we had. I was giving Bet here curry for having that worm in the house. That slimy son-in-law of hers. And I told her so. I'm not scared of saying what I think, whatever anyone else is.' She leaned over the arm of her chair and almost leered at Toby, stabbing her thumb in Betsy's direction.

'Madam here doesn't have me bluffed. I've wiped her bottom for her, and smacked it, too, in my time. She can't bully me!'

'Auntie Alice!' Betsy was scarlet. Mortification and rage struggled for supremacy in her face. Then she pulled herself together, with the enormous self-control Kate had noticed and admired before. Her face took on a tolerant and careworn expression. Her voice dropped.

'Please forgive my aunt, Sergeant Toby. She hasn't been herself lately.'

'There's nothing wrong with me that a bit of peace and quiet won't cure, Bet,' snapped Alice. She glared around the room, staring down the younger people one by one. 'You all think I'm going gaga, don't you?' she went on. 'Well, I'm not. I'm as sharp as I ever was.' Her hooded gaze came to rest on Birdie. Birdie returned the stare unmoved and showed no sign of embarrassment or restlessness.

'Excuse me, Miss Allcott,' said Toby quietly. 'But perhaps you could explain something to me at this point, just to get it out of the way.'

Alice turned back to him in silence. He continued, with a nod of thanks. 'Now, it looks as though Mr Damien Treloar died in your orchard after eating some apples off one of your trees. Can you tell me how long ago you sprayed the trees in that row, and what you sprayed them with?'

Alice moved impatiently, rubbing her heavily-veined hands against the arms of her chair. 'No, I can't,' she said, finally. 'Not for certain. The stuff's all in the storeroom. You can look for yourself. But when it was I did them middle trees last I just can't place now . . .' Her voice trailed off for a moment. Then vigour returned. Her head bobbed up and her eyes glared.

'But you can't blame me for what happened,' she said defiantly. 'I told them. I warned them all. You've got to spray or you lose your crop. Pests and parasites—they're everywhere, every season of the year. You've got to get rid of them. No choice.'

Toby smiled courteously at her. 'I understand, Miss Allcott. But I was just thinking that now is rather an unusual time to spray, from my experience.'

Alice paused and looked at him. 'You can't be too careful,' she said, and her mouth closed into a straight line. She turned back to the fire and hunched her shoulders.

Toby looked at the stubborn old back for a moment, a slight frown on his face. Then he sighed and turned to Betsy.

'So, Mrs Tender, by my notes it seems now that your son-in-law must have come back to the house maybe ten or fifteen minutes after he left the first time—allowing for your . . . discussion with your aunt, and Miss Delaney's tea-making. That brings us to 9.55 or ten o'clock. What happened then?'

'Well,' said Betsy. 'He explained what had happened—you know, the tyres being flat and everything. He asked if he could stay. In the garage. He had his sleeping-bag with him.'

'And you agreed? Even after your aunt had . . .'

'Auntie Alice had gone to bed by then, Sergeant Toby,' Chris interrupted. He put his hand casually on his mother's arm, and she glanced at him quickly and gratefully. 'And there really wasn't any alternative. The local garage was shut. Damien's van was full of goods he'd purchased and he couldn't sleep there.'

'I see.' Toby nodded slowly. 'And did Mr Treloar go straight out to the garage?'

'Pretty well,' said Chris, who seemed to have decided to become spokesperson. He was good in the role too, thought Kate. Fluent and confident—the popular, respected school teacher, Mr Tender, in action. She hoped the big, freckled detective was responding. He must have started thinking they were all mad as snakes by now.

Chris continued calmly, 'I suppose he would have been gone by 10.15. That'd be right, Jeremy, wouldn't it?'

'Yeah, I'd say so,' said Jeremy quietly. He was watching Simon Toby, sizing him up. Kate was wondering if he was finding him as impressive as she was.

'I gather he wasn't warned about the spray then, Mrs Tender?' said Toby, turning to Betsy.

'Well, no,' she said defensively. 'No, none of us thought of it. Of course he was here last year, and he knew that . . .'

Chris interrupted again. 'My aunt always warns us that the trees have been sprayed, Mr Toby. She has done so ever since I've been coming here, and that's many years. I'm afraid we've never taken the warning completely seriously. In fact . . .' he dropped his voice slightly, glancing at Alice's hunched form. 'I'm afraid plenty of apples have been eaten in previous years, by everyone, straight off the trees, with no ill effects. I still can hardly believe . . .'

'Sergeant Toby,' interrupted Betsy. 'You really mustn't blame poor Auntie Alice. *I* was the one who said Damien could stay. *I* didn't make sure he was warned about the spray. It's all my fault. Not Auntie Alice's. She's been overdoing things. She's got a bit mixed up, that's all. It was just a terrible accident.' Her voice broke and she buried her face in her hands. Chris put his arm around her protectively.

The big policeman leaned forward.

'Don't upset yourself, Mrs Tender. It's not necessarily a matter of blame.' He paused. 'Not yet, anyway. But I'm sure you understand I have my job to do. A man's dead, and I have to establish how and why he died. It's never a pleasant business.'

'But we *know* all that already, don't we?' Anna said, white and calm.

'Well, we think we do, Mrs Treloar, yes,' said Toby. 'But there are a few things I'd just like to check on.' He shifted in his seat, and ran a large paw across his lined forehead and the smooth brown skull above.

'Actually, Mrs Treloar, I'd appreciate a few words with you particularly, if you're up to it—just so we can get some details about your husband and so on.'

'Yes, of course,' said Anna quietly. Her eyes were huge in her white face.

Betsy sat forward and opened her mouth to speak, but Toby forestalled her.

'There's no need to bother anyone else at this stage, I don't think,' he murmured, squinting almost lazily around. 'Please don't disturb yourselves. Mrs Tender, is there a quiet room we can use? Anywhere will do.'

'Oh, well, really,' flustered Betsy. 'I . . .'

'Your bedroom will do, Mum,' said Anna flatly. She got up and turned to Toby. 'You don't mind the bedroom do you? There's a desk there and chairs and so on.'

'That sounds fine,' said Toby comfortably. 'I won't keep her away long, Mrs Tender. McGlinchy!' He escorted Anna to the door, the gangling constable hovering behind. The young man watched them disappear into the corridor, then slipped through the doorway himself, glancing almost apologetically back, and disappeared.

The door clicked shut.

'Well, honestly!'

Betsy's voice rang in the air between the three people in the dark corridor. Martin glanced at Anna and to his enormous surprise she smiled at him. She had a beautiful smile, despite the tension in her face, and

Martin felt himself blushing as though he'd been caught out.

'You'll have to excuse Mum,' she said to Toby. 'She's very protective. This is awful for her.'

'Oh yes, I know how it is, Mrs Treloar,' said Toby in a friendly, reassuring fashion. He pulled the cord by the bedroom door and the room was flooded with dusty yellow light.

Martin looked around. Heavy carved wooden furniture loomed from the walls, and the huge double bed had a lumpy, suffocating look. Suitcases and bags cluttered in a corner, and Betsy's cosmetics stood, prim and pink, amid an array of crystal and silver on the old dressing table. The room had the brown, silent, dead look of a folk museum in a country town—the evidences of habitation only emphasised its desolation. What a depressing place! He looked at the bed and imagined the rosy, black haired Mrs Tender and her grey, tired husband sitting up in it. He shivered. Hell, this place was getting on his nerves. He glanced quickly at Toby, but the bald head was turned away, as Toby settled himself into an old leather chair opposite Anna Treloar, perched before him on a hard chaise longue, her knees pressed together, her hands clasped.

Martin slipped over and sat quietly on a stool before the desk, shrinking, he hoped unobtrusively, into the woodwork, as he knew Toby wanted him to. He took out his notebook and pen, and started taking down the first routine questions and answers, his mind idling. He had no idea what Toby hoped to get from this interview, but hoped it wouldn't be too hard on the beautiful Anna, whom he felt, for some reason, he'd seen or met before. He couldn't have, though— he didn't meet classy-looking girls like her. It was hard to imagine her married to that ferretty little bloke out under the apple tree, with his weak chin and trendy moustache. No wonder it hadn't lasted.

Suddenly he felt a pang of sympathy for Damien

Treloar, so dead, damp shreds of grass clinging to that
gingery moustache, the hood of his pricey, padded
parka, fitting neatly over a smart ski-cap, framing an
agonised face, the carefully well-worn jeans smeared
with filth, the high-heeled boots scuffed and muddy.
Banished to the garage while his soft, lovely wife slept
tucked up well away from him with the rest of her
handsome family; caught out stealing apples, igno-
minious, humiliated in death; dying all alone, wondering what had gone wrong. And in the morning,
poked and prodded, explored, photographed and
talked over by men he'd never seen before—and Toby
running his fingers over the body, frowning, puzzled,
looking for something . . . what? Now he was on his
way to post-mortem, the final indignity. Probably no
one in this family had ever been post-mortemed.

'. . . so your husband wanted a reconciliation, Mrs
Treloar, and you refused?'

Anna looked up. She looked miserable.

'Yes . . . I . . . it was no use.' A dull flush spread
over her cheeks and forehead.

Go on, you old bastard, thought Martin. Help her
out. But he knew Toby better than that. He knew
he'd got more out of the girl if he let her talk un-
prompted.

'Anyway, in the end Mum went to the shop—his
antique shop—and asked him not to come anymore,
told him how it upset me. And he didn't come after
that. Until last night . . .' Her voice faded.

'When he came . . .' prompted Toby.

'To see Jill Mission, as she told you,' Anna said,
looking down at her hands again. Something strange
in her tone there, thought Martin. He knew Toby
would think she was looking down so he wouldn't see
her eyes. He was starting to wonder about Anna himself, actually. Whatever she'd felt about her husband,
it wasn't as lukewarm as she'd made out, by a long
shot.

'He said that, Mrs Treloar. But was that the real reason, do you think?'

'I'm certain it was,' the girl answered flatly.

She looked straight at Toby again. 'Look, Sergeant Toby, I'm sorry but what does it matter, all this? He's dead. It was an accident. That's that, isn't it?'

Toby leaned forward and put his big hands on his knees. The gap in his shirt where the button was missing parted to reveal a not-so-white interlock singlet. Martin watched Anna glance at the spot rapidly and then turn her eyes to Toby's face.

'That's the trouble, Mrs Treloar, I don't think it is . . . that,' he said quietly.

'Look, I don't . . .' Anna's eyes were wide, her cheeks flushed. She swallowed and went on. 'I don't understand. You think Damien was . . .'

'Suicide isn't out of the question, Mrs Treloar.'

'Suicide? Damien?' Anna sounded relieved, almost amused. 'Oh, no. Oh heavens, no. He'd never . . .' She stopped and paled a little.

'It was a possibility I hadn't dismissed,' Toby said smoothly. 'A man of intense temperament, having tried to win back his wife and failed, might choose to take his own life in a way and place that would impress her with her guilt. I've seen it before.'

Anna was silent. Her face was a study in conflicting emotions. She was obviously grappling with an idea that was new to her, thought Martin. A new way of looking at a man she thought she knew backwards, maybe. Finally she spoke.

'Well,' she said slowly. 'It's possible, I suppose. I mean, when you put it that way.' She smiled wanly at Toby. 'Damien was always fairly dramatic about things. You took me by surprise before, but I can see now that it's not totally out of the question . . . if it wasn't an accident. You think Damien took something?'

'Look, Mrs Treloar, I don't think anything just at the moment.' Toby spread his hands, and smiled at her. The warmth of that smile seeped right across to Martin in the corner, and he felt the tension in the room melt, saw Anna soften and relax. 'I'm just doing what I can to get to the truth of the matter.'

'Yes, I understand, Sergeant Toby, of course I do,' said Anna, nodding earnestly. 'Is there anything else I can do to help?'

'No . . . I don't . . .' Toby began looking at his notebook, and Anna started to rise from her seat. 'Oh, just a minute!' he exclaimed. 'That was silly of me. Of course . . . I do need to ask one more thing.'

Anna sank back down on the hard chaise longue with a smile of strained patience Martin thought she must have learned from her mother.

'Given what we've just been talking about I need to know when the people in the house last saw Mr Treloar.'

'But we've told you that!' said Anna quietly. 'He went out to the garage at about 10.15.'

'And that was the last anyone saw of him?'

'Well, I can't speak for the others,' said Anna, the flush mounting her cheeks again, 'though I'm sure they would have said. But I didn't see him again, anyway.'

'You went to bed about . . .'

'About eleven o'clock.'

'And you didn't go out?'

'No, what for? It was freezing cold, anyway.'

'Did you see or hear anyone else go out?'

'My door was shut. I'm a very light sleeper and I like to keep it shut.'

'So, you didn't hear anything all night. That's lucky, isn't it, in an old weatherboard like this, with no carpet. I would have thought a light sleeper . . .'

'Well, look, I suppose I must have . . . um . . . let's think . . . well, oh, yes, I heard some confusion in the hall, sometime after one. My brother's wife got a fright, or something, and yelled out and there was a bit of talk.'

'Any idea of the exact time, Mrs Treloar?'

'No. Except . . . it was just after, a few minutes after the quarter hour struck. So it must have been, say, twenty past one. But look, my brother can tell you . . .'

'Of course,' Toby was soothing. 'Well, thank you Mrs Treloar, I won't keep you any longer.'

He rose massively to his feet and held his creased arm out to the door. Ushering Anna out he didn't even look at Martin, hesitating uncertainly by the desk, but followed her into the living room leaving his assistant to trail behind with as much professional ease as he could muster.

7

Reaping the Whirlwind

666

'Now . . .' Toby leaned back in his chair. 'Before we go on, it seems to me that there's someone I haven't met yet. A Mr . . .' he ran a blunt finger down a list in his small notebook. 'Mr Nicholas Bedford. Where is he?'

There was a short silence. Kate looked at Jeremy. Ridiculous as it seemed, she'd forgotten about Nick completely in the horror and confusion of the morning. Jeremy looked apprehensive, and Jill was looking at her feet. Obviously they hadn't forgotten, and had been waiting for the question.

Chris spoke lightly. 'Oh, Nick went off somewhere last night. Went for a drive. It was quite late when he left. I suppose he decided to find a pub, and then couldn't face the drive back. You know the sort of thing.'

'Seems a bit unusual, though, Mr Tender, to take off in the middle of things like that. Had there been an argument of any sort?'

Suddenly the big, untidy policeman seemed to Kate like a bizarre old doctor, gently prodding apparently healthy flesh to find some sore sport. She felt herself stiffen in readiness for the sensitive stab that must come, and wondered at the feeling of foreboding that hung over her. She fought it off. It didn't *matter* that Nick had hated Damien. Damien had had an accident. Damien was dead. Other people's feelings about him were irrelevant, surely.

'Oh,' said Chris, smiling confidently, showing all his teeth. 'Oh, nothing like that.'

Why is he lying, thought Kate, confusedly. She glanced around. Jeremy was frowning. Jill was still, her freckled hands caught between her knees, her usually mobile face tense and expressionless.

'But, excuse me, um, why are you asking all these questions, Inspector?' Betsy's voice was querulous. 'I can't see the point.'

And at that moment, hearing her own thoughts spoken aloud in that brittle, stubborn tone so reminiscent of other moments, other Betsy-seeing-what-she-wanted-to-see moments, Kate knew why the police were lingering, understood Jeremy's frown, Jill's stillness, Chris's lie. Somehow or the other the big detective wasn't satisfied. For some reason he didn't think it was just an accident. He thought it was murder! She went cold.

'Well, Mrs Tender . . .' Sergeant Toby's mollifying rumble was cut off as they heard a thudding on the back path. Someone ran up the stairs.

'Who's that?' said Betsy sharply. She half rose. Chris put up a warning hand and after a moment's hesitation she sat down again. Kate and Jeremy twisted around in their chairs just in time to see the door fly open.

Nick stood there, a huge bunch of early narcissus in his hand. The deliciously sweet, heady fragrance washed into the room with the cool air. For years afterwards the smell of narcissus took Kate back to that shabby, cluttered room and Nick's face in the doorway. He looked haggard, his eyes were bloodshot and his hair stood out in all directions. But he was beaming, and he looked straight at Jill.

'Hello all. The prodigal returns.' He crossed the

room and thrust the flowers into Jill's hands. 'From the side of the road to you, picked with my own hands,' he said. 'Sorry I stormed off, Jillie. I was being stupid.'

The atmosphere in the room seemed at last to penetrate his consciousness, and his face fell a little. 'What's up?'

Simon Toby moved towards him, very quickly for a man whose movements had previously seemed so ponderous.

'Ah, you would be Mr Nicholas Bedford?'

'Yes?' said Nick. The bewilderment in his face would have been almost comical, thought Kate, under other circumstances. It was like a caricature—or a close-up in a bad film—dropped jaw, raised eyebrows, wide eyes. But there was no humor in the situation. Only a sudden wave of instinctive fear as the large grey-suited figure laid his hand on Nick's arm. Nick looked, suddenly, very small and frail.

'What's up?' he said again.

'There's been an accident, Mr Bedford. I'm Detective-sergeant Toby. Mrs Tender, if you don't mind I'll talk to Mr Bedford privately. In the master bedroom will be fine, if you've no objection. Mc-Glinchy!' The young detective sprang to his feet. Toby turned to Nick. 'Sorry for all the drama, Mr Bedford. It won't take long.' He held his free arm out towards the doorway in an inviting manner.

'It's Treloar, Nick,' said Jeremy clearly, looking him straight in the eye. 'We found him early this morning. Dead. Poisoned.'

Toby looked at Jeremy mildly. 'Thank you, Mr Darcy,' he said. 'Mr Bedford?'

Nick obeyed the direction and turned towards the door, moving slowly like a person who had just woken up from a heavy sleep. He looked back at Jill once, his face expressionless, and then went on. The door closed behind them.

'Well, what on earth!' Betsy's outraged and plaintive exclamation rose in the silence.

'Er . . . if you don't mind my butting in, Mrs Tender.' Everyone looked in some surprise at the slight figure sitting earnestly forward on her straight-backed chair, her eyebrows up and her forehead wrinkled over her glasses.

'Yes . . . ah . . . Verity?' Betsy was bemused. She looked at Birdie with politely, though transparently, veiled impatience.

'I've had a bit of experience in this sort of thing,' said Birdie hesitantly. 'Nothing as dramatic as this, of course, but . . .'

'Oh! Of course. You're a solicitor, Birdie. You know all the . . . Oh, Birdie!' exclaimed Kate. 'You should be in there now, with Nick! Oh quick, maybe we can . . .' She got up and started for the door.

'Calm down, Kate,' snapped Jeremy. 'You can't rush in like that, now.' He shot an unfriendly glance at Birdie. Smug little piece she was.

He entered the fray.

'Look, there's no point in panicking,' he said firmly, 'but it's obvious that this Toby doesn't think that Damien died by accident. So he's going to talk to all of us in turn, fixing times and so on. That's all he's doing with Nick now. It's obviously a poisoning—I mean, you could see that.' He paused, and everyone shuddered slightly. 'It's just a matter of whether it was an accident—or something else. Until he gets the post-mortem results he's working in the dark, you realise. He can't prove a thing until that report comes in—and it could take a week.'

'But,' said Kate. 'No one would actually have meant to hurt Damien—I mean, we're all here . . . none of us would . . . and anyway, why would we?' Her voice trailed off as she caught Birdie's golden stare moving around the room.

Anna, looking like a ghost! But Anna and Damien, she could have sworn, were heading for a reconcilia-

tion. It had looked like it last night, despite all the
nonsense with Jill. Birdie would have noticed that.
Anna was obviously still very much under her husband's spell last night. He knew it, too. Last night
even Kate had caught a glimpse of the sexual mag-
netism that lay below the rather specious personality
of Damien Treloar. She'd never understood it before.
Rather seamy, actually. Fatal for someone as inhib-
ited as Anna. No, Anna would go back to Damien if
he got her alone, away from Betsy. She'd have no reason to kill him.

But Betsy herself . . . Birdie's eyes were on Betsy
now. She was vehemently muttering to Chris and
Rodney, tucked down on the couch with them, her
bright brown eyes darting around occasionally. Betsy
had hated Damien, she really had. If she thought that
Anna might be thinking of going back to him . . . oh,
but surely not. Surely even Betsy wouldn't go that far.
But Kate had to drop her gaze as Betsy's busy, managing eye came round again. Betsy shouldn't be underestimated.

Sonsy was looking pale. Only natural. She'd been
the one who'd had to check Damien over, to make
sure he was really dead. For once in her married life
she'd been the centre of attention, poor little Sonsy,
kneeling beside the body sprawled face down on the
lanky green grass, her pretty red dressing gown gaping at the breast where a button had fallen off, so that
her nightgown, with its cheap blue lace, poked
through. Her little heart-shaped face had been set,
her pale fingers, pushing aside the damp parka hood,
had searched professionally for a non-existent pulse in
Damien's smooth, white neck, while they'd stood
around in a horrified, respectful circle in the mist.
Then she'd looked up at them and said yes, he was
dead, and Chris had said, 'He can't be!' and turned
the body over, and they'd seen the awful face. Then
someone had given a sort of shuddering sigh, and
Rodney had begun to retch, and suddenly everyone

was babbling about spray, and Alice being crazy, and
Betsy had screamed, 'What, in my place?' like Lady
Macbeth, and Sonsy had looked at her and started to
laugh, with tears pouring down her cheeks. And she'd
kept on laughing and crying while Chris hauled her
up and got her back to the house where Zoe and Alice
were waiting by the fire.

Kate looked at Sonsy's hands, limp and still in her
lap. She remembered them last night, plucking endlessly at the hem of her jumper. Her outburst down
in the orchard must have taken the pressure off a bit.
She seemed oblivious to Chris and Betsy now. Last
night she'd watched them constantly from under her
lashes, while jealousy gnawed away at her like a pink-
eyed mouse. Could she have had some sort of brain-
storm last night, and met Damien by chance and . . .
no, how ridiculous! Kate thought. You didn't poison
someone under those circumstances. You shot them,
or hit them on the head, or something. She had a
vision of a maddened Sonsy, wandering the orchard
with her dressing gown pockets full of poisoned apples, looking for a victim, her pale little face strained
in a smile, her eyes glassy—oh, stop it! she thought
savagely.

She watched Birdie's gaze move over Sonsy and linger on Alice by the fire. Anyway, if Toby thought
there'd been foul play, and that it wasn't an accident,
poor old spray-fiend Alice was off the hook. Unless . . .
She'd hated Damien, and who was better placed to
dose up an apple with something nasty than Alice?
But again, it was a bit far fetched, wasn't it? How
could she persuade him to eat one special apple, when
he was surrounded with them? And anyway, that was
all silly, because she hadn't even known Damien was
staying on the property. For all she knew he'd gone
for good when he left the first time.

So . . . who else was there? Nick? Kate refused to
consider Nick, whatever Toby might think. Nick had
always been the most genial person she knew. His be-

haviour the last couple of days had been uncharacter-
istic, that's true, but he couldn't kill anybody—not
poison them, anyway. To do that you had to plan and
plot and then coldly do the deed. Nick couldn't do
that.

Jill? She had no reason in the world to kill Damien
Treloar. In fact, she had every reason not to, with the
book and everything.

So—who was left? Chris? No motive at all, as far
as Kate could see. Rodney, mummy's boy? Could he
have done it out of some adolescent desire to rid his
family of a menace? Could he have noticed Anna's
glowing face, last night, and decided heroically to save
his sister from a possible, disastrous reconciliation?
Unlikely. He'd probably have been glad to see her rush
off, disgraced, with Damien, leaving the field at home
open for him. It must have put his nose out of joint,
when Anna came back to the family home and was
welcomed as a prodigal. Yes, he would have loved her
to go, leaving him to enjoy the little dinner-time lamb
chops, fatty and tender, all alone with Betsy again.

Hold on though, thought Kate irritably. I've done
it again! He wouldn't be alone with Betsy at all. I'm
always forgetting . . .

Anna's voice, clear and cold, cut through her
thoughts. 'Actually, you know,' she said. 'The detective, the big one, said he thought it might be suicide.'

'Suicide!' exclaimed Jill. 'But that's ridiculous. Damien wouldn't have . . .'

Anna looked straight at her, and curled her lip. 'I
don't think it'd be all that clever to say so, just at the
moment, Jill.'

Jill went red. 'What do you mean?' she said.

'Well, it's obvious, isn't it?' said Anna coldly, swiv-
elling her eyes to indicate the door through which Nick
had so recently been escorted.

'You bitch, Anna! You . . .' Jill leapt to her feet,
flushed to the roots of her hair.

'Oh, no! Don't fight, please Jill, please Anna!' Kate

found herself across the room with her arm around Jill before she had even thought about it. Her only feeling was horror at the dislike which had suddenly permeated the room. It made her queasy in the stomach to see those two familiar faces so changed, so strange. You don't really know anyone, she thought, as she led Jill out into the kitchen.

'I'll make some tea,' she said, and caught Birdie's teasing smile just as she closed the door.

Martin shifted uncomfortably on his seat and flexed his right hand. This note-taking was a rigorous business. Not that old Toby was getting much out of Nick Bedford. He just stuck to the same story—he'd driven away from the house at about 10.30. Yes, there'd been a bit of an argument, but it was nothing serious. He'd driven around for a while, then walked a bit to let off steam—oh, round the Atherton shopping centre, actually. He hadn't seen anyone. Then he'd driven out to Echo Point and sat for a while, then he'd simply gone to sleep.

'I woke up at about 5.30, feeling lousy, as you can imagine, cursing myself for an idiot,' he was saying now, leaning forward on his knees and looking at Toby frankly. You couldn't help but believe him, Martin thought. He seemed a genuinely straightforward bloke.

'Yet you didn't get back here till after nine, Mr Bedford. Why was that?' Toby enquired pleasantly. You'd swear the old bugger was just curious, thought Martin.

'Well, you know, I feel a bit sheepish about the whole thing and I wasn't really feeling like facing the music back here, to tell you the truth. I sat a while and listened to the radio, then I got a paper.' Nick Bedford sat up straighter, and his eyes brightened. 'Look, that bloke'd remember me, actually, because I bought chocolate too, and asked where I could get a coffee. At about seven, it was.' He turned to Martin. 'The newsagency at Bellbird Crossing.' He watched anxiously as Martin obediently wrote the details down. Poor sod, thought Martin, making his shorthand squiggles, what does he think that proves? The doc had said Treloar had been dead for hours by the time they got to the house at eight. This guy could easily have given him a dose of something and then shot off again so as to turn up at Bellbird at seven.

'Anyway,' Nick went on, apparently quite cheered at this newly-revealed proof of his movements, 'I had a cup of coffee at this garage—just out of a machine, it was. There was no one there at all, to notice I was there.' He glanced at Martin again, rather appealingly this time, and Martin lowered his head and took notes busily.

'So, you read the paper a bit, and had your drink, and then you came on, is that right?' mumbled Toby.

Nick nodded. 'That's all there was to it,' he said, spreading his rather grimy hands. 'Except that I stopped on the way to pick some flowers beside the road for Jill—we'd had this bit of a row . . .'

Toby smiled 'Ah, yes, of course.' He dropped his head and appeared to ponder for a moment.

'This bit of a row, Mr Bedford,' he said, without raising his eyes. 'Would I be right in thinking it was about Mr Damien Treloar?'

In the living room, Betsy had taken charge again.

'Now, the thing is,' she said determinedly, 'just to all be perfectly frank and tell the inspector—sergeant— whatever he is, everything he wants to know. None of us has anything to fear. *We* know that, but, un- derstandably, as Jeremy says, he doesn't and we must explain it all to him carefully so that he gets it clearly in his mind that this was all just a horrible accident. Or that poor Damien took his own life. He was an unhappy boy, we all know that. Right?' She looked around brightly, fixing them individually with her beady eyes, nodding enthusiastically at their dulled and exhausted faces. Kate felt a stab of pity for her. She was *so* determined that everything would be all right. So determined that her warm little domestic boat shouldn't be rocked, that Anna hadn't done something desperate, or Alice finally gone off the deep end, or even that Nick, that old and prestigious friend of her son's whom she had so often said was 'just like one of the family', had cast his lot with the criminal classes.

'It's all very well, Betsy, I mean, I understand what you're saying, but Nick's in there . . .' Jill began, looking from her to Anna and back again. Jill had been crying, and her eyes were pink-rimmed. She had no make-up on this morning and her pale orange lashes and brows had almost disappeared, leaving her blue eyes round, plain and defenceless.

'Nick will be *all right*, Jill—now, you *know* that. The police will understand once they've talked to him, that he couldn't possibly have had anything to do with what happened. I realise you feel responsible for the awkward position he's in, and that must be hard for you to bear. I know how I'd feel.' Betsy's eyes were cold and accusing, though her voice never lost its calm, responsible tone. 'But he's a grown man, a generous man, and he's obviously willing to forgive and forget. He'll be looking to you for calm, quiet support now. You have to pull yourself together and give it to him.'

Jill stood up and turned her back on Betsy. Her cheeks were flaming. 'I'm going for a walk in the orchard,' she said directly to Jeremy. 'If they want me, give me a yell.' She stalked out and shut the door behind her.

Betsy looked around. 'Reaping the whirlwind,' she said, shaking her head. 'A nasty lesson for her. Still,' she added in a livelier tone, 'Nick being the wonderful person that he is it'll probably all come out right.

These things often do. It might even be all for the best for dear old Nick and Jill. Stop them drifting along, as they've been doing. A good fright like this could really strengthen their relationship—I've seen it time and again over the years.'

Kate stared at her. She really was amazing, Betsy. She seemed to be able to convince herself totally of anything. Her absolute imperviousness to the feelings of other people was quite extraordinary.

The door into the hallway opened. Nick and the younger policeman stood there. Nick was pale and tense, but he grinned weakly at Kate, scanned the room and raised his eyebrows at Jeremy.

'She's out the back, mate,' said Jeremy, and Nick made for the door without another word.

'Could Sergeant Toby have a word with Miss Alice Allcott, please?' said the young policeman formally.

'Ah, my turn, is it, son?' grinned Aunt Alice, gripping the arms of her chair.

'I think I had better come with my aunt, officer,' said Betsy hastily. 'She's an elderly lady and not well.'

'You keep out of this, Bet!' retorted the old woman, heaving herself up. 'I'm not quite a crock yet, thanks, whatever you'd like to see me.'

'Auntie Alice, I'm only . . .'

'I said keep out of it!' thundered Alice, and Betsy shrank back. 'As a matter of fact, I want that lawyer woman there to come with me.' She pointed at Birdie.

'Well, um, ma'am, Sergeant Toby . . .' mumbled Martin.

'Look, if he wants me I'll come, but only if my lawyer comes too. And that's her. Right, missie?'

'Of course I'll come with you if you like, Miss Allcott, but . . .' Birdie began.

'Never mind all that,' interrupted Alice irritably. 'We'll talk about all that later—the fee and that. Just come along.'

She strode to the door, surprisingly agile once on her feet.

Birdie stood up and followed her, eyebrows raised quizzically. They disappeared through the door and Martin backed after them, avoiding Betsy's flashing eye.

8

Cobwebs

ⵔ

'We're all well rid of him, that's the point, well rid of him. If it was an accident, it was good luck, as far as I'm concerned. If it wasn't, well, for my money whoever did him in did us all a favour.' Alice glowered at Toby defiantly. Toby's gaze flickered to Birdie, sitting quietly studying her hands, half smiling. His brow wrinkled slightly.

'Miss Allcott, I'm going to be quite frank with you. I don't know yet whether this was an accident, or if it was suicide, or even murder. I feel worried enough by certain things I noticed about the body and its surroundings, not to jump to the conclusion that this is a case of poisoning by accidentally eating recently sprayed fruit. But I could have jumped to that conclusion quite easily, Miss Allcott, because there were several apple cores lying around the body when it was found, and the man had obviously been poisoned—had been sick, and so on. Also you had been heard to tell people that the trees had been sprayed and could be dangerous.'

Alice, breathing deeply, was listening intently to him.

'Now, Miss Allcott,' Toby went on, 'I want you to

think carefully and tell me exactly what you sprayed on those trees, and when.'

The old woman looked him straight in the eye, and spoke deliberately. 'I've told you, son, that I can't remember what I done with them trees, and when. If that little worm went and stole apples in the dark, that's not my fault, and I won't be held accountable. Hear me?'

'All right, Miss Allcott, we'll leave that for the moment,' said Toby, wearily running his hand from his eyebrows to his freckled crown as if to clear his head. 'Can you just tell me whether you heard or saw anything unusual last night, after you went to your room? I understand it looks out over the orchard.'

'Yeah, well, I can see a lot of the trees from there.'

'Did you see or hear anything?'

'Nope. Only what you'd expect, heard people trooping round, the toilet going and that. Heard poor little madam in the next room crying away to herself in bed. Dear oh dear, they've got no spunk, girls today. Boys neither for that matter.'

'That would be Mrs Susan Tender you mean, Miss Allcott, would it?' said Toby doggedly. Again his eyes flickered to the quiet, self-effacing figure of Verity Birdwood, and he was interested to see that her expression had become graver, all amusement extinguished.

'Yeah, well, there's only a bit of fibro between my room and the rest of the verandah. May as well be paper. You can hear straight through it, specially at night. I've heard funnier things before now than a poor girl crying, son.' The hooded old eyes looked at Toby and then at Martin in his corner, and the mouth twitched. Martin felt a flush rise and spread over his face and neck. Wicked old woman! It was awful, how crude some old people could be. At a time like this, too.

Toby remained unmoved. 'You heard Susan Tender

crying, anyway,' he said. 'When would that have been?'

'Oh, early on, you know, when I first went out to me room. She'd gone off before—Bet getting at her about making eyes at that pest—as if she was, poor little thing. Anyone with half an eye can see . . .'

'Making eyes at Mr Treloar, the deceased?'

'Well, he weren't deceased then, worse luck.' Alice snorted with mirthless laughter. 'Smarming all over every female in sight, he was. Darling this, sweetie that. The red-head one minute, his own wife the next, then making up to Bet, then Chris's wife, then the red-head again—even had a go at me, the little worm, much good it did him. Anyhow, however the other ones might have liked it, it was plain as the nose on your face that little what's-her-name, Flossie, or whatever they call her, didn't want a bar of it. Bet was just getting at her, out of pure devilry. Loves to stir people up, Bet does. It helps her get her own way. Always has. She'll go too far one day.'

'Her own way?' Toby pressed gently.

'Yeah, well, she wants young Chris to throw his little wife over, doesn't she?' sneered Alice. 'Wants him married to someone classier, I'd say, or maybe not married at all'd suit her better. Then she could run his life properly, couldn't she? She did a good job on Anna. Now she's having a go at Christopher.' She broke off, belatedly realising that she was perhaps letting a few unnecessary cats out of the bag, and abruptly screwed her head around to blink at Birdie.

'Is this all right, me saying all this?' she snapped.

'You can say as much or as little as you like, Miss Allcott,' said Birdie calmly. 'But perhaps for now it would be best to just go on telling Sergeant Toby about what you heard and saw last night.'

Alice faced Toby and hunched her shoulders. 'Yeah, well, I heard the girl crying, like I said, then a bit of talk and doors opening and shutting. House settled down after that. Chris came into his room, and I heard them talk a bit—low, like, but I could hear them—and the girl stopped crying. Heard the wind all right. Blew like a beaut all night. The old iron rattled on the roof. Sat awake listening to that for a while. The lights were all off then—all I could see, anyhow, at the side and the back. Heard the back door open and shut a few times—nothing in that, the lav's out there—and the old pipes thumping when people washed their hands. You know, the usual things. I got no more to tell you, son.'

Alice prepared to rise, but Toby's smile and raised eyebrows forestalled her.

'Miss Allcott, are you sure that was all? Anna Treloar mentioned some commotion in the hall at . . . sometime after midnight. Did you . . . ?'

'Oh, yeah, I heard a yell and a bit of talk, yeah. Well after midnight, though. Just after quarter past one, it was. Didn't last long. I guessed it was something to do with Chris's wife, because talk started again in their room just after—more crying and that. Anyhow, they settled down in the end.'

Toby looked at her thoughtfully. 'You disliked the dead man, obviously, Miss Allcott. Can you tell me why?'

Alice sniffed. 'No one with any sense would've liked him. Met him last year, and that was enough for me. In and out all hours of the night, sleeping half the day! Womanising, heartless little so and so. Decent women pay and pay when they get mixed up with leeches like him.' A dull flush had risen on her cheeks. Her deep-set eyes flashed.

'You're very fond of your niece's daughter, Miss Allcott?' Toby asked casually.

Alice shut her mouth, and the flush slowly subsided. 'Of course I am,' she said defiantly. 'Only natural, isn't it? I don't have much family left, you know.'

'Thanks, Miss Allcott,' said Toby pleasantly. 'That'll do fine for now.'

• • •

The morning wore on. Toby's shirt grew limp and gaped more widely, his tie was pulled a little askew. He had undone his top collar button. Martin's eyes grew wider and blacker and his hair woollier as the morning slick-down wore off. One by one the house party trailed into the musty bedroom, each to tell the tale of his or her night.

Kate was second last. Before Birdie, after Jeremy, who had come out looking rather grim. So far it had been easy to handle. Toby hadn't asked her opinion on whether Damien Treloar might have killed himself, so she hadn't had to worry about telling a lie and saying it might have been a possibility, when she knew in her heart that it wasn't. She'd been given the opportunity honestly to say that Nick was the gentlest man she knew, with only a few twinges as she recalled his angry, possessive face of the night before. Toby hadn't pressed her. Presumably he'd got an account of the quarrel from Nick and Jill, and the others. All she had to do was confirm the basic facts.

As she spoke she found her eyes wandering to the browning apple cores neatly reposing on the chests that stood on either side of the lumpy double bed. Betsy must be really flustered not to have got rid of those. Something about them made her feel sad. The apple beside each bed at night had been a real Betsy-type tradition. A nice thought for an apple-picking holiday.

'I gather your daughter is here with you, Mrs . . . Miss Delaney?' Toby said.

'Yes, um, Zoe's seven. She's over the road, with Theresa . . . um . . . oh, I've forgotten her last name. The lady over the road.'

'Yes. That would be the neighbour who used the phone here last night? I'm going to go over and see her later. Theresa Sullivan,' Toby said comfortably.

'Yes. Now, do you think Zoe would have heard or seen anything at all last night, Miss Delaney?'

'Well, I don't think so, Sergeant,' began Kate. 'No, I'm sure not. She would have said. Actually, I haven't asked her anything like that. I mean, I didn't want her to get thinking about . . .'

'No, no, of course not.'

'I mean, Jeremy and I slept through the whole night. Except for that thing with Sonsy—I gather everyone's told you about that. And even then Zoe settled again quickly. At least I presume she did. I was dead to the world five minutes after that business and so I'm afraid I can't tell you anything . . . And I'm sure Zoe can't.'

'Yes, well, that can't be helped. Same story with everyone, really, Miss Delaney,' said Toby, closing up his notebook and getting to his feet. 'I'll let you go now. I gather from your husband that you wanted to leave as soon as possible.'

'Oh, yes.' Kate was eager. 'Oh, absolutely. When can we go?'

Toby ran his hand over his forehead and thoughtfully rubbed his polished crown.

'To tell you the truth, Miss Delaney, as I said to your husband, I'd much rather you stayed, just for a while,' said the big man, and Kate's heart sank.

'But, really . . .' she began and then broke off. 'But why?' she said instead, rather lamely. So this was why Jeremy had given her that look of concern as she took his place in the interviewing room.

'The post-mortem's being rushed, but it could be days before I get the results,' Toby said slowly. 'Now, if they show what I think they'll show, I'll have to get in touch with all you good people again. It would be much easier for me if you were all here on the spot, and . . .'

Kate looked at her hands. The atmosphere of the musty room closed around her like cobwebs, as his matter-of-fact voice droned on.

• • •

Martin sipped his tea thankfully, warming his hands around the fat china mug. He watched Toby under his eyebrows. Toby crunched a biscuit and stared into space. The yellow light in the room made him look like a character in an old painting—a bushie in a pub, or something. The corners of his eyes turned down, Martin noticed, and his mouth turned down too, when he was quiet like this. He looked quite vacant, as though he hadn't got a thought in his head except maybe to wonder vaguely whether the rain would come before he got the wheat in, or if the brown dog he'd just got off a neighbour would come good.

Martin stirred uneasily in his chair, and it creaked. Toby turned his head.

'Well, got any ideas, son?'

'Uh, no, not really, sir,' said Martin, his eyebrows shooting up to meet his hair. 'It's a bit . . . they all say the same sort of thing, you know, about going to bed and sleeping through and everything. Um . . .' he hesitated. 'I'm not really sure . . .'

'You're not sure why I'm bothering with all this, I suppose.' Toby turned to face him, pulled at his rubbed brown belt and leaned back. 'Well, to tell the truth I'm not sure I'm not just making a mountain out of a molehill myself. I just wanted to talk to all of them before time got on and they'd had a chance to compare notes.'

'You think one of them's lying, sir?'

'At least one, obviously, Martin, if I'm right. Maybe more. Maybe all of them. Lying for themselves or bending the truth to protect someone else.'

'Yeah. Yes. Well, none of them seem to have had much time for the dead bloke, sir, do they?' Martin offered.

'That's putting it mildly, eh? He doesn't sound like he was much to write home about. I know that type.' Toby paused and the corners of his mouth twitched down. 'Still, that's not the point, is it, son? The point is, they didn't like him, but they all like Mr Nicholas Bedford, and maybe . . .'

'Oh, but he . . .' Martin broke in, and stopped.

'Yeah, well, go on, spit it out,' said Toby irritably. 'What?'

'He . . . he seemed an honest sort of bloke to me. I mean, his story's pretty stupid, but . . . well . . . people do stupid things like that. It sounded true to me . . . about the coffee and the paper and everything.'

'Oh yes, that rang true. Anyway, we can check, *you* can check, with the newsagency at Bellbird Crossing, can't you? It's the rest of the night I'm wondering about. What's to have stopped him nicking back here and doing Treloar in while everyone's asleep, and then going off again?'

'Well . . . yeah . . . but I just don't think he'd do that, sir. You know, poison a bloke. Anyhow, if they'd had a row, Treloar wouldn't be eating apples Nick Bedford gave him, would he? He'd think something was up. And Bedford can't have poisoned the whole orchard. I mean, I can't imagine how it could have happened.'

'Look, Martin, wake up and put this apple business out of your mind. You're thinking what you are supposed to think. If I'm right, you'll find out that the bloody apples had nothing to do with it,' Toby snapped, and then seemed to regret that he'd said anything.

'What?' Martin was truly stunned. 'But he was poisoned. The doctor said, he said . . .'

'Yes, he said the man was poisoned. God, boy, we all could see that. Of course he was poisoned, poor chap. Very nasty too. But that doesn't mean he got the poison in the apples, does it?'

'But he didn't eat anything else. They all said so.'

'They all said so! That doesn't mean anything for a start, Martin. Don't *assume* son, or you'll never be a detective's bootlace.' Toby paused, shook his head and went on. 'Look, it's probably true, by the look of the vomit. The PM'll settle that. Did you get a proper look at the vomit, by the way?'

'Ah, not really, sir,' said Martin unwillingly. 'I thought the lab would.'

'Of course the lab'll be looking at it. And at the apple cores. And at all the apples we picked off the tree. They'll look at everything. But we have to look at them too, in place, where they're found. Because we have to get a feeling for the thing. A bloke in a lab can't get a feeling. See? He's stuck in there with his test tubes and nasty bits of stuff on slides. We're the ones who have to use our wits and our instincts. D'you understand, Martin?'

'Yes, sir, sorry sir.'

Toby looked at him for a moment and sighed heavily.

Martin was silent. He looked down at his notepad and the thoughts chased themselves round under the brown frizz of his hair. Toby must be wishing he had Denver with him now. Denver had been boring and solid. Not much wit and instinct about Denver. But if he was a plodder, at least he was an experienced plodder. Denver would have looked at the vomit. Denver wouldn't have been so appalled by the sight of the dead man that it drove every other thought out of his head. But Denver had retired to grow orchids and watch TV six months ago. And Toby was stuck with him. Martin willed himself to think of something that would contribute. Something. Anything!

Toby shifted in his seat. 'The old lady especially seems to have hated the deceased like poison, doesn't she?' he said absently. Then he smiled. 'Huh, excuse the pun.'

'Yeah. Had a real thing about him. Funny, really,' said Martin slowly, remembering Alice's rage. 'All that stuff about leeches and women paying. It seemed . . . all out of proportion, didn't it, sir?'

Toby looked at him approvingly. 'Yes, it did. That's

good. Now you're thinking. Just try and keep your head clear, and don't assume *anything*. Now, look, call in Verity Birdwood and keep your wits about you. I want everything she says down in black and white. Hear me?'

Martin stared at him. The old bloke was getting a bit eccentric, he thought. The Birdwood woman wasn't a regular visitor. She'd barely met Damien Treloar, by all accounts. What was she likely to say that the others hadn't?'

He stared too long and Toby caught him at it. 'Look out or you'll catch a fly, son. Go on, get on with it.'

Martin shut his mouth with a click and scrambled for the door.

He found Verity Birdwood in the kitchen, deep in conversation with Kate Delaney, who looked up guiltily as he approached. Miss Birdwood was unmoved, however. Martin found himself being sized up by the strange golden eyes, clear and unblinking behind the glasses. He swallowed and cleared his throat.

'My turn?' asked the woman quickly. 'Fine. See you later, Laney.' She gave Kate a quick little smile, ducked the brown bush of her head and made for the door, with Martin trailing behind her.

Toby stood up gallantly as they entered the room. Verity Birdwood sat down collectedly. Her glasses flashed in the yellow light. Martin watched her curiously. Funny sort of person to find in a group like this. Like a little furry animal she looked, with a busy, wide-eyed face, small nose and chin, fluffy mohair jumper. She wore black Chinese cloth slippers on her feet, which barely touched the floor as she sat back on the chaise lounge. Her freckled, ringless hands rested calmly in her lap as she sat waiting for Toby to speak.

The old man took his time getting to the point. He repeated her name and address, asked a few questions about her movements the night before. She answered quietly, without supplying any trimmings, and waited again. There was a pause.

'Miss Birdwood,' said Toby finally, 'I've left talking to you till last because I think you may be able to help me—you particularly.'

She looked at him enquiringly. 'Oh . . . yes?' she said politely.

'Yes, I remembered where I'd heard your name before, while we were talking to Miss Allcott. You had something to do with my brother, Dan Toby, in Sydney a couple of years ago, didn't you? The Celia Morris case?'

She gave her quick smile and looked at him. 'Yes, that's right. I thought you must be related—Toby's not such a common name.'

'Yes, well, Dan still talks about what you did. Says that the Morris woman'd still be in stir today if you hadn't got into the act.'

Verity Birdwood flushed and smiled again, and this time her eyes smiled too, behind the protective glasses. She looked suddenly ineffably merry and mischievous. Well, thought Martin, startled. She's not so bad looking, really, once you get used to her.

'That's nice of him. I really only did a bit of research—it's my line of work. A few of the details seemed funny to me . . . and of course Celia works with me, so I wanted to help. I just passed a few bits and pieces on to Dan. He did all the work.'

Toby leaned forward. 'Look, Miss Birdwood, you must realise by now that I don't think this poisoning affair is as simple as it seems. Even if I hadn't heard of you before I'd want your views. You're the only outsider here, the only one with no axe to grind, if you get my meaning.' Toby smiled at her. She smiled rather thinly back. She wasn't exactly falling into his arms, Martin thought, even though he was turning on the charm full bore. She was sharper than she looked, all right.

'Oh, yes, I see. Well, I'll do my best to help, Sergeant Toby,' she said, and folded her hands.

'Er, right. Thanks. Now, uh, first of all I've got a straight question. The deceased—Mr Treloar—in your opinion, was there anyone in the house last night who would have liked him out of the way?'

'Just about everyone, I'd say.' She grinned, then sobered and settled back. When she began again she spoke seriously, her head on one side.

'He wasn't a likeable man, and his visit last night wasn't generally welcomed. That was obvious. Whether anyone disliked him enough to actually kill him—I suppose this is what you mean, Sergeant—I can't say.'

'You say "just about everyone". Who were the exceptions?'

'Well, Jill Mission seemed to get on with him quite well. They had a professional connection and this gave them something in common. But of course his visit caused a few problems for her because Nick Bedford, her defacto husband, was obviously jealous of him. Quite unnecessarily, I would think. I would have said Damien Treloar was one of those shallow men who feed their egos by compulsively flirting with anyone female. Jill seems sensible, and no doubt she copes with far more difficult cases than him everyday, in her job. I can't imagine her being taken in by him, really.'

She looked at them calmly. Martin, scribbling, hunched his shoulders. There was something about this woman that gave him the shivers.

'I, of course, had no reason to care about him one way or the other. All the others, though, obviously found his being around awkward or unpleasant.'

'And yet he was allowed to stay the night?'

'The idea was that there was no sensible alternative. He was more or less in exile in the old garage anyway, I suppose. And Mrs Tender felt she had no choice, apparently. At least that's what Kate Delaney says. I found it extraordinary she'd allow it, however hard to refuse, since it's common knowledge that she hated Damien Treloar and wanted to keep her daughter well away from him. Kate says I don't understand the social rules a woman like Betsy Tender lives by.' She smiled slightly, then leaned forward.

'Look, Sergeant Toby,' she said, 'I don't see that I'm being much help to you. I heard nothing at all last night. I know nothing about the relationships of all these people. Anna Treloar says you think it's suicide. Jeremy Darcy says you think it's murder. Betsy Tender is still convinced that it was an accident. Really, I . . .' She raised her hands and then dropped them back in her lap.

Toby looked at her in silence for a moment. He was obviously let down, thought Martin. No wonder. What an anticlimax. To be so unprofessional as to ask an amateur for help in solving a pretty simple old case. And then be knocked back, more or less. Poor old bloke must be losing his grip, listening to tall tales from his brother. Martin had met Dan Toby once and hadn't been impressed. Not his idea of a big city detective at all. Slow, heavy and grey as an old man wombat. Hadn't looked to Martin like the type to find out what day it was, let alone solve a crime.

Toby spoke slowly. 'Miss Birdwood, all I'm asking is that you keep your eyes open and have a think about it. OK? If the thing's what I think it is, then it's tricky. Almost everyone had some sort of reason, and some sort of opportunity, to make away with Treloar, if he was killed the way I think he was. You're one person I know I can trust. One person who is out of the running, you see, as a suspect. I just want you to stay a few days, and help me out if you can. Sure, you mightn't be able to. But then again, who knows what may turn up when I'm not around?'

The woman looked at her hands again. 'I can do that, of course. Look, I didn't mean to be awkward. Anything I can do, I'll do.'

Toby beamed. 'Right then,' he rumbled, planting two freckled hands on his ample knees. 'That's settled. Martin! Take these cups out to Mrs Tender, thank her, and tell her we're going over the road now, to talk to Theresa Sullivan.'

Martin hurriedly stuffed his notebook away and grabbed the tray. As he fiddled with the doorknob, tray awkwardly held against his hip with one hand, he heard Verity Birdwood speak again.

'Maybe I'll come with you, Mr Toby . . . just . . . to pick up Zoe. It will save Kate . . .'

'Of course, of course Miss Birdwood.' Toby's barely concealed triumph reverberated in the room as the door closed behind Martin with a disgusted click.

9

Tea and Sympathy

〰〰〰

As he emerged into the weak, chilly sunlight Martin blinked and stifled a sneeze. His stomach was rumbling. He hoped the interview with this Mrs Sullivan wouldn't take too long. Toby was standing with the Birdwood woman by the white van, talking earnestly.

The van was dusty and piled up inside it Martin could see a few boxes and roughly wrapped bits and pieces. These, he supposed, were the antique dealer's mountain purchases. For sure he'd paid peanuts for them. They were all crooks, those blokes. Old china, books, spotty pictures in fancy frames—bits of some old bachelor's family past, some old lady's lifetime. Like old Alice in there, they sat in the middle of it all like people in a time capsule up here. His mother had sold a whole houseful of stuff to some second-hand dealer when his grandmother died. Reckoned it didn't fit into their house, or wouldn't, or something. Fact was, she just didn't like it—too old and dusty.

Like that Mrs Tender. You could just see her itching to get her hands on Alice Allcott's place—clean it up, clear it out, put up bright flowery curtains and get in pine bunks. Still, she looked as though she knew what was what. Not like poor old Mum. She'd made fifty bucks out of Nan's furniture, and thought she was

135

Christmas. Mrs Tender would send it all off to auction, probably. That'd be the thing to do. Anna Treloar would score a couple of trendy things—that black iron pot in the kitchen, to put a palm in, a fancy chamber pot for an indoor plant, maybe; Mrs Tender would take a tea-set, or a picture; Alice would be left with a few bits and pieces to remind her of home, and the rest would be sold off, a little nest egg to keep her in whatever nice clean little box Mrs Tender put her in. Wouldn't need to be much. The old bird wouldn't live six months away from this place. Martin clicked his teeth and moaned softly to himself. He didn't really know why.

'Well, McGlinchy!' Martin jumped and cast his eyes guiltily up to Toby, standing massively beside him. He saw the slight figure of Verity Birdwood crossing the road. 'Come to any conclusions?'

'A . . . about the van, sir?'

'What else've you been staring at?' snapped Toby impatiently.

'Well, um, ah—the tyres are flat as pancakes, aren't they sir?'

'Sure are.' Toby waited.

'The whole car leans over. He must have seen it as soon as he came out.'

'Yes. Unless he was half blind. So?'

'Well . . . so . . .' Martin's mind raced. 'So why did he take so long to go back into the house?'

'Why indeed?' Toby waited again. Oh no, thought Martin. It's detective-lesson time.

'Probably he wasn't sure what he should do, sir,' he said after a moment. 'He probably thought about it for a while.'

'For fifteen minutes?'

'Yeah . . . well, maybe he . . .'

'Look, Martin. We've had trouble with kids letting tyres down before, haven't we?'

'Yeah, course. Gosh yes. Remember that whole

street in Katoomba, last holidays, and the traffic jam that . . .'

'Yes, exactly. That whole street. Have you ever seen just one car picked out of a whole long line like this for treatment?'

'Well,' Martin thought. 'No . . . no . . . except when it's a Rolls or a Jag or something . . . or some kid's got it in for someone specially.' He looked at Toby.

'Wouldn't have been much fun walking or cycling down this street last night in the cold and mist either, would it?'

'No . . . a kid'd be hurrying home, wouldn't he?' Martin's eyebrows shot up as he imagined the scene. 'He wouldn't be hanging around letting down tyres. He'd be . . .'

'Thinking of the fire and the telly, and a bit of hot soup, eh?' said Toby, smiling briefly at this boy, who wasn't much past the bicycling age himself. 'So?'

'So . . . say it wasn't a kid at all. And no one in the house went out while Treloar was there—they all agreed on that.'

'So who's left, Martin?'

'Treloar let down his own tyres,' Martin said slowly. 'Because he wanted to stay the night. But what for? What did he want to do?'

'Or who did he want to talk to without being over-heard? That's what we've got to find out, son,' said Toby.

Verity Birdwood and Zoe stood on the grass in front of the prim little house across the road, watching a huge black cat play with a piece of stick. Their voices reached Toby and Martin easily as they approached.

'Theresa says I can come back tomorrow and bathe Nel again. She said I was a great help,' the child was saying. 'Birdie?'

'Yes?'

'Theresa's got a doll's house with little wooden dolls and everything. She's going to get it out for me. Auntie Alice has a Noah's Ark, with animals that I've never seen, but she's lost it, and the train. Well, it's not lost. She's just forgotten where it is. So Theresa says I can play with the doll's house, until Auntie Alice finds . . .' Zoe turned her head and looked at Martin and Toby. Her eyes became wide and respectful.

'Zoe, this is Mr Toby, and this is Mr McGlinchy. They've come to have a word to Theresa.'

Zoe smiled, shuffled and said hello. Then, still trying to smile politely, she hissed out of the side of her mouth between bared teeth, 'What for, Birdie?'

Toby returned the smile. 'We just thought she might be able to help us, love,' he said, 'just because she's a neighbour of . . . Auntie Alice's.' He nodded to Birdie and strolled on up the path. Martin followed.

'About Damien, Birdie?' he heard the child ask. 'Why is everyone worrying about him dying so much? Yesterday he made everyone shout and cry and I woke up. Jill was crying. I saw her. And it was all his fault!' The shrill voice was rising.

'It matters when anyone dies, Zoe,' the woman said firmly. 'You'll understand when you're more grown up.'

'I'm seven and a half, you know, Birdie. I can play cards and ice-skate—a bit. I can stay up really late. I can stay awake when everyone else is asleep. I can do lots of things now. You think I can't but . . .'

Martin tucked his head into his chest and walked on quickly. He felt almost guilty overhearing the child put in her elders like that, in all innocence. As though he'd trapped her into it personally.

'Hear that?' muttered Toby as Martin joined him and they climbed the stairs together. 'Out of the mouths of babes. Shouting and crying till she woke up. Doesn't sound as though the little disagreement was quite as small-time as we've been told, eh?'

Martin nodded. 'Still . . .' he ventured. But whatever qualification he was about to utter was forgotten at that moment, for the front door opened, and Theresa Sullivan stood there looking down at them.

Years later both of them would remember that moment: the woman looking down at them, frowning a bit against the light. A heavy plait hung over one shoulder. She wore a thick woollen skirt, falling almost to her ankles, and over it a fantastically embroidered blue tunic with a high neck. She had on blue stockings and black walking shoes. It was a barbaric outfit, in a way.

She was big, tall, with full breasts and powerful arms, and in the crook of her elbow nestled a tiny creature in a red jumpsuit, its soft baby fingers gripping her strong hair, its short-sighted blue eyes staring at them.

'Er . . . Mrs Sullivan.' Toby shaded his eyes and squinted at her. For some reason his eyes had started watering, and he was forced to rub them with the back of his hand as he reached the verandah, on a level with her at last.

'Detective-sergeant Toby,' he said firmly. He felt Martin hovering at his elbow and introduced him too, feeling as usual a mixture of irritation and affection for the gangling boy, whose present lugubrious expression, no doubt intended to be businesslike and determined, wouldn't have deceived the baby. As if to prove his point the baby in fact noticed Martin at just this moment and beat its free fist at him. 'Aka,' it cried, in a welcoming and convivial way. The young detective grinned and held out a big, biro-stained finger. The baby, cross-eyed with concentration, grasped the finger and gripped with all its might. 'Azah!' it said, with enormous satisfaction, and resisted with all its strength when Martin, blushing with pleasure, tried to take his finger back.

'You seem to be stuck, eh?' said Mrs Sullivan. 'Look—come in and sit down.' She raised her voice.

'Birdie—coffee?' Birdie waved, said a few words to Zoe, and followed them.

Now Theresa Sullivan was warm and welcoming. The almost severe expression had completely disappeared—a slight line between her eyebrows and heavy shadows under her big eyes the only signs that her life was anything but serene. She laughed at Martin who, anxious not to upset his new friend, stumbled along close beside her, following his captured finger.

'I've just made a pot of coffee,' she said, leading the way down the hall.

The house, so prim and neat on the outside, was friendly and warm. It smelled of the new rush matting that covered the floors, and of fresh coffee. They walked past two small bedrooms on the left of the corridor, a sitting room on the right. The front bedroom was painted white, and through the open door Martin could see a single bed, a bassinet with rockers, a change table stacked with nappies and a beautiful old dressing table. A soft-looking armchair piled with cushions faced the window. There was something sad about that single bed and the bassinet side by side. He couldn't have put the thought into words, though.

The corridor led into a tiny, dark kitchen. The friendly coffee-and-groceries smell didn't conceal here the aroma of old stove, gas and damp linoleum. Above the sink was a small window, and beside it a door with coloured glass panes led out to the side passage of the house, dark, overgrown with shrubbery and dominated by the hulking shape of the gas cylinder. The woman led the way quickly past this depressing scene onto an enclosed back verandah, and stood back to usher them in.

Martin blinked. This was like another world. It wasn't a large room, but white walls, a blue and white Indian rug and plants in baskets gave the effect of light, air and space. Blue curtains were drawn back from glass double doors leading out to an overgrown garden, full of old fruit trees and bushes through which lanes of mossy stepping stones meandered. The sun filled the room with light. It supplied no warmth, but an old gas heater whispering in a corner made up for that.

'Sit down,' said the woman, gesturing towards a couch along one wall. She gently disengaged the baby's fist from Martin's finger, and carried her to a multicoloured rug lying on the floor near the doors in a pool of sunlight. From the ceiling hung a mobile. The baby lay back and kicked her floppy little legs, and multicoloured fish, translucent in the sun, swam solemnly above her.

'I'll just get the coffee,' said Theresa. She went back into the kitchen and they heard her clattering cups. Birdie stood for a moment, then sat down at a table by the wall. Martin sat uneasily, fingering his notebook. He looked out of the corner of his eye at Toby. He was watching the baby, smiling. What a turn-up! Theresa reappeared with a tray of coffee in pottery mugs. Toby half-rose from his seat.

'I'm fine, thanks' said the woman, and set down the tray, smiling. Toby smiled back and settled down into the cushions again. Martin couldn't believe his eyes. What had got into the old boy? He'd never seen him like this before. If he didn't know better, he'd think old Simon Toby was a bit struck with this arty lady in her embroidered smock.

'Look, ah, Mrs Sullivan,' Toby began, still smiling, 'we won't keep you long. Just a few points . . . ah, now, ah, first of all, you were at the house across the road last night?'

'Yes. To make a phone call. I don't have the phone on yet, and I often use Miss Allcott's . . . Alice's.'

'Right . . . ah . . . and you stayed for how long?'

'Oh, well, I don't know. About fifteen minutes, I suppose—maybe even less, maybe ten. Alice had people there and I just wanted to get in and out—you know.'

Toby's eyes twinkled. 'You hadn't met Mrs Tender before?'

She flushed a little, and then compressed her lips into a small answering smile. 'No,' she said slowly. 'I'd heard quite a bit about her, from Alice, but I hadn't ever actually met her before last night. Last night I just had to ring up the girl who looks after my shop, about arrangements for next week—oh, I won't go into all that—anyway, I just had to ring, so—I went over.' Her voice trailed off. She looked as though she was remembering something not very pleasant. Her eyes moved to where the baby lay, waving its hands, beating off shadows.

Toby waited a minute, then prompted her. 'So you left, at about, say, 9.45?'

'I suppose so, yes. It'd be about that.'

'And Damien Treloar left with you?'

'Yes . . . he left at the same time.'

'Did you have any conversation at all?'

Theresa stared at him. 'Just goodnight . . . you know. I was anxious to get back home. It was all misty, and I had Nel with me, and anyway she was due for a feed.'

'So you didn't notice if his car had flat tyres?'

'Well . . .' she seemed to be thinking. 'Well, no I didn't, actually. I suppose the mist . . . it was quite dark too, of course.'

'Right.' Toby sounded neither pleased nor disappointed.

'Why are you asking all this, Sergeant Toby?' said Theresa, looking into her coffee cup. 'I was told there'd been an accident.'

'I'm almost sure there wasn't, in fact,' said Toby deliberately, staring into his own mug. 'I'm operating now on the assumption that Treloar was murdered.'

Martin looked up from his notes and was shocked. The woman had gone white—really white. The lines in her forehead and the shadows under her eyes looked charcoal grey.

'You don't think . . .' she began, and shook her head. 'Oh, no, you couldn't.'

'What, Mrs Sullivan?'

'You know, that *Alice* . . . oh, look, she *wouldn't* Sergeant, honestly. She's a bit eccentric but she'd never deliberately hurt anyone. Never. I leave Nel with her—she's kindness itself . . . she's . . . anyway, she'd have no *reason* . . .' she stopped and looked confused.

'I've really got no firm views, Mrs Sullivan, at present,' said Toby mildly.

'Oh . . . good. For a minute I thought . . .'

The baby gurgled in her corner, and Martin saw Theresa's eyes move quickly to the spot and linger there. Her hand went to her breast. She turned back to Toby.

'It's just that Alice has been so terrific to me . . . to us. Ever since I moved in here . . .'

'And how long has that been, again, Mrs Sullivan?'

'Well, let's see. Nel was twelve weeks on Friday, and I moved into the place a month before she was born, so that's four months, about, that I've known Alice.'

'And Nel's father?' Toby asked gently.

'Dead,' said Theresa quietly.

'I'm sorry.'

'Yes. Thanks. Well, we manage fine on our own, really. Nel's a treasure. We manage.' The woman fell silent, her eyes on the baby again. The little jump-suited figure called out, and began to beat its hands in the air. Theresa put her hand to her breast again.

'Look, ah, actually, I don't want to rush you, but she's going to want her lunch soon. She's a real little clockwatcher. So if there are any . . .'

'Oh, yes, of course Mrs Sullivan.' Toby seemed a bit flustered, and Martin bent over his book, in mingled embarrassment and mirth.

'Just, if you could tell me if you heard or saw anything at all out of the ordinary last night. Any cars coming or going . . . anything like that.'

'Oh, I don't think . . . out here I can't hear the road, really. I usually sit out here at night. I leave the door open, to listen for Nel, but I don't really hear cars. In the bedroom I can, of course. Let's think. Well, I suppose I heard a few cars passing once I was in bed—I suppose I got into bed sometime after twelve. The lights were all off across the road then. I read for a while. I didn't pay much attention to the time. At two I got up to feed Nel—I say two—it could have bit a before or after, but she really is like a little alarm clock, every four hours almost to the minute, so it probably was two. There weren't any cars passing then. No cars. But there was one thing—oh, maybe I should have mentioned it before. I looked out the front window after I picked Nel up, and I saw, um, the man who died . . .'

'Damien Treloar?' Toby sat forward eagerly, and Martin felt his heart jump. So Treloar was alive at two, anyway.

'Yes, of yes. It was awfully dark but no mist anymore. The wind had blown it all away, I suppose. He was getting something out of his van, I think . . . anyway the doors were open.'

'What happened then?'

'Well, I don't know. I mean, I didn't stay and watch. I went and sat down in the chair to feed Nel, and I couldn't see out of the window from there . . . Is what I saw important?'

'Well, it shows the man was still alive at two. We knew he had gone back to the van sometime during the night, because his keys were inside it in the morning, and I gather when he left the Tenders for the garage he was wearing them clipped to the waistband of his trousers . . . his jeans.'

'Yes, . . . he did that . . . I remember.'

'Now, look, Mrs Sullivan, this is quite important. Your statement . . .'

The back door rattled. Zoe elbowed her way through, firmly clutching the black cat around the chest. Its legs dangled in an undignified fashion, its eyes glared accusingly at Theresa.

'It might rain, Theresa, so I thought he'd better come inside,' said Zoe responsibly. She stared at the detectives, then looked round for Birdie.

'Say hello to Nel for me, Zoe,' said Theresa quietly, smiling at the child. 'She's getting cross, and she'll be quiet if you play with her. OK?'

Zoe carefully put the cat down and went over to the baby's rug. The cat walked away from her stiff-legged, stopping as soon as dignity allowed to begin licking its ruffled fur back into place.

'Right, thanks, sorry Mrs Sullivan.' Toby cleared his throat. 'Now, as I said, your statement is that you saw Damien Treloar at his car at 2 am . . .'

Theresa sounded flustered. 'Well, when you say statement, I told you I was just guessing at the exact time, really, because of Nel, but . . .'

'Oh, yes, I understand that, certainly, but in general . . . it wouldn't for example, be earlier than twelve?'

'Oh, no, it was *around* two. Because I've just thought, after I'd put Nel back into bed I did look at my watch and it was only two-thirty. I looked outside again, you know, like you do. I wasn't sleepy at all—I hadn't really slept before Nel woke, to tell the truth, and I was just looking out . . .' Her face changed and she hesitated.

Toby prompted her. 'No sign of Damien Treloar then?'

'Oh no. But, look, you'll think I'm mad not to have remembered it before. There was a funny thing. That's really why I looked at my watch. I remember now. When I looked out there was a car parked just outside my place, where your car is now, and I'm sure it wasn't there when I looked out the window before, you know, before I fed Nel. I remember thinking that it must have cruised down the hill with the engine off, because I hadn't heard it at all, and I looked at my watch automatically, to see how late it was. Anyway, I didn't think much about it—forgot it, actually, until just now. The car was gone this morning, but I didn't hear or see it go. But, you know,' she added diffidently, 'it's really nothing. It was one of Alice's cars, one of the guest's, I mean, not a strange one. I'd seen it there, parked on the other side, earlier, so really . . .'

'What sort of car was it, Mrs Sullivan?' Toby asked. Martin held his breath. This was it, he thought, and waited. When the answer came he felt that strange thud of the heart you get when you hear something you half expect, half dread.

'It . . . it was the VW. The green . . .' Theresa was faltering now, her confidence draining away as she realised what her testimony might mean.

'The green VW. You're sure?'

'Oh . . . well . . .' She looked at him, frowning. 'It was dark, and I . . .'

'Please think carefully, Mrs Sullivan.' Toby was all intent now, serious and sober. The obvious goodwill and interest in Theresa herself that had been radiating from him was gone. Now he was just willing a witness to cooperate, with all his force.

She gave up. 'I'm pretty sure . . .' Then, as he leaned back, glancing at Martin, she went on, 'Look I don't know whose car it was. I said it was the car I saw earlier, but really it could have been anyone's, couldn't it? I . . .'

Zoe looked up from her corner. 'It must have been Nick. He's got a green VW. He wasn't home when I got up, though, so he must've come home and gone away again. Why would he do that?'

'We'll have to ask him, won't we, lass?' said Toby.

*   *   *

'Very gently, now, Zoe. She's full of milk and we don't want to get blurk all over your jumper.'

'Yuk, no!' Zoe clasped the baby bundle gingerly, and rocked it awkwardly, her face serious. 'Oh, look, she likes it. She's going to sleep.'

'Yes. It's her sleep time and you've rocked her off beautifully. Give her to me, I'll put her down in her bed, Zoe.'

Zoe surrendered the baby and watched as Theresa disappeared into the hall. She leaned back in her chair and looked vaguely around the room. This was a funny holiday. She wondered where Birdie had got to. She'd been supposed to go home with her, but somehow or other she had disappeared when the policemen went, and Zoe had been left with Theresa again. Theresa was nice, but she seemed a bit far away now. She'd forgotten about the doll's house, and Zoe hadn't liked to remind her. Still, it had been interesting watching Nel having her lunch, sucking her milk from Theresa's warm breast, holding on with her little hands, bright little eyes peeping up and toes kicking and curling inside the jumpsuit. She worked very hard at it. Her face was pink, and you could see sweat like dew on her forehead and wetting her fluffy orange hair all around. Babies were nice. She wished Mum would have another one. But Dad said over his dead body, one was bad enough and he wasn't going through all that again. If he'd seen Nel sleeping in her arms like that he might have changed his mind.

At this point in her cogitations there was a knock at the back door and she looked up to see Jeremy smiling at her. She ran over and slid the door open.

'That was a coincidence, Dad. I was just thinking about you.'

'Were you . . . well!'

'Yes, I was thinking . . .'

'Look, darling, you can tell me in the car. I'm taking you to the Scenic Railway. How about that?'

'The train that goes right down the mountain? Where you have to really hold on?'

'Yeah. OK?'

'Great! I'll just tell Theresa.'

'I'll tell her, Zoe, don't worry. She'll understand.' Birdie had appeared behind Jeremy. 'You go off with Jeremy now, and I'll thank Theresa for having you. I'm going to have a cup of tea with her.'

'Oh. OK.' Zoe took Jeremy's hand and slid through the half open door. 'Bye, Birdie,' she said cheerfully.

'See you, Birdie,' said Jeremy rather grimly, and they set off down the path. Birdie waited a minute.

'And a waffle at the Paragon after?' Zoe's voice floated back to her. The bargaining had started. She smiled, and stepped into the room as Theresa came tiptoeing through the hall door, and pulled it nearly closed behind her.

'Oh—all's well?'

'Yes, Jeremy's taken her off to Katoomba. Kate's with Jill.'

'Look . . . I hope they all understand—I mean . . .' Theresa looked exhausted and pale. The shadows under her eyes were dark grey. 'I had no idea the car was . . .'

'Nick Bedford's? How could you know, Theresa? You had to tell what you saw.'

'What's happened?'

'He's gone with them. "For further questioning", as you can imagine.'

'Oh, God!' Theresa sank down into a chair and bent forward, her hands clasped between her knees. 'Oh, how awful!'

Birdie looked at her for a moment, but made no move towards her.

'They won't hold him,' she said at last. 'They haven't got the post-mortem results yet. Look, there's just no point in worrying, Theresa. Kate and Jill are in a terrible flap, but they don't blame you in any way. Nick would have been much more sensible to tell the truth from the beginning.'

'What *is* the truth? Look, come and sit down. I'll make some tea.'

'Thanks.' Birdie sat down and raised her voice slightly so that Theresa could hear her in the kitchen. 'Well, I can really only tell you what Nick said. You've heard that he went off in a rather bad temper earlier in the evening, and that he said he hadn't come back. He now admits that he did in fact return to the house after driving around for a while, having cooled down after the argument I told you about. He apparently turned off the car engine and cruised down the hill to Alice's place, so as not to advertise his arrival, and pulled up outside your place, as you said, sometime before 2.30. He said he saw that all the lights were off. He thought it probable that the back door had been locked, as it usually is, apparently, once everybody's in bed. He'd vaguely planned to slip into the house and make up with Jill without an audience, but this now seemed impossible. So he sat there in the car and wondered what to do for a while, five minutes or so, and then simply put the car into neutral, took off the brake again and slipped away past the house and around the corner. He started the engine there and drove off to some lookout where he had an uncomfortable few hours' sleep. Once it was light he found a shop and bought a paper and some coffee. Eventually he decided it was a respectable enough hour to come home, and did so, to find the police in the house.'

'But why didn't he just tell the truth before?' said Theresa. She stood in the kitchen doorway, a cup of tea in each hand, tall in her fantastic blue and black.

'He says he panicked—thought from the detectives' manner that they suspected foul play and that he was the natural suspect.' Birdie paused. 'True enough, as it happens,' she added drily.

Theresa sat down beside her on the couch and put down the tea, looking at her curiously.

'But surely you don't think he did . . . hurt the man? Isn't he a friend of yours?'

'Not of mine. Of Kate's and Jeremy's. The question is, did he actually just sit in the car and then drive off, or did he in fact get out, find Treloar, kill him, or at least arrange for him to die during the night, and then just slip away again. There are no witnesses one way or the other. Unless you . . . ?'

Theresa shook her head. 'No. Honestly I saw nothing at all. Just the car sitting there. I got some tea and got into bed then, and finally I went to sleep. I didn't hear or see anything more till morning.'

Birdie moved slightly in her seat, and reached for her cup. 'The baby keeping you awake a bit, is she?' she said sympathetically.

'Oh, no!' Theresa smiled. 'She's honestly an angel. Sleeps like a baby in a book. I've been feeling marvellous.'

'But last night, you . . .'

'Oh—yes, well, last night I just couldn't get to sleep somehow. I always sleep in the afternoons, as Alice might have told you—round about this time, actually, and I must have overdone it yesterday. You know, I just kept thinking, turning plans over in my mind. Nothing special, but, you know, it's a precarious business, managing on your own.' She pushed a couple of strands of hair back from her cheek and looked at Birdie from under her heavy eyebrows. Then she lifted her chin. 'On your own with a baby, I mean,' she said with quiet dignity. 'It's a responsibility. I want her to have a good life.'

'Well, a kid couldn't ask for a better place to grow up than here, could she?' said Birdie, her eyes friendly behind the spectacles. 'Did you come up here from Sydney?'

'Oh no, no . . . I've lived in the mountains almost all my life. I worked in Sydney for a while, but came

back up here to look after Dad ten years ago, after
my mother died, and when he died I stayed on. I had
a shop, you know, and I was settled.'

'It's an antique shop, isn't it?'

'Oh, I'm not in the same one now. I moved—when—
after I found Nel was coming, and everything. The one
I've got now is smaller. It's more crafts and craft materials and things like that. Less investment, and really
more in my line. I keep a few little old things, though.
People like them, and it gives the shop variety. I told
Alice I'd take any bits and pieces she wanted to sell on
consignment. I think she needs the cash. Apparently Mrs
Tender—Betsy—suggested the same thing to her over a
year ago. Her son-in-law, about whom Alice was very
scathing, had . . . oh, my heavens . . . Mrs Tender's
son-in-law!'

'Damien—the man who died,' said Birdie calmly.

'Yes, it must have been, of course. Apparently he'd
told Betsy Tender that there was a great market for
old household bits and pieces, and poor Mrs Tender
confronted Alice with a list of dealers he'd given her
and everything, and Alice blew her top. "Gave her a
piece of me mind", as she put it. As you've probably
noticed, Alice is a bit, um, contrary where her niece
is concerned.' She smiled a trifle mischievously.

'Yes,' Birdie grinned in response. 'Seems a good idea,
though. The old house is bursting at the seams.'

'It's a muddle, all right. Reminds me of Mum and
Dad's place. Alice agrees, actually. It's often the way.
People will often listen to an idea from a friend, where
they'll resist a relative. Don't I know it!' She laughed.
'Dad was a terror for that. So now Alice's threatening
to have "a good clean out", as she calls it. All that
happens, of course, is that she unpacks a drawer or
two, has a good afternoon's daydream over the things,
and then puts them all back intact. Just like Mum.'
Theresa laughed quite gaily this time, and for a moment the line between her brows disappeared, and the
edges of her eyes wrinkled in genuine pleasure. She

turned smiling to Birdie. 'I really love old Alice. She's great, don't you think?'

Birdie smiled back. 'She's an original all right.'

'She's been really good to me. When I moved in here I can tell you I needed a friend. You can imagine—eight months pregnant, and the house, honestly, was in the most disgusting mess. Not that I wasn't lucky to get it. I really wanted to buy a place, but I didn't have much money to play around with. This place was so cheap, I couldn't believe my luck!'

'Cheap—with that fantastic garden, and that bush next door and all?' Birdie looked at her disbelievingly over the rim of her cup.

'Oh, *yes.*' Theresa hesitated, glanced at Birdie's friendly eyes and went on in a burst of confidence. 'Actually, the thing was, the poor old bloke who owned it lived by himself, and apparently he died suddenly. Gastric flu and a heart attack or something—I didn't really listen to the agent. Anyway he died in the loungeroom and wasn't found for a day or two. And word got round so people didn't like the idea of the house, and no one would buy it. Then I came along, and look, it didn't worry me. I'd have taken a converted funeral parlour if that would have meant a safe roof for me and my baby.' She stopped. 'I suppose you think it's awful. I don't usually tell people. I mean, it puts people off, but really . . .'

'It doesn't put me off. People die every day, and presumably their houses go on being lived in. Usually you don't know about it, that's all.'

Theresa looked at the thin figure gratefully. Shadows fell on Birdie's face as she sat there, frowning into the cup clutched in freckled fingers. Something about this woman was intensely reassuring, Theresa thought. What was it? She hadn't talked to anyone about this house, except Alice, of course. She'd shied from the agent's smooth glossing-over the subject, hadn't responded to the feelers put out by Pat in the shop, dying to discuss the price of the house, wondering why it was so cheap. Yet here she was revealing herself to a complete stranger. It was just that this Birdie was so—honest. No gush or pretence about her, so you didn't feel you had to gush or pretend.

'Anyway, Alice was great. Apparently she was glad to have a new neighbour. I gather she and the old fellow who died weren't the best of friends.' She laughed. 'She's a terror, Alice. Apparently when she heard the old bloke had gone she more or less said "good riddance". An old terror, but marvellous to us. You know, always wandering over with soup or eggs or apples, and once with a couple of exquisite crystal bowls full of junket "to keep my strength up", she said.'

She sighed. 'It's not the food, you know. It's just nice to know someone knows you're alive, and cares.' She fell silent. Again she almost bit her tongue, cringing with a feeling of exposure, a loss of hard-won dignity. But Birdie sat nondescript, unmoved and quiet. No condescending half smile of understanding, no impetuous, kindly, meaningless reassurance. Just interested, undisturbed ease.

Birdie put down her cup and stretched, running her fingers through her tousled hair. 'Look,' she said, 'I'd better get back. Thanks for the tea.'

'Thanks for the sympathy,' said Theresa, smiling, and showed her to the door.

10

Girls Together

𝄚

The old house opposite was still when Birdie slipped
in the back way. It was a heavy, uneasy silence. Birdie
crossed over to the half-dead fire and crouched in front
of it, absent-mindedly poking the embers with a stick.
The kitchen door opened with a click and she turned
to see Kate peering at her, eyes black and wide.

'What's doing?' said Birdie.

Kate put a finger to her lips and stepped into the
living room, crossing the carpet on tip-toe and squat-
ting beside the crouching figure.

'Alice is in her room,' she hissed. 'Jill's gone for a
walk and so have the others except for Betsy and Wilf.
They're asleep. For God's sake don't wake them. Bet
sy's being outrageous. One minute she's threatening
to ring up someone she knows in Parliament, because
Nick's being victimised, and the next she's giving Jill
little homilies about standing by your man whatever
dreadful thing he's done for the love of you. God,
Birdie, Damien was a pain, no doubt about it, poor
bloke, but Betsy's a pain and a half. If there's a murderer loose I can't imagine why it wasn't Betsy who
got the chop. There'd be at least two perfect suspects.'

'Laney, you're babbling,' said Birdie calmly.

Kate dropped her head to her knees. 'Oh, I know,'

she said. 'But Birdie, poor Nick. Poor old Nick. Birdie, what if . . .' She raised her face and stared at Birdie with tears brimming up in her eyes.

'Come on mate!' said Birdie, and her glasses flashed. 'What if what? What if he did it?' She shook her head as Kate opened her mouth to speak. 'Don't tell me you aren't scared to death he did! You and Jeremy wouldn't be nearly as upset as you are if you were sure he had nothing to do with it. Jeremy's got a good poker face but I know him too well to be fooled. He was scared of that this morning.'

Kate nodded miserably. 'Yes, he said that before he left. How he could I don't know, really, Birdie. Nick's his oldest friend. And look, Birdie, I said to Jeremy, Nick was really surprised when he saw the police here. Really surprised. You could tell.'

'Yeah, he looked incredibly surprised. Quite amazed, really,' Birdie said slowly. 'I remember thinking that at the time.'

'So you see, I'm sure *really* that everything is OK, in my heart. It's just that things look so bad for him. I mean, why didn't he just *say* he'd come back for a few minutes, instead of lying about it?'

'I suppose he didn't think he'd been seen, and just wanted to keep clear of the whole thing. He's a quick thinker. He must have realised he'd be suspected, if foul play, as they say, was a possibility.'

Birdie turned back to the gloomy grate, selected a few bits of kindling and began stacking up the fire. She stared into the blaze, and didn't notice the mohair of her jumper beginning to curl and singe. Kate pulled at her arm.

'Move back, looney, you smell of singed goat!'

The door opened and Jill stepped into the room, her face rosy from the cold. She pulled off her striped woollen cap and shook her head so that her wiry hair stood out like a red nimbus round her head.

'It's freezing!' she said. 'And the mist's coming down again.'

She walked over to the fire, stripping off her gloves, and held her hands to the blaze.

'It's freezing,' she repeated, then looked at Kate. 'Any news?'

'Not a word. But Jill, you know, no news is good news,' said Kate.

The other women looked at her. 'Betsy been giving you cliche lessons?' said Jill, and plumped down on the floor.

'Look,' she said in a level voice. 'I've been thinking. Looking at all this rationally, I can see why the cops might think Nick bumped Damien off. But I know he didn't do it. I'm certain. The thing is, how do we prove it?'

'Assuming that someone did bump him off, and it wasn't an accident, or suicide, you mean?'

'Yes. Look, it's obvious *they* think it was murder. So let's assume what they're assuming, and see where we are.'

'Good,' said Kate. 'That's just what I was going to say to Birdie before. Birdie's good at these things, Jill. You know, I've told you, she got someone else off a murder charge a couple of years ago.'

'It wasn't quite the same thing, Kate,' said Birdie warningly. 'And . . .'

'Yes, I know,' Kate brushed her demur aside. 'You're going to say that you only research the facts, ma'am, and can't be held responsible if in the end it turns out that Nick *did* do it. Right?'

Birdie nodded, one side of her mouth turning up in a wry smile.

'But that's OK, isn't it Jill? Because we're sure he didn't do it.'

Jill nodded slowly. She looked tired to death now that the flush whipped up by the cold breeze had gone. Her nose glowed pink, but the rest of her face looked bleached, and her cream eyelashes and eyebrows could barely be seen.

Kate looked at her and her heart turned over. To see Jill like this was almost as bad as seeing joyously independent Nick carted off, shaken and unresisting, between two policemen. Both of them were being robbed of the very thing that made them themselves, different from anyone else. She spoke directly to Jill, urgently trying to break through.

'If we accept it's murder, and we want to prove Nick's innocent, we've got two alternatives. One, we can prove Nick *didn't* do it, which is apparently going to be difficult, or two, we can prove that *someone else did*. I think that's what we should aim for.'

Birdie looked at her. 'You realise that whoever did it was almost certainly someone who was also in this house last night?'

'Yes, of course I do. We'll find out who, and get Nick off.'

'It's not a game.'

Kate flared. 'Don't be so bloody condescending! I'm not saying it's a game or anything like a game. Whoever did it I'm sorry for them in a way, but they must be lousy to let Nick get lumbered with the blame.'

'Maybe they think the police won't be able to prove anything, and he'll go free,' said Birdie quietly.

'And be half suspected of murder all his life? That'll be great for his academic career I don't think,' Jill snapped.

Kate drew closer to them both. 'The thing is,' she said seriously, 'I actually think I know who did it. Really. You'll think I'm mad, but the more I think about it, the more I think I'm right.' She paused.

'Well, who, who, for heaven's sake?' hissed Jill.

'I think it was Betsy.'

'*Betsy!*' Jill's eyebrows disappeared into her hair.

'Yes. Listen. Don't look at me like that, Birdie, just listen. I know Betsy and you don't. She's besotted with her children, fanatical about running their lives and keeping them under her thumb. Jeremy told me that even Chris was saying his mother had done everything she could to get Anna away from Damien, and that she'd finally succeeded. And Sonsy told me—in confidence, so don't repeat it—that Betsy was playing games and trying to break up her and Chris.'

'Oh, but that's . . .'

'It's not ridiculous, Jill. I really believe it's true. Now, obviously Betsy thought Damien was gone for good and she was rid of him. Then he turns up here, at apple picking, breaking into one of the cherished family traditions. There's Anna, safe back in the Rose room in her little single bed and in comes Damien, all flags flying, exchanging burning glances with Anna across a crowded room.'

Jill looked up sharply. 'What burning glances?'

'The real old come-hither. I saw it with my own eyes. Come on, Birdie! You saw it too, didn't you?'

'Yes,' admitted Birdie slowly. 'I saw it, but not knowing the bloke I couldn't really tell if it was serious. Frankly, I mean, not meaning to be offensive, Jill, he seemed to be turning the charm on every woman in the room, especially you.'

'He was like that,' said Jill drily, and Kate nodded vigorously.

'I wasn't really sure myself, about him. There was no doubt, though, about *Anna's* side of it, was there, Birdie?'

'No. No, she seemed to take it seriously, all right. And return it, with one eye on her mum, if you know what I mean.'

'Exactly!' hissed Kate.

'I didn't notice a thing!' protested Jill.

'You had plenty to think about without noticing what Anna was doing,' Kate pointed out. 'What with Nick pulsating and glowering behind you and Damien being all proprietorial between flirts with everyone else.'

'With friends like you, Kate, who needs enemies?' Jill was only half joking. 'But look, say this was all happening—over my head, as it were—so what? It would only be important if . . .'

'If Betsy saw it too! Right! And I think she did.'

'She didn't seem to, Laney,' said Birdie. 'And most important of all, she let him stay the night. She wouldn't have done that, surely, if she suspected he might try to see Anna, or spirit her away or something. I found her agreement inexplicable as it was!'

'That's just it, Birdie. She let him stay the night so she could get rid of him once and for all. She hates to be thwarted. She's ruthless when she's threatened or crossed.'

'Yes, Katie, I know—in her own sphere she is,' said Jill, her brow wrinkled. 'But murder! It seems fantastic.'

'Lots of women have done murder to protect their children,' insisted Kate. 'And that's how Betsy'd see it. If I could see so clearly that Anna was charged up by Damien, then Betsy could too. That woman's got x-ray vision where her children are concerned.'

'Well, *how* did she do it then?' said Birdie.

'Got to Alice's poison cupboard and put a dose of something nasty in the coffee . . . oh, no, he didn't take the thermos with him, in the end, did he? Well . . . well, in an apple maybe, that she gave him before he went out.'

'I didn't see her give him anything,' said Jill, 'except the cake and coffee, that he left behind anyway.'

'Well, she managed it somehow,' said Kate firmly.

'Kate, it just doesn't ring true. I know you know Betsy better than I do, but the motive seems . . . I mean, she's got Anna away from him before, and I gather he was a bit of a pain anyway. Why shouldn't she just sit back and let nature take its course for a while, and then move in and get Anna back?'

'Because she wanted to protect her, Birdie. Mothers are like that. Betsy's just an exaggerated case—perverted, even, if you like.'

'Well, maybe . . . we'll see. You tell a good story, Laney. It's a theory, anyway,' said Birdie. 'Certainly Betsy's got the best running knowledge of the house, other than Alice, and the most right to be in any room in the house at any time. And she did go into the store cupboard to get the kerosene lamp for Treloar. I suppose she could have nicked the poison then.'

'Right! I hadn't remembered that,' said Kate eagerly.

'But still . . . I don't know.' Abruptly Birdie pushed her glasses up on her forehead, and rubbed her eyes. 'I'm not convinced.' She put her glasses back in place, and wrinkled her forehead.

Jill shook her head slightly, impatient. 'Look, this isn't getting us anywhere. The others'll be back soon. We've got to decide how we're going to tackle this.'

Birdie sat back on her heels and stirred the fire. 'Well, the first thing is not to go running round trying to play detective, all three of us in different directions, half cocked. If there's a murderer in this house that'll just put the wind up them. I want you both to leave it to me.'

'Oh, come off it, Birdie!' exploded Kate.

'No, Laney, look, it's important,' Birdie said firmly. Her glasses flashed in the firelight and for a moment she looked blind. 'I'm used to digging out things, and I'm used to working alone. This is research work like any other, right? You'll have to brief me on some things, but I probably know more about other things than you do, because Simon Toby was quite forthcoming when I went over to Theresa's with him. His brother was the detective in charge of that other murder case I was involved in, and obviously he thinks I'll be able to do him some good by keeping my eyes open here. The deal is, I'd say, that I tell him what I know, or work out, and he returns the compliment. If what we're after is the truth of the matter, we're in an ideal position, but not if you blow my cover, as they say, by drawing attention to the fact that work's being done here in the house as well as in the police station. See?'

She stood up, turned her back to them and walked towards the verandah doors.

'Where are you off to?' Kate demanded.

'I want a word with Alice. See you,' Birdie said,

and slipped out into the chill air, shutting the glass doors behind her.

Kate and Jill watched in silence as the tousled little figure knocked at Alice's door. Beyond the verandah the mist was rising. Alice's door stayed firmly closed. Birdie bent and called and knocked again, and the door slowly opened, light leaking out into the dusk. They saw her speak, then nod and step forward into the room. The door slammed shut.

'She's a funny girl, Kate, isn't she?' said Jill, care-fully non-critical of a friend's old friend.

'How do you mean?' said Kate defensively. She knew what was coming.

'I mean, she looks so . . . so sort of . . . quiet . . .'

Such a boring nobody, you mean, thought Kate. 'Yes,' she said, and waited.

'But once you get talking to her, she's really, really . . . confident, isn't she?'

Abrasive and bossy? Not to put too fine a point on it? 'Yes,' said Kate again. 'The thing is, she's got a lot to be confident about, you know. In her own line she's really good. She's had terrific offers from the commercial channels, but she stays with the ABC, lucky for it. I don't think commercial TV could handle her, anyway. She's a devil once she gets on to something. Won't stop digging until she's absolutely got everything, no matter who tells her to stop, or how long it takes, or how em-barrassing it becomes for everybody. Jeremy says she'd have been sacked from anywhere else long ago. She's always been like it. At school she was like it.'

'What's that she calls you?'

'Laney. It's a school thing. From Delaney. You know. Like I call her Birdie. I never think of her as Verity at all. It's always quite a shock to hear other people doing it.'

Jill looked at her curiously. 'You've never said that much about her.'

'No,' said Kate thoughtfully. 'Somehow she's not someone you do talk about much. She's . . . she's a

bit of a solitary. I mean, people find her eccentric . . .
I just don't feel she'd like me babbling on about her
to friends she doesn't know. You know?'

'Sort of,' said Jill, staring. She moved impatiently.
'What do you think she's talking to Alice about?'

'Poison, I suppose,' said Kate.

Alice Allcott's bedroom was a long section of the
closed-in verandah. Along the side and back walls
were windows, uncurtained, through which the apple
trees could be seen whispering their leafy branches
together, up to their waists in mist.

Alice sat in an old seagrass chair, the twin of the
one by the fire, right down to the soft, washed-out
cushions. Fierce blue eyes glared at Birdie under their
wrinkled hoods, and her strong, skinny hands clutched
the arms of the chair.

'I told the police and I'm telling you . . . I don't
know what . . .'

Birdie leaned forward and the old iron bed on
which she was perched creaked intimately.

'Miss Allcott, please listen to me. This is really serious. Your family's involved in a murder case. Nick
Bedford's in danger of being arrested for killing Damien Treloar. The police know he came back to the
house in the middle of the night, and Damien was
seen alive just before that time.'

Alice's eyes glittered and her hands tightened on the
chair. 'Who told them that?'

'Theresa Sullivan. She saw Damien, and then she
saw Nick's car. I was there when she told them.'

'Ah.' It was almost a sigh.

'Now, the thing is, Nick swears he didn't go near
Damien, or even get out of the car, but you can understand the police thinking what they do. They see
jealousy as a pretty good motive for the murder.'

'What do you think?' Alice looked straight at her.

'It's as good as any. And it's certain that Nick's not as mild-mannered as Kate makes out, by any means.'

'Piffle!' said Alice firmly. 'Any fool can see . . .'

'Miss Allcott, the police aren't fools, but they don't know Nick Bedford and they're going on what they've found out. He lied, remember, about coming back. Now, I've told Kate—Kate's an old friend of mine—that I'll try to do a bit of work at this end, and try to get Nick out of the mess he's in. I want you to help me.'

'I can't.'

'Yes, you can, Miss Allcott, you have to!'

Alice pushed herself up from her chair. She stood looking down at Birdie, tall and gaunt, her face in shadow. Birdie had a flashing sense of her own frailty. It happened sometimes, usually with men, and she didn't like it. She hated her tough, active mind being locked in a small, thin body, so easily broken and restrained. Theresa would have made two of her. So would Jill, almost. Now Alice, eighty if she was a day, was towering above her, bullying and aggressive. She fought the feeling down, forced herself to stay absolutely still.

'I say have to, Miss Allcott, because things are different now,' she said calmly, looking straight ahead. 'I think you've decided not to cooperate with the police because you think whoever did Damien Treloar in should get a medal, not a prison sentence. Look, I understand that—I don't agree with it, but I understand it. But you've got to face the fact that if the police don't get all the information—if you, or any of us keep quiet about anything at all that might help—it's on the cards that some poor sod like Nick Bedford'll get it in the neck when he's done nothing at all to deserve it. Do you want that?'

Alice looked at her in silence, and then sank back into her chair. Suddenly she grinned, showing uneven white teeth. 'Well, you're a funny one, eh?' She put her head on one side and looked at Birdie slyly. 'Where'd you come from? You're not the type Bet usually drags along here. Don't talk like it, anyhow.'

'I'm a friend of Kate's, like I said.'

'Well, she's got good taste, eh? All right. What do you want to know?'

'First, *did* you spray the trees just before we came?'

'Nope, 'course not. The fruit was going to be picked. Think I've got a screw loose?'

'You said you had.' Birdie grinned. 'Sprayed, I mean.'

'I say that to stop them young ones eating the apples. I've always said it. Every year I say it. They wouldn't know—well, now I find they've been eating them anyhow, pack of parrots—but I thought they wouldn't know. The point is, I never sprayed.'

'Apparently Mrs Tender was concerned that this year you'd really . . .'

'Oh, Bet's a fool. She thinks I'm gaga, see? Wishful thinking.' She cackled. 'I let her think what she likes. I don't say I don't give her a bad time, bung it on a bit. But she brings it on herself, gets on me nerves. Her stuck-up kids get on me nerves. Her dad kept a little corner shop up here at Birk's Crossing all his life. Me sister Lily married him. Never had two pennies to rub together. Bet was their only child, and, 'course, they doted on her. She married poor old Wilf straight out of school, practically, and got him to move down to the city. Then she nagged and pushed and worked part-time in a shoe shop herself till they had a house and a car and everything else, and the kids at private schools.'

The old woman moved restlessly. 'Look,' she said. 'All credit to her. Wilf wouldn't have been much help. He's not a fighter, Wilf. A couple of years ago his business nearly went bust, and he's been more or less useless ever since, as far as I can see. No, all credit to her. I don't know how she's managed. But the way she carries on you'd think she'd been born with a silver spoon in her mouth, silly biddy. Looking down her nose at Christopher's girl, and at this house, that she was glad enough to come to as a girl—a cut above poor Lil's little place, it was. Airs and graces, plummy voice to keep in with those women she meets through Rodney's school. What for? Oh, it makes me laugh . . .'

'About the poison, Miss Allcott,' Birdie prompted. Betsy would be up and around by now. Any minute she might knock at the door, and that would be the last of any useful information from Alice.

'Oh, yeah. Well, the fact is I didn't spray. Right. The young copper, forgotten his name, young woolly-haired bloke, looked through the storeroom, wrote everything down in his little book. Ha! Much good it did him! The horse had bolted, hadn't it?'

'You mean there was something missing?'

'Yeah. A little bottle of Parathion. Concentrate.'

'Parathion? I've heard of that somehow or other. It's deadly. What were you doing with that, Alice? Oh . . . sorry, I mean . . .'

'Call me Alice, for heaven's sake. We always used to use it. Worked like a charm for all sorts of bugs. Better than most of this modern rubbish. But there's no doubt about it, it's nasty stuff to have around the place. Had an old dog years ago got some on his paws out the back. Dead as mutton in five minutes. Some fool had spilled some, filling the sprayer. There was a terrible hue and cry because of course it could've been any of us, easy, stepped on it with bare feet. Anyhow, we didn't use it much after that, and I haven't used it for years. But the bottle was there in the storeroom all right. Right at the back, up high. Saw it only yesterday, when I was showing young Zoe round me chamber of horrors.'

She looked at Birdie, her head on one side. 'What's more,' she said slowly, 'I mentioned it to that crew in there the first day. I remember now. They all blooming knew it was there. And it isn't there now. I looked for it first thing, before the cops got here. I reckon that's what was used on Treloar. I saw him stretched out. Looked just like that old dog. Nasty way to go. Painful.' She looked at Birdie and her eyes were cold. 'Served him right,' she said.

11

Birdie Makes a Phone Call

〰〰

In the kitchen Anna was washing up and Kate was making custard. Anna was silent and Kate, after a few attempts at conversation, gave up and let her thoughts drift. Thank heavens Betsy had decided to go to the shops and buy takeaway food for dinner. She'd been so afraid that Betsy would discover Birdie talking to Alice. She'd felt absurdly guilty about it, her heart beating wildly, as if she'd somehow arranged the whole thing. And now, with Betsy safely off in the car, Wilf, grey and querulous, buckled in beside her, Kate was feeling guilty again, and embarrassed at having so foolishly and emphatically insisted that the woman was a cold-blooded murderer. There beside the fire with Birdie and Jill it had seemed so simple and obvious. Now it seemed childish. Birdie was right. She'd been treating it as a game. Murder in the dark. Damien Treloar screams in the night. Betsy has a motive, Betsy has the card with 'murderer' on it. Let's catch Betsy. Betsy with the lines around the eyes, Betsy with her little world shifting around her.

Kate felt a sudden longing for Jeremy and Zoe. They were her little world. How far would she go to protect them?

Birdie slipped in through the door and winked at Kate. Anna spun round, looked at her coldly for a couple of seconds and then turned back to her suds.

'Birdie, stir this while I do some apples, will you?' said Kate. Birdie obediently took the wooden spoon and began moving it around ineffectually in the thickening yellow mess.

'I never want to eat an apple again!" said Anna without turning around. 'I don't see how you can!'

'Zoe loves apple crumble and custard,' said Kate apologetically.

Anna grunted. 'Oh, blast, these thin gloves Mum buys are hopeless. Now this pair's got a hole in it, and it was the last one.' She stripped the gloves off and examined her nails.

'Where is everyone?' she said fretfully. 'It's getting dark.' She slammed the dishwashing brush down crossly and unplugged the sink. 'Why couldn't that woman across the road keep her mouth shut? What was she doing spying through her curtains in the middle of the night, anyway?'

'She was up feeding the baby, she said,' said Birdie. 'Kate, should this be doing . . . ?'

'Oh, Birdie, you've let it go lumpy. Oh, gosh, look! You're supposed to keep . . . here, give it to me! You finish the apples.'

'You should have explained, Kate,' said Birdie reasonably.

'Haven't you ever made custard before?'

'No. I never eat stuff like that. Looks horrible.'

'It looks horrible now, yes, thanks to you. I'll have to beat it up with the egg-beater.'

'Is Theresa Sullivan sure it was Nick's car she saw?' said Anna, wiping her hands.

'It doesn't matter if she is or not. Nick admitted that he came home at that time,' snapped Kate, whirring away at the lumpy custard.

'Is she sure she saw Damien?'

'She saw someone at Damien's van,' said Birdie,

looking at her over her glasses. 'She says she's almost sure it was him.'

'It must have been dark, Birdie,' said Kate.

'Yes. She said it was. And he was leaning into the van, getting something out, or putting something in. Anyway, she saw a person in dark blue pants and a light blue parka, and shiny boots, at the van. His keys were in the ignition in the morning. She assumed it was him, and the police think so too.'

'I don't see why they should,' said Kate excitedly. 'It could have been the person who killed him!'

'Are you still on about that, Kate?' Anna's voice was cold. 'It's ridiculous. He could just as well have killed himself. Why don't you just leave it!'

'For God's sake, Anna! Nick's suspected of murdering him. Of course I can't leave it.'

'They'll let him go, surely. There's no hard evidence.'

'People are in gaol for murder now on circumstantial evidence!'

Anna was silent. Kate turned to Birdie.

'Did Theresa see his face?'

'No. His parka hood was up, tight around his face.'

'Is that what she said?' Anna's voice had changed. They both looked at her.

'It's . . .' she hesitated, and flushed a little. She went on uncertainly. 'It's just that, really, he hated wearing it up. He never did.' She swallowed.

'It was awfully windy, Anna,' said Kate gently. She cursed herself for starting this. She'd gone after her hare without even thinking about Anna's feelings on the matter. This afternoon she'd harangued Birdie and Jill about Anna's reaction to Damien the night before. The poor girl had really cared about him, creep as he was, and now she was being forced to talk about him.

Anna's voice roused her. 'He *never* wore it up,' she was insisting, well in control now. 'It made him feel claustrophobic. If he was cold, he wore a woollen cap, a blue one, that he bought in Ireland. Even skiing.'

'His parka hood was up this morning,' said Birdie quietly. 'This morning in the orchard.' She paused. 'There was a blue cap underneath.'

'I *know* it was up this morning. Everything was so strange, so awful, this morning, that I didn't think of it especially. But I'm thinking of it now. I can't understand it. I've never known him to wear it like that before . . . Oh, what does it matter, anyway?'

She brushed past both of them and left the kitchen, slamming the door behind her.

'Poor Anna,' said Kate, and tears welled up in her eyes.

'Kate, can you finish these apples? I've got something I want to do,' said Birdie. 'And anyway, I've cut my finger.' She put down her knife, sucked her fingers and left Kate blurrily staring at the mess of half-peeled, blood-stained apples on the kitchen table.

Birdie walked across to the garage, through the mist. The police had spent hours in there this morning, and the doors were firmly closed. She wasn't interested in going inside, anyway. She picked her way through the lank grass, her eyes fixed to the ground, her hands plunged deep into her duffle coat pockets. The mud soaked into her cheap, soft shoes, but of this she was oblivious. She reached the garage and began pacing around it, paying attention to the soft earth that lay along its sides and at the back—water-washed earth pitted with little round stones, and disturbed every now and then by a straggly shrub. There were shutter windows at the back of the garage and on the side wall near the front entrance. They were half open, but much too high to see through—almost at roof level. Beneath the side windows an ancient cassia grew. Birdie stopped and crouched, and in the earth beside the bush found what she was looking for. She wandered around to the back of the garage, squatted, and then stood up and thought for a moment. She moved away and came back with some pieces of bracken fern. When she had arranged these to her satisfaction she turned and walked briskly off towards the road.

Kate, looking out the bathroom window, saw her go. She looked like some hunched, black-hooded gnome, alien and strange in the dusk. Kate bit her lip and went to turn the stewed apple down.

Martin thankfully reached for his jacket. He'd had it, well and truly, and it would be another early start in the morning. Nick Bedford had been taken home, and his typed, signed statement was safe in Toby's desk. Martin felt strangely depressed. It looked as though Bedford was for the high jump, all right. Toby was whistling through his teeth as he looked through his notes. Obviously he thought it was just a matter of time.

The phone rang, and Toby answered it. He glanced at Martin and put up his finger, signalling him to wait. Martin stood by the door, fumbling for his car keys.

'You were quick. I told them it was urgent . . . Right. Right. Yeah, I thought that . . .' Toby was nodding. It must be the first autopsy results. They'd pushed that along. Martin had always heard that it took twenty-four hours at least. He moved over to Toby's desk, stumbling against a chair as he did so. Toby shot a frowning look at him.

'Nothing? For God's sake! Did you try . . . Right, I see . . . But look, it must be somewhere . . . Look . . . I know you can, but there isn't time, is there? Well, you do your best . . . yeah . . . talk to you in the morning. Thanks . . . Yeah . . . bye.'

He hung up, and banged his fist on the table. 'I was bloody certain . . .' he began, and the phone rang again. He swore in annoyance and grabbed at the receiver. 'Yes!' he barked. 'Oh, hello, Miss Birdwood. What can I do for you? Why the public phone? Is . . . ?' He listened, frowning for a moment, then his eyebrows shot up and his mouth opened slightly. 'Eh? My God . . .

What? No, not yet . . . My God. Of course it does. Makes terrific sense . . . Well, we'll try it. I'll get on to them now . . . yes, I hope so too, love. Thanks . . . what? You *what?* Blow me down. Ah . . . oh, are they? Well, yes, as you say it's very late. It's not going to rain, anyhow. Morning'll do. Yes. Especially . . . yes . . . might be better if we got the other straight before . . . yes. OK. I'll ring before I come. OK. Bye.'

He cut the connection and immediately redialled, his eyes bright. He hunched over the handset, his elbows on the desk, pulling at his tie as if it was strangling him. The receiver clicked and twittered. 'Silvestro, thanks,' said Toby, and waited. 'Hello, Dr Silvestro, Toby here again. Looks like it's Parathion. Just heard from someone in the house that there's some missing. And look, try the back of the neck. I'll explain later. OK. Good. Ring me at home, will you? You've got the . . . Good. OK. Bye.' He put down the receiver and grinned at Martin.

'That woman's on the ball, all right. She got the old woman to admit that a bottle of Parathion was missing from the storeroom. D'you know Parathion?'

'I've heard of it. It's pretty powerful, isn't it?'

'Bloody lethal—for bugs and people. Used to be used all the time. Anyhow, seems the old Alice had a bottle of concentrate stuck away in the storeroom, and it's missing now. It's exactly the sort of stuff I had in mind.'

Martin had been thinking fast. 'Because it poisons you if you get it on your skin, just as though you'd swallowed it.'

'Right. Got there at last, son. See, I never really went for that poisoned apple business. For one, the cores around the body were really brown and shrivelled up. Didn't look to me as if they were from apples eaten last night. Then, bloody hell, the bloke obviously died quickly and in a lot of pain. He'd thrashed around quite a bit, grass was all flattened and so on, branches of the tree broken.

'The poison worked fast, then, and if it was an ordinary spray he'd have had to eat a lot of apple skin bloody quickly to get that sort of dose. And why would he? He'd taste the stuff on the first bite or the second and spit it out, then go looking for help if he started feeling funny. He was only about a hundred metres from the house. So I decided the accident theory was no go. That left suicide or murder. Suicide by eating apples that may or may not have been sprayed is an idiotic idea. He could have gone out to the orchard, eaten a few apples, and then taken some cyanide or something, but as I say, those apple cores bothered me. They looked so obvious—there were so many, for one thing. So,' said Toby, rubbing his hands over his bald pate with great satisfaction, 'I reckoned it was ten to one it was a murder case, and because I didn't believe Treloar had eaten those apples, and everyone else in the house agreed he hadn't had anything else, except a glass of wine. I thought it was a worthwhile idea that he'd got the poison into him some other way.'

'Someone could have gone out in the night and given him something,' said Martin, wanting to contribute.

'Of course,' snapped Toby impatiently. 'I'm not an idiot, McGlinchy. But in fact my idea was spot-on because there was bugger-all in the stomach, according to Silvestro. No signs of anything but the wine.' He recovered his temper and leaned back in his chair, hands behind his head.

'Anyhow,' he went on, 'I told the mob doing the PM to shake a leg, because if the poison was on the skin it would be easier to find traces of it today than tomorrow, or Tuesday week, or whenever they'd normally decide to get down to the job. And for once they took notice.'

'You reckon someone sprayed him? Like a bug?' Martin's eyes were wide and black, his eyebrows lost in his bushy hair. His spine was crawling.

'That's what I thought, yeah. But seems I was wrong. They couldn't find any traces of anything on his face or hands. That's what Silvestro was saying just now. Then little Birdwood rang. You heard. She told me about the Parathion. *Then*, and this is the important part, she said that Treloar's wife, ex-wife, claimed he never wore his parka hood up. Never. Gave him claustrophobia, or something. Anyhow, I never thought about the bits of him that were covered up. When I spoke to Silvestro first, I assumed it was only his face and hands that were possibilities. But there's nothing on his face and hands, boy. There's nothing in his stomach. The poison got into him somehow. Right. He never, according to his wife, wore his hood up, yet it was up and tied this morning. Right!' Toby leaned forward, his big hands planted on his knees.

'What if, Martin, he had the hood down last night, like normal, and was just wearing a cap? What about if someone sneaked up on him and gave him a good slosh of Parathion all over the back of the neck? That'd do for him all right. And quickly. I'll have to check on it, but Birdwood reckons that a large quantity directly on the skin'd start working almost immediately, and that he'd be stone cold dead in ten or fifteen minutes. Then, when it was all over, the murderer could put up the hood, tie it, so as to throw us off the scent, and scatter a few apple cores around for good measure, hoping we'd think he'd eaten something that disagreed with him, and it'd go no further. How about that?'

Martin nodded thoughtfully. It was clever. It could have happened like that. For the first time that day he forgot the personalities involved in the case and experienced a surge of the pure thrill of the chase. He looked quickly at Toby.

'Mrs Sullivan said that the bloke she saw at the van had his parka hood up, sir' he said.

'She did too,' said Toby, banging his fist on the desk. 'She bloody did!'

'So it's possible that wasn't Treloar at all?'

'Yeah—more than possible.'

'So . . . so . . . Treloar—so Treloar could have been dead before Nick Bedford came home?'

'You're right, Martin. It's wide open again. Silvestro says he could have died at any time between midnight and 4 am. Bedford could have done it. Of course he could. He was seen outside the house at two-thirty. But Treloar could have been dead for hours by then. Hours.'

'Sir, if . . . we're assuming now that the person at the van wasn't Treloar . . . because of the parka hood and all . . .'

'Yes.'

'That means that the bloke or the woman, or whoever it was, at the van at two, was probably the murderer.'

'It'd be a reasonable theory, Martin, but of course it could've . . .'

'So,' Martin went on, determined to follow through his train of thought, 'as Bedford didn't get home till just before two-thirty . . . doesn't this actually let him off the hook, sir?'

Toby was silent. He looked at Martin, wild-haired and earnest, and tightened one corner of his mouth in a tolerant half smile, half grimace.

'Like the look of that bloke, don't you?' he said quietly. 'But you're right, Martin, you're right. If Theresa Sullivan's times are correct, and the post-mortem blokes ring up tomorrow morning and say there is poison on the back of Treloar's neck, so we know his parka hood was down last night, that'll give us a very good reason to think that Bedford's in the clear.'

Martin felt a wave of satisfaction. His lips trembled as he struggled to restrain a grin. He'd shown Toby he could work something out, and put in a good word for the amiable Nick Bedford as well.

'Right, McGlinchy, you get off home now,' said Toby indulgently. 'We've got a job ahead of us in the morning. Verity Birdwood came up with another detail our wonderful police seemed to've missed.' He grimaced as Martin stared at him enquiringly. 'You'll find out about that tomorrow. On your way!'

Martin went home with a light heart, the car radio blaring, looking forward to the huge plate of Mum's lamb stew, being kept warm in readiness for his coming. Toby sat in the office for a while, his feet on the radiator, and looked through his notes. Then he too went home, stopping on the way for Chinese take-away which he ate with a spoon in front of the television set. The house was shadowy and prim, and smelt closed up and stuffy.

In the bedroom he changed into striped pyjamas. He considered his shirt and decided it would do for another day. A button was missing, but his tie would cover it, and the collar wasn't too bad. He carefully hung the shirt over a chair. From the dressing table, the black china cat, his dead wife's sentimental joy because he'd given it to her during their engagement, stared at him from slanted emerald eyes. He turned off the light and crawled into bed, pulling the covers and the pink chenille bedspread up under his chin.

He stretched out in the cool, empty bed. He didn't have to put a pillow beside him to get to sleep anymore. Five years was a long time. He'd got used to having the whole double to himself. He turned heavily on his side, suddenly weary, and closed his eyes. In the morning, first thing, he'd hear from Silvestro. Then he'd go out to see the Tender family again. And Theresa Sullivan— he'd probably be able to see her too, to see if she could remember anything more about the figure at the van. Good-looking woman, that. There was something about her . . . With his eyes closed, he smiled.

A few kilometres away, in the old part of Atherton, Theresa sat and embroidered wattle sprays on a baby's jacket—a little padded grey jacket with a hood lined in yellow. It was warm in the back verandah room. The old gas heater hissed. The curtains were drawn and the misty night excluded.

The little coat was soft in her fingers, and the sprays of yellow and blue-green stretched out and fastened to grey beneath her needle, magically fast. She pictured Nel in the jacket, in a month or two, rosy and laughing. A little wattle baby. The needle faltered and she put the sewing aside, took off her glasses (Nel didn't like her wearing her glasses), and walked quickly to the front bedroom, her heart beating fast.

But all was well. The baby lay on her side, sleeping peacefully, warm and safe. Theresa parted the curtains and looked at the house opposite. The lights were still on at the back. The garage was a black shape, isolated and grim-looking. She shivered. She wondered what was happening; whether the man the police had taken for questioning had returned. She thought about Zoe—funny, old-fashioned little thing—and remembered the doll's house she'd promised to show her.

Zoe would be in bed now, good-nighted by her grown-up friends, tucked in by Kate, kissed goodnight by her dad—Jeremy, wasn't it? Zoe had told her about a granny, a grandpa, uncles and cousins. Theresa let the curtain fall and turned again to the bassinet, dropping her hand and touching the baby's neck. Nel screwed up her face a little, curled and uncurled her hands, and relaxed.

'It's just you and me, Nel,' whispered Theresa. 'But we're all right, aren't we?' She touched the baby's soft head and quietly left the room. It was well past eleven, but again tonight she had too many thoughts for sleep.

12

Fun and Games

In the house across the road restlessness prevailed likewise.

Alice sat by the fire, apparently oblivious to everything around her. She sat so still that she looked like a carving, only the occasional slow blinking of her eyes showing she was alive and awake. Her head thrust forward on her long neck, she looked more than ever like one of those giant tortoises, hundreds of years old.

Kate turned back to the scrabble board, and tried again to arrange her unpromising letters into some kind of order. Jill, Nick and Chris were playing with her around the table. Sonsy was sitting next to Chris, watching. She seemed quieter and more settled after her afternoon walk. There was a pale dignity about her, in fact, a separateness, Kate thought, rejoicing as Chris occasionally spoke to his wife and received a quiet, unflurried response.

Jill and Nick were treating each other gently too—speaking quietly, calling each other 'sweetie' and 'darling'. It should have been nice, but it wasn't, somehow. It was as if they were recovering after a serious operation that may or may not have succeeded, as though only time would tell if the disease would take

hold once more and sweep them away, and they were
encouraging one another to hope for the best, in a
rather artificial and unconvincing way.

Jeremy was immersed in a huge old book he'd found
under their bed. Birdie was reading too, but every
now and then Kate saw her look over her glasses and
take a quick look around.

On the couch Betsy knitted, talking in a low voice
to Anna and Rodney who were sharing a pile of ancient *Reader's Digest* and *Believe It Or Not* magazines, and drinking wine, rather quickly. Wilf sat in
his usual place by the curtains, his mouth a little open,
his pale eyes staring into space.

Chris moved restlessly. 'It's getting late. Hadn't we
better break this up and get to bed?'

Nick stretched. 'Yeah, well, I s'pose we should. I
have a feeling it's going to be a long day tomorrow.
The coppers haven't finished with me yet, I dare say.'
He tilted his head and finished his drink.

'Surely they have, Nick!' said Betsy sharply. 'You
were there all afternoon. Surely they must be satisfied
by now?'

'Satisfied I'm innocent or guilty, Betsy?' said Nick
mildly.

Betsy opened her mouth and looked flustered. 'Well,
I mean, innocent of course,' she squeaked.

'I'm going to make some tea,' Anna announced
brusquely. She strode unsteadily across the room and
into the kitchen.

Betsy began to pack up her knitting.

'Yes, well, it's very late, but I think I might have
my shower. I missed out this afternoon, what with
one thing and another. I don't think it will disturb
Zoe, Kate? She seems to be sleeping peacefully tonight
anyway, poor little thing. It must be the clean air.
They say inner-city children are very often hyperactive because of the lead in the petrol fumes.'

'Zoe's not hyperactive, Betsy!'

'No, no, of course not, Katie. Not *truly* hyperactive.

Just a little bit nervy. She'll probably grow out of it. I wouldn't worry about it too much, dear. You've got enough on your plate, with your job and the house and everything.'

Kate bit her tongue. No point, no point at all in trying to argue with Betsy in this mood. Just let it go, she told herself. She forced a smile and said nothing.

Betsy hovered a moment, then, seeing nothing further was to be got out of that conversation, turned to Wilf.

'You'd better get off too, Wilfie.'

He jumped. 'Oh, yes, right. Ah . . . goodnight all.' He trailed after her as she bustled towards their bedroom.

The younger people watched them go in silence.

Kate sighed. 'Isn't it incredible to think that it was only last night that we were all sitting round like normal?'

'As normal as we ever are,' said Chris wryly. 'We weren't exactly a happy little group, even last night, were we?' He didn't look at Sonsy.

Kate smiled. 'Well, no, but at least . . .'

'At least we weren't murder suspects,' said Jill.

'*We* aren't murder suspects, my love,' said Nick drily. '*I* am murder suspects. Suspect one, two and three, it seems. Whose go is it?'

Kate pushed her letters away. 'Mine, and I can't go. Look, Nick, do you think there's any doubt in their minds at all that Damien was killed purposely?'

'Absolutely none, I'd say.'

They fell silent as Betsy appeared in her dressing gown and slippers, smart royal blue ski pyjamas over her arm and a spotted sponge bag clasped in one hand. She nodded to them brightly and went into the kitchen. They heard her speak to Anna and go into the bathroom. Anna brought in a tray and distributed mugs of tea and coffee, then settled back on the couch, legs outstretched, looking determinedly uninterested in her surroundings.

Birdie spoke from her chair across the room.

'I don't know much about Damien Treloar, but from what people have said he seems to have been a controversial sort of character, and I was wondering . . .' She paused and her glasses flashed.

Everyone was looking at her now, Anna with her fine eyebrows raised. Birdie wasn't a prepossessing figure, her bespectacled pointed face pale in the lamp light, nondescript corduroy jeans with rubbed knees clothing legs twisted back into the rungs of her chair. She looked about twelve, for a start, thought Kate. But Birdie seemed unabashed by the attention.

'I was wondering,' she continued, 'whether he could have had a visitor last night that none of us knew about. Someone from outside with a grudge against him, say, who knew he was coming here.'

'But they couldn't have known that he was going to stay!' objected Chris.

'Someone let down his tyres,' Birdie pointed out.

There was a small silence. Kate's brow wrinkled. This was unlike Birdie. The mysterious stranger theory was one she herself had thought of, but she'd quickly dismissed it as wishful thinking, and she hadn't even mentioned it to Birdie, thinking she'd scoff. What was she up to?

'But how could someone come and go without being seen?' said Jill. 'They'd be taking an awful risk.'

'Not much if you think about it,' said Anna grimly. 'Nick came home and was seen by the merest chance. You came home earlier, and no one saw you. No one *saw* you at all!'

Jill flushed. 'What . . . ?' she began angrily.

Kate rushed in. 'Anna just means that in the mist and the dark it would have been quite possible for someone to slip from the road into the garage, at least, without being seen. You were coming to the house and no one saw you. The garage is fifty metres off, with no lights around it. If someone arrived on foot, or cruised down the road, like Nick did in his car, they could very likely get to the garage and out again without a single soul knowing.' She hesitated. 'Except Damien, of course,' she finished lamely, glancing at the frowning Anna.

It sounded weak even to Kate, but to her surprise Jeremy put down his book and came to her rescue.

'It's not beyond belief that that's exactly what happened,' he said firmly. 'In which case we're all off the hook.'

'The cops'll take some convincing,' said Nick, with a weak grin. 'They think it's an inside job, well and truly.' He glanced at Jill, and she put her hand on his, over the scrabble board.

'How about, then,' said Jeremy, 'we give them a bit of a push in the right direction? Let's pool all our information about last night. I gather the Sullivan woman only remembered about seeing Nick's car when she really thought about it. Maybe one of us noticed something, without registering it as important. Let's go through last night, once more, and see what comes of it.'

'Oh, Jeremy—no!' groaned Anna. 'It's stupid. We've been through everything with the police. I can't bear . . .'

'Well, I think we should,' said Jill energetically. 'I'd like to hear what everyone else saw and heard, anyway.'

'Are you sure, Jill?' said Anna, her lovely face almost sneering.

Jill's blunt features looked blank for a minute, then she drew herself up. 'I don't know what you think you're on about, Anna, but you're barking up the wrong tree if you're hinting that Damien and I were on together, or something . . . No, Kate, I'm sick of this, I won't put up with it. We worked together, that's all. For God's sake, Anna, you lived with the bloke for eighteen months, or whatever it was. You must have known what he was like?'

Anna looked at her proudly, her cheekbones flushed.

'Of course I knew him, better than you'd know him if you tried for a year. He liked collecting women, especially women who took themselves seriously. Specialised in single professionals who were hard to get.' She laughed, rather unpleasantly. 'He was an attractive man. They went for his brand of sex like a ton of bricks.'

'Anna . . .' Kate began, and was silenced by a flashing glance from Birdie. She bit her tongue.

Anna leaned back, putting her hands behind her head. Her superb body arched and relaxed. The wine had darkened her eyes, loosened her hair and flushed her cheeks and lips. She looked beautiful, spiteful, and slightly out of control.

'What they didn't know, those women,' she drawled, 'was that he always came back to me. Always, Jill. Always. Whatever he said to them, whatever fantasies they had together, he'd always come back when it was over, and he'd tell me about them—about the sex, about everything. About the plans they'd made, the houses they'd buy after he left me, the babies they'd have, the trips they'd take. I could always tell when he was infatuated with someone. It lasted a night, a week, or a month. But then, when he had them well and truly, he'd just lose interest. That's how it always was. He'd keep a photo or two, to be sentimental about—I saw a few of them—and that'd be that. I was the only one who lasted.'

There was a shocked, uncomfortable silence.

'Anna, that's . . . that must have been awful for you,' said Kate, filled with pity.

Anna looked at her scornfully. 'Kate, you wouldn't know,' she almost sneered. 'You wouldn't have the faintest clue. Plump little mum, with your cosy domestic set-up, your precious little Zoe. Damien wanted me to have a baby, begged me to have one, but I knew what that would mean. He wanted a baby, but he didn't want a mum for his lover. Who would? I'll bet Jeremy hasn't let the grass grow under his feet all these years. Men aren't like that. Men worth their salt, anyway. You just prefer not to know about it, like most women. You just want your baby and the house, and for everything to go on in a rosy glow. Whatever Jeremy has on the side's his dirty little business.'

Chris stood up, his mouth open, his eyes furiously angry, but Jeremy forestalled him.

'I'm sorry to disappoint you, Anna, but you over-estimate my potency,' he said, leaning back in his chair, his eyes bright blue chips. 'I don't have the time or the energy to seek excitement away from home. Kate's a devil when she's roused, you know.'

'Jeremy!' cried Kate, blushing to the roots of her hair with mingled embarrassment and pleasure.

Anna stood up angrily. 'Oh, how sweet!' she hissed and left the room, brushing past Betsy just toddling in from the kitchen in her dressing gown, with damp curls and a shiny nose.

'Oh dear . . . oh . . . has there been an argument?' said Betsy, looking worried and somehow smaller in her night attire.

'Sort of, Mum,' said Chris. 'Anna's been running off at the mouth. She's been getting stuck into the wine, I fear.'

'Oh, Christopher, she's upset. You really must all treat her gently. Now, please! Oh dear, poor Anna.' She shot an angry look around the room and followed Anna into the hall, closing the door sharply behind her.

'Poor Anna's right,' said Chris, half to himself. 'What a performance! I'm sorry, Katie. She didn't . . . you know she's not usually like . . . She's had a real knock, knocked right off balance by this business. Sorry Jill, too. She seems to have the knife into you all right.'

'And quite right too, in my case,' said Jill. She looked down at her hands. 'I was stupid. I should have given that idiot—poor Damien, I mean—the cold shoulder. But Nick had got me all cross, and . . .'

'We understand,' said Sonsy in a small voice. It was the first time she had actually spoken aloud the whole evening, and Jill looked at her in surprise. 'It was an awful night last night,' the girl continued, pale but determined. 'Everyone was upset. The house wasn't friendly. I felt Chris's mother wasn't being friendly. I made a fool of myself, too.'

'No you didn't, Sonsy,' said Kate gently. 'Everyone saw why you were upset, and we were sorry.'

'Everyone but me,' said Chris grimly. 'Anyway, I see now and I'm sorry now. I must have been . . .'

'Blind! That's right, son!' Alice's harsh voice broke in. She had turned in her chair to face him. 'Come to your senses, have you? Not before time. Too late, maybe.' She looked at Sonsy, still and white-faced, strangely unmoved by her husband's unprecedented humility. Chris looked at Sonsy too and his face sagged. He put his arm around her and she sat unresisting and still under his fingers.

Rodney looked up from the couch. His face was angrily flushed. 'Are you saying Mum did something wrong?' he demanded. 'What did she do? She didn't do anything!'

'Look, mate, don't worry about it,' said Chris kindly. 'I forgot you were there. It doesn't matter.'

'Everyone always forgets I'm here. It does matter. I can't understand you!' He fought back angry tears. 'Last night you were all over Mum like a rash. Now you're turning on her like she's not worth that much to you.' He snapped his fingers.

'Rod, go to bed,' Chris said. 'You've had too much to drink.'

'I won't go to bloody bed!' Rodney's voice broke to a squeak. 'You can't boss me. You and Anna, you're both the same. You take up with other people and then turn on Mum. She's told me. She tries to please you and you go off as if she's nothing. She cries sometimes, you know. She says I'm the only real help she's got. I'm the one who chops the wood, and gets the hoppers out, and puts up the ladders and does all the dirty work. She'd never ask you to do it. You never do a bloody thing for her, and she still loves you the best. You and bloody Anna.' The tears were flowing now, and he childishly brushed them away with the backs of his hands, leaving dirty smears.

'Rodney,' Chris began helplessly, but Alice rose from her chair. She walked over to the trembling boy and put her hand on his head.

'Go to bed, son,' she said gruffly. She stooped and eased him to his feet, and put her arm around him. She was as tall as he, and she bent towards him as they walked towards the kitchen door, protecting him from the eyes of the others in the room.

'Wash your face, boy, and go to bed through the storeroom door, so you won't disturb your mother. Go off, now.' She set him on his way and shut the door behind him. Then she plodded back to her chair and sank back into it, staring into the fire.

'For God's sake,' groaned Chris, and put his head in his hands. Jill looked at Kate and raised her eyebrows. Kate raised her eyebrows back and behind Jill's head caught Birdie's expression. Definitely smug. Kate felt suddenly furious. For Birdie all the world was a stage, all right, but she herself was safe in the audience. An audience of one. Nothing touched her. She watched the antics of less composed creatures with a detachment that was nothing short of inhuman. I've never, ever seen her cry, Kate thought. Never once. Not even at school, bullied by the tough, budding society beauties, irritated by her plainness and her brains. There she was, the little recorder in her brain going click click click behind those clever amber eyes as they watched undisturbed through panes of thick glass the comedy of errors being played out for her edification and amusement. Well, bum to Birdie!

Kate turned to Nick—fallible, nice, loving, human. 'Let's have a drink,' she said.

'I'll drink to that!' he grinned. 'The two departed have a long start on us.'

He put his hand on Chris's shoulder as he squeezed past him and went over to the sideboard. 'Wine and soda?'

'Yes, please.'

'You'll find something stronger in the cupboard,' said Alice, without looking round. 'You're welcome to it, if you fancy.'

Nick poked in the sideboard cupboard and whistled. 'Chivas Regal,' he said. 'You don't mean that, do you Alice?'

Alice grinned into the flames. 'Why not?' she said. 'Been there donkey's years. Mightn't be any good, anyhow. Open it and see. The whisky glasses should be there at the back. They were Dad's. There's brandy, too, on the other side. You can give me a nip of that.'

Nick rummaged further. It was like a treasure hunt. Bottles of spirits and liqueurs, most unopened, stood and lay amongst the glasses, a silver ice bucket and tongs, crystal decanters and piles of miscellaneous junk that had nothing whatever to do with drink—packs of cards, stuffed toys, several books and a couple of exquisitely embroidered tablecloths reeking of mothballs.

'Come on, Nick,' said Jeremy, who had opened the whisky. 'Alice, this smells fantastic!'

'Nice to see someone enjoying it,' said Alice, looking thoroughly sane and human. She seemed to like playing hostess in her own home again.

'I can't find the whisky glasses . . . oh, damn,' said Nick, as a box of Chinese checkers slid out and showered the floor with coloured marbles.

Jill laughed and dropped down to the floor to help him pick them up. She looked at Nick's finds. 'I'll have

Green Ginger Wine, can I, Alice? I haven't had that for years.'

'Help yourself, love. Anything that's there, help yourself.' Alice waved her hand. 'Just don't forget me brandy!'

In the end, everyone drank from little green sherry glasses, of which there seemed to be a profusion. Nick, Chris, Jeremy and Birdie had the whisky. Jill had her Green Ginger Wine. Alice and Kate had brandy, and Sonsy good-humouredly but determinedly stuck to soda.

'Drink up,' said Alice. 'Bung ho!' She drained her glass. 'What about another?'

Jill leaned towards Kate. 'You know,' she said, 'This is the first time I've felt normal this whole holiday. Yesterday—last night, even before Damien came—it was as though everything was out of kilter. As though we were all playing parts. Do you know what I mean? But now it's OK.'

Kate smiled and nodded. Yes, she thought. And I know why. It's because Betsy isn't here, Anna isn't here, Rodney isn't here. Wilf isn't here either, though really he makes so little contribution that it shouldn't matter if he's around or not, poor bloke. And yet, she realised, almost with surprise, that lugubrious figure radiated some sort of negative energy. The room was brighter and lighter by his absence. The Tenders' loving, close-knit world had somehow got off balance, despite Betsy's efforts to keep it in its familiar, safe orbit.

Jeremy spun the golden fluid in his glass and broke the silence.

'Just so you won't get too used to feeling good, Jill,' he said, 'how about trying out my idea of going through last night from each person's point of view?'

Jill's face fell, and Chris groaned.

'Just,' Jeremy went on persuasively, 'to test out Birdie's "outsider" theory. I don't want to be a pain over this, but it's not as though we've got all the time in the world. If there's anything to discover, we need to discover it now. The PM results could be in in a few days and even before that the police could take someone in.'

'Me, you mean,' said Nick, in a pleasant voice. He looked around at their watching faces, and his grey eyes, usually so frank, were unreadable. He dropped his head and stroked his beard thoughtfully, then he looked up again and grinned.

'I'll be glad of any help I could get, as it happens. Being charged with murder, even if I wasn't found guilty, might just have some small effect on my brilliant career. This might amaze you, but I hadn't quite intended to be a lecturer all my life. All my academic ambitions haven't quite been sublimated in the university dramatic society, star that I am.'

'But some people aren't here!' said Jill, distressed.

'We'll make do with what we have,' said Jeremy energetically, dragging his chair over to them. 'Come over to the table, Birdie. Do you want to join us, Alice?'

'You go ahead,' said Alice from her chair. 'I'll listen from here. I'll give you my bit when you're ready.'

'Jeremy, you can do shorthand, can't you?' said Chris. 'We should take notes.'

'I can,' said Jeremy. 'And I suppose you can too, Birdie?' She nodded. 'How about we take it in turns, then?' He pulled the scrabble scoring pad and pencil towards him, turned to a blank sheet and looked up at them.

'Katie, why don't you start, to get the ball rolling?' He headed the paper 'Kate'.

'Oh, um . . . where will I start?' said Kate, feeling self-conscious.

'Where Damien went out to the garage.'

'Oh, right, well . . . um . . . heavens, it's quite hard to remember. Oh, I didn't actually see him go, because before that Zoe had woken up, hadn't she, and she was upset because Jill was upset. She thought it was Damien's fault, which I suppose it was, really, and she called him various abusive names which I think . . . I think she'd heard from Alice.' She broke off and shot Alice a hunted look, but the old lady only smile to herself.

'We have to be honest, Kate,' said Jeremy impatiently. 'Just say what happened flat and don't worry about hurting anyone's feelings, just for a change.'

Kate cleared her throat. 'OK. So I got her back to bed, and tucked her in, and . . . oh!' she stopped again.

'Honestly, Kate, you're hopeless,' cried Jill. 'Get on with it!'

'I saw Sonsy, in Betsy's room, across the corridor,' said Kate flatly, looking at the table.

'What?' Chris said. 'But Sonsy was in bed! Weren't you darling?'

Sonsy was red to the roots of her hair. 'I had no idea you saw me, Kate,' she whispered. 'How did you . . . I was so careful.'

'In the wardrobe mirror, just your reflection. I really forgot about it till just now.'

13

The Night in Question

'What on earth were you doing in Mum's bedroom?' said Chris, bewildered. 'Sonsy?'

She didn't look at him. 'I told you—last night, I was really upset,' she began, in a level voice. Her face was pinched. 'I'd gone into our room. I . . . cried a bit. I heard someone tap on the front door and wondered who it was. I got into bed and just lay there, thinking, you know. Then a bit later I heard Damien's voice talking and the front door open and close, so I knew he'd gone. Then there was quiet again. I counted to a hundred, then counted backwards again to one, but I couldn't go to sleep. I . . . I was . . . I wanted to know what was going on.'

Her voice fell to a whisper. 'I thought you might be talking about me to the others. I wanted to find out. I couldn't stand just waiting there for you to come.' She looked at Chris then, and he dropped his own eyes.

'So,' she went on more firmly, 'I got up and put on my dressing gown. I looked through a hole in the front windows, to make sure Damien had gone. I saw a woman walking across the grass strip opposite, and into that house's gate. Damien's van was still there, and I could see him kneeling down at the back wheel. He was on the road side, not the kerb side, so I couldn't see him all that well, but his parka was pale and showed up, even in the mist.'

'He must have been looking at one of the flat tyres,' said Chris.

'I didn't know what he was doing. He stayed there, quite still, for a minute or two, then he got up and went to the front of the van and knelt down again.'

Jeremy looked up from his notes. 'Sounds to me as though he was letting his own tyres down, mate,' he said to Nick.

'Does, too,' said Nick thoughtfully. 'Obviously he wanted an excuse to hang round a bit longer.'

No one looked at Jill.

'What happened then, Sonsy?' Kate prompted, anxious to move away from this delicate ground.

'Well, as I said, I didn't know what he was doing, and I didn't care much,' said Sonsy, 'as long as he was well out of the house. I crept round the verandah and into the front hall. I was going to listen at the door into the living room, to see if I could hear anything.' She shook her head wonderingly. 'I must have been mad,' she said. 'It was like being in a nightmare. The whole of the last six months has been like a nightmare.'

'Sonsy, I . . .' Chris put his hand on hers but she withdrew it almost unconsciously.

'It's all right,' she said. 'I've woken up now. Finally.' She turned to Kate.

'Anyway, I got to the door, and I listened. You weren't talking about me, but I still listened. I heard Damien come back, and Chris's mother say he could stay. I couldn't understand how she could, with Anna the way she was and everything. Then I thought, she's letting him stay so she can go on teasing me about him in the morning. It's the sort of thing she does.' She drew breath, and looked down at her hands, folded at her waist.

'Then,' she said, looking up, 'I heard the argument start and I heard a thump from Kate and Jeremy's room. I realised Zoe had woken up, and was getting out of bed. I didn't want her to see me there and tell everyone. I . . . I rushed back up the hall and into the big bedroom, Chris's parents' room, and hid behind the door. Zoe went out and complained about the noise. I couldn't get back to bed because the door to the living room was wide open, and I thought someone might see me. But I hated being in that room. It was stuffy and smelt of Betsy's face cream and that jasmine powder and old apples. I was nearly sick.'

She gave herself a little shake and her voice grew calmer. 'When Kate and Zoe were in their bedroom, and the door to the living room was closed again, I slipped out and round to the verandah. I didn't know that the mirror would give me away. You must all think I'm pathetic. I *was* pathetic! But I couldn't help it. I was all mixed up.' She shook her head. 'I just waited for Chris to come then. That's all.'

'Did you tell the police all this? About seeing Damien at the van, and so on?' asked Jeremy.

Sonsy shook her head. 'There didn't seem any need to,' she said, and her voice was tired and flat. 'It was easier just to say I went to bed and stayed there, without having to explain—everything else.'

'I'm sorry you had to go through it all now,' said Jeremy, professionally sympathetic. 'But you can see already that it was worth it. The stuff about Damien and the tyres, for instance. That's something that we can tell the cops tomorrow. We needn't go into all the rest. Right'. He consulted his notes. 'Now . . .'

'I hadn't finished my bit,' Kate pointed out. 'Do you want me to go on? I don't think there's anything interesting in it, but still . . .'

'Yes, of course, Kate, go on. We've got one good piece of information already.'

'Or two,' said Birdie absently. She looked up. 'Sorry,' she said brightly. 'Go on, Laney.'

'Well,' Kate began, 'when I got back to the living room Damien had gone, Rodney had gone to bed, I think, Jill had gone for a walk . . . um . . . You were in the bathroom cleaning your teeth, Birdie. Betsy was clearing up. She was a bit grumpy, and was irritated because she'd made Damien supper, and he'd forgotten to take it.' She hesitated. 'What happened to that, by the way?' she said casually.

'What?' said Jill.

'The supper he forgot. The fruit cake and coffee. What happened to it?'

'What does that matter?' asked Chris.

'Oh . . . oh, I was just wondering . . .' said Kate lamely, and looked at Birdie who, to her disgust, gave her no help at all—just a rather amused wink.

Sonsy looked up. 'At morning tea, this morning, when I was putting out the food, I found two slices of fruit cake, wrapped in foil, in the cake tin. Maybe that was it. The packet wasn't there yesterday, anyway.'

'That would've been it, I suppose,' said Kate, a bit let down. 'You put the sliced cake out for morning tea?'

'Yes, with some other slices, and some rock cakes. You had some.'

'You might have eaten the very slices in question, Laney,' said Birdie mischievously. 'How do you feel?'

'Look, what's all this?' Jeremy interrupted. 'Did you think someone'd got to the supper, and Damien came back for it, Kate?'

'Something like that,' Kate muttered.

'The small thermos was on the draining board this morning,' said Jill. 'Did Betsy make Damien's coffee in the small thermos?'

'She would've,' said Kate. 'Look, this isn't getting us anywhere. Sorry.'

Jeremy moved impatiently. 'Right, well, Betsy was clearing up, Kate. What happened then?'

'I went to the loo—there was a *hideous* caterpillar on the wall. Did you see that, Sonsy?'

'No, no . . . ugh,' Sonsy shuddered.

'Sonsy's got a thing about caterpillars,' said Chris indulgently. 'Once, she . . .'

'It was *hideous*,' said Kate, not to be put off. 'It was crawling . . .'

'You ninny, you don't have to go into every bloody thing,' exploded Jeremy. 'Get on with it! Could you see the garage? Was there a light on?'

'Look, you said . . . oh, all right. I don't know if there was a light on then. I couldn't see, really. But when I went and cleaned my teeth I could see a little light from the window there, flickering through the garage door, and showing at the top windows. It was still quite misty then, and the windows were still a bit steamed up from the showers, but someone had rubbed a hole to look through.'

'Could you see anyone on the road, or a strange car or anything?' Jill put in anxiously.

'You can't see the road from the bathroom window,' said Jeremy, drawing lines on his pad. 'Right, Kate. What then?'

'You know what then,' said Kate, rather tartly. 'I went to bed. Once I got into our room I couldn't see a thing. I could hear Rodney turning over in bed, through the wall. Anna's door was shut. She'd gone to bed just before I went out to the toilet, I think. I heard Birdie go through to the front verandah. She whispered goodnight. Betsy and Wilf were already in bed. I could hear them talking, a bit, across the hall. Chris came through and said goodnight to his parents, and then you came and shut the door after you, and thumped around getting changed. I heard the clock strike eleven, and very soon after that I must have gone to sleep, because I don't remember anything else until, you know, there was a bit of a commotion in the hall.' She glanced at Sonsy, hunched on her chair.

'Yeah, well, we'll leave that for a minute,' said Jeremy. 'That was about, when? Midnight or so?'

There was a general murmur of disagreement.

'Oh, later than that,' said Jill. 'I came in about twenty past twelve, by my watch. And I definitely heard the clock strike one before the noise started.'

'That's right, lass,' agreed Alice.

'I really don't know what the time was,' said Kate, 'because I wasn't wearing my watch, and I was dead asleep. All I know is that there was a noise. Zoe woke up and cried because she was frightened and I remember cursing because sometimes she can't drop off again if she wakes frightened in the night. She'd already been upset. Anyway, I covered her up again and got back into bed, and I went straight back to sleep. So I suppose she did too. Anyway, I didn't hear a car or a noise or anything else till morning when . . . when Chris came and told us . . . to come.'

'OK, then,' said Jeremy, breaking the heavy silence. 'Birdie?'

Birdie turned and looked at him, but her eyes were abstracted behind the glasses. A small furrow had appeared between her brows.

Jeremy pushed the pad over to her a little crossly. 'Your turn to take the notes,' he said.

'Well, why don't you say your piece now,' said Birdie quietly, picking up the pencil.

'Oh, OK . . . Most of my stuff's the same as Kate's, so it won't take long.' He leaned his head on his hand and began.

'Treloar went to the garage about quarter past ten, while Kate was putting Zoe back to bed. I wanted to make sure he was doing what he was supposed to, so I went into the bathroom, rubbed a clear patch on the window because it was still steamed up from the great shower orgy, and saw Treloar go along the side of the house to the front.'

'What? Not to the garage?' exclaimed Jill.

'No . . . I realised after a minute that he'd gone to get his sleeping bag, because I saw him come back from the direction of the van carrying it, and some sort of shoulder bag, and go into the garage. It was misty, but he had the kerosene lamp and I could see it bobbing up and down from where I was.'

'You're sure it was him, mate?' asked Nick anxiously.

'I've thought about that . . . but I really think it was. I could see the light shining on his parka. His face was in darkness, but it was Treloar, I'm sure. It was his walk.'

'Was his parka hood up or down?' asked Birdie.

Jeremy looked at her. 'I don't . . . oh . . .' He half-closed his eyes. 'Down, I think, otherwise the light would have reflected on his head too, and it didn't. Look, it was him, I'm sure of it.'

'Maybe he left his keys in the car then,' said Kate.

'Why would he do that, though?'

'Well, no one could steal it with flat tyres. He might've just forgotten them, and not bothered to go back.'

'He did go back, Kate, anyhow. The woman across the road saw him in the middle of the bloody night!'

'We don't *know* it was him,' said Kate calmly. 'It could've been someone else. We were only saying this afternoon . . .'

'Let's get on with this now we've started, eh, Laney? No point in chasing every herring that comes our way,' said Birdie sharply, looking up from her notes. 'It's getting late.'

'*Honestly!*' Kate hissed and almost ground her teeth.

'Treloar went to the garage,' said Jeremy, slightly raising his voice, 'and went inside. I saw the light shining through the windows, and through the door. Then Rodney came in, on his way through to his room. I felt pretty funny being caught out peeping through the bathroom window. Anyway, he stared and didn't say a thing. Just went into the storeroom, stumbled round a bit, got the old door open and went into his hideout on the side verandah. I'd seen Treloar safely bedded down, I thought, so I went back out to the kitchen. Our little mate here was waiting there. She went into the bathroom to clean her teeth, and I . . . started talking to Chris, I think. Yes. Betsy started tidying up. Anna was just sitting, staring into space. Jill went off for a walk. Then Kate came back, and Betsy and Anna had a little set-to about the cake and coffee Treloar forgot. Everyone but Chris and I drifted off. I went and had a pee.'

'See any caterpillars, Jeremy?' asked Birdie, without cracking a smile.

Kate snorted.

'By the time I came back inside,' Jeremy went on, 'everyone had gone to bed. I left the back door unlocked for Jill and Nick and went to bed myself.'

'No mysterious strangers on the horizon yet,' said Nick grimly. 'This doesn't seem to be getting us far.' He smiled wryly. 'My fate is sealed, I fear.'

'Come on, Nick, we've barely started,' said Kate anxiously.

'OK, Katie, OK . . .' Nick pulled out his wallet and took out a sheet of carefully folded paper. 'These are my notes of what I did last night. The police have a lovely tidy typed copy, with my signature at the bottom. I may as well give you this, eh? To save going over it all again, Jeremy?'

'Yeah, OK, mate,' said Jeremy, attempting to appear careless. 'We'll put it with the others.' He passed the paper over to Birdie, who folded it inside the pad.

'It basically says, leaving out the details, that I left when I left, came back at about 2.30, saw all the house was dark—and the garage too, incidentally—sat in the car for about five minutes and then went off again. It was dark, windy and bloody cold. That's all. I didn't see anyone. There were no strange cars parked. So that's me.'

'Birdie, why don't you go next, then,' said Kate.

'OK,' said Birdie, and pushed the notebook over to Jeremy. 'I went into the bathroom after Jeremy, like he said, and I had a sticky-beak out the window too, and saw the light in the garage. I didn't see anyone around. When I went to bed only Chris and Jeremy were left in the living room. I went through to the front verandah. I could see a light showing through the glass from the house opposite. I looked through a hole in the window, just like Sonsy, but, in my case, from pure curiosity. There were no strange cars or people in the street—at least the part of it that I could see. While I watched, the light over the road went off. Theresa must have been checking the baby. Then Chris came through on his way to bed, said goodnight and so on and went round to his bedroom, so I changed and got into bed too.' She paused.

'I didn't go to sleep straight away. I had a feeling people were moving around, somehow, but right down in the corner of the verandah there you can't hear or see much. I did hear Jill come in. At 12.20 it was, by my watch. It's pretty accurate.' She indicated her wrist and Kate noted with amusement Jill's eyebrows go up at the sight of the simple, beautiful and very expensive-looking circle of gold revealed under the tatty jumper. Birdie noticed too, and flinched slightly. She folded her arms again, firmly hiding the evidence of great and powerful friends. 'So,' she said firmly, 'Jill came in and got undressed and got into her bed.'

'*Onto* my fiendishly uncomfortable camp stretcher, yes,' said Jill glumly.

'Right . . . onto her stretcher,' said Birdie. 'Then I heard someone come from Chris and Sonsy's end of the verandah, and go into the hall. I didn't see who it was, but later it became clear that it was Sonsy.' She gave Sonsy a friendly, casual glance, but Sonsy just looked at her, expressionless. 'That would have been just before one. I didn't check my watch. I was feeling sleepier by then. But I heard the clock strike one just after. The wind had started up and the house was full of creaks and bangs, and the roof was banging too.

'I think I dozed a bit, and then there was a yell, and I woke up. A yell, and another, in the hall. The hall light went on and I sat up and saw Jill sitting up too, and Chris come pounding round from his room and go into the hall. I gathered something had happened to Sonsy, because he came back with his arm around her, and she was crying. He was trying to calm her down. He was almost carrying her. Anyway,' she paused, and the room was dead silent, 'anyway, Chris took Sonsy back to bed. Betsy came halfway through the door and looked after them, and Jill and I got our heads down fast, didn't we Jill?'

Chris was slightly flushed, whether on Sonsy's, Betsy's or his own behalf, Kate couldn't say. A bit of all three, probably.

'Anyway, after that things really did settle down. I went to sleep, and in the morning—well—you all know about that!'

'Yeah.' Jeremy said slowly. 'OK. So that's Kate, me, Nick and Birdie. Now, Jill?'

Jill flushed. She was looking better, strangely enough, thought Kate. She'd lost that helpless, rudderless look.

Birdie, repossessed of the notepad, looked at her enquiringly. Even more like a possum wearing glasses than usual, thought Kate. Her hair stuck out in a brush around her small face, and the pupils in her golden eyes had dilated till they appeared huge and black. Even her hands clutching the pad looked like little paws. What was going on in her head—tick, tick, tick? One almost expected her nose to twitch.

'Well,' began Jill, almost cheerily. 'I went for my walk, as you know. I went before Damien, so I didn't

see him go to the van or the garage. I walked fast, up
the street, towards the shops. I . . . I thought Nick
might have gone up there, really. For coffee . . . or
cigarettes, since a fight was as good an excuse as any
to take up smoking again. Anyway, I got up there—
would have taken about ten minutes, I suppose—and
of course I'd missed him. That place where we get the
barbecued chicken was open, and I went in and had
a coffee, just for something to do, really. I didn't feel
like coming back here. I'd really had it. I was so
cranky with Nick and . . . oh . . . everyone and everything . . . and myself, I suppose. So I had another
coffee, and then I just wandered around for a while,
and finally came home. It was well after midnight.
There was no one around.'

'Was the garage light on?' asked Kate.

Jill paused. 'Yes,' she said slowly. 'There was a flickering light there, but the last thing I wanted was to
see poor old Damien. He'd got me into enough trouble.' She compressed her lips. 'I slipped in the front
gate and down the side path to the back door. I left
it unlocked, in case Nick . . . anyway, I didn't bother
with my teeth or anything, just tiptoed down the hall.
I didn't turn on any lights. I was feeling dead tired,
suddenly. I got into bed and lay for a while. I think
I heard the clock strike one, but I must have been half
asleep because I didn't hear Sonsy go out, though she
must have gone straight past me. But I heard the yell
and the fuss later, well and truly. I sat straight up
thinking Nick had frightened someone, creeping in
with his shoes off, you know. But . . . well, of course
I realised straight away that it wasn't Nick at all. It
was Sonsy screaming. Chris came round, like Birdie
said, and took Sonsy back to bed. Betsy was talking
sixteen to the dozen by then. I didn't go straight back
to sleep . . . I was a bit disappointed that it *wasn't*
Nick, actually . . .' She looked at her feet and Jeremy
cleared his throat warningly. She rallied. 'And . . . I
could hear Sonsy crying and Chris talking. But any-

way eventually I did go back to sleep. I woke up before it was light. Nick wasn't in his bed. I opened the front door and looked out and saw his car wasn't there. It was misty and cold, the wind had gone. The house was incredibly quiet. I got back into bed and ate my apple—my Betsy-apple I hadn't eaten the night before—and then I went back to sleep again.' She shivered. 'God, thank heavens I did. I nearly went out to the kitchen to make a cup of tea, but then I thought I might wake people, so I didn't. I might have seen . . . you know . . . out of the kitchen window.'

'Yeah, well, poor old Rodney copped that,' said Chris quietly. 'Just for the record, he says he went to bed, slept like a log all night, didn't even know about our little fracas in the hall till I told him about it this morning. He got up early, went out to move the ladders and so on—he's right, poor little bugger, he does all the slog around here—and saw Damien lying stretched out, face down, in the orchard. Apparently he got a terrible fright at first because from the back stairs he thought it was Mum lying there. Because of the body being in her favourite spot, I suppose, and of course her parka is pale blue, like Damien's was. He thought she'd had a heart attack, or something. He was terribly upset, even telling me about it.' He tightened his lips.

'Anyway, he ran down and saw straight away who it was. He touched the hand and it was freezing cold, he said. He said he just turned round and ran back to the house, and it was all he could do not to yell. He had the sense to come round and get me out of bed. Didn't go straight to Mum, like you'd think. Came and got me and wouldn't say a word till we got out to the kitchen. Then he really let go.' Chris shook his head. 'He's not a bad kid, you know, Sons.' He looked at her almost pleadingly. 'Just young. He's always been the baby.' Sonsy nodded absent-mindedly. She was very pale. She licked her top lip quickly and the flash of pink tongue was quite startling.

'I'll go next,' she said. 'For what good it will do. I didn't see or hear anything strange, except Chris's mother in the hall.' She smiled nervously at her own small joke. Kate's heart went out to her immediately. From Sonsy that little pleasantry was very courageous, and quite a step forward.

14

A Few Home Truths

'I've told you what happened earlier,' said Sonsy, 'so I'll go from when Chris came to bed. We talked for a while. I was upset. He was angry.' She smiled sadly. 'We kept our voices down, but I suppose Alice could hear a bit.' She looked at Alice, but the old woman's face didn't change, or move from its contemplation of the fire.

'Chris said she could, anyway, but I didn't care, really. I just wanted to talk it out this time. I honestly felt I was going mad, or I was mad, or something. You know Kate. I told *you*.'

Everyone looked at Kate in surprise, and Kate nodded, feeling embarrassed and guilty under Chris's eye.

'Anyway,' Sonsy went on, chin up, 'finally Chris said that he was going to sleep, and turned over and wouldn't speak anymore. I lay there. I heard the clock strike twelve, then twelve-fifteen. The house was creaking, and the roof started to rattle. I thought . . . my friends at school and in training liked me, and the other girls at the hospital seem to think I'm nice, and funny, and . . . and good at what I do. And I wondered why at home, or here, I was so unlikeable—I mean, such a problem, and so hopeless at everything. And it came to me that here I was a fish out of water, and that was the trouble. Maybe with my friends, and in my world, it'd be Chris and his family who'd be out of place and awkward.'

She paused. No one said a word. What could one say? thought Kate, keeping her eyes down. But Sonsy wasn't looking for a response. She drew breath and continued.

'I heard Jill come in, I think. I heard her get onto her stretcher. I thought how ridiculous it was that Chris's mother made Chris and me a special bedroom, because we'd been married nine months, but made Nick and Jill sleep separately, when they'd lived together for ten years. I wondered why they came. I heard the half hour strike. Half past twelve. I wondered how Kate could stand Betsy calling Zoe "poor little thing" and saying she was nervy and deprived, just because she's not being brought up Betsy's way. I thought I couldn't stand her saying things like that to me, about any child of mine.' Sonsy's cheeks weren't pale now. They were flushed, and her eyes were bright with remembered anger. Her little hands clenched and unclenched, the knuckles changing from white to pink, pink to white.

'Sonsy.' Chris put his hand on her shoulder and she took a gulp of air and quietened immediately.

'Sorry,' she said, moving away from him. 'I'm only saying all this to explain what happened next. See, everything was just going round and round in my head. I couldn't sleep. After a while I wanted to go to the toilet. Chris was asleep—at least, I think he was. I slid out of bed quietly and put on my dressing gown and slippers, because it was really cold. I went round to the front of the verandah and I could see Jill and Birdie were asleep. Nick's stretcher was empty. I listened at Betsy and Wilf's window, and heard Wilf snoring a bit. I went on and turned into the hall. Halfway down the clock struck one. It seemed so loud, but no one moved, and the bedroom doors were shut. It was pitch dark. I walked very quietly through to the living room. I pulled the hall door to behind me, and went on out the back door.' She stopped. Her voice was calm and steady, but she was breathing fast.

'The door was unlocked, so it didn't make any noise. You see, the thing was, I just couldn't have stood seeing anyone. I was so mixed up, and angry and ashamed for rushing out of the room like I'd done. Anyway, I went to the toilet, and . . . and all the thoughts I'd been having were sort of echoing in my head. I came back in the back door. Inside was darker than outside, and I could barely see my hand in front of my face. I went to open the door into the hallway and it seemed stuck. I pulled at it, and it flew open— and Betsy was standing there, with her hand out, staring right at me. I just screamed! I couldn't help it. It was a terrible shock, because . . . as though I'd made this monster appear out of my head, you see? I screamed a few times, I know, and she just stared at me, with her mouth open. Then Chris came running, and Betsy started talking, and I must have fainted, or anyway everything went very woozy. Chris took me back to our room and took off my dressing gown and slippers and put me into the bed. I was shivering all over. I could hear everyone talking, and Zoe calling out, but all very far away. And then I must have just gone to sleep, because I don't remember another thing till morning.' She looked at them gravely. Her cheeks were wet. 'People do that sometimes, when they're exhausted, or they've had a shock,' she said.

'Sonsy, my darling . . .' Chris began.

She turned her head to look at him and smiled. She put her hand on his arm. 'It's all *right*, Chris,' she said. She turned back to face the centre.

'In the morning Chris came and told me what had happened. So I went out, and Damien was there. He was quite dead. He had been dead for hours, I'd say. Chris's mother was upset. I see now that she just said the first thing that came into her head, but when she said "Oh, not in my place!", or whatever it was, like

that, I just thought, I can't believe it! The man's dead.
His life's over. And all she can think about is that he's
had the bad taste to die in her favourite spot, so now
one of those endless family traditions will be spoilt.
And it seemed to sum up everything, somehow, and
it seemed so funny and I started to laugh. I couldn't
stop. You all saw. You must have thought I was mad.
Chris did, for sure. He's been treating me like a cot-
case ever since.' She lifted her eyes and looked around.
'I can't explain it, but somehow after that I felt different. Like I said, it was as if I woke up . . . woke
up like a delirious person who's fever's gone down. All
the monsters have shrunk down to normal size, now.
Soon I'll be up and walking.' She smiled.

Walking out of Chris's life, I'll bet, thought Kate,
if he's not careful. And he knows it too, and he's
scared. He's suddenly discovered he cares about her
much more than he thought, now that she's not on
tap. Why do people go on doing that? I wonder if it'd
last if she went back to trusting him again. I suppose
that's what she wonders. She looked curiously at Sonsy's calmer clear-eyed little face, and at her still hands
lying so quietly, folded one above the other on her
lap. If she was wondering, she didn't look as though
the answer to the question was of enormous impor-
tance to her, anyway. Something stirred in Kate's
mind. Some memory she couldn't quite place was
roused by that expression, those hands. She racked her
brain, but she was tired, and she couldn't find the
picture she was looking for, or put a name to it.

There was silence. Everyone was looking tired and
pale under the lights. Kate looked at Birdie and caught
her exchanging a glance with Jeremy. Jeremy frowned
slightly and cleared his throat.

'Ah . . . Chris,' he began, and Kate suddenly realised that Birdie's look had been a prompt. This mysterious stranger business was a set-up! Birdie was
fact-collecting, about the people in this room, keeping
a low profile while she did so. And Jeremy was co-

operating with her—what a turn up! Kate knew that her irritation was unfair. She'd wanted Birdie to get involved. But it was awfully galling to be tricked along with everyone else. Obviously Birdie had felt she needed a sensitive instrument to start this conversation off. So she'd primed up Jeremy, confidently relying on Kate to rush in enthusiastically and back the scheme, thoughtlessly loyal, full of goodwill and energy, like some clumsy puppy. And how right she'd been, thought Kate bitterly. I was much more convincing as a dupe than I'd have been as an accomplice. She simmered. Suddenly she'd lost all desire to participate in this enterprise.

Chris looked rather ill. His handsome dark-complexioned face seemed to sag a little. His jawline was blurred just slightly. There were pouches under his eyes. Not such a great catch, after all, thought Kate, with her new-found cynicism fresh upon her. I've been believing Betsy's propaganda. One of the best and the brightest? An English master in a snobby boys' school. His world was sweat and chalk, that institutional smell of bananas and running shoes. A place where sarcasm passed as wit and the one-eyed man was king. As Chris began to speak, stale words corroborating everything said previously by everyone else, her distaste for the situation grew, and her jaundiced eye flicked round the company, disliking what it saw.

Birdie, scruffy and hunched over her pad, looked absurd. Why did she insist on dressing like that? She could have any clothes she wanted. It was reverse snobbery of the worst kind. And a weird kind of malice, thought Kate, with a flash of bitter insight. She loved being able to laugh up her tatty sleeve at people like Betsy—'scholarship girl, I suppose?'—knowing how they would fawn if they knew who her father was.

Jeremy was enjoying his part in the comedy, disengaged, playing games, eyebrows raised, feeling superior, she'd bet, to everyone in the room, including Birdie. Jill was listening intently, her face thrust forward, chin resting on one fist. Her eyes were unreadable under the pale orange brows. With her free hand she grasped Nick's arm, occasionally patting or stroking it. All a bit overdone, surely.

Nick sat passively beside her, but his small clever eyes were watchful. Sonsy looked at her hands, still folded on her lap, so that her face was hidden, conveniently perhaps. Alice faced the fire. She could have been a statue, except for the slow, tortoise-like blinking of her eyes. Her whole position though, the set of her head and neck, showed she was alert. She was listening hard. There was something very creepy about Alice. Kate gave herself a mental shake, and forced herself to tune into Chris's monologue.

'. . . I eventually went to sleep,' Chris was saying, determinedly calm, 'oh, at about twenty to twelve, I'd say. I heard and saw nothing after that until I heard Sonsy scream and then I wasn't thinking about the time, and who was where. I went out and got her back to bed, as she told you, and that was that for me.' He leaned back in his chair and yawned, and put his hands behind his head. 'Sorry,' he said, 'not much help, eh?'

'Well,' said Jeremy, 'no, not much. Still . . . Alice, you're the last. D'you want to have a go?'

Alice turned her head towards them just sufficiently to look at Jeremy out of the corner of her eye. Her neck wrinkled into a hundred folds and creases. Her single visible eye, watery and half-hidden by a deeply-folded eyelid, shone slyly in the firelight.

'I told the police blokes I didn't see or hear a thing except the wind and the trees all night,' she said. 'Well, I'm not saying any different now. My windows face the other side of the orchard, don't they? No way I can see the garage or anywhere round it. Even if I had I wouldn't have told the police. Far as I'm concerned Treloar deserved everything he got.'

'It's different now, though, Auntie Alice,' murmured Chris persuasively, 'now that Nick's suspected.'

'Yeah, well, that does make a difference,' said Alice, turning her head back to the fire. 'Fair's fair. Wish I could add in some titbits, but I can't. I heard the yelling in the hall at quarter past one. I heard the young ones next door go on a bit after that. Christopher, actually, doing a solo. But after about half past the hour I was history, I reckon. Can't help you, little madam.' She turned from the fire and grinned wickedly straight at Birdie. 'Can't do anything but wish you luck.'

Kate's heart gave a lurch. Birdie was returning Alice's look calmly enough. But her eyes were a little wider than usual behind her spectacles, and her eyebrows were high.

'I'm going to bed,' Alice announced, and struggled to her feet. She shuffled across the room towards them, a tall, eccentric figure in her long, floppy skirt, men's boots and multicoloured vest. She was still grinning widely as they cleared a path for her. She went out the back door without another word, and they heard the toilet door slam.

'She's barmy, poor old Alice,' muttered Chris. 'Nutty as a fruit cake.'

'I don't think so.' Sonsy looked almost amused. 'It's just a part she likes to play. We're such a good audience, see? Almost as good as your mum. Not quite so easily shocked, but almost!'

Kate would have cheered, if she hadn't been so tired. She got up and went into the kitchen to make a cup of tea.

She was just filling the kettle when Alice came in. The old woman nodded gravely at her and strode into the bathroom, shutting the door firmly behind her. Water ran and the pipes thumped. Tonight there'd be nothing to see from the bathroom window. The garage would be dark, shrouded in mist, and cold. Like Damien, cold on some table down in Sydney.

• • •

Birdie, Kate and Jeremy saw the others off to bed, and sat together, drinking their tea.

'Well, pretty useless exercise all round, really,' said Jeremy, and yawned.

'I don't know,' said Birdie complacently. She was sitting cross-legged by the dying fire, looking through the notes, the evening's harvest of times, places and motives. 'Now we know what everyone was doing, or claims to have been doing, in detail, for the whole evening.'

'Not Anna, or Rodney, or Wilf—or Betsy,' Kate pointed out.

'No,' admitted Birdie cheerfully. 'But we know them in general. According to old Toby, Anna says she went to bed and stayed there, and heard nothing but the Sonsy business all night. Betsy says ditto, and also swears that neither Anna nor Wilf could have left the house without her hearing them. She says she got up to go to the toilet and was just opening the door to the living room when suddenly it jerked out of her hand and flew open, and there was Sonsy screaming at her. Gave her the fright of her life. After that business she said she was so rattled that she and Wilf both took sleeping pills and sank into a dreamless slumber until morning. So that takes care of them. Rodney didn't even hear the rumpus in the hall, apparently. He was tired and went straight to sleep as soon as he got into bed.'

Kate sat forward. She'd remembered something she'd been saving up.

'Birdie, Rodney—I meant to say . . . you remember Chris saying that Rodney first took Damien's body for *Betsy's?* The same colour parka and all, same height. The person at the van—well, I know you're being cautious, but it could've been Betsy easily.'

Birdie looked at her, expressionless. 'Well?' said Kate stubbornly. 'What do you think? We don't know

Betsy took a sleeping pill. She says she did, but she could've easily . . .'

'Of course she could, dummy,' snapped Birdie. 'Any of us could. Think about it.'

'For that matter,' Kate persisted, 'she, or someone else if you like, could have left poison for Damien to take himself. Tampered with pills he was taking, or given him some specially doped apples to eat later, or anything. In fact, that must have been how it was. No one could have poisoned a whole tree of apples, and just left it to chance that he'd eat one.'

'Now look, Laney, I told Jeremy but I haven't had a chance to tell you yet. I'm almost sure Damien didn't take the stuff by mouth at all. I told Toby that and he agreed with me. We think it was put on his skin. There's a bottle of Parathion missing. Even a small splash of that on the skin is deadly. Alice told you all about it, remember? They're rushing the post-mortem so that traces on the skin will still show up.'

'On his skin?' Kate felt sick. She looked at Jeremy, and his face was grave.

Birdie was unmoved. 'Why is that nastier than dosing an apple for him to eat?' she said coolly. 'I thought at first that someone may have sprayed him in the face, or on the hands, because they were the only exposed parts of him, but then Anna went on about the parka hood, about it never being up. It seemed funny. He did have the cap on under the hood. Why break his own rule and put the hood up last night?'

'Birdie thinks somebody put it up for him,' said Jeremy quietly, 'after splashing the back of his neck with Parathion and watching him die. To throw the cops off the scent, just in case they did suspect poison on the skin, and weren't taken in by the apple cores lying around.'

'Oh . . . oh, how disgusting!'

'Fairly disgusting. Fairly crafty though, you must admit,' said Birdie, looking through her notes. 'And

I'm not sure about the watching him die part. It's all just a theory. It might be completely wrong.'

'But you don't think so, do you?' said Kate.

'No. No, I think I'm right. It fits.'

'Well, that means . . .'

'It means the murderer didn't set a trap or leave a time bomb, so to speak, or anything like that. It means the murderer equipped himself, or herself, with the poison and some rubber gloves, and some apple cores, probably painted with the nasty stuff, before-hand. Then whoever it was sneaked over to the garage, some-time between midnight and about three, and lured Damien out to the orchard, or met him there by ap-pointment, and sloshed him in the neck. He would have died in about ten minutes, according to the book Alice showed me this afternoon. Fits and vomiting, then loss of consciousness, then death.'

Birdie looked at them over her glasses and fingered the notepad. 'Fairly quick, see? So, Laney, as you say, Betsy could've stayed awake, and gone out to the or-chard while Wilf slept on. Conversely, my dear, Wilf could've palmed his pill and gone out after Betsy had dozed off. His parka's blue too. Anna could have slipped out anytime, and used her mum's parka. We only have her word for it that she heard the Sonsy business. She didn't come out of her room. She may not have been there at all, and just heard about the thing this morning. Sonsy herself could have been out killing Damien instead of going to the loo as she claimed. Chris could have slipped out and done it af-ter Sonsy went to sleep, or fainted, or whatever she did. Rodney could've slipped out the back via the storeroom and the kitchen, picking up the poison as he went. No one would have heard. No one would have heard Alice, either. We all thought Alice didn't know Damien was staying overnight. But Chris and Sonsy were talking about it when Chris got into bed, and if the wall's as thin as they claim, Alice'd have heard about it too.'

'Now, who else . . . Jill . . . Jill didn't get in till twenty past twelve. She could've done the poor bloke to death before coming inside. Nick admits he came home at two-thirty, but says he didn't get out of the car. He could be lying, or he could have visited earlier, unseen by anyone. Quite a few people have motives, of sorts. Anyone could've got hold of a pale blue parka. There are two in the house, easily accessible, and everyone had the opportunity.'

'You left out Jeremy and me,' said Kate coldly. 'And Zoe.'

'And yourself,' added Jeremy. 'You aren't very thorough, for a hot shot.'

'Look, there's no good being cranky with me,' snapped Birdie. 'Someone bloody did it! Someone round here poisoned that man like a bug. Do you want to know who, or not?'

15

Developments

The next day dawned bright and clear. A perfect
mountain morning. But at breakfast most people were
looking decidedly seedy. The combination of a very
late night and Alice's spirituous refreshments had had
a dampening effect on some and an irritating one on
others, while high emotion had left Anna and Rodney
sulky and out of temper. Only Zoe and Alice were in
their normal states, and they had left the table as soon
as possible to have a private conference by the fire.
Zoe was whispering insistently and Alice was shaking
her head. What on earth was Zoe up to now, thought
Kate.

Betsy made it clear that she was disappointed with
her group, and made a short speech about making an
effort and pulling together, closely followed by another about burning the candle at both ends. Finding
that this had no effect on the prevailing gloom, and
that Birdie alone was paying her any attention, she
became irritated herself, and looked around for a victim. She fastened on Sonsy who, looking rather
queasy, was nibbling on a piece of toast at one corner
of the table.

'Sue, dear, don't just have toast, please! Have some
egg. Look, it's lovely, and it's all going to waste.' She

dipped a spoon into the quivering yellow mass of scrambled egg on the platter and held it out invitingly. 'Pass over your plate.'

'No, Betsy, thank you, really, I . . .'

Kate saw Alice glance in their direction and frown. She said something to Zoe who looked up, her face wreathed in smiles. They both rose and walked quickly to the back door, Zoe self-conscious, Alice's face unreadable. Betsy watched them leave with eyebrows raised, but said nothing. She turned back to Sonsy.

'Don't be silly, dear. Eat up now. Short, fair people like you need a bit of weight on, Sue, I always think, or they just lose their looks completely.' She looked around the table, head on one side.

'Don't you think so, Katie? You never watch your weight, do you?'

'Of course I do, Betsy, or I'd be fat as a pig,' said Kate, with what she hoped passed for a jovial grin. It felt more like a grimace, and in fact probably was, because Betsy stared at her for a moment before going on vivaciously.

'My friend, Judy Perlez, who's a trained beautician, always says just what I'm saying now. She's small and fair, well, fairer than you, Sue. More a real blonde blonde than that in-between colour, but she always says how she envies Anna and me, being brunette, because it's so much easier for us to keep ourselves looking at least passable. "I'd just fade into the woodwork, Betsy," she says, "without a bit of colour and a bit of curve. The colour comes out of a bottle," she says, "but the curve's all mine!".' Betsy laughed. 'Oh, dear, she's a witty woman, Judy. All the personality in the world.'

She turned her smiling face to Sonsy again. 'You were such a pretty little thing, Sue, when Christopher first brought you home. We didn't like to say so, dear, but Wilf and I were shocked when we saw you the other night. Your face has all fallen in. Come on, be a sensible girl.'

'Mum, give it a rest,' said Chris nervously. But Betsy didn't even look at him. She just held out the spoon, heaped with cooling egg, and waited.

Sonsy looked at the face across the table, at the smiling, lipsticked mouth, the engagingly raised eyebrows, the hard, dominating eyes. Her own face was very pale. She shook her head and didn't speak. Then suddenly she rose from the table and made for the back door. She went out without looking back and they heard the toilet door bang behind her.

Betsy looked down at the rejected spoonful of egg and gently lowered it back to the platter.

'Anyone else?' she said, carefully casual. 'Jill? Nick? Oh dear, what waste.' She shook her head and rose from the table. 'I'll let you clear away, if you don't mind, Anna,' she said. 'I think I'll go and do our room while I have the chance.' She moved quietly away from the table without waiting for an answer, and disappeared with upright dignity into the darkness of the hall.

'Poor old Mum. She's having a hard time,' murmured Anna. 'Sonsy's being a bit unfriendly, isn't she, Chris? Couldn't you ask her to lay off for a bit?'

Chris was silent. He looked rather shocked. Kate wondered if he'd seen what she had. She would have been with Anna all the way, just for the sake of peace, would have thought that Sonsy should humour old Betsy, just to be friendly, if she hadn't been placed so that she could see Betsy's eyes during the exchange, cold as little sharp stones, they'd been. Betsy had learned, early probably, to muffle her iron fist in a velvet glove. To use guilt and other emotions to bend people to her will, instead of physical force or outright threats. But the implacable need to be right and boss people around burned as strongly in her as in the toughest street bully or the maddest dictator.

How frustrating she must find her chosen, or rather,

her only appropriate and available, weapons. How she would love to stamp her foot and say 'Off with their heads!', when people crossed her. Then Kate's thoughts reached the point to which any musing about Betsy's psychology had inevitably led them in the last couple of days. Had Betsy, in fact, finally found herself in a position to say just that, about Damien Treloar? Had she decided to get him out of Anna's reach once and for all? It was possible. It was more than possible. She wouldn't jib at poisoning. Not Betsy. She was already an old hand at poisoning of a different kind.

She'd succeeded in bringing Anna to heel, anyway. Anna was sticking to her like glue, as if all the stuffing had been knocked out of her and she needed a support to stay upright. My God, thought Kate, what if Betsy really *did* do it? What if the police found out? What would happen to Anna? And Wilf? And Rodney? She was the mainstay, the family's axis. What would they do if she ended up in prison? Betsy in gaol—it was unimaginable. She suddenly, desperately, hoped that the police wouldn't find out. That the whole thing would just die down, unsolved. After all, whoever did it—Betsy or . . . or whoever . . . it was just an isolated thing, to do with Damien Treloar. No one else would be in danger, if the person who killed him just went their way.

But even as the thought crossed her mind the memory of Birdie's hard voice shot it through.

Someone poisoned that man like a bug . . . like a bug. She shivered.

Running steps thudded on the back stairs, and the door flew open with a crash.

'Mum, Mum!' Zoe stood in the doorway panting, her eyes wide and bright with excitement.

'Hey, take it easy!' shouted Jeremy.

'Mum, Dad, we found the Ark. It was under the house. It was right there, and we found it. Oh, I can't believe it!' She leaned in a dramatic fashion against the door, her hand on her heart.

'OK, OK, no need to overdo it,' growled Jeremy repressively. 'Just act normal, will you? And I thought we told you not go under the house. Or was Alice with you?'

Zoe rolled her eyes heavenward. 'Of course she was. Dad, it's incredible, you don't . . .' She hesitated, looked at Kate, and then, for some reason, at Jill, and sobered down.

'Well, anyway,' she said with dignity, 'let me tell you calmly, Dad, that we've found the Noah's Ark at last—and here it is!'

With a touchingly embarrassing flourish she introduced Alice, coming through the door carrying what looking like a painted box with a handle.

Sonsy came in behind them, looking very pale and pink-eyed, and disappeared without a word into the kitchen. She had obviously been sick. They heard her close the bathroom door behind her, and the pipes thumped as she turned the taps on.

'Isn't it lovely? Whoopee!' Zoe clapped her hands as Alice carried her burden to the rug before the fire. 'Come and look, Mum.'

'Hold on, hold on!' cried Alice excitedly. 'I've got to fix it up!'

Kate sighed and slowly pushed herself up from her chair. Honestly, Alice was as bad as Zoe. Maybe now at least she'd stop the endless searching for toys to entertain the child who after all needed no extra entertainment up here. It made Zoe so overexcited, this constant turning out of cupboards and dragging out of things. Not to mention what it did to Alice's house, already a disaster area.

'Now then,' said Alice to her as she approached, 'what do you think of that, eh?'

She moved aside, exchanging proud glances with Zoe.

Kate looked at the Noah's Ark sitting on its gritty

rug, and her bedroom and irritation fled. The firelight flickered on its soft, faded colours and the beautifully proportioned curve of the rainbow arching over it. At the highest point of the rainbow perched the white dove, wings outstretched, a green twig in its beak.

Almost involuntarily, Kate dropped to her knees and stretched out a hand to touch the old wood.

'Alice, it's beautiful,' she breathed. 'It's—is it?—it's hand carved!'

'That's right,' said Alice delightedly. 'Friend of Dad's made it for me while he was staying here once. Took him six months, working of an evening . . . oh dear, when I was six or seven, just a little thing, anyhow. Mum and Dad had lots of friends good with their hands. Lots of crafty types lived in the mountains in those days, real artists, some of them. Poor as church mice, of course.'

'Artists, I'll say,' said Kate, looking at the tiny animals Alice had begun to arrange on the deck of the Ark.

'Hope it's still all here,' said Alice. 'Used to be two of every animal, 'course, but some might have gone missing. It's been packed away for donkey's years. I wanted the little lass to see it. She's old enough now to take care of it, aren't you, love? Glad I found it at last?'

'I'll say,' said Zoe eagerly. 'Why don't we arrange all the animals now, Auntie Alice, and make sure they're all there?'

'Righto then, love.'

Kate looked at their shining faces, savagely innocent, both of them, patted Zoe's shoulder and stood up. The people around the kitchen table had lost interest, and were finishing breakfast in a half-hearted way. She walked back to them. No point resisting it. She couldn't go back to Zoe's state of grace, and almost certainly she'd never attain Alice's. Life was too complicated for that now.

• • •

They stood around the kitchen table, some wiping dishes, some just lounging, somehow happier there, even standing up, than sitting in the living room with Alice and Wilf, and Betsy buzzing in and out.

'Who feels like getting some picking done this morning?' Chris asked. 'Rodney's down there already. I gather it's OK to go into the orchard, as long as we keep away from the marked-off area . . . um . . .'

'Sure, mate,' said Jeremy, stretching. 'Good idea.'

'Anna's not feeling up to it, she said. Mum said she might come down later,' Chris went on. 'So it'd just be us. But we could make a dent in it. The point is, the trees have to be stripped, even if . . . ah . . . the apples have to be dumped. So . . .'

'Let's get on with it then, mate!' Nick was already making for the door, delighted to have something positive to do.

In a few minutes only Kate and Birdie were left in the kitchen, drinking their third cup of tea for the day in companionable silence. They both jumped as the phone rang.

'I'll go!' Betsy's voice shrilled from the depths of the house.

'I'll get it,' said Birdie, with a gleam in her eye. But just as she took the first step Wilf appeared at the kitchen door. He shuffled rapidly to the phone and lifted the receiver.

'Hello?' he said vaguely, and listened. He stared straight ahead, his pale, watery eyes unfocused. 'Oh, yes . . . oh, yes . . . yes, that'll be all right,' he said dully. 'Yes . . .'

Betsy arrived at the door, one side of her head studded with hot rollers, and crossed quickly to his side. She began mouthing to him, but he waved her away irritably. She almost danced with impatience as he turned away from her, the receiver glued to his ear.

'All right, then. We'll see you then, then . . . all right
. . . goodbye.' He hung up.

'Wilf! I said I'd get it! Who was it?' snapped Betsy.
'Really, I wish you wouldn't . . .'

'It was that Mr Toby,' said Wilf. 'The detective
chap. He rang to say that he was coming over here
again. He said there'd been developments.'

'Developments? What developments?'

'He didn't say really. Just that the first results of the
post-mortem had come to hand, that was what he
said, and he wanted to come over and have a few
words with us. Nice polite sort of chap, isn't he?'

'Wilf! For goodness sake! Why didn't you let me get
the phone? Didn't you ask him . . .'

'I didn't ask him anything, Bet. I was a bit flustered. He'll be here soon, anyway. He said they were
leaving now.'

'Oh, heavens! My hair . . . oh, it's always something!' Betsy threw a reproachful glance at Kate as
though somehow it was all her fault, and trotted back
to her bedroom, clutching the plastic-armoured side
of her head with one hand to protect the smoothly
developing curls.

'I'll go down and tell the others,' said Kate.

Birdie nodded. 'Kate, before you do, though, I'd
take Zoe over to Theresa's again, if I were you.'

Kate looked at her friend. She was very serious, but
was obviously going to answer no questions.

Kate shrugged and went on her way and Birdie
stood still for a moment, looking after her. Then she
picked up their tea mugs and absently clinked them
together before putting them on the sink. The thought
of rinsing them out never crossed her mind, but she
did arrange them neatly, with both handles facing the
same way. Through the window she watched Kate
lead Zoe, protesting vehemently, down the back steps,
and heard them clatter up the side path. She ran her
fingers through her hair so that it was flat on the top
and stuck out in two great tufts behind her ears,

brushed some toast crumbs off her jumper and, thus groomed, slipped out the back door and up to the road, to await the police.

A few minutes later Kate was crossing the still dewy grass of Theresa's front lawn, having left Zoe happily folding nappies in Theresa's lovely back room, the Ark and its delights temporarily forgotten. Theresa looked tired but had welcomed the little girl warmly.

'I'll be having a sleep this afternoon, after Nel's feed,' she'd told Kate. 'I really need my naps. As soon as Nel goes down, so do I!' She smiled. 'It's the mornings that I get everything done, and Zoe's no trouble at all. She's good company.'

Good company, Kate thought, was something that Theresa had been doing without for a while, it seemed. She appeared to be quite alone in the world, except for her little Nel, and Alice who, after all, she'd only known for a few short months.

The police car was parked outside Alice's house, and Kate could see Birdie, hands deep in her duffle-coat pockets, talking earnestly to the big detective under the arch of the gate. She quickened her steps, determined to get in on the conversation, but as she hurried across the road Toby nodded his head slowly and moved away from Birdie's side. His assistant immediately slipped through the archway and followed him like a gangling shadow. A sandy policeman in uniform brought up the rear. Birdie swung the gate closed and leaned over it, looking up at Kate as she approached.

'Zoe stowed?'

'She's OK till lunchtime. What's up, Birdie? Come on—what's up?'

'Better not to say, Laney, really. I'm not sure if it'll all come off. You'll soon see, anyhow.' She swung the gate open to let Kate through. Kate looked towards the garage. The big detective, Mr Toby, was walking

along its side wall, his eyes to the ground. In his hands
were two pieces of bracken fern, and he was beating
them absent-mindedly against his shiny trouser leg.

Kate and Birdie moved round to the side path, and
watched in silence. Toby got to the end of the ram-
shackle building, rounded the corner and paced along
behind it, casually looking at the ground. He stopped
at about the halfway mark, under the high windows.
At a word from him the younger man bent and picked
up two more stalks of fern. Apparently losing interest,
Toby immediately turned and strolled back towards
the house.

'Stay here,' hissed Birdie as Kate began to move.
'Just watch. Listen.'

'Mr Toby!' Betsy's brittle voice rang out in the clean,
bright air. Her little boots clattered on the stairs and
rang on the cement path as she appeared at the corner
of the house, pink and white, hair black, crisp and
wavy in the sunlight.

'Ah, yes, Mrs Tender,' Toby was formal but
friendly. 'You know why we're here?' It was a question, but only just.

'My husband told me you were coming. He wasn't
quite clear on the reason, I'm afraid. Poor Wilfie isn't
always . . . I mean, it's just as well, Mr Toby, to ask
for me when you ring, if you don't mind. It saves . . .'

'Ah, well, I'm sorry, Mrs Tender, but I was in a bit
of a rush this morning, to tell you the truth.' Toby's
rumble rose and drowned out the gradually rising note
of complaint in the high voice. 'Now, the fact is,
things are looking a bit more complicated than they
were yesterday, Mrs Tender, and I'm afraid we're going to have to talk to a few people again.'

'More . . . ? What do you mean?' Betsy's voice rose
in a squeak. Kate was sure there was real fear there,
and her stomach contracted. Oh, no, it couldn't be.
Betsy really had killed Damien, rather than let Anna
go back to him.

Such was the rushing in Kate's ears that she missed

Toby's next words. Her mind cleared suddenly
'. . . speak to your daughter, Anna Treloar, please,'
Toby was saying.

Anna? Surely they weren't going to make Anna give
evidence against her own mother? She wouldn't. Or
would she, if she was told what Betsy had done?

'No, I'm very sorry, but Anna is resting this morning. She's not very well,' said Betsy icily. If there had
ever been panic in her voice, it was gone now, ruthlessly suppressed, with that iron control that was her
greatest weapon in crisis. She was standing with her
back to them, but Kate could see her shoulders squar-
ing under the thin sweater, her fine white neck rising
out of the green wool collar, her black head high. Her
eyes would be flashing, her small mouth set.

There was a small silence, then Toby moved his
shoulders in a sort of shrug.

'Mrs Tender, I wouldn't be troubling her if I could
avoid it,' he said, 'but I have my duty to do as I'm
sure you understand, and . . .' He broke off. His expression didn't change, but his eyes moved, and Betsy
slowly turned to follow his stare. In profile her face
was a study in baffled anger and something else—
despair?

'Anna!' she snapped. 'Darling, I told you to stay
. . . in bed. Anna? Don't come down into the air.
Anna, go straight back . . .'

The heavy booted steps continued down the stairs
and along the path, and Anna, looking fragile and
heavy-eyed, moved into view. She put her hand on
her mother's shoulder.

'It's OK, Mum, it's warm. I'm warm. I couldn't just
stay inside while you . . . I'm . . . I was Damien's
wife. I've got to be in this.' She looked straight at
Toby.

'"Dad said there had been "developments",' she said.
'What does that mean, exactly?'

'It has been found by the men doing the post-
mortem, Mrs Treloar, that your husband's death was

not accidental. He was deliberately killed by someone unknown, someone who smeared a contact poison on his skin. I'm sorry to have to tell you this . . .'

'What!' Anna stared at him, wild-eyed. 'But there were apple cores everywhere. He ate . . .'

'The apple cores were a blind, it seems. They'd been clumsily dabbed with the same poison that was found on his skin, but it was obvious that they were at least a day old and the poison was distributed randomly over the flesh. Also, your husband had in fact eaten no apples at all. Hadn't eaten anything in fact, since late afternoon.'

Kate nudged Birdie, who put her fingers to her lips.

'I want to show you something, Mrs Treloar,' said Toby slowly. 'This way.' He held out an arm and she obediently moved forward and walked beside him over the grass, towards the garage.

Betsy stood irresolute for a moment, then turned back towards the house and began beckoning wildly. More slow steps sounded on the stairs. She bared her teeth in impatience and spun to watch her daughter and her escort, who had by now almost reached the garage doors, where Detective-constable McGlinchy was waiting.

Birdie gripped Kate's arm. 'Come on,' she whispered.

They moved across the grass. Anna and Toby were talking now. Both had their hands in their pockets. Their heads were bent. Then Anna shook her head and moved away.

'Mrs Treloar!' The words were sharp in the air, and Anna stopped and turned. As if in a dream Kate saw Betsy and Wilf approaching, hurrying, from the back of the house. Betsy and Wilf, she and Birdie were walking along opposite sides of a triangle, converging on the apex where Anna and Toby stood looking down at a patch of mud under the high side windows of the garage. In the orchard, seemingly far away, Nick, Jill, Jeremy and the others were gathering into a knot, staring up at them. As she glanced again the knot split into pieces, and the apple-pickers began moving towards them.

Now she could hear Anna's voice, low, insistent.

'I'm telling you again, Mr Toby, and it's not at all pleasant for me. There was no chance whatever of a reconciliation. My mother told you that and I told you. I don't know why you keep on about it. He . . .'

'What's happening here?' Betsy's voice was shrill. She clutched Wilf's arm and actually seemed to be leaning on him for support. Her cheeks were blazing red and she was panting.

She's not a young woman anymore, thought Kate irrelevantly. You forget that all the time. This will kill her. My God. She wished herself anywhere but where she was, but couldn't tear her eyes off Betsy's working face. There was such fear. Fear that had almost burnt out the fight. But not quite.

'This is quite absurd. You're overreaching your authority, Mr Toby, completely. You can't come here and badger a sick girl like this! It's ridiculous! Come away, Anna.'

Anna stepped towards her but Toby looked at Betsy lazily out of half-closed eyes, his forehead wrinkled up to the smooth brown skin where his hairline used to be.

'Mrs Tender, a murder has been committed. There's no doubt about that now. I have told your daughter, and I'm telling you, that if you want a solicitor to advise you, you're perfectly free to call one in. But I'm also free to ask questions, and it's my duty to do so. I'm not accusing anyone of anything. I'm just clearing up a few puzzling details. Such as this one— I simply want to know why, if your daughter did not go out of the house after going to bed the night before last, her footprints are clearly evident in the mud beside the garage—here, under the window.'

He indicated the spot. There in the rain-washed mud, where smooth little stones glittered, the indentations of two booted feet showed as sharply and clearly as if they'd been cut by a sculptor about to make a plaster model. The toes were rounded, the heels were narrow and had plunged deeply into the soil. The person who'd made those prints had stood as still as a statue, for quite a few minutes. Kate glanced involuntarily down at Anna's feet. Her boots could have made those prints. Easily. Probably. They were stained in a narrow band all round, just above the soles. The high heels were muddy. Those boots were a give-away. But much more of a give-away was Anna's face, dissolving as she watched into soft, enraged and baffled tears.

'I told you,' she sobbed. 'I told you I never . . . I never came out here. Why should I lie? You . . . it's my business. My marriage is my business, and I want . . .'

'Mum! For God's sake, what's happening?' Chris was at his mother's shoulder. Other faces bobbed behind him. Rodney, pink and anxious, Jill pale, Nick grim.

'Go away!' Anna almost screamed. 'Everyone go away. Look, I . . . I won't have this. It's . . . ridiculous. I'm sick . . . God knows how those marks got there. *I* wasn't there . . . leave me in peace!'

'Where? Where was Anna?' Rodney's face was avid.

'Rodney, go into the house!' It was Wilf. Rodney looked at him with astonished resentment, and stepped back. He made no move to go, but the overexcited, unpleasantly eager look left his face, and he grew sulky, silent and quiescent. Wilf shuffled forward, shaking off Betsy's arm. He cut a ludicrously unprepossessing figure alongside his dark, beautiful daughter. His grey hair stuck out a little at the sides and at the top, his warm cardigan stretched over a little tub of a belly and baggy trousers flapped around his thin legs. Anna clutched him, burying her face in his grey woollen shoulder.

Any old port in a storm, thought Kate, and was shocked by her own meanness, because the tenderness and proud protectiveness of that paunchy grey figure made it immensely moving.

Fathers, too, thought Kate. Of course . . . fathers are passionate about their children too. Only so often they're elbowed to one side. Wilf has been one of those fathers. But he's coming out of the shadows, into his own. Asserting his right to protect, and to love too. She remembered Wilf steadying Anna in the living room, dabbing at her bleeding leg where the leech had been. That's twice in three days.

'Wilfie!' Betsy's voice was calm, persuasive, controlled. 'Take Anna inside. She's had it. She needs to lie down. Take her in, darling.'

'I'd like to go, Dad,' snuffled Anna, into his cardigan. Wilf put his hand on her shining black hair.

'No, Annie,' he said gently. 'I think we'd better clear this up, you know, love.'

Her head jerked in surprise against his shoulder. Kate saw her eyes widen.

'Wilf!' Betsy was dangerous now.

'I'm sorry, Bet, but I don't like this. I don't like Anna being in a false position *for any reason*. She's done nothing wrong, and nothing to be ashamed of, and she's going to tell this gentleman so. Aren't you, Anna?'

'Dad, I . . .' Anna's head was up now, and she was staring at him, dry eyes startled.

'I know how you feel, love, but it's got to be done. Otherwise this gentleman will be imagining all sorts of things about you. It's gone too far now, Anna. Your footprints are there, clear as a bell, for everyone to see. It's time to tell the truth. Don't worry about what anyone else will think. Just tell the plain truth, and everything will be all right.'

Anna spoke only to him. 'Dad, I don't understand. What do you mean? I told you, I told everyone. I didn't see Damien that night.'

'You didn't *see* him, that's right. But you came over here, didn't you? And heard something.'

'How . . . ? How could you *possibly* . . . ?'

'Your mother told me. She followed you out, Anna, and saw everything. She heard everything. She came back after you, and told me. We know all about it already, love.'

Betsy's furious voice ripped through the air.

'Wilf, you bloody fool!'

16

Happy Families

🔥

Anna began to speak in a flat, colourless voice. She looked at the ground.

'All right,' she said. 'I did come over. I wanted to talk to Damien. He was my husband, you know. I had no idea I was followed.' She raised her eyes briefly and looked at Betsy with something like hatred. Betsy shrank back. Suddenly she seemed smaller. The silence was complete. Everyone seemed to be holding their breath, and no magpies called.

'I came over to the garage and went towards the door. I heard Damien talking to . . . someone.' She tightened her lips.

'*Talking* to someone? Who?' Chris burst out. Anna ignored him.

'I stopped. I didn't know what to do. I stood there, under the windows, trying to hear who it was, and what they were saying . . .' Her voice trailed off.

Toby waited a moment, then prompted. 'Go on, Mrs Treloar.'

Anna's eyes widened. She wrapped her arms across her breasts and tugged at her shoulders in an agony of remembered shame and pain. Then she spun round and pointed at Jill.

'Ask her!' she choked. 'Ask her what they said, the

bitch. She'll remember every bloody word! Go on, smart-bloody Jill Mission. Tell them what that bastard said to you, tucked up there with the fertilisers and empty bottles. Always lovey-dovey after a bit of the other, wasn't he? We must compare notes sometime.' She spun round to face Toby again. 'Or ask my mother, why don't you?' she spat. 'She'd be a great witness. She probably had her ears out on stalks. My God, she must have been dancing for joy. How right she'd been, all along. Oh, how right! No chance of Damien darkening our door after that, eh Mum? Weren't you thrilled? All you had to do was be nice to me, and I'd never suspect for a minute that you knew why suddenly divorce seemed such a good idea. Everything would have been lovely. What a shame he got done in! What a spoke *that* must have put in your wheel, eh? Mucked everything up again.' She shook off her father's restraining arm, and turned towards the house. Rodney and Betsy moved quickly out of her way, as she strode off without a backward glance.

Just before she got to the path she turned.

'Lover's quarrel was it, Jill?' she shrieked. 'Everything going so well too. Great plans and all. Bad luck! Sounded heavy. Wanting to make it legal, was he, and stop you having your cake and eating it too? Dear, dear. Watch out, Nick. Poisoning men might be a habit with her. Watch out!' She laughed, turned again and ran for the house.

They heard the door slam behind her. A car hummed past. No one moved or spoke. Jill was white as paper, her face dotted with pale freckles like rust marks. Her mouth was slightly open. Nick's face was a mask.

Jill tried to speak but no words came. She swallowed and tried again.

'She's mad,' she said. 'She's crazy. I . . . I never saw Damien Treloar that night. I never went near him. She's mad. We weren't . . . I mean, I hardly knew him. Only through work. Nick, honestly.' She turned

to him and spoke pleadingly. 'Honestly, it's all mad
. . . it's a lie.'

'No, it isn't!' Betsy's voice rang out. 'I heard it all.
Every word Anna heard I heard.'

'You were standing behind the garage, under the
back windows, weren't you, Mrs Tender?' Toby said
calmly. 'You could hear from there?'

'Oh. I see. I left footprints too, did I?' snapped
Betsy. 'Yes, well, I could hear perfectly. He was talking to this young woman,' she looked coldly at Jill.
'Obviously planning to set up house with her as soon
as he could. He spoke very insultingly of Anna, and
of the whole family, and made it very clear that
whatever my poor, beautiful girl had thought, he
hadn't cared about her *that* much!' She snapped her
fingers. Her eyes were blazing.

'I knew what he was. I knew. I tried to tell Anna,
but she thought, you all thought, I know you did,
"overprotective mother", "Betsy tying Anna down to
her apron strings again". I know. I'm not stupid!' She
blinked and looked around, her face strangely puck-
ered.

'My heart nearly broke for her,' she said. 'I couldn't
even go to her and comfort her, because I knew she
would be so, so angry and ashamed if she found out
I'd heard. She wouldn't want *anyone* to know. So I
just followed her back to the house quietly. She was
back in her room when I got in. Wilf was awake.
He'd heard her come in. I told him about it. I had to
tell someone. I was so terribly upset.'

'You were glad!' Wilf's thin voice cut through the
air. 'In your heart you were glad! Anna's right. I
couldn't understand you! I never have understood you.
I always thought you knew best, about the children.
I always left it to you. I know I'm nothing much. Not
much of a provider, or much of anything. You've always been the one the kids have turned to, Bet. I
haven't been much help. But when you came and told

me about what that . . . that man said about my daughter, and you *smiled*, you . . .'

'I didn't!'

'Yes, you were smiling all the time, that way people do, with your hand over your mouth so I wouldn't see. But I saw. You were sorry for Anna, I'm not denying that, not for a minute. But you were glad too because you knew that now she'd *never* go back to him. You even said, "Maybe it's all for the best". *The best!* With Anna crushed and trampled on like . . .' he stopped, choking with angry tears.

They stared at one another, apparently oblivious to their riveted audience, while Wilf fought for control.

'Surely,' said Betsy coldly, at last, 'you would rather Anna saw the man in his true colours, however painful it might have been for her. I suppose you would rather she'd gone back to him not knowing he had a red-haired floozie dangling on the side to joke about her to.'

'For one thing,' said Wilf, 'from what you said there was no way he was going to *take* her back. He was planning to run off with his lady.' He blinked vaguely at Jill and shook his head slightly as if to clear it. 'And for another, yes, I'd rather *anything* than that she'd suffered the blow she did. My Lord, Betsy, she'll never feel the same about herself again! Our beautiful, proud girl. Can't you see that? That man's destroyed something in her. It's gone. Lost. My little girl . . .' He covered his face with his hand. 'And you say "all for the best". Best for who? You say, "let him go, it's really over now. He's burned his bridges without knowing it. Good riddance". What about Anna? Eh? She goes on like before, does she? With the man she loved and trusted and was . . . and had . . . had been so intimate with, Bet . . . off cavorting with other women and giggling about her to them. I . . . it's disgusting! It's too much . . . for anyone to . . .' He trailed off, panting. His face was terribly pale. His forehead gleamed dully with sweat under limp strands of hair and little flecks of saliva bunched in the tight corners of his mouth. He looked around vaguely and suddenly staggered a little.

'Chris!' cried Betsy urgently. Chris reached his father in two strides and put his arm round him. The older man tossed his head and mumbled irritably, but finally let himself be led away to the house.

Kate left Birdie's side and crossed over to where Jeremy was standing with Nick and Jill.

It was an odd little group. The two men had drawn together, leaving Jill as isolated as if she was on the wrong side of an invisible line. They weren't touching, but were standing shoulder to shoulder, their obvious suspicion damning and chilling. Jill had stopped expostulating and was standing very tall, hands on her hips, just staring at them. She hardly moved, and didn't look around when Kate touched her arm.

'Jill . . . what is all this?'

'I haven't got the faintest idea. Not the faintest.'

'But she said . . . they said they heard . . . Jill, the police are going to . . .'

Jill turned slowly and looked at her. Her colour was high and her mouth firm, but her pale eyes were wide and startled-looking. 'I know,' she said, with dry lips. 'They're bound to question me again. I've got nothing to tell them. None of it was true.'

'But why would they . . . ?'

'Why Anna and her mother and father would say anything is beyond me, Kate. But I tell you I wasn't in that garage with Damien Treloar for a single moment at any time. It's either a story they cooked up, or someone else was there, and they mistook her for me. That's all.'

'They said it was you. They were certain.'

Jill's control snapped at last. 'Well, I'm telling you it wasn't me! I wasn't there!' Angry tears welled up in her eyes. 'Believe me or believe them. There's your choice! OK? Nick's obviously made up his mind. Didn't take him long, did it? His loyalty's sensational!

How about you?' A single tear brimmed over and ran down her cheek.

'Excuse me . . . ah . . . Miss Mission, I wonder whether we could have a bit of a talk.' It was Toby.

'Yes.'

'I thought, if you wouldn't mind, we might have a word together in the car. A bit cramped, but I'm not keen on going all the way back to town, you see, at this point. Obviously I have other people to talk to here, later on.'

'Yes, OK. Sure.' She turned and began to follow him. Nick, looking up and blinking in the sun as though he'd just woken up, called urgently.

'Jill! You don't have to, you know. Answer any questions. You don't . . .'

'I know all that, thanks. I've got nothing to hide.' She stalked off, tall and very upright beside Toby's massive grey back. The young detective moved like a shadow from the side of the garage and fell in behind them. The sandy man in uniform stood impassively by the garage door, hands behind his back. He seemed to be looking at the view.

Jeremy caught Kate's glance. 'Guarding the evidence,' he said drily, 'in case any of us decide to rush in and jump up and down on their precious footprints.'

'Birdie's precious footprints,' said Kate bitterly. 'Oh, what a mess. Nick, surely you don't believe that Jill . . .'

'I don't know,' muttered Nick, running his fingers through his sparse front hair. 'I don't know what to think. That bloke . . . he was a womanising bastard and he fancied her all right. She's been funny lately. I don't know. God! And why would Anna make it up? Look, I know she's neurotic, but come on, she's not as cracked as all that!'

He fell silent, and Kate became conscious that Birdie had joined them. Jeremy looked at her distastefully and she grinned at him.

'Let's go to the pub, mate,' he said, clapping Nick on the shoulder. 'Have a quick one.'

'Oh, I don't know, mate. I should wait and find out . . .'

'Come on, let's get out of here just for half an hour. Kate'll look after Jill if she gets back before we do.'

They wandered off towards the car, self-consciously supportive, not touching, with an air of leaving the women and all their works behind them.

Kate watched them go.

'So,' said Birdie, with a self-satisfied smile. 'It's moving along.'

'Yes,' said Kate flatly. 'So it seems. You needn't look so pleased with yourself, though, Birdie. Anyone'd think you'd planned the whole thing.'

Birdie looked injured. 'But I did plan it,' she said. 'From start to finish. I thought it would have been very strange for Anna to just go to bed and sleep the night through like she said she'd done, after the obvious signals between her and Treloar. The way her mother felt she'd obviously wait till people were asleep and then pop over on the quiet, to see him. Anyhow, as soon as I found the footprints there—Anna's at the side of the garage, under the windows, and Betsy's at the back, under the windows again I saw what had happened, as clear as day. I couldn't think of any reason why Anna should have stood there so long that her boots had sunk right into the dirt except that she was stopped from going into the garage by something she could hear through the windows or the open door. The only sound that would have stopped her there was Damien talking to someone. Right? So I had to get Toby to confront her with it, to try and make her tell what really happened. I didn't know Jill was involved, but even if I had known . . .'

'But Betsy . . .'

'Betsy's been radiating worry and concern ever since that night. Leaving aside the possibility of her own guilt, which despite your accusations to the contrary

I hadn't dismissed by any means, the probability that she knew more than she was telling, and that her knowledge affected one of her children, was high, I thought. She'd been absolutely firm to Toby that Anna had stayed in the house all night. Too firm, it seemed to me. I decided that *if* Anna had sneaked out it was quite on the cards that Betsy would follow, maybe to interfere, maybe not. Just to keep an eye on her, anyway. So I checked and sure enough there were Betsy's neat little gumboot prints behind the garage. Just where she would have stood to keep out of sight and just under the windows where she could hear what was going on, too.

'I was pretty sure Betsy would have told Wilf. He's been jittery too. What's more, he's been terribly tender to Anna, and a bit defiant of Betsy, in a rabbity, sly sort of way. I thought that of them all he was the likeliest to crack, so I arranged a fairly public confrontation, and hoped for the best . . . and there you are . . . it worked a treat, eh?'

Kate stared at her. 'Except that now Anna's in trouble. And poor Jill!' she said.

Birdie wrinkled her nose. 'Yeah, well . . . they're the breaks, frankly,' she said. 'I didn't know who it was with Damien. I had to find out. And if Jill wants to play the fool . . .'

'I can't believe it, Birdie! She says that she wasn't there. She swears it. I can't believe it.'

'Well, you have to, Laney. Heavens, you're hard to please. Anyhow, Anna's not necessarily in trouble. The field's wide open again, that's all. Anna lied and was out at the garage, sure. And sure she's got a fantastic motive for murder. If she slipped out once, she could slip out twice. She could pick up the poison on the way. Damien wouldn't know she'd overheard him and Jill. He wouldn't suspect a thing. She could suggest a walk in the orchard, sit down with him, put her hand up to the back of his neck without it looking funny at all. A quick splash of the nasty stuff, and bye bye Damien.'

Kate shuddered.

'But Jill lied too, apparently,' Birdie went on. 'And so did Betsy, who swore neither she nor Anna had left the house.'

'But now Betsy's got no motive, and Anna was hinting that Jill might have done it,' Kate wailed desperately. 'Birdie, this gets worse and worse!'

'Yes, I must admit it's not very nice. Jill's position's tricky, though not as tricky as Anna's. But look, Laney, one bit of good news for you—the cops seem to have dropped Nick as a serious suspect.'

'What!'

'Yeah. They've finally decided that the person at the van probably *wasn't* Damien—because of the parka hood business—but was probably his murderer. So Nick's times, supported by Theresa, don't fit in.'

'Oh, heavens, that's terrific, Birdie. Because I was thinking if he'd heard Jill and Damien too, or seen her coming out of the garage . . . If he'd come home earlier, say . . .'

'Yeah, well . . . it's still a possibility as far as I can see, whatever Toby's decided. I'll have to think about it.'

'Birdie, whose side are you on?'

Birdie went very still. 'I told you, Laney, before. I'm not on anyone's side. Quite a few people seem to have had good reasons for disposing of Damien now. It's not as simple as it was. But Laney, you can't expect me to prove it was Betsy, or Rodney, or someone you don't happen to care about particularly, and then get dark if I can't. OK?'

'Yes, of course. Of course. Birdie. I'm not stupid.' Kate paused. 'That's what Betsy said.'

'What?'

'I'm not stupid—when she was talking about being thought of as an overprotective mother. She obviously knows exactly what people think. I suppose I really did think she was pretty stupid. But she's not, is she?'

'No. She's just got tunnel vision. What *she* wants is right.'

'Well, she's done it this time, with Anna *and* Wilf, apparently. The worst thing was Wilf saying she was glad about it. I mean, she must've been, but imagine letting the mask slip and *showing* it.'

'Yes. I suppose she's got used to Wilf just being an extension of herself. She was looking very shocked when he started raving about Anna being crushed and violated and all that.'

'I don't blame her. He was just about demented . . . I wonder . . .'

'What?' said Birdie, looking slightly amused.

'Nothing.'

'Come on, you think you've found another ram in the thicket, don't you?'

'I don't know what you mean,' said Kate with dignity.

'Wilf'd fill the bill, wouldn't he? Now you've had to drop Betsy because her motive's up the spout? Wilf's the perfect answer. The man who wasn't there, coming out of the woodwork to do the murder for the love of his daughter, and then settling slowly back.'

'Birdie, there's no need to laugh at me. I didn't say a thing. But it's not inconceivable, is it?'

' 'Course not! Nothing's inconceivable at this point. Look, I want to go and have a word with Alice, so will you . . . ?'

'Heavens. I forgot about Alice. Where is she?'

'Round in her room, I think. She came up from the orchard to find out what was going on and nicked round the side of the house when Wilf started to yell. Wanted to keep right out of the way, I'd say. Mind you, she was grinning—loves an argument, the old devil.'

'Yeah, she does. She is an old devil, too.'

'Anyway, will you go inside and see what's up there

while I go round to Alice? I can't be in both places at once.'

'No. Well, I'll do my poor best to substitute. I'll try hard not to miss anything,' said Kate sarcastically.

'Good-oh,' said Birdie gravely. 'Thanks. See you later then.' She set off across the grass, whistling.

No sooner had Kate entered the house than she was pounced on by Betsy.

'Katie, I'm glad . . . look, come into the kitchen where we can talk.'

'How's Wilf?'

'Oh, he's all right. He's overdone it, that's all. He shouldn't get so worked up.' Betsy rested her hand on the kitchen table and began smoothing the checked tea-towel that lay there. The clock in the living room struck the hour. Kate waited. Finally the words came.

'Katie, I can't tell you how sorry I am that you've all walked in on such a shambles.'

'Betsy, heavens, don't apologise. It's . . .' Oh, thought Kate, this is bizarre. I nearly said 'it's not your fault,' and only half an hour ago I was sure as I could be that it *was* her fault, in the worst possible way. Now I'm busy suspecting her husband! She became aware of Betsy staring at her. 'It's just one of those things,' she finished lamely, forcing herself to look up.

Betsy shook her head. Her mouth drooped. 'I'm not just talking about . . . the terrible thing that's happened . . . the death. It's everything.' She sighed. 'The last six months have been so . . . difficult, Kate. We used to be such a happy family, and now, I don't know, everything seems to be falling to pieces. I was really hoping this holiday would help us all to get straightened out again. It's always been such a happy time, hasn't it? I thought with you and Jeremy and Nick here, doing what we've always done, since the children were little, we could go back to the way

things used to be. But you can't go back, can you?
You just can't.'

'No, I suppose not,' said Kate, feeling sympathy rise
in her and fighting it down. She desperately wished
for someone to come in and break Betsy's mood, but
the house was quiet. The tap dripped into the sink
and a fly buzzed at the window. Betsy looked her
straight in the eye.

'Kate, when Zoe grows up you might understand
me a bit better. When she's a young woman, and she's
got boyfriends, and thinking about getting married,
maybe you'll remember me at this moment and think
"poor old Betsy Tender. She wasn't so crazy after all."
This is hell!'

'Betsy! I . . .'

Betsy put her hand on Kate's arm. 'It's all right,
Katie. Don't say anything. I know how you feel. It's
just that you have to go through it to know. Like
childbirth. No one but a mother knows. You put so
much into your children. You see them growing up
beautiful and healthy and strong. And then . . . then
they fall in love, which is nature's way, and a wonderful thing. Heavens, do you think I didn't want
that? Don't you think I long for grandchildren . . .
Oh dear, and to see Anna and Chris and Roddy settled and happy? Of course I do. But Kate, to see your
children choose—and just have to stand by and watch
them choose—people who you know aren't going to
make them happy . . . it's the hardest thing, Kate.
You can't imagine.'

'I can, Betsy. I can, really. But . . .'

'Yes, I know, I know.' Betsy looked at her, watery-
eyed. 'I've done it badly. I made a mess of it. But
Kate, Damien, he is . . . was . . . dreadful. Honestly,
wasn't he? You should have heard him, Kate, talking
to that girl. I know, I know, I shouldn't have listened.
I shouldn't have followed Anna. She's right to be angry. But I admit it, what Wilf said. It sounds dreadful, but I was glad Anna heard. Saw him in his true

colours at last. Oh God . . .' She buried her face in her hands. 'If I'd known what was going to happen I'd have done anything in my power to stop it. But after I thought, well, God moves in His own way. Everything is meant. This will free Anna to go on and live a new life once and for all. And suddenly I felt quite peaceful in myself. Everything would have worked out. I know it would. And then, in the morning . . . and now . . . oh, it's so unfair!' Tears brimmed over in her eyes and she pulled a tissue from the sleeve of her jumper and dabbed at them. She fought for control over her trembling lips.

'Betsy, sit down. I'll make you a cup of tea,' said Kate in a panic. 'Don't cry. Please don't. Sit down.'

She guided Betsy to one of the kitchen chairs, noting with pity the frailty of the shoulders under the smart pullover. She grabbed the kettle and went over to the sink, glad of the opportunity to turn away, and at the same time guilty at the slight feeling of repulsion the sniffling figure engendered in her. She put the filled kettle on the stove and knelt down beside Betsy, awkwardly patting her knee.

'It's OK, Betsy, Anna'll get over it.'

'I hope so. Surely she will, oh surely.' Betsy blinked. 'Oh dear, how awful to break down like this. I can't imagine . . .' her eyes brimmed again, and Kate turned quickly to the cupboard.

'I'll make teabags,' she said. 'Quicker.'

'Now there's all this business with Jill to contend with,' said Betsy, drearily sniffing. 'I was so hoping it wouldn't ever come out—for Nick's sake really, because I've never been all that fond of Jill, to be honest. I've always found her rather . . . hard, you know what I mean?'

'No, not really, Betsy. Jill's a good friend of mine.'

'Oh of course she is. Of course. You're a loyal friend. A good loyal friend.' Kate sat down and carefully pushed a mug of tea over to Betsy's side. Betsy took her hand and gripped it. 'You don't know, Kate, how many times I've wished that Christopher could have found a girl like you. A good, honest, intelligent girl who'd be a real companion to him.'

'Oh . . . look . . .'

'But he met Sue and she got her hooks into him and that was that. She saw he'd be a step up for her, no doubt about that! Oh, dear, oh dear, and poor Christopher had no idea. No idea . . .'

Kate, ridiculously holding hands with Betsy over the kitchen table, buried her face in her mug of tea and tried to turn off. This was making her quite sick in the stomach. Betsy's voice went on and on, a low, feverish mutter.

'. . . most peculiar. I've been quite frightened. The other night, for example. That screaming. After all the business with Anna, I just couldn't drop off and Wilf couldn't either. We decided to take a pill. So I got up to fill our water glasses. Well, I came into the kitchen and filled the glasses, and just then the clock struck one and what should I see through the open door but Sue creeping through the living room in the pitch black.

'I hadn't bothered to turn the light on so she didn't see me and to tell you the truth, Katie, I didn't want her to. She's been so strange and so nervy, I really felt I couldn't face her. So I just stood there by the sink and I heard her let herself out the back door. So I thought, well, I'll just pop quickly back to the bedroom while she's in the toilet, and I won't have to meet her. So I did that, and got back into bed and gave Wilf his pill and everything and then I lay there and after a while I thought, gee, she's been out there a long time. The clock struck the quarter hour, you know, and I thought, I wonder what she's doing? I was actually very worried, Kate. She's very unstable. I thought she could have wandered off, or fainted, or anything. Well, to tell you the truth, she seemed rather obsessed with that wretched Damien and I thought she might even have gone over to the garage . . .'

'But why would she have done that?' asked Kate, helplessly drawn in despite herself.

'Oh, I don't know . . .' Betsy seemed flustered. 'You know how your imagination works at night. I just thought . . . well, she'd been away for over fifteen minutes, and it doesn't take that long to . . .' she blushed. 'Well, does it? To pay a visit, you know . . . So I thought, well, I'd better go and see if I could see her.' Her blush deepened, and she avoided Kate's eyes. 'Busybody Betsy again, I suppose, but, I mean, *anything* could have happened, Kate, couldn't it? I got up again and went down the hall, and I was just opening the door into the lounge when all of a sudden the knob was just *ripped* out of my hand and there was Sue standing there. Goodness knows it gave me a fright. You can imagine! But she, she *screamed*. She looked at me as if I was a *ghost*, backing away and flapping her hands and *screaming*. Oh, it was awful. She wouldn't stop!' Betsy's face was filled with a kind of horror and her voice dropped. 'I've been wondering whether she's quite, you know, *all right*, Kate. What do you think? You've talked to her, haven't you?'

'Yes,' said Kate slowly, images of Sonsy's drawn, heart-shaped little face flashing into her mind. 'I think she's a bit overwrought, certainly. A bit jumpy. But I think Chris's the best person to . . .'

'Oh, yes, yes, I know. I'll keep out of it, don't you worry. I've learnt my lesson . . .' Betsy wiped her eyes determinedly, sniffed, and put the tissue away. 'Well, this isn't the way to behave, is it?' she said with a smile. 'I'd better go and get some war paint on. I must look awful.' She carried her mug to the sink and stared for a moment out the window.

'This house has been a second home for me, since I was a little girl, you know,' she said quietly. 'The old log under the tree—Dad put that there for me when I was Zoe's age. The tree hung down even more then, and it was a real cubby. I'd play there with my dolls for hours, and the log would be a table or a stage or a seat or a bed, or anything I liked. And then later on, before I married Wilf, and after, too, I'd go and sit there when we came up, and think and plan. It always made me feel safe and peaceful, that place. And now it's all spoiled.' She turned and looked at Kate, expressionless. 'I keep thinking—it's silly, you'll think—that now it's gone, there's really nowhere for me to go now, to feel quite safe. It's given me a funny feeling.' She shivered. 'Silly,' she said. 'Goose walking over my grave.'

She left the room, and Kate sat looking after her, for quite a long time.

17

Shadows

🔥

In the orchard it was green and still. Down in one corner Kate could see Rodney, stolidly, silently, picking apples. He saw her watching but made no sign. Just looked, and turned back to work. The sweet smell of rotting apples mixed with damp grass and earth. A thin blanket of cloud had faded the gloss of the sunshine, so that now the apples and the green leaves of the trees no longer sparkled, but hung secretly glowing.

Kate wandered, bemused and incapable of a single straight thought. Somehow she'd even lost the desire to get away from this place. Or maybe, in her strange state, it was just that she'd lost the hope that they ever would. She would have to talk to Jeremy about it. Because Zoe had to be thought of. This atmosphere was bad for her. It would be nightmares, next. But Jeremy seemed far away, caught up for the moment in Nick's worries and Nick's world. He'd drawn back from her at the moment Anna had accused Jill. She'd felt it, seen it in his face. *Women!* The age-old rage of men against unfaithful women, against the *potential* unfaithfulness of women, and the drawing back into male solidarity.

Weak tears formed in Kate's eyes. I'm going soft in

the head, she thought, rubbing them away. A couple more days of this and I'll be great company for Alice. We all will be. We'll be in some home doing basket-weaving and lining up for our pills every evening. She jumped violently as a hand touched her shoulder.

"It's only me,' said Jill. 'Didn't you hear me?' Her grip tightened slightly and then relaxed, and her arm dropped.

'No. I was thinking. Jill, what happened? What did Toby say?'

'Oh, we just went through the whole thing again. He invited me to come clean about Damien and I said there was nothing to tell, and so it went. He's grilling Anna now. Betsy's having kittens in the living room. She's finally woken up to the fact that Anna's position's a bit dangerous. Anyway, look, I've come to say goodbye. I . . .'

'What?'

'Well obviously I can't stay here after what's happened. It'd be ludicrous. I told Toby I'd hang around for the moment but I needed somewhere else to stay, so he suggested that boarding house place just up near the shops. You know, the mock Tudor with the big pine trees at the gate? So I rang them and it's OK. I'm off now. Come and see me there, eh? It'll be great. I've always wanted to stay at a place called The Pines.'

'Jill, what about Nick, he's . . .'

'Noticeable by his absence.'

'He's gone with Jeremy for a drink.'

'Ah, beer and misogyny. How nice. Well, tell him where I've gone, will you? If he asks?' Just for a moment the brazen, haughty look flickered and a vulnerable, much younger face came into focus. Then the lips tightened. 'You can ring me there, if there's any news. I've put the number on the noticeboard by the phone.' She looked around and shrugged her shoulders as if getting rid of a heavy coat.

'Come and see me off, eh?'

• • •

Kate stood on the grass outside the house and watched Jill out of sight. The tall, gaudy figure turned and waved once, then set off over the brow of the hill.

Nick's battered VW still sat grubbily by the kerb, nose to tail with Damien's van. Moved by a morbid curiosity she inwardly despised, Kate moved closer to the van. The police had been over it with a fine tooth comb, taken things out of the glove box, noted the other contents, then locked up the van and left it. It was still redolent of Damien's personality—gave her an unpleasant feeling just looking at it. Kate circled the van, noting the flattened tyres on the road side, the lambswool steering wheel cover, the foam rubber mattress that fitted into the back so neatly that it had obviously been cut carefully to size.

A few cartons, rugs and packages littered the back now. Not so many, though, that Damien couldn't have slept in the van if he'd really wanted to. Obviously he'd preferred to spend the night in a more accessible, less public spot, where an assignation would be easily accomplished. Assignation with Anna? Or with Jill?

Kate crouched and stared into the back of the van in fascination, as if somehow the answer to all this lay in that untidy and dreary interior. And slowly, as she squatted there, she became aware of a prickling in the back of her neck. She stood and turned, rather more quickly than she'd meant, and saw Sonsy standing staring at her from the front gate. She'd moved as silently as a mouse. Her little hands rested on the top bar of the gate and as Kate watched she moistened her top lip with a small pink tongue.

Kate restrained a jump and forced a smile. 'Hi,' she said. 'I didn't hear you. You gave me a fright!'

'Oh, yes? Sorry,' said Sonsy, blinking.

There was a short silence. For some reason the moment was intensely awkward. Feeling as though she'd been caught out in some unworthy action, Kate bit her tongue to stop herself from explaining and making things worse. With relief she saw Chris appear at the front door. He grinned at her and swung down the path, car keys jingling. He reached Sonsy and his leather jacket creaked as he put his arm round her.

'Kate, I've been looking for you. I've just been to see Theresa. I suggested to her that we might take her and Zoe and the baby to the park. Sonsy and I felt like getting out for a while. Is that OK with you? We thought we'd get fish and chips or something for lunch.'

'Oh, that'd be terrific, Chris. Zoe'd love that.'

'We'll be back before two,' said Sonsy carefully, 'so Theresa can feed the baby at home. She's a bit shy about it, I think, in public.'

The front door of the house opposite opened and Zoe appeared, hopping up and down with excitement. She clumped down the stairs, proudly swinging a bulging bag. Behind her Theresa emerged from the dark hallway, carrying the baby basket. She turned to pull the door shut and slowly descended, following the flitting figure of the little girl. Zoe ran to the road's edge, self-consciously looked both ways and walked quickly across. Kate went to meet her.

'We're going to the park to feed the ducks!'

'I know, darling. That's good, isn't it? I want you just to come quickly inside and get a coat, in case.'

'Aw, Mum!'

Theresa came up to them, her strong face slightly flushed. Today her heavy hair was looped loosely over her ears from a soft centre parting, and wound into a knot at the back of her head. She smiled gently and tentatively at Kate.

'I can't thank you enough, Theresa, for looking after Zoe so . . .' Kate began, and then saw Theresa's eyes flick away, and her lips part, and heard her take a quick breath. Turning, she saw Simon Toby standing at the open front door, looking at them with a rather curious expression. He smiled and lifted one

finger to them in a sort of greeting salute. He turned
back into the house, said a few words and stepped out
onto the path, hitching up his trousers and then but-
toning his coat. The dark young detective followed
him as usual, stuffing a notebook awkwardly into an
inside pocket, and Betsy, sharp-eyed and sharp-nosed,
brought up the rear.

'Ah, Mrs Sullivan, I was just coming over to see
you. You're on your way out?'

'Yes, we're going for a drive,' Theresa said quietly.
'Is there anything . . . ?'

'Ah, look—it was really only a double-check. I
wanted to ask you just to think again about . . .
ah . . .' he glanced at Zoe, who was staring at him
with passionate curiosity, 'the night in question, if you
see what I mean. And if you can remember any little
detail at all that hasn't already been brought up, I'd
be grateful if you could let us know—no matter how
unimportant it seems.'

Theresa's brow wrinkled. 'I'm sorry,' she said, 'but
I really think I've told you everything.'

'You'd be surprised,' he said genially, 'how little
things can get forgotten and then just pop back into
your head. How the person at the van was dressed,
exactly, for example, or how the road looked, or the
van, anything.' He beamed at her.

'Yes . . . yes, of course, Mr Toby,' Theresa murmured, and dropped her eyes. Following her glance
he looked into the baby basket where Nel lay, staring
at him with unwinking blue eyes, her fluffy head se-
curely encased in a red and white striped woollen
bonnet.

'How's the young lady?' he said, and smiled.

Nel smiled back.

'Look at that!' said Toby, really touched. 'I think
she remembers me. Eh, blossom?' He put a big, careful finger down and brushed the baby's cheek. Then,
recollecting himself, he straightened rather self-
consciously and pulled at his belt again.

'Well, we'll be off. Thank you, Mrs Sullivan, Mrs Tender.' He nodded to Betsy, who looked at him severely and made no reply.

They watched the two detectives make their way back to the police car, waving in a pally way to the sandy man still standing at his post by the garage.

'Well!' said Betsy, as the car doors slammed. 'He really is a most peculiar man.'

'No, I think he's sweet,' said Kate. 'That was sweet, with the baby, wasn't it, Theresa?'

Theresa nodded and smiled, but her eyes were watchful. Betsy opened her mouth to argue, but was forestalled.

'Ooh hoo!' Alice waved a grubby man's handkerchief from the front door. 'Theresa! Come and have a look at this.'

'Auntie Alice, they're just going,' called Betsy impatiently.

'Theresa! Won't take a minute. Come in.' Alice ignored her niece and beckoned wildly at Theresa. 'Come in!' She turned away from the doorway, and made off back into the house.

'This bloody expedition's doomed,' groaned Chris.

'It's the Ark. She's so proud of it. She wants to show it off. Look, Zoe's got to get her jacket anyway,' said Kate. 'Just pop in, Theresa, and out again.'

Theresa picked up the baby basket and moved quickly towards the house, her booted feet sinking into the soft grass, her dark red skirt whipping in the breeze. Zoe walked beside her, her hand on the basket, talking to Nel.

'I want a leak now, anyway,' said Chris. 'May as well all go in.'

'Christopher, don't use language like that, please. What you do in your own house is your business, but please don't . . .'

'OK, Mum, OK . . .'

They trailed back to the house. It was dark in the hall after the veiled brightness of the outside air. The house smelt enclosed, dusty and of old carpet. From the living room floated the sounds of Zoe exclaiming and twittering, Theresa murmuring softly and Alice's raucous, gratified laughter. They entered the room and found Anna and Wilf sitting staring impassively at the enthusiastic three clustered around the Noah's Ark, now standing in state on a low table by the French doors, the thin curtains drawn behind it. Alice's idea of dramatic effect, Kate thought. If they'd been red velvet curtains instead of faded cotton it might have been more effective. As it was the unusual dimness of the room was rather depressing.

Birdie stood against one wall, her eyes twinkling behind her thick glasses. Betsy brushed past her into the kitchen, her mouth set.

'There's two koalas, and two kangaroos, two elephants, two of everything. Look, Theresa!' Zoe's fingers were everywhere, stroking and pinching the faded wood.

'Oh, I wish I had my glasses, Alice. It's really beautiful. Oh, what a nuisance.' Theresa knelt by the table and, as eagerly as Zoe, picked up and handled the little figures. 'I'll have to come back and look at it properly. Oh look, Zoe. Look at this little hippo looking over his shoulder.'

'He's looking for his wife! Here she is coming—plomp, plomp, plomp!'

Chris looked at Kate resignedly. 'Should we drop the idea of this trip, d'you think?' he said.

'Oh no!' said Theresa, scrambling up. 'We're all packed and ready. Sorry—I'll be back tomorrow to have a proper look, Alice. With my glasses I'll be able to see the detail properly. When Zoe told me you'd found it I was so pleased, but I've waited this long, I can wait one more day!'

'You're looking all in, Theresa,' said Alice gruffly.

'Oh, I'm all right.'

'Feeding takes it out of you, doesn't it, Theresa?'

sighed Betsy. She was standing by the kitchen door with a glass of cloudy liquid in her hand.

'Oh . . . I don't . . .' Theresa smiled uncertainly.

'You're drinking plenty of fluids, aren't you? That's what keeps the milk up. Before every feed, you should have a drink.'

'Oh yes, I always drink a glass of milk before every . . .' Theresa was fidgeting by now, but Betsy nodded approvingly, impervious to the woman's obvious discomfort.

'Mind you,' she said, 'baby's three months now, isn't she? She should be sleeping through, naughty girl.'

'I know,' said Theresa ruefully. 'But she'll come to it, and I sleep in the afternoons to catch up, you know. On the back verandah. It's so warm and lovely there. I do fine.'

'If I were you,' said Anna, lifting her eyebrows, 'I'd just take a sleeping pill and not worry. She'd soon go back to sleep once she found you weren't going to oblige.'

'Anna! Theresa couldn't do that!' Betsy was greatly shocked. 'A nursing mother can't take sleeping pills. In fact, you shouldn't be taking them really, a young woman like you. None of us should. But a nursing mother—heavens! You won't do that, will you, Theresa? Now don't you dare!'

Theresa flushed, but managed a small smile. 'I've never taken anything like that,' she said. 'I haven't got anything stronger than aspirin in the house, so you don't have to worry.' She turned to Alice. 'Where did you find the Ark in the end, Alice?'

'Under the blooming house! It was Zoe's idea to look there and I only looked to please her, she was that keen to try everywhere. We both got the surprise of our lives when we actually found it though, didn't we, love? Piled up with a lot of other good stuff around the side there, behind the door, it was. Some people've got a hide. Worth fifty quid, probably, and stuck under there to rot.' Alice looked daggers at Betsy.

Betsy's eyes widened.

'Don't look all innocent at me, Bet! I know you. I'll thank you to leave my things in their places. No wonder I can't ever lay me hand on anything round here anymore, with all your blooming poking around and cleaning up. Time for that when I'm dead, my girl. Hear me?' Betsy was scarlet now, and everyone looked away.

'Auntie Alice, you're very unfair,' said Betsy, her voice high and trembling. 'I've come up here to see you and help you every month when I could easily have been looking after my own house, or even . . . even having a rest, just quietly, or doing something I'd like to do. You're very unfair, and very ungrateful. I'm sorry, but you are.' Her voice strengthened. 'Why on earth would I put that thing under the house? You've put it there yourself and forgotten about it. You're always doing that. It's no good blaming me. You're getting terribly forgetful. You've burnt out two kettles in the last six months, you know you have. I lie awake thinking about it! You'll burn the house down one day. Why don't you admit it, and stop blaming everyone but yourself for everything that happens? It's naughty of you, very naughty.' She ran her hand over her forehead.

'Steady on, Mum.' Chris walked over to her and gave her a pat. 'Look, what's this? Have you got a headache?'

Betsy nodded.

'Take the stuff then and go and lie down for a while, eh?'

She obediently swallowed the mixture and handed him the glass. 'I'll just sit for a minute, Christopher,' she said, to him alone. 'Thank you, son.' She squeezed his arm and looked into his eyes, then she walked to the table, and sank down on one of the chairs, holding two fingers to her forehead.

Why was it, thought Kate, that you could never feel as sorry for Betsy as she probably deserved?

'The police on to you again, Theresa?' Alice said. 'What for?'

Theresa lifted her hands helplessly. 'They just wanted me to think again about what I saw that night. You know, how the van looked, the person I thought was . . . was your friend Damien. All that sort of thing. But honestly, without my glasses I can't be relied on, especially when the light's bad. I really just see shapes. On the way out I barely looked at the van. Just saw a few things sticking up against the windows, you know, in the back part, and the shape of the steering wheel. I didn't see anyone in it, or anything like that. And when I looked out later—again, it was just shapes I saw, really. The white van, the hump of the steering wheel inside, and someone in a light blue or, anyway, light-coloured, coat, standing at the back, leaning over.'

'I don't know why they're still fussing about the van,' said Anna in a bored voice. 'They've been over it and over it. His wallet was still in the garage, full of cash as usual, because he liked to pay cash. People sold things more cheaply that way.'

Kate felt restless, and glanced worriedly at Zoe. Oh, to be far, far away from here.

Chris obviously felt the same restlessness.

'It's too dark in here,' he said.

He wandered over to the double doors and pulled back the curtains. Weak light streamed into the room and fell on Zoe's face as she kneeled before the Ark, to all appearances deeply absorbed in some game with two tiny sheep. Kate felt relieved. Almost certainly she was hearing nothing. Silhouetted against the glass panes the rainbow arched above Zoe's head, and the dove spread its wings joyously. The child's hair shone golden in the pale light.

Anna was still talking. '. . . and the keys were there, with the keys to the shop and everything, so there's really no question of robbery as a motive, Toby said. Everything seemed completely intact, right down to his bundle of candid snaps in the glove box. All his lovely ladies, all named and dated on the back, and all the negatives complete in his wallet.' She laughed rather unpleasantly, and put her hands behind her head.

'Even I hadn't realised my dear late husband spread his net so widely. I think Toby thought I'd be shocked into baring my heart and confessing all when he showed them to me this morning. He seemed rather shocked himself when I didn't turn a hair. Poor old boy.' She stretched her arms carelessly and yawned.

'My picture wasn't there. I suppose I should be flattered I wasn't regarded as one of the club. Toby would've been even more shocked if he'd seen that. It was rather frank. And of course the star turn was missing,' she added airily.

'What do you mean?' Kate snapped, dreading what was to come, but impatient beyond all endurance with innuendo.

'Well, Jill Mission, of course. He must have had a picture of her, too. And it wasn't there, in the collection Toby found in the glove box. It had completely disappeared. I can only think of one way that could have happened. What about you, Kate?'

'One way . . . look, Anna . . .' Kate felt the blood rush to her cheeks and ears. She bit her lips. This scene was not going to escalate in Zoe's presence. Or Theresa's, for that matter. Theresa was staring fixedly at Zoe and the Ark, as if they were of absorbing interest to her. Two bright spots of colour had appeared on each cheek, and the rest of her face was very pale, showing up the blue circles under her eyes.

'Cut it out, Anna!' said Chris violently. He turned to Theresa. 'Sorry about all this. Will we go?'

Theresa turned stiffly towards him. 'Oh, right.' She bent and picked up the baby basket.

Alice strode to her side and laid a horny hand on

her arm. 'Now, you'll come back and look at the Ark tomorrow, won't you love?'

'Yes, Alice.' Theresa looked gravely at the old woman for a moment, then bent and kissed the wrinkled cheek.

Alice's face registered in turn brief surprise, then pleasure, then a shadow of doubt. 'See you soon, then,' she said, dropping her arm.

'Oh, Auntie Alice—perhaps it would be nice if Theresa joined us for dinner tonight,' said Betsy, with the strained air of rising to an occasion, and offering the pipe of peace at some personal cost.

'Oh, no, really, I . . .' stammered Theresa, the dull flush rising in her cheeks.

'We'd love to have you, Theresa, really. It would be lovely, wouldn't it?' cried Betsy, looking around for support.

Everyone murmured polite agreement, but it was so obvious that Theresa was very far from considering it lovely that it was impossible for most people to even raise a smile.

'Right,' said Betsy cheerily. 'Wilf or Rodney or someone will come over and get you, say at six-thirty? We eat early, because of little Zoe. Baby will have been fed at six, so she'll sleep in her basket here for you, and you can be home by ten for the next feed, can't you, with no trouble. How about that?'

'Mrs Tender, really I . . .' Theresa glanced helplessly at Alice who looked back, expressionless. Suddenly she gave in. You could almost see her shoulders sag under the weight of Betsy's bright will, thought Kate. Poor woman. Long service to parents in poor health had obviously rendered her biddable, despite her appearance of strength.

'Yes, all right. Thank you,' Theresa said to Betsy, almost sullenly. 'That would be nice.'

'Good, fine. See you later, then.' Betsy smiled warmly.

Theresa weakly ducked her head in everyone else's

general direction and moved quickly out of the room, the baby basket bumping against her knee as she walked. Chris, Sonsy and the freshly jacketed Zoe followed her. The front door slammed. Everyone was silent, waiting for the inevitable. Betsy wasn't one to let them down.

'*What* a *peculiar* woman,' said Betsy.

18

Sleep and His Brother

Kate and Anna strode down the bush track, arguing. At least, Anna strode. Kate had almost to trot to keep up with her long-legged companion. Birdie trailed them, hands behind her back, head down, stumbling slightly on the roots and stones that littered the path. Kate's voice became impassioned.

'Now look, Anna, I'm not saying you're a liar. It's just that . . . think of my position. Jill's a friend, an old friend, and she says she wasn't there. I just want to know exactly what you heard. I owe it to her to get it straight in my own mind. See?'

Anna suddenly capitulated. 'OK, OK, I'll go through it once more,' she said sulkily. 'Only for God's sake let's sit down. I'm hot, and full of lunch. Why in heaven's name you insisted on going for a bloody bush walk at this time of the day I can't imagine.'

She flung herself down onto a flat rock beside the path. There was only room for one. Kate perched uncomfortably on a smaller, rather pointy, stone. Birdie sat on the ground, careless of any mud, leeches and ants, and drew up her knees so she could rest her chin on them. She stared at the other two in the blind, politely interested way that showed Kate she was in fact listening intently.

'All right,' said Anna, 'I went out to the garage. I got to the point where you saw my footprints, behind the old cassia bush, and I heard Damien laugh, so I stopped. It was a shock. I didn't particularly want to listen but the windows and door were open, and I could hear what he said without even trying to.' She moved restlessly.

'What did he say, exactly, Anna?'

'I'm telling you! Don't push me, Kate. He laughed and then he said, "Don't make problems, old girl. It's out of your hands. I know what I'm doing," or something like that. Then Jill said something I couldn't quite catch and he went all lovey-dovey and . . .'

'If you couldn't catch it, how do you know it was Jill?'

Anna turned on her furiously. 'Do you want to hear this or not, Kate?'

'Yes. OK . . . you tell it. Sorry.'

'He was in his sentimental mood. Kept calling her darling and honey and his beautiful red-headed girl. The relationship was perfectly clear. He said they were a great team, and that they had already produced one terrific thing together. God, I wish I'd burnt that bloody book before I left. That would've put a spoke in his wheel!

'Jill seemed to be having a few small twinges about me—nice of her, wasn't it?—because at one point he said that whatever he may have thought, with her around he and I were finished and she wasn't to worry about that. Actually, I think he'd just got a bit too hot to handle. I don't think she'd been banking on him getting all worked up and wanting to make a permanency of the whole thing.'

She laughed bitterly. 'I think she was trying to wriggle out, but he wasn't having any of that. Half by the he-man approach, and half this mucky sentimental stuff.' She dropped into a bad Humphrey Bogart impression. 'You mightn't have planned for this,

you mightn't even want it, but you've got it, old girl.
There's no turning back.'

She looked at them through slitted eyes, and took
on a melodramatically tender, crooning lisp. 'Now I've
found you, I'm not going to lose you, am I? No one
can take you away from me, ever again, sweetheart
. . Oh!' She rubbed angry tears from her eyes. 'Sickening!'

'I'm sorry, Anna. You'll think I'm dreadful, but
honestly, did he actually ever say Jill's name?'

Anna looked at her tight-lipped for a moment and
finally shook her head. 'My God, you take some convincing, don't you, Kate? Well, I don't actually think
he did, as a matter of fact. It was just so obvious to
me that it *was* Jill. But look, if you're so determined
to get her off the hook you'll do it one way or another,
won't you?' She slipped off her rock and made off
down the path, her head high.

'Let her go, Laney,' said Birdie thoughtfully. 'She's
said all she's going to say. Let's go back.' She lurched
to her feet and half-heartedly brushed clinging earth
and leaves and little sticks from the back of her jeans
before setting off up the track, the way they had come.

'It might not have been Jill at all, Birdie, from that
report,' said Kate hopefully, trudging along. 'It could
have been anyone.'

'Yes,' said Birdie seriously. 'It could have been anyone. As long as they had red hair and had worked on
a profitable project with Damien recently.'

Kate stole a look at her face. She didn't seem to be
being sarcastic, but one never really knew with Birdie.
She sighed, and Birdie looked up at her.

'Laney, d'you reckon Jill really cares about Nick?'

'Of course she does.'

'Say—don't blow up, Laney—say Jill did have some
sort of fling with Treloar. Do you think it's likely,
knowing her, that she'd want to leave Nick for him?'

'Birdie, the idea's ridiculous. It really is. Jill really
loves Nick. I know she comes on a bit strong, in a

way, but she deals with men at work all the time, like
I do. She's friendly and nice to them, and I suppose
it's conceivable that someone like Damien Treloar
might read too much into that, but I've thought about
it and I'm positive that . . .'

'What if you're wrong, Kate? What if Jill did fall
for Treloar's line of chat, even once, and found she
was in deep water with someone who wouldn't retire
gracefully? Someone who wasn't above a spot of moral
blackmail?'

'But look, Birdie, Jill wouldn't fall for that sort of
stuff. She's not some naive girl.'

'But if Damien threatened to talk to Nick . . . I'm
just wondering what a person like Jill does when
something she despises stands up on its back legs and
gets between her and something she really values.'

For the first time Kate felt a stirring of doubt. Nick's
feelings ran very deep. If he found out for sure that
Jill had been unfaithful to him it was quite on the
cards that whatever the practical results were, he'd
never feel the same about Jill again.

Jill herself, warm-hearted, confident, generous,
would, after a period of hurt, be able to forgive and
to a very large extent forget a disloyalty or even an
outright betrayal. But Jill knew the man she was dealing with too well to assume he'd react as she herself
might. Would she . . . could she possibly have
summed the whole thing up and decided to protect
her happiness in what might have seemed the only
way left to her?

Kate looked at Birdie sideways. Birdie's glasses
flashed in the sunlight that was once again piercing
the trees. She was a drab enough little figure, treading
the yellow clay of the track in her shabby canvas
shoes. A different species to the flushed, healthy, earnest bushwalkers one met sometimes on mountain
paths.

The road came into view, and beyond it the first of

Alice's trees, and the house. Kate barely held back a shiver.

'So?' Birdie stopped and looked at her. 'What do you reckon?'

'I suppose it's possible,' said Kate slowly. 'Possible Jill might have hit out at someone if they threatened her like that. If they threatened her and Nick. She might.'

'Yeah, I think so too.'

'D'you think the police do?'

'To tell the truth, I think it's a bit too subtle for Toby. I'd say Anna was the one he had his eye on. The woman scorned, and all that. He obviously showed her the charming Damien's photographs to get her reaction.'

'Apparently he was disappointed.'

'By her account, yes. Still . . .'

'Don't you believe anything *anyone* says?' cried Kate irritably. 'It makes it impossible to work anything out. We haven't got any "givens". I'm so confused.'

'Of course we've got givens. We've got masses of givens. Do you want to hear a few?' Birdie squinted into the apple trees looming ahead over the strip of bitumen with its deep unkerbed gutters.

They crossed the road and climbed the orchard fence.

'You love murder mysteries, Kate. Use your brains on this lot. OK . . . um . . .' Birdie checked the points off on her fingers.

'Anna's separated from Damien, because of his philandering, but still has a yen for him.

'Alice despised Damien and doesn't seem particularly fond of Anna.

'Damien is murdered by someone annointing the back of his neck with a contact poison. Everyone in the house knew that the poison existed and approximately where it was kept.

'Alice said she'd recently sprayed the trees, but has now admitted to me she hadn't.

'Damien was killed in a place that was regarded as special in the Tender family, where Betsy was wont to sit and muse of an evening, feeling the wind in her hair, as it were.

'Damien wore high-heeled leather boots.

'Damien kept photos of his mistresses in the glove box of his car. Jill's picture wasn't in the collection. Neither was Anna's.

'Damien's keys were found in his van.

'Jill has red hair.

'Damien had a gingery moustache.

'Damien didn't really have to bring the transparencies he gave to Jill as a matter of urgency. It's almost certain, therefore, that he wasn't "just passing on business", as it were, but came up to the mountains purposely and used the pictures as an excuse to get into the house. His van wasn't as crowded as he claimed, so he could have slept in it if he wanted to. He preferred the garage.'

'Yes, I was thinking that earlier,' began Kate, but Birdie went on ticking off her 'facts'.

'Betsy thought Damien was a hopeless character and wanted Anna to keep away from him.

'Betsy picks on Sonsy, her other adult child's spouse.

'Nick was jealous of Damien, who he thought was carrying on with Jill.

'Sonsy is in a highly nervous state, and jealous of Betsy's domination of Chris.

'Wilf is passionately devoted to his daughter.

'Alice loathed Damien and raged at Betsy for allowing him in the house. Alice said Damien preyed on women . . .'

Kate shook her head. 'This isn't helping,' she groaned. 'They're not in any logical order, and you're leaving out things like Damien flattening his own tyres.'

'That's not a fact. It's only a suspicion, with Sonsy's word to back it up. Anyway, now you see that we're in fact confronted by hundreds of "givens". Anything that we all saw or heard, or that we know to be the case . . . Ah, I see our sandy-haired friend's given up guarding the footprints. They must have done their stuff with them already. Look, Laney, I'm not going back to the house with you. I'm going for a drive. I want to see some people.'

'Good, OK,' said Kate vaguely. 'But look, Birdie, what about the things that trustworthy people saw, or worked out, by themselves. You can't leave those out.'

'Who's trustworthy?'

'Me, for instance,' said Kate with dignity.

Birdie looked at her mischievously. 'Oh, of course, Laney. I believe in you, thousands wouldn't, as Dad would say. Let's see, then. Clues vouched for by Kate Delaney—um—I know! Damien was given supper by Betsy, but didn't eat it. It could have been poisoned, but wasn't, because the next day we ate it for morning tea and no one croaked. How's that?'

'Birdie,' said Kate dangerously. 'I'm serious.'

'It's OK, I've got another one. There in fact *was* a huge, hairy caterpillar on the toilet wall on the night of the murder. A vitally important fact vouched for only by Ms Delaney, but accepted wholeheartedly by the jury because of Ms Delaney's undoubted integrity and . . .'

'Oh, drop dead!' said Kate and left Birdie cackling with laughter among the apple trees.

Kate reached the house. It was very still. A smell of damp and dust rose from the junk piled between the brick pillars that lifted the house clear of the earth. She trudged up the stairs and opened the door.

'Hi, Mum!'

Zoe was again kneeling before the Ark. She still had her jacket on and had obviously flung herself down to play immediately she came in.

'Hello, my love. Did you have a good time? I didn't realise it was so late. Where is everyone?'

'Theresa took Nel home to feed her. I think she was a bit cross. She wasn't really, you know, really *nice* like she was yesterday. I think she was bored, at the park. I don't know why. Nel was as good as gold. And I was.'

Kate sighed. Was nothing simple anymore? Not a trip to the park? Not anything?

'Sonsy's gone to have a sleep. She said she couldn't keep her eyes open. Auntie Alice is having a sleep, too, and so is Anna. Everyone's having a sleep except Auntie Betsy and me. We've got lots of energy. Where's Dad?'

'Out with Nick. I wish he'd get home.'

'Well, where's Jill? I want to show her . . .'

'Hello, Katie. Back again? You look tired.' Betsy's black-capped head peeped out from the kitchen doorway.

'I am tired, Betsy. You must be, too.'

Betsy sighed. 'No rest for the wicked, they say. I thought if I could get my casserole on now, there'd be no rush tonight. Theresa's a bit difficult to make conversation with, isn't she? I'd rather not be doing too much cooking while she's here. I'll get an early night tonight. Why don't you take the chance and have a rest now, Katie? Before the others get home.'

Wilf wandered into the room from the hall and looked around vacantly.

'I'm restless,' he complained fretfully. 'I think I'll go for a walk.'

'Oh, don't do that, Wilfie,' said Betsy solicitously. She smiled at him encouragingly. 'Look, if you feel like stretching your legs, why don't you pop around the side and get a nice bunch of parsley for me? Near the old tank there.' She returned to her cooking, satisfied, as Wilf obediently shuffled to the door and went out.

Kate looked after him. He seemed much older than

he had a few days ago. Quite like an old man, in his cardigan and grey-socked feet pushed into smart leather slippers.

'I think I will have a sleep, Zoe,' she said quietly. 'Will you just stay here and play with the Noah's Ark?'

Betsy clattered in the kitchen. 'I'll keep an eye on her, Katie, don't worry,' she called. 'Christopher's gone to do the shopping for me, so I've got no reason to go out. I'll have my shower and do my hair when I've finished this, I think.'

The back door opened and Wilf returned, bearing a single stalk of yellowed parsley. He carried it into the kitchen.

'Oh, Wilf, that's not nearly enough!' Betsy's exasperated voice rose. There was a mumble. 'There must be more. There was a whole lot there the other day. Oh, for goodness sake. I suppose a snail or a dog or something's got to it. Now what'll I do? Where on earth will I get parsley? I couldn't stand going up to the shops just for that!'

Apologetic mumbles from Wilf. A little pause.

'Maybe Theresa would have some. Oh yes, she's bound to. Would you mind awfully popping over Wilfie?'

'She'll be asleep,' said Zoe. 'She said she always goes to sleep after feeding Nel in the afternoon.'

Wilf and Betsy appeared at the kitchen door, Wilf looking rather bemused, still clutching the rejected parsley stalk.

'It's only two-thirty now,' said Betsy, bustling him to the door. 'Get on quickly and maybe you'll catch her before she settles down, Wilf. Go round the back. Don't ring at the front and wake the baby, whatever you do.'

'I'll go, Betsy,' said Kate.

'No, no, Katie, I'm right as rain,' said Wilf, already on his way. 'You stay there and keep warm.' He stepped outside. 'You know that boy's picking apples again, Bet?'

'Yes, I know,' said Betsy softly. 'Rodney's a good boy, isn't he Wilf? The image of my dad. Just getting on with the job. He'll be a man before we know it, won't he?' She turned away, her eyes brimming.

Wilf's reply was lost as the door slammed behind him.

Betsy pulled a tissue from the sleeve of her pullover and dabbed at her eyes. She sniffed and faced Kate and the curious Zoe with a wobbly little smile.

'I'm an old donkey, aren't I, Zoe?' she said.

Zoe looked at Kate for a prompt and, getting none, smiled uncertainly back.

'We're all a bit overwrought,' said Betsy. 'I'm glad Anna and Sue are having a lie-down. And Auntie Alice too.' She sighed. 'My big boys are still going, though. They're real standbys. I'm proud of them both. Jeremy and Nick are at the hotel, I gather, Kate.'

Kate nodded.

'Ah, well. Nick has been through a lot. You can't blame them. Men have their own ways of coping.' She paused. 'Um, your little friend, Verity, she didn't come in with you.'

'No . . .' said Kate slowly. 'She's gone for a drive. She said she'd be back for afternoon tea. I'll be up by then.'

'Oh good, then . . . I mean. I don't mean . . . it's not that I'm not *comfortable* with her, Kate, but I'm not up to conversation just at the moment.'

'Betsy, I quite understand, really. I'll look after Birdie.'

Betsy smiled wanly. 'I'm sorry, Kate. I'm not myself, today. I've got the strangest feeling. A nasty prickling feeling. As if someone's not wishing me well. I look round, and there's no one there. Well, you know, no one but us.' She gave a self-conscious little laugh. 'Going bonkers, as Rodney would say.'

Not so mad, I'd say, thought Kate guiltily. I don't

think there's anyone here but Rodney and Chris who haven't wished you ill sometime in the past few days.

'I was feeling pretty bonkers myself today,' she said aloud. 'It's been an awful couple of days, Betsy. It's no wonder.'

'It hasn't been all awful,' Zoe piped up from her station by the Ark. 'The fairies found the Ark for me.'

'The fairies did?' Kate smiled. 'I thought you and Auntie Alice found it.'

'Oh, yes, we *found* it, and brought it in. But the fairies put it there.' She went back to putting a small red hat on Mrs Noah.

'Of course they must have, darling,' said Betsy playfully. 'I hope they won't take it back again. Fairies are tricky.' She winked at Kate over Zoe's head.

Zoe looked at Kate in alarm and clapped a hand over her mouth.

'I wouldn't worry, sweet,' said Kate, irritated beyond measure by Betsy's automatic, coy needling at anyone who seemed unaffectedly happy. 'Just enjoy your game. I'm going off now. See you later. You can come and wake me at four and I'll make some afternoon tea. OK?'

'OK, Mum.'

Wilf's slippers flapped on the stairs and he pushed through the door looking more than ever like an aged mopoke. But his cheeks were slightly flushed, and he carried a healthy bouquet of parsley, which he held out proudly to Betsy.

'How's that?' he said. 'She had plenty.'

Betsy stared at him disapprovingly. 'Oh, Wilf, that's far too much. You must have picked her plants bare. What on earth am I going to do with all that? Was Theresa asleep? I hope you didn't wake her?'

Wilf's shoulders sagged a little, and he dropped his arm to his side. 'Oh, no,' he mumbled. 'She was just lying down, on the back verandah couch. She was sleepy, but not asleep, you know. She certainly rushed me, though. Wasn't going to ask me in or anything.

Said I was to pick what I liked, and yawned in my
face. I mean, she covered her mouth and everything, but it was a bit rude, I thought. So I got a
good lot. I thought I may as well. I thought you'd be
pleased.' His voice dropped. 'You bustled me and then
she bustled me, and now I'm breathless, really. I think
I'll just go in and lie down, if you don't mind, Bet.'
He hung his head.

'Oh, Wilfie, I'm sorry!' Betsy was now all tender
concern. 'Come, on, old boy. I'll take you in. I
shouldn't have let you go. Here . . .' She took the
hard-won parsley from him and cast it on the table.
Then she took his arm and led him to the bedroom,
almost crooning. The games people play, thought
Kate, almost in wonder.

It was dim and stuffy in the Chinese room. The feather
mattress billowed up on either side of Kate's body,
enveloping her in warmth. Kate lay on the edge of
sleep, eyes closed. The noises of the house swam, muffled, outside the yellowed walls. The oven door opened
and closed with an impatient bang. Betsy labouring
on alone on dinner—a twinge of guilt, suppressed by
irritation. Really, Betsy didn't have to go to so much
trouble. And she hadn't *had* to invite Theresa for dinner. The hall door opened and steps creaked up the
corridor—oh, no, Zoe, not now . . . but the creaks
stopped and went back whence they'd come. Betsy
checking on Wilf, maybe, or picking up her dressing
gown and sponge bag. Yes. The shower was running
now. Betsy looked after herself all right. No three-
minute evening showers for her. Oh, to be back home
and out of this. Soon . . . tomorrow morning . . . Kate
slept . . .

The rain beat down. Forty days and forty nights, endless, endless rain. In the distance stood Mrs Noah in a

red hat, a short, plump figure in a long red coat with a scaly, bulging sack on her back, weighing her down. Kate walked towards her, paddling in the wet. She must ask her where Zoe was. Mrs Noah turned and stared at her. Not Mrs Noah—Sonsy. How could she have been mistaken? Somehow her eyes weren't properly open, that was the trouble. She couldn't get them to open wide. Everything was misty and out of focus. She struggled, but her lids were too heavy. Sonsy, strangely double-jointed, reached an arm over her shoulder, deep into the sack. She held out an apple, glowing and red. It wouldn't be polite not to take it. Kate bit deep into the scarlet skin. It was soft and bitter on her tongue. Then her eyes opened and she saw that the apple was black to the core, and in the centre a bloated leech wriggled. She spat and screamed, and Sonsy laughed. But now it wasn't Sonsy but Alice, Alice with no teeth, laughing like a witch and pointing, and somewhere Jeremy was calling her name.

'Kate! Kate! Wake up, darling. Kate!' He was leaning over her. She grasped his hand.

'I'm OK . . . oh, what a terrible dream. Oh it was horrible!' She sat up like a spring. 'What's the time? Where's Zoe?'

'Don't panic, don't panic. It's ten to four. Zoe's outside gorging on rock cakes and lemonade and making some elaborate thank you present for the fairies or something. Betsy's making tea. I came to get you, and just as I reached the bloody door you started screaming like a banshee. You gave me the fright of my life. What in God's name were you dreaming about?'

'Noah's Ark and apples with leeches in them and ghastly things. Oh!' she shuddered. 'I'll tell you later. I'd better go and help. I've been asleep for an hour. Jeremy, we've got to get out of here. Out of this house at least. I can't stand this.'

'Yeah. I'll ring Toby. As soon as we've had some

tea, I'll ring.' He smiled and patted her shoulder.
'You've got feathers in your hair again, you know.'

'You smell of beer and garlic.'

'How appalling of me. Come on, get some tannin
into your system and you'll feel better.'

19

Breathing Out

\/\/\/

'Well, I think the least he could have done was ring up this afternoon, after carrying on with all that hooha this morning. Surely he knows we're on tenterhooks.' Betsy's voice, high and querulous, dominated the gathering round the afternoon tea table.

'I imagine he wants us that way, Mum,' said Chris, smiling tiredly. 'Waiting for the murderer among us to crack.'

'Christopher! Don't say things like that, please. Not even in a joke. He can't think that. It makes me sick to think about it.' Betsy certainly didn't look well, Kate thought. She was pale and tired, and now that her lipstick was mostly on her tea mug, her mouth looked defenceless and almost grey. Even her hair, still damp from the shower, drooped lankly on her head instead of springing into a cap of curls as it usually did after a wash. She kept glancing rather pathetically at Anna who appeared not to notice.

Sonsy looked ill and tired too, and Alice had grey circles under her eyes. This afternoon sleep business wasn't all it was cracked up to be, thought Kate. It didn't seem to have done anyone the slightest good.

Rodney munched rock cakes stolidly, cheeks bulging, eyes flicking around watchfully. He looked healthy enough, anyway. He seemed to have put on weight in the last few days. He looked beefier, heavier in the face, older, as if the strains and shocks under which they'd all rocked had steadied him. Nick and Jeremy looked slight beside him, and Chris slightly effete, puffy and jaded.

'All I can say,' said Anna in a bored voice, looking at no one, 'is that for God's sake let's not talk about it anymore. Particularly tonight when Theresa what's-her-name's here. She obviously thinks we're beyond the pale already. I thought she was going to faint this afternoon when we were talking about Damien's charming sexual habits. She's a large lady. I don't fancy having to haul someone twice my size home in the mist with bubs bawling in the rear. Do you, Rodney?'

'Anna!' Alice's voice was low and venomous. 'I'll thank you to watch your nasty little tongue. You're talking about a friend of mine, girl! She'd make two of you all right. Easy. But not the way you mean.'

There was a very unpleasant silence. Anna maintained her bored expression but she breathed quickly, and her cheeks burned. Betsy looked startled and almost frightened.

'Auntie Alice, I'm sure Anna didn't mean . . .' she began, and seemed to lose heart.

Wilf cleared his throat and sat forward. 'Ah . . . look, we're all a bit nervy, aren't we, eh?' he said anxiously. 'Let's all calm down and talk about something else. I wouldn't be surprised if Theresa didn't come over tonight anyway, Bet, after all.' He turned to his wife.

'Why on earth not?' snapped Betsy. 'She said she would. I've made . . .'

'I know.' Wilf nodded slowly. 'But I got the feeling when I was over there that she was going to try to give it a miss. She looked like death warmed up. She said she was terribly tired and didn't feel well, and when I said I hoped she'd be well enough to come

over and see us tonight she just sort of smiled and
muttered and shook her head. I meant to tell you, but
I came over a bit queer myself, if you remember, so
I forgot all about it. Funny woman . . . a nice
woman, Alice,' he added hurriedly, '. . . but a bit
unusual. You'd say that, wouldn't you?'

Alice grunted and hunched her shoulders.

'Well . . . that's extraordinary. I mean, I've gone
to trouble over the dinner and everything.'

'Well, no one asked you to, Bet, did they?' snapped
Alice.

Birdie muttered something and slipped from her
place, squeezing behind Sonsy's chair to get to the
back door. 'Back in a sec,' she said to no one in particular, and went out. They heard her pad down the
stairs.

Sonsy stood up and started to clear the table. Her
hands trembled slightly and Kate moved to help her.

Jeremy wandered into the kitchen with them, and
went to the phone.

'I think I'll see if I can get onto Toby, Kate,' he
said. 'Where's the number?'

'Card on the wall there. Near the hook with the key
on it.'

'OK.'

Kate left Sonsy disposing of crumbs, pushed open
the bathroom door and slipped inside. Crossing
quickly to the window she looked out on green grass,
dark shrubs, the garage looming up, Zoe sitting in
luxury on a crocheted rug, surrounded by scraps of
coloured paper, lemonade and cakes by her side. No
sign of Birdie at all. What was she up to? Kate sighed.
The bathroom smelt damp and stale, like old linoleum
and wet dust, with drifts of flyspray and metho from
the storeroom adjoining. Bathrooms and kitchens were
always where you came down to earth in old houses.
Faded charm was fashionable, but mildew and smelly
drains were quite another thing.

She craned her neck to see down towards the orchard and up towards the road. Nothing. Nothing but Zoe, absorbed in her work. She heard Jeremy put the phone down. 'Engaged,' he said to Sonsy. Something niggled at the back of her mind. What was it? Something that didn't fit in. She wandered back to the kitchen, deep in thought. Jeremy was just about to re-dial.

'Jeremy,' she began, and then, weirdly, there was a muffled echo from the front of the house—'Jeremy, Jeremy!'—and a wild banging at the front door. The doorbell shrilled.

'God! Who's that?'

Jeremy banged down the phone and dashed for the hallway. Kate followed.

Rodney had got to the door first and was staring bewildered as Birdie strode down the hall, her face pale.

'Jeremy! Quick! Theresa . . . there's something wrong. She's on the back verandah. She won't wake up. The door's locked. We'll have to break in. Kate, ring an ambulance.'

'Birdie . . . but why? Are you sure? What if . . .'

'Do it, Laney! Please! I'm certain.'

Kate turned to the kitchen, to the ring of shocked faces in the living room, and Sonsy, eyes dilated, standing with wet hands still in the sink.

Alice supported herself on her chair. Her cheeks were bleached.

'No need to break in,' she said gruffly. 'The key's hanging on a hook by the phone. The side door key. Ah . . .' she shook her head. 'Ah . . . Theresa . . .'

Betsy went to her, and for once wasn't turned away. The old woman sank back into her chair, and her niece kneeled beside her, patting her arm.

'Sonsy!' Kate grabbed the key and ran to the girl. 'Quick! If she's sick or had a heart attack or something you'll know what to do, won't you?'

Sonsy stared at her dully. 'Yes, yes . . . but . . .'

'Well go! Here.' Kate wiped Sonsy's hands as if she

were a child, and gave her the key. 'Go. I'll ring. I'll
get an ambulance. Oh, God, the baby . . .'

Sonsy's brow wrinkled as if she was going to cry.
She spun round. 'Ring now,' she said, and fled from
the room. Chris, Jeremy and Birdie closed around her
like a bodyguard, and within seconds they were gone.

Kate turned to the phone.

'Kate, why don't you wait until we know if Theresa's really in trouble,' Anna said coolly. 'It'd be terrible if this was all just a false alarm. I mean, imagine
how embarrassing it would be.'

Kate hesitated. That thought had already crossed
her mind. Anna went on persuasively, 'Birdie couldn't
be that sure it's something serious, could she? I don't
know why she's panicking. Just because Theresa
couldn't hear her knock it doesn't mean she's dying,
for heaven's sake. Just wait a few minutes.'

Kate made her decision. 'Birdie doesn't panic easily.
I think I'd better ring,' she said, and dialled emer-
gency.

She had barely put the phone down when Rodney's
feet thudded back down the hall. His red, sweaty face
confronted her at the kitchen door.

'Kate,' he stammered. 'Jeremy says to come. For the
baby. And he says, have you rung?'

'Yes. They're coming. The baby? What's happened?'

'It was gas. The place was full of gas. The heater
was on full, but it wasn't lit. She's . . . we had to
carry her out. We nearly choked, no air . . .' He swallowed and shook his head, and the whites of his eyes
showed. 'She's a goner, I think. Sonsy says she's really
bad. She's doing mouth to mouth on her, trying to
bring her round.'

'How terrible,' said Anna. 'Why would she do such
a thing?'

'I'm going over there,' said Alice, struggling from
her chair and shaking off Betsy's restraining hand. She
walked stiffly towards the door, brushing past Anna

without a word. Nick came quietly up beside her and took her arm. They moved on down the hall together.

Kate put her hand on Rodney's shoulder. 'The baby?' she said urgently.

'It's asleep. Sonsy says it's just asleep. But Jeremy said you should come and look after it, and . . .'

'Of course, I'll come now. Betsy?'

'I'll watch Zoe, dear. Don't worry.' Betsy spoke through dry lips.

'Jeremy said could you ring the police, Mum,' said Rodney.

'I've done it already, Rodney,' said Kate from the door. 'I rang them after the ambulance. Mr Toby's on his way.' She ducked round Anna in her turn, and made for the front door.

Jeremy paced Theresa's front garden, a swaddled bundle in the crook of his arm.

'Fast asleep,' he said, handing it over to Kate. 'We took her out straight away and Sonsy thinks she's OK. The front of the house was practically clear. But she didn't have much time to check. Theresa just wasn't breathing when we got here, and she's busy with her.'

'Not *breathing*. You mean she's *dead*?'

'It looks as though Sonsy's keeping her going. But only just. She seems pretty bad to me.'

Kate looked down at the tiny features of the baby, brow wrinkled in concentrated sleep. 'This is like a nightmare, Jeremy. Why would Theresa do this? Could it have been an accident?'

Jeremy shook his head. 'The gas was full on, and there was a rug up against the hall door, to block up the crack. The windows in that part of the house are tight as drums, too. She'd have been dead by now if Birdie hadn't dropped in when she did.'

In the distance they heard a siren, coming closer.

•   •   •

Strapped to a stretcher, oxygen mask obscuring her face, Theresa was carried away. Not alone, though. At the last minute Sonsy had taken the baby from Kate. 'We'll go with her,' she said crisply, to the ambulance man. 'The baby should be checked over . . . and she'll need it if . . . when . . . she recovers consciousness.' Pale and determined she'd climbed into the back of the ambulance with her burden. She nodded to them as the doors banged shut. The ambulance shot away silently. They watched it out of sight and heard the siren start at the top of the hill.

Kate drew a deep breath. 'Jeremy, I'll go into the house and get some of Nel's clothes and some things for Theresa, to take over to the hospital.'

'OK . . . but Kate . . . you do realise that Theresa mightn't make it, don't you?' Jeremy put his hand on her arm.

'Oh, she's got to! Poor little Nel. No Mum, no Dad . . . well . . . no point in all that, is there. I'll get the things. Look, here come the police. I'll go in. You deal with Toby. He's not going to like this at all, you know.'

'In what way? What do you mean?'

'I think he was getting a bit keen on Theresa—and the baby.'

'In a personal way you mean? Oh, come on!'

'He *was*, Jeremy.' They turned to watch Toby get out of the car. He certainly looked shaken. His face was grave and he held himself stiffly as if braced against a blow. 'See!' Kate whispered, and fled to the house.

The front door stood open. The smell of gas was still fairly strong, even here. It must be worse out the back, thought Kate, and tiptoed down the hall. Why she was creeping like a burglar she couldn't say, but the sight of the open door leading into the kitchen drew her like a magnet. A gay rug lay on the floor in the doorway.

The side door was open, too. It was through that

door that the others had come, to meet the flood of
gas that had set them reeling, Jeremy said, and gasp-
ing for air.

Kate shook her head slightly and walked through
the tiny kitchen. At the doorway to the back room she
stopped, and stepped back. With a shock she realised
that the house wasn't empty as she'd thought.

Someone was in the back room. Alice. She was
standing by Theresa's work table, staring straight
ahead sightlessly, hands plunged deep in her skirt
pockets. As Kate watched she moved wearily, and
gave a low moan, deep in her throat.

'Alice!' Birdie stood by the French doors, shoulders
hunched. Alice made no move.

'Alice, there's still gas in here. It'll make you sick.'

'I'm all right,' the old woman muttered.

Birdie crossed the room to her. 'Alice, please, don't
play silly buggers. Come out. And give it to me.'

Alice raised her gaunt face and stared at Birdie
fiercely. 'Give you what?' she said.

'You know what. Toby's here. He'll have to see it.
He'll have to, Alice. There's other people to think
about. Nick, Jill, Anna . . . all of them.'

'What do I care about them!'

'Come on, Alice. Hand it over. You can't help Theresa now. It's all going to come out, whether she lives
or dies. It's not up to you anymore.'

The firm old lips trembled. Slowly Alice drew
something from her pocket and tipped it into Birdie's
hand. Then with great dignity she walked from the
room into the garden.

Kate shot from her hiding place and ran forward.
Birdie jumped violently. 'Laney, where did you spring
from?'

'What on earth's going on? What's that?'

Birdie walked to the table, pushed Theresa's sewing
out of the way and put two pieces of card down on
the smooth brown surface. She pushed them together.

'I saw this here when we came to get Theresa. I

thought Alice might try to make off with it, and in fact she did. It wouldn't really have mattered, I suppose, if she'd got away with it. I've got the story worked out and it'd be easy to check. Don't touch it, Kate. Just look.'

'A photograph.' Kate bent forward. 'Someone's torn it in half.'

Theresa's image, black hair loose on bare shoulders, smiled self-consciously at her, holding up a glass of wine. Behind her, artfully soft focus, was grey-green bush and a white van. The sky was very blue.

Kate stared. 'But . . .' she began.

Birdie turned the pieces of photograph over by their edges without a word. On the back someone had written, in fountain pen, 'Theresa—Blackheath', and a date.

'Just over a year ago,' said Kate wonderingly. 'Theresa . . . and Damien?'

'Yes,' said Birdie. 'And Nel's just three months old. All fits, doesn't it?' She sighed. 'Let's get out of this gas, Laney, I'm getting a headache.'

Jill and Nick, Kate and Jeremy, Chris and Birdie sat together in the living room. It was late, and everyone else had gone to bed. The wind blew outside and the house creaked.

Jill shook her head. 'So it was Theresa all the time. The one person I never thought of. It never occurred to me she might have—known—Damien before.'

'It didn't occur to anyone, except Birdie, apparently,' said Nick, stretching out his legs and frowning at the rubbed toes of his boots.

'Alice knew, though,' said Kate. 'She knew from the beginning. She just wasn't going to say. She was—is— very fond of Theresa. She fought tooth and nail to stay at the hospital, but Toby made her come home.'

'Good thing,' said Chris. 'She was exhausted. Sonsy

too. She wanted to stay as well. God, what a day. I'm
glad it's over. I'm glad this whole thing's over.'

The others nodded. All evening an undercurrent of
relief had swept below all the other feelings, the feelings of pity, sadness and anger Theresa's pathetic little
story had engendered in them all.

'Now that it's just us, though,' said Jill, leaning forward in her chair. 'I mean, now that Alice and Betsy
and Sonsy and everyone are in bed, could someone fill
me in? I was in glorious solitude at The Pines. I only
know the bare bones. By the time I got here everyone
was keeping quiet, because of Zoe, and Alice, of
course.'

'I don't know it all myself,' said Kate. 'Birdie's the
one.'

'I'd like to know,' said Jeremy, turning to the
hunched, skinny little figure by the fire, 'why you suddenly jumped up from the afternoon tea table and
went across the road to Theresa's when you did.'

'When I did . . .' Birdie drawled. 'Yeah.' She
rubbed her forehead. 'Too late. Terrific timing.'

'Birdie, she's not dead. They've got hopes she'll pull
through, haven't they?' said Kate.

'Oh, yeah. There's a chance. A slim chance.' Birdie's face was pale. She took off her glasses and held
them in her lap. Her beautiful eyes stared at them
sightlessly. 'I was so stupid. I thought I had more time.
She was coming over here for dinner, for a start. But
while we were sitting there Wilf was talking about
how she'd said she mightn't be over after all. And
Anna—Anna was talking about how upset she'd been
during the afternoon, you know, just when we were
talking about Damien and his photographs . . .'

'The photographs!' exclaimed Kate. 'That's right!
We thought she was just embarrassed about the scene,
but of course, Anna was talking about the photographs Damien kept in the car. The photographs,
named and dated on the back, and the *negatives*.
Theresa had taken the print, but hadn't realised the

negatives were in Damien's wallet. It must have hit her like a thunderbolt. She must have known it was only a matter of time before the police realised that all the prints weren't there, and searched the negatives for the missing one. Oh, poor woman!'

'Yeah, well, don't forget she was willing to let one of us take the rap for killing Damien, Kate,' said Chris tartly. 'You can't help feeling sorry for her, but I don't think we ought to overdo it.'

'If one of us had actually been arrested I'm sure she'd have come forward,' said Kate. 'She was like that. She was, is, a *nice* woman.'

'But listen, I don't *understand*,' said Jill impatiently. 'Start at the beginning. Birdie? What put you on to the Theresa-Damien thing in the first place?'

Birdie put her glasses back on and looked into the fire.

'In fact,' she said, 'I was pretty slow. I noticed a few odd things but I couldn't see they meant anything. It wasn't until Anna told us what she'd actually heard Damien say in the garage that night that I put everything together. I realised that the woman in there with him was Theresa.'

'All that stuff about red-headed sweeties?' said Jill, not looking at Nick. 'Theresa's got black hair. You're not telling me it's dyed?'

'No, of course not,' snapped Birdie impatiently. 'See, Anna repeated the one-sided conversation she'd heard, or bits of it anyway, and it seemed to me there was something funny about it. Half the time Treloar was all lovey-dovey and crooning—*that* was where the beautiful red-headed girl stuff came in. The other half of the time he seemed to be bullying the person he was talking to. Calling her "old girl", rather contemptuous, really, and saying that she mightn't have planned for this, but she'd got it, things like that. I thought, well, maybe it's not as schizo as it sounds. Maybe he was talking to *two* people, instead of one. Then I remembered that Nel has red hair.'

'*Nel* does? The baby?' exploded Jill.

'Yes. We saw it that first night. Fluffy, gingery hair. Just the colour, actually, of Damien's moustache.' She looked at Kate. 'I did give you that hint, Laney.

'Anyway, I remembered a few things then. Anna saying Damien was always on at her to have a baby. Alice saying that when Damien was up here a year ago he was always nicking out at all hours, woman-ising, she implied. A year ago . . . and Nel's just three months old. Theresa was running a little antique shop a year ago. Damien used to call on little shops like that to buy things to sell in the city. He could easily have met her that way. She was middle-aged, intel-ligent and sensitive but not, I would think, terribly confident, and probably quite lonely. He turned on the charm, such as it was, and they had some sort of fling. He probably used his time in this house to see a lot more of her, revelling in doing it under his wife's nose.'

She looked at her hands. 'Well, so they have this affair. The photograph's taken, to add to Damien's collection, and the affair fizzles out, or he drops her, or she wakes up to herself, or whatever. So he disap-pears from the scene.

'Then Theresa discovers she's pregnant. What does she do? She sells her shop, and moves. Not right out of the mountains. She loves it here, and she can't face that. But over the other side of the ridge, where she buys a house and sets up as a widow with a handicraft shop—out, she thinks, of Damien's ken. She never wants to hear of or see him again. And the last thing she wants is for him to find out she's got his baby, the baby he always wanted. Nel's hers, and hers alone.'

'That's right. That's exactly how she'd feel,' mur-mured Kate.

'Yes. And then, one night, she decides to go over to the house opposite, to use the telephone. And there she meets the one person in the world she never wanted to see again—the father of her baby. Remember how she came in quite serene and relaxed? She wasn't wearing her glasses. She was quite happy at first. Then Betsy insisted on introducing her all round, and suddenly she was on tenterhooks. I thought about it afterwards. It wasn't because of all that nitwit stuff about Kate and her maiden name and illegitimate babies. It was because she'd just been introduced to Damien Treloar. Treloar, who suddenly started looking like the cat who'd swallowed the cream.'

'But he wouldn't know the baby was his,' said Jeremy. 'Not for sure.'

'Oh yes, he'd be pretty sure. He could count. He must have known that such a little one could only have been conceived round the time that he was on the scene. And if he had any doubts, Theresa's own behaviour that night would have put paid to them.

'I didn't see all that then, of course. In fact, the first inkling I had that something might be going on between Damien and Theresa came on the night *after* the murder, when Sonsy told us she'd seen Damien letting down his tyres. Sonsy said that she'd heard Damien and Theresa leave. She said she'd then counted to a hundred and then backwards to one again. That takes a few minutes to do. Then she got up and put on her dressing gown and went to look through the hole in the front windows. That all probably took another minute. And she saw Damien kneeling down by his car and Theresa walking across the grass strip on the opposite side of the road and into her gate. In other words, Theresa hadn't gone straight from this house to her own—a walk that takes about thirty seconds—but had hung around with the baby in the dark and cold and mist for some minutes, presumably talking to Damien. Unlikely she'd indulge in small talk with a stranger under those circumstances. And anyway, she claimed to Toby that she hadn't hesitated, but had gone straight home. I just filed it away for future reference at the time, but later . . . oh, it just joined up with a lot of little things, like Theresa say-

ing so firmly to Toby that Damien carried his keys on
his belt. Well, it was a funny thing to notice about a
man one had only met briefly and walked down a
hallway with. Things like that.'

'You're a bloody dangerous person to have around,
Birdwood,' said Jeremy sincerely. 'So you're betting
that Damien tackled Theresa once they were outside,
and got her to agree to a meeting later that night, in
Alice's garage. Then he let down his tyres, came in
with his story, and went out there and waited for her.'

'She kept the appointment sometime before midnight, obviously, because Anna came out then and
heard her and Damien talking. Nel would have been
there, sleeping in her sling, and what Anna heard was
Damien ooh-aahing at her and at the same time telling Theresa he was back on the scene for good. Asserting father's rights, I would think, not lover's.
Imagine how she felt. Talk about trapped.'

'He said they'd produced something wonderful together! Anna thought it was his *book* they were talking about,' cried Kate. 'And instead he was talking
like a soap opera about the baby.'

'Yes,' said Birdie, wrinkling her nose.

'And,' said Chris, 'I've just remembered that stuff
he was saying to Mum before he went out to the garage. About getting things straight and starting out
fresh. He must have planned to have a showdown in
the morning, and tell everyone about Nel being his.
He was a great one for the emotional scene. Theresa
must have really panicked, and decided there was only
one way out. To kill him. It would have been a cinch
for her. No one was watching *her* comings and goings.'

'Birdie,' Jeremy leaned forward. 'You said Alice
knew about Theresa and Damien from the beginning.
Did she tell you so?'

'Oh, no.' Birdie grinned tiredly at him. 'She
wouldn't have told anyone. It's just that some of *her*
reactions to things seemed strange. Like, for example,
she seemed to really loathe Damien. She kept calling

him a worm and saying he dragged decent women down, and such things. I mean, it was a bit excessive, if it was only because he'd given Anna a hard time. She *said* she was fond of Anna, but I couldn't see any evidence of it. She seemed to me to move between indifference and outright dislike as far as Anna was concerned. But she's obviously *very* attached to Theresa. I'd say Theresa confided in her about the baby's father early on—maybe described him, maybe even mentioned his name. Alice didn't let on she knew the man, and just thought he was well off the scene and nothing to worry about. But then, out of the blue he turns up, and by extraordinary bad luck Theresa comes to the house at the same time. Remember how angry Alice was after he and Theresa had gone?'

'It was all conjecture, of course, till I went back into the house after Theresa had been taken off to the hospital and found Alice hiding the torn photograph that'd been left on the work table.'

'I gather the photo *was* one of Damien's?' said Jeremy.

'Oh, yes. Exactly like the others, with his handwritten note on the back. Taken from the glove box of his van.'

Jeremy sighed. 'Well,' he said, looking at Kate, 'that's that, then.'

'Yes. And thank goodness!' said Jill. She stretched self-consciously and yawned. 'I'm really tired. It's a long walk back to The Pines, kids, so I think I'll go.'

'I'll drive you,' said Nick formally. He stood up, looking rumpled and somehow pathetic as he searched for his keys.

'No need, Nick. I'll be fine,' said Jill, attempting breeziness.

They stood together, hovering and uneasy.

'Stop fencing you two, and get along,' said Jeremy, grinning.

The tension was broken.

'Jeremy, you're trampling on our sensitivities,' complained Nick, with a wry smile.

'Ah well, mate, I've only got your interests at heart,' said Jeremy. He rounded on Kate. 'What are you grinning and nodding and mouthing at Jill like that for? You look like someone's old granny.'

'I can grin and nod at my friend if I like,' said Kate with spirit. 'All this bluff masculine stuff is all very well but surely you can't expect me to go in for it.'

'Come on, Nick, we'll leave this sordid domestic squabble,' said Jill. She pulled on her hat and coat. 'Bye, all. We'll see you in the morning.'

Nick grinned almost shyly and ducked his head. He grabbed his own parka and held the door open for Jill. She winked at Kate as she went out. The door slammed.

'Well, they're all right again anyway,' said Kate, pleased. 'She's forgiving him.'

'Forgiven, I'd say,' said Chris.

'Oh, no. But in the meantime she'll act as though she has, so it'll happen more quickly.'

'I've finished, sir.' Martin rubbed his eyes and pushed his chair back.

'Good-oh, Martin. Thanks. You can go now. Sorry I had to keep you back.'

Martin looked sideways at his superior. Toby looked grim and tried, and somehow older.

'Will you be leaving soon, sir?'

'I'll leave with you, boy, and you can lock up. I'm going back to the hospital for a while.'

Martin hesitated, then took the plunge.

'I'm sorry, sir.'

'Yes.'

20

Night Owls

§§§

Kate lay in a body-sized trough on her side of the
feather mattress, wide awake. Jeremy breathed quietly beside her. Zoe's camp stretcher creaked as she
turned over, sighed, and was silent. Tomorrow they
would go home. They'd help Betsy shop, have lunch
somewhere nice, and then go home. That was the
plan. The Tenders would go on with the picking, by
themselves. It was all over.

The house was quiet. The air was so heavy and still
it was almost hard to breathe. The thought of Theresa, drifting unconscious through the night hours, her
baby cared for by strangers, preyed on Kate's mind.
Pictures of the woman, tall and strong, her arm curv-
ing so protectively around that little ginger-haired
bundle strapped to her chest, kept rising in her mind.
She saw that big, light, blue and white room, the new
seagrass matting, the bedroom with its cot and single
bed, the little grey jacket half-covered with embroidered yellow blossom lying on the work table—all el-
ements in a fragile, quiet and happy life, now smashed
and broken. No, it was no use. She couldn't sleep.

She crawled down to the foot of the bed and quietly
slipped to the floor. Jeremy turned over and, sighing
with satisfaction, spread himself over the newly en-

larged space. He'd spread her dressing gown over the bed for extra warmth. Kate decided not to disturb it. She found her jacket on the floor, and silently let herself out of the room clutching it. She turned to pull the door shut and almost jumped out of her skin as she heard an apologetic sniff behind her.

Wilf, tousled in striped pyjamas, was standing at the entrance to the living room. He blinked at her.

'Oh, Wilf! You gave me a fright!' whispered Kate.

'Oh, sorry, Kate. I've just been, um, had to get up for a minute,' Wilf whispered in his turn. 'I'm a bit of a night owl, you know. Often lie awake for hours.' He hesitated and looked at her sideways. 'Ah . . . I'd appreciate it if you wouldn't mention this in front of Bet. Me being up, I mean. She'd be a bit crooked.'

'Oh, sure, Wilf,' Kate murmured, bemused.

'See, I didn't take my pill,' said Wilf, and covered his mouth with his fist like a naughty schoolboy. 'Don't like those pills, do you? Bet relies on them too much, in my opinion. Gets through them at a great rate, Bet does, though she wouldn't admit it, mind you.' He turned to open his bedroom door and paused for a final word.

'Your little friend, Biddy, is it? She's still up and about in there,' he gestured towards the living room. 'She's a bit of a night owl too, apparently. Well, goodnight.'

The bedroom door closed behind him. Kate waited for a moment, then shivered a little. After the heat of the feather bed the hall was chill. She slipped on her jacket and went into the living room.

Birdie was curled up in front of the fire, poking at a log she'd just added to the coals. She was still dressed. She looked up in surprise as the door opened. Her glasses flashed as a flame ran up the back of the log and caught.

The clock on the sideboard struck two.

'It's late,' said Kate. 'I can't sleep.'

'Neither can Wilf.'

'I know. I saw him in the hall.' Kate giggled. 'He swore me to secrecy. Terrified Betsy'll find out he palmed his pill and stayed up past his bedtime. What a family! Have you noticed Betsy's embroidery hasn't been seen since Sonsy showed hers off? It's been secreted away, lock, stock and barrel, because it was overshadowed.'

'Mmm.' Birdie was obviously only half listening. The fire crackled. 'What's worrying you, Laney?' she said at last.

'Oh, you know, Theresa, I suppose.'

'You're sorry for her.'

'Well, of course I am. Of course. But it's not just that.' Kate's brow wrinkled. She chewed a thumbnail. 'I suppose she did it because she was desperate. I suppose she just felt she couldn't bear it any longer, the guilt, and so she just . . .'

'Oh, you mean the suicide thing? I thought you were talking about the murder.'

'Oh, no, I can imagine how *that* happened. I can understand how she could have thought about killing him—and done it, too. But imagine her suiciding, Birdie, with little Nel up there in the front room, such a tiny baby, so defenceless, so dependent on her.'

'The crack under the door into the hall was well covered with the rug. The baby wasn't really in any danger, you know.' Birdie leaned forward, watching Kate intently.

'Oh, I know, I don't mean that. In fact, if Theresa had taken Nel in her arms and turned on that gas, because she couldn't face what was to come for both of them, well, that would have been ghastly, Birdie, but in a way it would have been more natural. Oh, I don't know. I can't explain why it seems so frightful. It's not that I knew her at all well . . . but for *her*, that kind of woman, to leave her baby sleeping and lie down to die not knowing what was to become of it, or who was going to look after it, knowing that it was going to wake up and be hungry, and want her, and cry in the dark, and she wouldn't be there . . . oh, she must have lost sight of everything so completely, so utterly. It's hard to imagine.'

Kate felt the tears filling her eyes and rubbed at them.

'You get yourself so worked up about things like this, Laney,' said Birdie reasonably. 'You're identifying with her, Theresa, too much. That can lead you up all sorts of garden paths, that sort of emotional storytelling that has no basis in known fact.'

'Oh, that's all very well,' snapped Kate. 'Sometimes instincts are just as important as facts, as you should know, since you said this afternoon you'd been concerned about Theresa. If you'd followed *your* instincts you might have got over there in time to . . .'

'For God's sake, Kate! Shut up!' Birdie ran her fingers back through her hair and tugged at it. 'How do you think I feel?' She dropped her chin to her chest, still clutching her hair.

The burning log fell in a shower of sparks, making them both jump. Birdie brushed some tiny lights from her grubby mohair chest, frowning fiercely. Kate looked at her for a minute, cursing herself for a fool, yet again. Why couldn't she defend herself without lashing out like that?

'Come on, Birdie. You know in your heart you couldn't be expected to have done more. Don't thrash yourself. Look, how about some cocoa or something? It's awfully late, and we've got to get some sleep. I'm not really tired. I slept this afternoon, that's the trouble. Oh, and I had the most frightful dream. I dreamt it was raining, pelting down, and I was . . .'

Kate led the way to the kitchen, talking as though she'd been wound up and couldn't stop. Birdie followed, arms folded, half listening.

' . . . and inside the apple there was a leech, curled up and thrashing its tail, oh, ghastly, like that caterpillar I saw in the loo. Jeremy said I was screaming the place down. He'd just got back and . . . are you listening, Birdie?'

'Yes,' said Birdie vaguely, then pulled herself together. 'Sorry, I was just thinking about something. So, Jeremy woke you up. Was Nick with him?'

'Of course not!' Kate snapped.

'I mean, did they come back home together?'

'Oh, I don't know! Probably. He was at afternoon tea, wasn't he?'

'Yes . . . yes, we all were, except Jill. She was up at The Pines, or whatever it's called.'

'I wish I was at the bloody Pines,' said Kate irritably, clattering the cups, 'or anywhere except this depressing, horrible place. You know, I really used to like this house. But now it just seems old and creepy. I was standing in the bathroom this afternoon, just after you'd left to check on Theresa, watching Zoe playing outside. She was sitting there making something for the fairies—a thank-you present for finding the Noah's Ark, I think. It was a lovely scene, really, but I was looking at it through dusty glass, stuck in this dank-smelling, cold room, and suddenly I got the strangest feeling that something was wrong . . . wasn't as it should be.'

'Why? What else could you see out there?' asked Birdie curiously.

'Well, nothing. Zoe on this crocheted rug, making something with paper and scissors and tape, you know how she does. There was no one else. Nothing to be seen at all except grass and trees and the garage.' She shrugged her shoulders. 'Just a weird feeling. It's no wonder, really. We've all been jumpy. Even Betsy was saying that she kept feeling as though someone was giving her the evil eye. Remember, I told you?'

'Oh, yes. All that about her special place being spoiled, and so on.'

'Yes. Funny. You know, like I said, Betsy's such a self-dramatiser but this time she seemed really sincere. Here, take your cocoa.'

Kate stalked back to the fire. Birdie followed her thoughtfully.

'I thought, you know, Birdie,' Kate went on, 'that maybe all this business might have really jolted Betsy, so that she's suddenly starting to feel people's dislike, and it's giving her the heebies.' She looked at Birdie sideways.

Birdie squinted at her cocoa. 'There's skin on this!' she announced in disgust. She picked up a twig from the woodbox and began to dab at her cocoa with it. 'Go on,' she said, without looking up.

'I mean,' said Kate determinedly, not commenting on this unhygienic display, 'that before Betsy just loved stirring the pot. She didn't feel threatened by anyone, no matter how they felt. She was always so . . . so supremely confident. But maybe Damien's death, under the tree where she always sat, too . . . maybe she suddenly realised what high emotion can lead to, that people who sow the wind can reap the whirlwind. I think she suddenly feels vulnerable, and scared.'

'Could be . . . she looks fraught, certainly.'

'I don't actually mean in terms of "Maybe I'll be next," or anything dramatic like that. Just the feeling that violence is possible, when violent feelings are in the air.' Kate yawned and then jumped. 'Oh, heavens, I nearly forgot the fairies!' She scrambled to her feet and made for the back door, feeling in the pockets of her jacket.

'Kate, have you lost your marbles?'

'No, no. It's the fairies, Zoe's present for the fairies. She finished it and left it out at the foot of the stairs for them. I've got to get it. She told me about it when I was putting her to bed and swore me to secrecy. I'd completely forgotten about it. Oh, have you got a silver coin? Anything'll do.'

'There's some money on the sideboard,' grunted Birdie disapprovingly, and watched as Kate selected a coin and rubbed it on her sleeve to polish it.

Kate laughed at her sour face, and went out into the cold night.

It was still misty, and the back steps glistened. Kate gathered her nightdress around her and walked down gingerly. On the grass by the beginning of the path a little heap of miniature lanterns, stars and origami swans lay, with an envelope made of green cardboard, carefully sealed up and addressed 'FOR THE FAIRIES' in decorated felt-tip pen capitals, already blurring and dissolving in the misty air. Kate gathered up the treasures and left the silver coin where they had lain. She stuffed her haul into her jacket pocket and went back up the stairs. As she pushed quietly through the back door she thought how strange it was that she could even be considering things like presents for the fairies in a place where a man had been poisoned like a bug and left to die in convulsions, and a terrified, lonely woman had laid herself down to die in a room full of gas. A wave of revulsion swept over her.

Birdie was sitting staring into the fire, her pointed chin pressed into her fist. Kate crossed the room quietly, knelt down beside her and gripped her arm.

'What's biting you?' said Birdie.

'Birdie, stop thinking about it. Stop brooding about it. If Theresa dies, as you obviously think she will, it's after all what she wanted. Your torturing yourself over it won't help her, will it?'

Birdie didn't answer.

Kate looked at her for a moment, and then slowly got up. 'See you in the morning,' she said quietly, and went back to her room, and the warm, soft breathing of her sleeping family.

21

The Party Goes to Town

The magpies were calling in the morning, filling the air with liquid, throaty sound. It was going to be warm. The mists of the last few days had lifted and vanished. A lovely day for getting out of here, thought Kate.

Despite her late night she'd woken early, and an unpleasant restlessness prevented her from just lying still and enjoying the unaccustomed peace. She crept to the kitchen for bread and butter and a cup of tea, and sat on the little back verandah, listening to the magpies, watching the apple trees, and understanding how Alice felt about them.

A click warned her that another early riser had entered the living room. She heard the back door open, a scuffle as someone put gumboots on, and a clumping down the back stairs. She eased herself out of her chair and leant over the verandah rail. As she'd suspected, Zoe was crouching by the bottom step, eagerly searching the grass.

A flicker of movement deep in the orchard caught Kate's eye. A movement, and a flash of glass. Birdie was prowling among the trees. Kate went back to her chair and closed her eyes, suddenly and perversely weary, now that escape back to bed was virtually impossible. She barely heard the boots retrace their steps. She was only faintly aware of the back door opening and closing again.

'Mum!' The piercing whisper penetrated her self-imposed stupor. 'The fairies have been. Look what they left me this time!' Zoe came out to the verandah, eagerly holding out her hand to display her prize.

'How terrific!' Kate held out her arms and Zoe crept into them. For a moment Kate clung to the firm, warm little body, patting and rocking, gripped by a sudden surge of feeling—of love, protectiveness and, somehow, fear.

'I saw you weren't in bed. I came . . .'

'Listen, Zoe, let's move inside. We might wake Alice if we talk out here.'

They went back to the living room.

Zoe knelt in front of the Noah's Ark and began idly fingering the little animals. Kate sat at the table, thinking of Theresa.

'Will Theresa die, Mum?'

'No one knows, Zoe,' said Kate, wondering, not for the first time, if Zoe was psychic. 'She's very sick. The doctors say she would be very lucky to recover. She breathed in a lot of gas, you see, and that's poisonous, so . . .'

'Yes, Mum, I know that,' said Zoe patiently. 'We learnt at school about it in Safety in the Home. Mrs Stanley said a person in a room filled with gas would be dead in about two hours, and a budgie in much less—a few minutes, probably. She didn't know how long a cat would take. Or an elephant.'

'Oh,' said Kate, somewhat disconcerted.

'When will Nel be coming back?' said Zoe, stroking the little figure of Mrs Noah.

'Well, darling, she won't be coming back without Theresa. Who would look after her?'

'We would, of course!' said Zoe scornfully. 'You and me—and Daddy. She can come and live with us, and be our baby, if Theresa goes to Heaven.'

'Darling,' said Kate helplessly. 'It doesn't work like that.'

Zoe turned to look at her, lips quivering, wide tragic eyes suddenly brimming with tears.

'But Mum, *of course* she'll have to live with us. I've got it all worked out. She'll need a family to love her and look after her. You said we'd have another baby one day. This way we can get one we know is nice, without you having to be pregnant or have sore legs or anything! Mum, please!' The tears splashed down.

'Zoe! Come here darling.' Again Kate held out her arms and Zoe ran into them.

'Dear, dear, now stop crying. Goodness me, silly old thing. Look, we'll talk about it later, will we? Everything's going to be all right. We're crossing our bridges a bit, my love. For all we know Theresa isn't going to die at all. Oh, look!' Kate took the wooden Mrs Noah from Zoe's hand. 'Look, Mrs Noah's hat's fallen off. Pick it up. There it is, under the chair.'

'It's not really her hat,' sniffed Zoe, getting off Kate's lap and reaching down for the little red object on the floor. She took a shuddering breath and sniffed again. 'It's . . . it was outside under the trees. Down the bottom of the orchard.'

She fitted the round red object on Mrs Noah's head again. A bottle cap or something, Kate thought. It looks quite smart, actually.

Alice's door opened and she appeared at the French doors.

'Early birds!' She greeted them almost cheerfully. She was dressed in an ancient navy skirt and coat, with brown stockings and shoes. On the lapel of her coat was pinned a beautiful cameo brooch. Her grey hair was twisted into a bun, exposing quite a bit of grubby neck. She looked rather magnificent.

Kate whistled and Alice looked pleased.

'Going into town,' she said. 'I got a few things to see to.'

'Can we go into town too, Mum?' asked Zoe eagerly, brushing at the last tears.

'Yes, we're going too, darling, after we've packed. We'll do some shopping for Betsy, and then go to lunch with Nick and Jill before we drive home.'

'Oh, but . . .'

'Still like the old Ark, I see, love,' said Alice to Zoe. 'Tell you what, I've been thinking that when I'm gone, I'd like you to have it, all for yourself. What d'you say to that?'

Zoe flung her arms around the old woman's waist. 'Oh, thank you, Auntie Alice!'

'Steady on, steady on, I'm not dead yet!' said Alice, grinning from ear to ear. 'But I wrote it down, that you were to have it, last night. So it's all settled.'

'Oh, I knew the Ark had come back specially. I told you. I told . . .'

'Well, isn't that lovely, Zoe.' Betsy's voice, brittle as cracked china, piped from the doorway. She came into the room, smiling, freshly lipsticked, eyes cold as little black stones. Anna, sullen, walked behind her.

Alice grinned at them. 'You'll get all me other things, Bet, in the end. I can't last forever. No need to be jealous of Zoe 'cause she's pipped you on the Ark.'

'Auntie Alice!' Betsy struggled with rage, self-pity and embarrassment and after a few seconds bolted for the kitchen, face red and set. Anna followed, looking like a thundercloud. As she closed the door on them she looked back, and Kate was shocked to catch the glare of real dislike directed her way. She'd done nothing at all to deserve it, and felt rather ill-used. Anna and Betsy must think she'd hinted to Alice that Zoe would love the Ark. No doubt it was quite valuable. Oh, how mortifying. She felt the blood rush to her cheeks, and looked helplessly around, not knowing what to do next. She sat down heavily in a chair. Now they were locked in the kitchen and she couldn't even go and get another cup of tea! She thought enviously of Nick and Jill, probably still sleeping in their comfortable bed at The Pines. They'd probably get early morning tea on a tray.

Sonsy appeared, wrapped in her red dressing gown and looking like a ghost. She nodded briefly to Kate and escaped out to the lavatory. She obviously has a virus or something, thought Kate irritably. Why doesn't she just go to the doctor, instead of creeping around like a stricken shadow?

The house was stirring now. Kate heard Chris call out to Jeremy and to his father on his way down the hall. In a few moments, she thought drearily, someone will ring the hospital for news of Theresa, unless Birdie's done it already. But they don't care if she lives or dies, really. They're just glad because Damien's murderer's been found and they're free to go on their selfish, squabbling little ways. Even Alice, who was supposed to have been her friend, seemed to have wiped her hands of the whole affair.

'Kate, wave to Zoe. She's waving at us, see?' Jeremy sounded the horn and the small figure in the back seat of the car in front signalled triumphantly.

'Birdie's driving too fast,' he grumbled. 'I wish you hadn't said Zoe could go with her. What for? Birdie could have come with us. That car of hers sounds dreadful. It's a wonder it goes at all, let alone at that speed.'

'Oh, Birdie wanted the company. She's very depressed about Theresa, you know. She was on to the hospital at the crack of dawn, and the news was so bad. She's going to get her car looked at in town, so . . .'

'Yeah, well, it doesn't matter. Why we're all trailing into Katoomba anyway I can't see. We could've bought everything at the local shops. Are we still going to lunch? Who's coming?'

'Just you and Zoe and me, and Chris and Sonsy and Nick and Jill.'

'What about your little mate?'

'Birdie didn't want to come. She said she didn't feel like talking. She said she'd catch up with us back at the house, before we all went home.'

'It's all a bit awkward, isn't it?'

Kate sighed. He was perfectly right. The plans for the day were awkward. But somehow, last night, a trip to the local big town had seemed so agreeable to everyone else that she hadn't been able to keep clear of it. One last effort to pretend this was a happy, normal house-party. One last effort to ignore the apples hanging unpicked, heavy on the trees, Damien in cold storage in the Sydney morgue, Theresa drifting towards death . . .

'This is a really nice milkshake,' said Zoe. 'Not too sweet. Just right. Oh!' She stood up and waved. 'Hello, Jill!'

Jill and Nick came into the coffee shop, grinning.

'Chris and Sonsy aren't far behind,' Nick said. 'Betsy, Wilf, and Anna are trailing, but will be here anon.'

'Zoe, why don't you go and mind that booth for the others? We won't all fit into one. Will you? Thanks, darling.' Jill slipped in beside Kate as Zoe scrambled across the aisle to extend their territory. Jill's eyes were sparkling, and her colour was high.

'Isn't it *great* to be out and about?' she carolled gleefully. She flung her arms into the air, fists clenched, and two old ladies on the other side of the room looked at her in alarm.

'Stop attracting attention to yourself, you madwoman!' said Nick calmly.

Jill smiled and dropped her arms, leaning forward on the polished wood of the narrow table top. 'A drive and a walk and a lovely long boozy lunch at Fredrica's is just what we need,' she said. 'To celebrate. Should we book, Nicko?'

She's trying too hard, thought Kate.

'Yeah, I reckon we should,' drawled Nick. 'Chris and Sonsy said they'd come, didn't they? And Jeremy and Kate. That's six, seven with Zoe. We'd better book.' His watchful eyes flicked to the doorway.

Chris and Sonsy walked in and crossed the room to their booth. Sonsy looked white and peaked, and sat down thankfully next to Nick.

'Weak black tea, please,' she said, as a plump waitress in a mauve cardigan jiggled up to take their orders.

'You still icky in the stomach, Sonsy?' said Jill sympathetically. 'You should go to the doctor, or something. You shouldn't let these things go on and on. I edited a book once . . .'

'I'm OK, it's OK,' murmured Sonsy. 'Thanks. Really, it's nothing.'

'Did you get what you wanted?'

'What? Oh, the wool. Yes, I got some that'll go all right, and the red buttons. They had quite a good range.'

'Where's Jeremy?' Chris asked.

'Oh, I don't know, he ducked off somewhere. So did Birdie. They hate shopping,' said Kate. 'So do I, actually. But they've got no conscience. They just disappear and then turn up again when it's all over. Betsy's groceries are slowly defrosting at parcel pickup as we speak. I couldn't stand the thought of moving the car and having to find another parking space. It's so crowded.'

'Hello, all. Oh, Zoe, thank you dear.' The Tender contingent had arrived. Betsy sank into the booth Zoe had been minding so gravely and slid along the seat beside her to make room for Rodney, Wilf and Anna. They gave their orders to the plump waitress.

'We're late, I know. Sorry, Katie,' said Betsy to Kate across the narrow passageway between their tables. 'Never mind! We're here now. A quick coffee and we'll move off home. As soon as Auntie Alice gets here, anyway.'

Wilf looked at his watch. 'She's supposed to be here now,' he said fretfully. 'Eleven-thirty sharp, we said. I want to tell her about Theresa.'

'She'll be here soon,' said Betsy comfortingly. 'She won't want to miss her lift home, will she? Oh, thank you,' she added graciously, as the waitress returned with coffee and raisin toast. There was silence while the Tenders imbibed.

'What about Theresa?' said Kate at last, unable to wait another second.

'Oh,' said Wilf eagerly, clattering his cup down. 'We met a nurse from the hospital at the butcher. An old friend of Bet's. Sylvia something or other, and . . .'

'Sylvia Block. Sylvia Stephens that was,' said Betsy impatiently, dabbing her lips with a paper napkin.

'Seems she saw Theresa this morning,' said Wilf, not to be squashed, 'and *she* says she's sitting up and talking.'

'What!' exclaimed Jill.

'But, Dad, this morning they said . . .' Chris leaned forward, brow wrinkled.

'Said she was critical, didn't they?' nodded Wilf triumphantly. 'Yes they did, but there's been a mix-up somewhere. Sylvia said that she was told that last night it was touch and go. Those were her very words, weren't they, Bet? But this morning when she saw the patient, she was improving every minute. Awful headache, of course, but . . .'

'Oh, I'm so glad!' cried Kate. 'Oh, Birdie will be so relieved. And Alice. Sonsy, if she's alive it's all thanks to you. What a terrific thing to have been able to do.'

Sonsy flushed and smiled.

'Yes,' said Anna. 'Now she'll be able to stand trial, won't she?' She smiled at Sonsy, like a cat playing with a mouse. 'I wonder if she'd thank you?'

'That man Toby is extraordinary,' said Betsy

quickly. 'Why on earth he saw fit to lead us astray like that I can't imagine.'

With relief, Kate saw Jeremy coming towards them. He stood by their table.

'I saw Alice in the street, Betsy,' he said. 'She asked me to tell you she'd meet you at the car in half an hour. She's still got some things to do.'

Betsy sighed. 'Dear oh dear. All right, Jeremy, thank you.' She turned to the others. 'I'll have to wait here for a while, then. Now, Anna, you and Rodney are going to the pictures, did you say?'

'Yes, why not,' said Anna coldly. 'Nothing else to do. That's why I brought my car. Chris is taking his off to this lunch, isn't he?'

'You'll have to ask him, darling. I don't know what his plans are.'

'Oh, don't be so coy, Mum. You *heard* him say he was having lunch with Nick. If I don't care that he obviously doesn't want Rodney and me there, I don't see why you should.'

Betsy hunched her shoulders, looking hunted.

'You can come if you like, Anna. Don't be so childish,' growled Chris.

'Oh, lunch is still on then?' asked Jeremy, brightening up.

'Why not?' said Jill. 'After all, here we are in the mountains. It seems a waste not to go to Fredrica's. People drive up from Sydney just for lunch there, and here we are five minutes from the place. I thought it was all settled. They'd have something Zoe could eat, for sure. They don't actually cater for children, but . . .'

'Oh, Mum,' called Zoe from the opposite booth. 'Couldn't I go home with Auntie Betsy? She said I could, this morning. I don't want to go to some boring old lunch. I want to play with the Noah's Ark. One last play,' she added melodramatically, 'before I go. Please, Mum.'

'Zoe!' Jeremy began warningly.

There was a groan from Wilf. 'I've broken a tooth,' he mumbled. 'Aargh—look at that. Broken clean off!' He held out a piece of toast crust with a chip of yellowed enamel embedded in it. Everyone recoiled.

'Dad, put it away!' hissed Anna.

'Well, all right, it mightn't look the best, but I can tell you it doesn't feel the best either, Anna,' moaned Wilf. 'It's aching already. I'll have to get to a dentist. Oh, my Lord . . . it's very painful.'

'Oh, Wilf!' For Betsy this seemed to be the last straw. 'Oh dear, what am I going to do now? I've got Alice to meet, and all the frozen food . . .'

Chris stood up. 'I'll take Dad to that dentist up on the corner, Mum. They'll be able to fit him in. I'll wait with him and bring him home afterwards,' he said firmly. 'Now don't worry. Just take Alice and Zoe home, and all of you have a quiet afternoon.'

'Christopher . . .' Betsy began to protest but was too obviously relieved to be able to carry it off. 'What about your lunch?' she said lamely, at last.

'Can't be helped,' he said cheerfully. 'I'll get a sandwich while Dad's being operated on. Sonsy can go with the others to Fredrica's.'

'Actually,' said Sonsy quickly. 'Actually, if you don't mind, Betsy, I'll go back to the house with you. I'm not feeling all that well.'

Everyone looked at her. She was certainly very pale, and she must have been feeling absolutely dreadful to go anywhere voluntarily with Betsy.

'Oh. Oh, of course, Sue dear. What a shame.' Betsy herself seemed nonplussed, and a little nervous at the idea.

Sonsy turned to Chris. 'You go with your dad now, Chris,' she said, putting her hand on his arm. 'I'll wait here with your mother until it's time to meet Alice.'

He looked at her quizzically. 'OK, then,' he said slowly. 'We'll see you at home.' He leant over and kissed her pale cheek.

'Well, we might go now, eh, Nick?' said Jill, moving her long legs restlessly. 'We can ring up and book and then have our walk before lunch.'

'Jeremy, you coming?'

'I guess so, mate. Zoe, you'll have to come with us, darling. Betsy's tired, and . . .'

'Auntie Betsy doesn't mind! She doesn't!' Zoe insisted urgently. 'I'll be good as a mouse. Mum? Please!'

'Betsy?'

'If my little girl wants to come of course I'm glad to have her,' said Betsy warmly.

There seemed nothing more to say. Everyone stirred, gathered up bags and parcels. Kate felt irritated, guilty, and cross with everyone, including herself. She gave Betsy the parcel pick-up tickets and followed the others to the door. She looked back at the little party in the booth, and Zoe gave her a happy wave. Kate lifted her hand in reply and went out into the street.

Two hours, half a bottle of wine and a light, elegant, expensive lunch later, things seemed much brighter to Kate. They hadn't talked of murder, or suicide. They hadn't even talked about the Tenders, except in jokey, peripheral fashion.

Looking for uncomplicated conversation, they'd slipped effortlessly into the tried and true remember-when, to the days when Jill's flamboyant clothes came from second-hand market stalls, and Jeremy had a full head of hair; when Nick was a vegetarian and she herself was pinched on the bottom three nights a week by the Dutch cook at the cafe where she earned her rent. Life had seemed very fraught and complicated then, but looking back it all appeared so simple.

She'd looked forward, in those days, in a vague sort of way, to career, marriage, a house of her own, children, independence. She hadn't realised that the first four things, particularly the fourth, made the last functionally unobtainable. In fact, it wasn't really until Zoe was two or three weeks old that she had suddenly realised that she had blithely put her heart in bondage to a small, anarchic creature, and endangered her peace forever.

'Excuse me,' said a voice. Kate looked up. A waiter, coffee pot in hand, was bending confidentially towards their table. 'There's a telephone call for a Miss Kate Delaney. Would . . . ?'

'Oh, yes. That's me,' said Kate, jumping up hastily and knocking the table awkwardly with her knee.

'Who would that be?' asked Jeremy, looking worried.

'It must be Zoe. I hope nothing's wrong.' Kate followed the waiter to the reception desk and picked up the receiver. Her heart was beating fast. What on earth . . .

'Hello?'

A deafening roar drowned out the voice at the other end of the line. Kate strained to hear the faint piping vaguely discernible under the din and suddenly recognised it for what it was.

'Birdie?'

'Yes!' Birdie sounded extremely ruffled. 'Kate, I'm talking from a phone box. Can you hear me? The traffic . . .' Another roar muffled her voice. Kate crammed her ear flat to the receiver and covered the other ear tightly. '. . . outside the hospital. You've got to come now. I've got to talk to you and Jeremy anyway, and my car . . . bugger these trucks, can you hear me?'

'Just. Birdie, what . . .'

'Just listen. You've got to come and get me. My car's packed up completely, and there's not a cab in sight. I want you to come now. Can you do it?'

'Yes, I suppose we . . . but . . .'

'Good. Quick as you can. See you soon. Bye.'

The line went dead. Kate hung up. Jeremy wasn't

going to be very pleased, being dragged off so soon.
Outside the hospital. What did that mean? Kate
walked back to the dining room, to break up the
party.

'High-handed little minx! I tell you, Kate, one of these
days . . .'

'There she is! By the bus stop.'

Birdie was leaning against the bus shelter, hands in
pockets, head down, looking rather like a small derelict keeping a sharp eye out for cigarette butts. She
looked up as Jeremy irritably sounded the horn, and
ran to clamber into the back seat of the car.

'What took you so long? Did Zoe go with Nick and
Jill?'

'What d'you mean so long?' Jeremy snapped.
'You've got a bloody cheek . . .'

'Where's Zoe?'

There was a short pause.

'She's at home, with Alice and Betsy,' said Kate at
last. 'She didn't want to come to lunch. Sonsy went
home too, because she wasn't well.'

Birdie's face was pale, as though she'd had a great
shock. She licked her lips. 'I thought she was going to
lunch with you. That was the plan. I never dreamed . . .
Are you sure she's in the house with Alice and Betsy and
Sonsy—and no one else?'

'I don't think so. Wilf broke a tooth and Chris took
him . . . Birdie, what is this? What's wrong with Zoe
being back at the house? Why were you at the hospital? Is Theresa . . . ?'

'Jeremy, get back to Alice's, as fast as you can!'

'Listen, Birdie,' Jeremy began warningly.

'Oh, Jeremy, *please!*' The urgency in Birdie's voice
cut through Jeremy's irritation. The car shot out into
the traffic, just missing a couple of dawdling pedes-
trians.

Kate twisted herself around so that she could look at Birdie huddled on the back seat. Birdie looked back at her, speechless.

'Birdie, for heaven's sake! What's the matter?'

Birdie hunched forward tensely. 'You were right about Theresa, Laney. Quite right. She didn't try to gas herself. Someone tried to kill her.'

'*What!*'

'*Someone tried to kill her!*' She was drugged up with something, they think sleeping pills. In the milk she drank before she breastfed at two, maybe, or maybe sometime before that. She was drugged, and after she and the baby were asleep someone came into the house, planted the photograph and turned the gas on.'

'How can you possibly know all that?' barked Jeremy.

'I've just been with her, and with Toby. The photograph didn't have Theresa's fingerprints on it, Jeremy. Just Damien's and some glove smears, and a set of Alice's that I saw her put there. Smears on the gas knob too, over Theresa's own prints. And she swears . . . oh, sorry, I forgot. I told Alice early this morning, but not you. She's not nearly as sick as we pretended. She . . .'

'Yes, we heard. Betsy met a friend of hers who works in the hospital, and she told us all . . .'

'*What!*' Birdie shook her head despairingly, unbelievingly. 'This is—oh, my God.'

'Why on earth did you try to lead everyone up the garden path, Birdie?' Jeremy turned recklessly to stare at her. 'What's the point?'

'Toby and I thought she'd be safer if people thought she was done for,' said Birdie distractedly. 'We were afraid someone might try to get at her again, in hospital, if they knew, and . . .'

'My God, Birdie. Are you saying someone tried to kill Theresa because she knew something? Are you saying there's a killer on the loose and Zoe's . . .' Kate felt her voice cracking.

'Laney, I had no idea she'd be out of your sight! You were having lunch together. That's what I thought. I thought . . .'

'Well, you thought wrong.' Jeremy pushed down the accelerator. They were out of the town now. His knuckles were white on the steering wheel and his mouth tightened as the car screeched round the winding mountain roads. Beside them the gullies dropped away from the road in folds of green. The white trunks of gum trees flashed by like a many-poled fence. Kate leaned back and shut her eyes. Her heart was pounding.

This was like some terrible nightmare. Birdie—she'd never seen Birdie like this. Birdie was terribly afraid, afraid for Zoe, for Zoe who they'd left so happy, two hours ago, in the care of people she trusted—Alice, Betsy, Sonsy. They were all at the house together. What could happen? They were all there together. Wilf and Chris—they were at the dentist's, weren't they? Anna and Rodney were at the pictures. Or . . . two hours. How long did it take to get in to Atherton from town? Twenty minutes? Fifteen? Or . . .

The monsters that had been shut away when Theresa's sad little story was revealed pushed their way out again and loomed up at Kate, darker and more menacing than ever. Her eyes opened, but she didn't see the road ahead. She fought the panic down. They were all there together. What could happen?

They were in Atherton. The pub, the chicken shop, flashed by. Kate clutched at Jeremy, he glanced at her and a flash of terror jumped between them.

'Get ready to move fast,' he said. Nothing else.

What did he . . . ?

Please let it be all right, oh, please. Please, Sonsy,

Betsy, Alice, whoever, whoever I can trust, look after my Zoe.

The car rounded the corner, into Alice's street. A dog raced out and snapped at their wheels. It was all so ordinary. Hope stirred, fluttered. Surely nothing could . . . and then Kate saw the smoke. Smelt it.

'Fire! A bush fire!'

The car thundered over the brow of the hill, and at the bottom they saw the heavy brown fog spiralling up, but not from the distant trees. It was Alice's house.

The car hurtled forward, skidded to a stop in the road, and they fell stumbling from it, running without thinking, eyes already stinging as the dusty, dry old wood roared and crackled, going up like a bonfire before their eyes.

Kate threw herself against the closed front door, hopelessly beat on it, saw Jeremy and Birdie streak past her, down opposite sides of the house. She ran after Jeremy, towards the kitchen, calling Zoe's name, hearing the house groan and crack, knowing that it was hopeless.

Flames leapt from the shattered kitchen window and a terrible roaring filled the air. Jeremy was heaving at the back door, cursing and crying. He turned to face her, hesitated, then set his jaw and sprang down the stairs again, and together they sprinted further around the house, to the open back verandah.

The French doors were ajar and smoke rolled and billowed through the gap. Behind the smoke orange light flickered and grew like a garish sunset. Without a word Kate braced herself to support Jeremy's desperate leap to the wooden railing, and as she did saw, like a vision, a tall figure, huge, impossibly broad in the flickering light, moving through the smoke-filled room. She screamed aloud. Poised on the railing, Jeremy jerked up his head. And so it was that they both saw Alice step out into the sunlight. Alice, face blackened in streaks, hair falling witch-like around her shoulders, with Zoe unconscious in her arms.

She looked round, eyes streaming, stumbled as she saw Jeremy, then moved to meet him, handing over her burden, barking a few words, then turning back to plunge once again into the smoke.

'Zoe!' Kate clung to the railings, shaking them. 'Jeremy! Give her to me! Oh God! Is she all right? Oh, Zoe!'

'She's unconscious, but she's breathing OK. Put her on the grass away from the house. I'll have to help Alice. She says Betsy's in there, and Sonsy. She's trying to get them out.'

He lowered the small body, heavy and still, into Kate's hungry arms. Zoe's fair hair was dull and smelled of smoke, and her arms hung limply. But she was warm and breathing without effort, and as Kate gripped her she sighed and turned her face into the cloth of her mother's jacket like a baby nuzzling for milk.

Trembling, legs turned to water, Kate staggered away from the house and sank to the cool, green grass at the fringe of the orchard. Insane that it should be cool and green . . . crazy that it should be damp. Ash floated in the air like the snow that Zoe had never seen, and settled quietly on her sleeping face.

The house glowed at every window, hideously, weirdly reminiscent of a cosy cottage on an English Christmas card.

'Jeremy! Come out!' Kate screamed. But even as she took breath to scream again, Jeremy and Alice were moving to the verandah railing. They were alone. Alice was shaking her head at Jeremy, arguing with him. He needed help, but Kate was terrified to leave Zoe, so strangely limp, breathing so deeply. With relief she saw Birdie appear around the corner of the house. She heard Jeremy shout and Birdie ran to the verandah, holding up her arms to steady Alice, and help her to the ground. Jeremy jumped to safety. He turned to look at Kate, then, with a word to Alice, followed

Birdie around the side of the house from which she'd come.

Kate stood up. Alice walked towards her, stumbling a little on the grass. Behind her there was the crash of timber falling. The living room blazed now. Just for a moment Kate could see it in clear detail, brightly lit. Then the glass in the French doors cracked and fell away, and there was nothing to see but orange and red, masked by smoke.

Alice didn't even turn her head. She stumbled on towards them, the wrinkles on her weatherbeaten face etched out with smoky black, her eyes under their hooded lids grave, her mouth set.

'He was right. It's too late. I couldn't hear her anymore. No one could live in that. Zoe OK?' The words snapped out.

'Alice . . .' Kate took a few steps towards her. She wanted to throw herself into the old woman's arms, to thank her, bless her passionately for saving her little daughter, say she was sorry about Betsy, about the house, about everything—but something in Alice's expression held her back.

'She looks all right, anyway,' said Alice, looking down at Zoe almost absent-mindedly.

Kate opened her mouth to speak, but suddenly her stomach gave a lurch and the words died in her throat. Over Alice's shoulder she saw Jeremy and Birdie appear around the side of the house, holding between them Sonsy Tender. Half dragging, half supporting her, they moved across the grass. She looked dazed. Kate watched her pale, peaked face with its huge glazed eyes and half-open mouth bob up and down through the drifting smoke.

Alice saw Kate's face change and turned slowly around.

'So they got her, too,' she breathed. She drew herself up and looked vaguely back to the house. 'Good,' she said, almost to herself.

Sonsy sank to the ground near to the old woman's feet. Jeremy crossed swiftly to Kate's side, as the noise of sirens sounded in the distance, growing louder by the second.

Alice watched impassively as her home of eighty years burned to the ground.

22

Final Assembly

Toby put his big freckled hand on Zoe's.

'Well, love, Constable McGlinchy and I'll let you have a word to your Mum, now. Thanks for your help.' He rose to go. Zoe struggled up on her white pillows.

'Is Auntie Alice's house all burnt up?' she asked quietly.

Toby glanced at Kate. 'I'm afraid it is, yes.'

Kate leaned forward.

'It was a terrible fire, Zoe darling,' she said. 'But you and Auntie Alice and . . . the people in the house were what really mattered. We're so lucky that you're safe.'

'I thought firemen came and stopped fires. I didn't think fires burnt houses all away. I thought that only happened in the olden days.'

Zoe's eyes brimmed over, and tears splashed down her pale cheeks. 'So the Noah's Ark's all burned. And the mittens. And all our clothes and my treasure box, and . . .'

'Look, my love,' crooned Kate, her heart wrung for so many different reasons. 'We can buy new clothes. And Daddy and I will buy you a special toy to make up for the Noah's Ark. I promise.'

'Mum,' Zoe whispered. 'Mum, I've thought of something awful.'

'What, darling? Don't be upset. Tell me what's the matter.'

'The brooch Daddy bought me at the scenic railway was in my treasure box. It'll be all burnt up too. Will Daddy be cross?'

'Of course he won't. Zoe, you don't understand. We're so happy to have you we don't care what else was lost . . .' Kate broke off with a pang and turned away. She had forgotten for a moment about Betsy.

But Zoe didn't know about Betsy, and now was not the time to tell her. She'd always liked Betsy. Betsy had been a kind and lovable companion for a little girl. She must have been a marvellous mother, when her children were young. It was only when they grew up that the trouble had started.

What had she thought about, in those last moments before the fire raged through the bedroom in which she lay? Her body had been found, crouched against the iron frame of the bed. Did she suspect that the fire had been deliberately lit? Did she smell the kerosene that Toby said had been used? Did she know . . . ?

Kate turned back to her daughter's bed, suddenly weighed down with almost overwhelming fatigue. She laid her head on the cool, white sheet. Zoe patted her elbow.

'Mummy? Don't cry, will you?' she said anxiously. 'I tell you what . . . Mum? . . . I'll get a new treasure box. A tin one, this time, like Auntie Betsy's. Then if there's another fire it won't get burned. I'll hide it under the bed, or somewhere where a burglar won't get it and then everything'll be all right. See?'

Kate laughed a little hysterically. 'I'm glad we've got that settled. I'm glad everything's all right. Oh dear, oh dear . . .'

Toby stepped forward and put a hand on Kate's arm. His touch sobered her immediately, and she sat up, smoothing her hair.

'I'm a bit tired,' she said ridiculously. She glanced over to the corner where Martin McGlinchy sat, brows knitted, looking a bit bemused. He saw her looking and suddenly smiled, a shy smile of extraordinary sweetness. She smiled back gratefully.

'Well, we're really on our way now,' said Toby briskly. 'Come on McGlinchy! We've got a couple of hours to put in at the office before we can get back here.'

He gave Kate a little bow. 'Goodnight, Miss Delaney. We'll be seeing you later.' He touched Zoe under the chin, nodded at them both and shambled to the door, hitching up his trousers. Martin ducked his head and followed him, lifting up a hand in a vague, friendly farewell. They disappeared into the corridor.

'They're both very nice, aren't they?' said Zoe, and suddenly yawned hugely. 'I can hear the rain outside.'

'Yes, so can I. Time for sleep, darling.'

Kate settled Zoe down and held her hand. In two minutes she was asleep. Kate moved away and went to turn off the light. Night had fallen, and the room was dark. She leaned against the doorjamb and looked down the brightly lit corridor. Somewhere Jeremy was talking to the doctor who'd treated Zoe when she first came in. Somewhere Theresa lay in bed, with Nel by her side. Somewhere Birdie prowled, still tormented by guilt over what had happened. Somewhere Alice tossed on a bed in an observation ward, complaining probably, and giving the nurses hell. Insisting she was all right and wanting to go home, though she had no home to go to. Somewhere Chris was sitting with Sonsy, Wilf, Anna and Rodney. What were they feeling? Kate shuddered, and closed her eyes.

'Oi!' Jeremy's whisper startled her, and she jumped violently. He walked down the corridor towards her, his shoes squeaking on the polished vinyl floor.

'Little one asleep?'

'Yes. Just dropped off. She seems fine. Just tired out. Maybe still a little bit of the other.'

'Apparently she had quite a dose. Not too much, thank God. Just enough to ensure she slept through . . . whatever was being planned.'

'Oh, Jeremy.'

'I know. Apparently the old house is burned out to the foundations. The fire blokes didn't have a chance of stopping it.' He paused. 'They found Betsy,' he said awkwardly.

'I know. Birdie told me. Have you seen Birdie?'

'Yeah. She's around somewhere. She said she and Toby were going to talk to us after dinner. Are you up to that?'

'Talk to us? Why?'

'They're not saying. Everyone'll be there. Except, I gather, Rodney, who's terribly cut up about his Mum, and Zoe of course. We're meeting in Theresa's room. She's in a three-bed ward now, and the other beds are vacant.'

'Jeremy, I can't go and sit through . . . One of those people, one of them . . . How can you even think of it? With Zoe lying here.'

Jeremy's face darkened. 'Well, for God's sake, Kate, how do you think I feel?' he said angrily. 'But if Toby's going along with it, I am too. I'm not going to miss a bloody thing from this point on. There's been too much mucking around already. My God, there's got to be proof somewhere. Someone did this, and some-one's going to pay!'

Kate looked at his frowning face and recognised what she saw there. His eyes were still bloodshot from the smoke, his clothes smelt of smoke and sweat.

She put her arms round him and held him tightly. After a moment he relaxed and held her too. His head rested on hers. 'Oh, Kate, five more minutes . . . five minutes, two minutes, and we would have lost her. I keep thinking . . .'

'Don't. It's all over,' she whispered. 'Don't, Jeremy. It's all right.'

• • •

'Well,' said Toby, standing up and reaching for his jacket. 'It's time to get a bite to eat, boy, before we go up to the hospital. D'you want Chinese, fish and chips or a hamburger?'

'Ah, um . . . I was wondering if I could, um, have an hour off, sir,' Martin mumbled. 'I just want to, ah . . .'

'Oh, I suppose so,' said Toby irritably. 'If you've got something better to do, go and do it. We don't have to be at the hospital until eight-thirty. I'll have dinner by myself.' Just for a change, he could have added, but Martin's hangdog expression took the edge off his irritation. 'Shake a leg, then,' he muttered, in a more friendly fashion. 'Don't be late, though, eh? I don't want to be left taking my own notes.'

Martin was already scrambling into an all-weather coat. Outside the rain was falling, and occasional rumbles of thunder could still be heard.

'And whoever she is,' Toby went on drily, 'just try and get her out of your system in this hour, eh? For tonight at least. You've been wool-gathering ever since we left the hospital. You'll be worse than useless to me later if you can't pull yourself together.'

Martin mumbled incoherently and backed out the door. His ears burnt red as though Toby's jibe had hit the mark, but of course it couldn't have been further from the truth. For a moment doubt assailed him. Was he making a fool of himself? Well, if he was, no one would ever know. And if he wasn't . . . Martin braced himself against the wind, and made for his car.

Toby looked around the brightly lit room, and cleared his throat in the expectant silence. 'We're all present, I think, so we'd better make a start,' he rumbled. 'Unfortunately my young off-sider seems to have gone missing, er . . . I daresay he'll be along shortly.'

His formal manner could not disguise his irritation. He'll be in for it, poor Martin McGlinchy, thought Kate, exchanging glances with Jill across the room.

Toby cleared his throat. 'I'm very sorry to have asked you to meet here like this, particularly you, Mr Tender, Mr Tender, Mrs Treloar. You've had a terrible shock, and you have all our sympathy.' He gave Wilf, Anna and Chris his little bow. Wilf stared vacantly at him. Anna murmured, and bent her head. Chris tightened his lips and nodded.

Toby cleared his throat again and raised his head, carefully looking at the wall. 'But we felt, I felt, that just because of everything that has happened over the past few days, and because various people, ah, various people in this room, have been under suspicion of a series of particularly unpleasant and callous crimes, it would be best, in so far as we can, to try to clear the matter up tonight, at least to our own satisfaction.'

Anna looked up. 'Do you actually mean you're intending to tell us, now, who you think did these things? Who killed my husband—and my mother? How is that *possible*? Has someone confessed?'

'No, Mrs Treloar, no. I'm afraid it isn't as simple as that, no.'

'Then what *is* this? Can't you see we're . . .'

'Mrs Treloar, I know this is hard for you. Could I ask you just to listen for a moment to your friend Verity Birdwood, who has agreed to give you the outline of the whole story as we see it.'

Anna's beautiful eyes widened. She looked at Birdie in undisguised surprise, and her lip curled. Birdie remained impassive. Toby coughed self-consciously and went on.

'Now, we've talked to quite a few of the people in this room over the past few hours, and feel we have a very clear picture. I want you all to listen carefully to what Birdie, Miss Birdwood, has to say, and by all means add anything you wish to add, or ask questions—whatever you like. I'm just going to sit back here and be a fly on the wall.'

And watch us like a hawk, thought Kate. She kept an eye on Toby as, true to his word, he retired to an upright chair in the background, and slipped a notebook and the stub of a pencil from the inside pocket of his jacket.

A feeling of apprehension settled on the room. Everyone looked grave, except Wilf, who still looked as though he was on another planet, and Anna, who looked positively stony. People were rather too obviously not looking at one another. Jeremy reached across and took Kate's hand.

Sitting shabbily on her straight-backed hospital chair, Birdie looked unprepossessing enough to shake anyone's confidence in her conclusions. She looked straight ahead, and began to speak.

'I suppose that as the stranger among you I had the chance to see what's happened over the past few days with a different perspective. That's made it easier for me to put together details that you all probably wouldn't notice or consider important.' She looked down and absent-mindedly scratched at a rough spot on her corduroy jeans.

'The fire this afternoon, as you all know, was definitely not an accident. It was lit by someone who wanted to do two things—destroy damaging evidence of a crime, and destroy someone who was a potential danger. I was sure even before the evidence of arson was found that the fire was set deliberately. This was because such a fire fitted perfectly the pattern set by the murderer on two previous occasions—the murder of Damien Treloar, and the attempted murder of Theresa Sullivan.'

'What pattern?' asked Anna impatiently. 'The three things were totally different!'

Birdie smiled. 'Well, so far as means is concerned,

of course they were. But the mentality behind all three was the same. All three were accomplished with very little time to plan, and involved seizing opportunity with both hands, acting boldly, and quickly, using means to hand and trusting enormously to luck. This in fact is one of the reasons why it was so hard to investigate these crimes in the normal way. There were no plans, very carefully worked out beforehand and overcomplicated. So often people trip themselves up like that. Timetabling was hopeless. It was such a large party, and no one could be sure where anyone else was unless they were actually talking to them.' She drew a long breath.

'This afternoon, for example, the house-party was spread all over the place. Most of us, in fact, were in Katoomba, fifteen minutes by car away from Alice's house. But cars were available, and despite the fact that people were for most of the time in company, we've established this evening that almost everyone had at least three-quarters of an hour alone. Chris while his father was having his tooth repaired, Anna and Rodney who . . .'

'We were at the pictures!' snapped Anna.

'But you sat apart, didn't you?' said Birdie quietly. 'Rodney said you argued about where to sit and you ended up . . .'

'Oh, yes . . . yes, but . . .'

'Look, this is just an example, Anna,' said Birdie, leaning forward. 'I'm not making a big thing of it. And anyway, just for now I want to concentrate on the thing that started all this. The key to everything. The killing of Damien Treloar.'

There was a heavy silence.

'OK, then,' said Birdie firmly, tucking her hands into her jacket pockets. 'At first there didn't seem much of a reason to think too carefully. There were two very obvious suspects for the murder of Damien Treloar.

'The first was Nick Bedford.' She looked at him gravely, and he smiled wryly at her.

'Nick,' she went on, 'was obviously furiously jealous of Treloar, because of a real or fancied relationship between him and Jill, and . . .'

'I don't understand how you could have *possibly* suspected Nick, at *any* time,' cried Jill, who had been listening with growing impatience. 'He was obviously totally amazed when he arrived the next morning and found the police in the house, and Damien dead. Anyone could see that!'

'He certainly looked amazed,' said Birdie, unruffled. 'But then, he's quite a good actor, I think you said. Doesn't he do a lot of amateur theatricals? And he would have had quite a few hours to practice his act for the morning.'

'For God's sake!' hissed Jill, flushing with anger. 'You . . .'

'Look, let me finish, please. If everyone's going to blow their stack every time I mention what I thought about them we'll be here all night!'

Nick turned his freckled, good-humoured face to Birdie and smoothed his beard with a steady hand. 'Fair enough,' he said calmly. 'So what were your thoughts on suspect number one, if I may ask?' Did Theresa's evidence about seeing me arrive home after we know Treloar was already dead have any effect? It got me off the hook with the police.'

'Yes, it did. But I didn't pay much attention to that. You could have come and gone beforehand without being noticed by anyone. But I didn't raise any objection when Detective-sergeant Toby dropped you as a suspect. I'd thought about you carefully by then, and talked to Kate and Jill—and Jeremy—about you, and frankly I couldn't see you as the type of bloke who'd creep up behind someone, slosh poison on him and run off.'

'Thanks a lot,' said Nick drily. But he was relieved all the same, thought Kate. His hand on his knee had been clenched, the knuckles white. Now it was slowly relaxing.

Birdie leaned forward, and put her hands between her knees. Her eyes, slightly magnified by her strong glasses, were fixed to the floor.

'The second obvious suspect was Betsy Tender.'

Kate had been waiting for this, but her stomach lurched. She heard Jeremy groan softly under his breath, and stole a look at Wilf. He was looking at Birdie in a puzzled sort of way. Anna, beside him, was deadly pale, her lips slightly parted.

'Betsy disliked Damien Treloar intensely. She was very keen to ensure that Anna did not go back to him. It was possible that Betsy had decided to get rid of her troublesome son-in-law for good, and seized the opportunity presented to her by his staying overnight.'

'This is monstrous!' breathed Anna.

'Betsy was as tall as Damien, and she had a pale-blue parka like his. She could, therefore, have easily been the mysterious figure seen by Theresa at the van. But though I thought about Betsy very seriously, for this reason, and because I thought she would be capable of the quick and decisive action the murder required, I was unhappy about her motive, when all was said and done. The more I thought about it, the more I saw that Treloar was really more useful to her alive than dead. Alive he was an unsatisfactory ex-husband, a constant reminder of what ignoring a mother's advice could lead to. He was a genuinely unpleasant and unstable character, so that even if Anna occasionally went back to him, she would almost be guaranteed to return to the nest within a fairly short time. Dead he could have become an attractively unconventional and glamorous figure. Anna might even have turned on her mother and blamed her for the breakup of her marriage, once she was freed from the necessity of ever returning to it.'

'Hey, Birdie, hold on!' Jeremy glanced uneasily at Anna, who was now white as paper. 'No need to . . .'

'Oh . . . sorry,' said Birdie, looking at him blankly. She's well in her stride now, thought Kate. She just expects everyone to be as absorbed as she is in the riddle. Never mind their feelings. She's inhuman. But even as the thought crossed her mind the memory of Birdie's hands cupping Zoe's sleeping face, just before the little girl was lifted into the ambulance, crossed with it. Not inhuman all the time, then.

'Finally, of course, we found out that Betsy was actually there when Anna overheard Damien's conversation with someone in the garage. At that point, Betsy's motive disappeared. Totally discredited, Damien was now no threat. Furthermore, everything she had ever said about him had been proved correct. Her advice would not go unheeded again, and whatever Damien did, his very existence would be a constant reminder to Anna of her humiliation and misplaced trust.

'So, I started looking further afield. The conversation in the garage made two more suspects worth considering. Anna herself, for a start, now had the best of reasons for killing Damien.'

'Yes, I did!' spat Anna. Her hands were clasped together so tightly that her nails were digging into the flesh. 'The best of reasons. But I didn't kill him. It never occurred to me. I did think of killing her.' She directed a poisonous glance at Jill, who flinched.

'But of course we know now that it wasn't Jill in the garage at all, but Theresa,' Birdie pointed out calmly.

'So I hear,' said Anna coldly. She didn't look at Theresa, sitting high in her hospital bed, with Alice close beside her. Theresa bit her lip, and glanced quickly at Alice who muttered something indistinguishable.

'Your eager acceptance of Simon Toby's suggestion that Damien might have suicided seemed a bit suspicious. Everyone else who knew him claimed it was an absurd idea. You were quite tall enough to have passed for Damien at the van. You were obviously very, very keyed up in the days that followed the murder. The attempted murder of Theresa could have been nothing to do with Theresa's having some information about the murderer, but might have been another expression of jealous rage.'

'So it could, I suppose,' said Anna, smiling rather horribly. 'So I was your pick, was I?'

'No, you weren't. For three reasons. One—you mentioned, quite of your own volition, that Damien never wore his parka hood up, thus drawing attention to both the murder means, and the fact that the person seen at the van was probably not Damien at all. Two—you seemed to have no doubt in your mind whatsoever that Jill had been in the garage with Damien that night. I couldn't believe you were acting. The person who killed Damien Treloar went to his van and found there a photograph of Theresa. If you were that person, you would, surely, have at least wondered whether it was Theresa, not Jill, who you'd heard in the garage. I don't think you had the faintest suspicion. You talked about the photo collection in front of Theresa absolutely naturally. I don't believe you could have done that if you knew the truth, and had her photograph in your possession.'

'I see. Well, thanks for nothing,' said Anna childishly. 'What about reason number three?'

'Well, it doesn't really . . .'

'Go on, spit it out, why don't you? Was it, perchance, that you couldn't quite see me burning my mother to death?' Anna was very close to breaking point. Her voice was trembling and shrill.

'No,' said Birdie. 'If you must know, it wasn't that. It was because when the gas was turned on in Theresa's back room, someone went to a lot of trouble to cut the front of the house off from the gas. I don't think it was just to make the gas work faster. It's a tiny house. I think it was also to protect the baby.

And if you'll forgive me, I don't think you would have done that. In fact, I think . . .'

'You think I would have made bloody sure that the brat went the way of its mother. Well, you're right. I would've done just that!' Rigid with hate and anger, Anna gripped the arms of her chair as if to spring to her feet. Then, as if an invisible string had been cut, she slumped back, and turned her face to the wall.

23

A Friends-and-Family Affair

Simon Toby watched Anna warily out of the corner
of his eye. He was feeling sick and tired of this whole
enterprise already. He was also worried about Martin. Where was the young devil? He was having grave
doubts, too, about the wisdom of all this explanation.
Explanation? Theory, more like it. They should have
waited until a few hard facts had come to light.

Birdie had thought it was important to give people
the facts as they saw them, to stop rampaging suspicion
and rumour. She'd said it was unfair to keep people
guessing in the dark, filled with vague doubts and fears,
when she and Toby were sure they were right.

He'd been persuaded, and Martin had been eager.
He was a soft-hearted lad under that vague exterior.
Toby had been swept along by their enthusiasm, and
the possibility that out of all the dramatics would
come a few shreds of proof. He wasn't used to being
swept along, though, and it made him nervous.

It was making Theresa Sullivan nervous, too. He
could tell. Amazing how he'd got to know that woman
so well, in only a couple of days. He looked at her
thoughtfully. Her heavy, handsome face pleased him.
She was listening intently as Birdie summarised their
previous discussion, leaning back on her pillows, her

337

black hair, streaked with grey, hanging over one shoulder. Her nightdress was cream, and came right up to her neck, in a fold of heavy cream lace. Hand made, he supposed.

'And so, naturally, we then had to consider Jill.' Birdie's voice finally impinged on his consciousness, and he came to himself with a little shock. By the Lord, he was getting as bad as McGlinchy, with his daydreaming. He pulled himself together, and looked about him, forcing himself to concentrate.

'After Anna, Jill was the most obvious suspect, simply because, from the conversation overheard by Anna, it sounded as though she was being bullied, blackmailed, threatened, into making a casual liaison a permanency. Again, I thought about her seriously, because I found the motive plausible, and she was out of the house on the night of the murder, and I thought she had the pragmatism to do what was necessary to ensure her own survival and then put it out of her mind once it was done.'

Jill looked rather pleased. She obviously took that as a compliment, thought Kate.

'However,' Birdie went on, 'I found it hard to believe that Jill would leave so much to chance. She seems scatty, excuse me Jill, but in her line of work you can't be that. Attention to detail is a prerequisite, as it is in mine. I kept her in mind, though, because the motive was there. That motive was, however, completely destroyed once it was discovered that it had not in fact been Jill in the garage at all, but Theresa.'

Birdie moved restlessly in her seat, and looked around at the circle of watchful faces. 'So,' she said, 'I went on thinking. The scene outside the garage, when Anna and her mother reported the conversation they'd heard on the night of the murder, made me realise that there was another possibility. Someone I'd overlooked before. Someone that possibly everyone overlooks, as a matter of course.'

Oh, here we go again, thought Kate, not daring to look at Wilf.

'Wilf Tender was obviously extremely upset about the sneering way Damien had spoken about his daughter, to whom he is passionately devoted. He may well have thought that Anna could only be revenged, and her humiliation eased, by the death of the man who had betrayed her so shamefully. He felt he had not been a good provider, or protector, and may have decided that at last he had an opportunity to act decisively on his own account, to rid his family, particularly his beloved daughter, of a menace.'

Wilf stirred, but said nothing. He no longer looked vacant, though. Just inexpressibly sad. Beside him, Anna was very still, listening.

'Wilf complained of insomnia, and was often up and around at odd hours of the night. He said he sometimes didn't take the sleeping pills Betsy gave him. He could have lain awake after Betsy had taken her own pill and gone to sleep. He could have gone quietly out to the orchard and killed Damien, without anyone knowing.'

The silence in the room was oppressive. Everyone became aware that Alice was breathing heavily. Kate stole a look across the room. Chris was leaning forward, his dark, heavy brows knitted. He held Sonsy's hand tightly. She looked frightened, her mouth a little open. White mouse, thought Kate.

Birdie continued, 'Wilf, of course, was the only member of the party officially to visit Theresa on the afternoon of her supposed suicide attempt. He went to borrow some parsley from her garden, and came back saying Theresa had seemed very tired, and was going to have her afternoon sleep. Theresa confirmed that this morning. Wilf hadn't attempted to do her any harm then. It was still possible, however, that he could have been checking on her, intending to go over later, when he himself was supposed to be asleep, to stage a suicide.'

Anna spun round in her chair. 'That is ridicu'
she snapped. 'Absolutely ridiculous! Dad could ne
I mean, would never do all that! You must be crazy.
Chris, for goodness sake, tell her.'

'I had to consider every possibility, Anna,' said
Birdie steadily. 'I'm sorry to upset you, and Wilf, especially now, but I've got to go through everything. I
agree with you. I don't think your father could have
acted in the way I've described. It is possible that
driven by very passionate feelings he could have killed
Damien. But I think that the effort would have left
him incapable of further action. He was obviously
very shocked by the events of the murder night, and
has really been a semi-invalid ever since. I therefore
decided he was emotionally and physically incapable
of planning and carrying out the attempted murder
of Theresa, and certainly of the burning of Alice's
house. And on mature reflection, I found it pretty unlikely that, whatever his feelings, he could have successfully murdered Damien either. Inaction has
become so much of a habit with him, that I think that
however emotional he might have become, he would
not have been able to take the fast and decisive steps
necessary.'

Wilf looked at her hopelessly. Oh God, thought
Kate. She could have left him with something. She
could have left him with the idea that someone
thought he could stand up and fight for his daughter.
I think he'd have preferred a murder charge to this.

'Now,' said Birdie. 'All through this whole thing
there was at least one very important red herring,
which was distracting, to say the least.' She glanced
at Theresa.

'Me,' said Theresa ruefully. Then she smiled. 'The
scarlet herring, you might say,' she added surprisingly.

'Yeah, well . . .' Birdie looked a little nonplussed.
'Yeah, you were the big problem. Once I heard Anna's
report of the conversation she'd overheard I was

sure Damien had been talking to you and Nel, not Jill, as she'd thought.'

Theresa nodded. 'He made me promise to meet him in the garage at eleven-thirty, when he thought everyone would be asleep. Now it's over I just keep thinking what a fool I was to . . . to get so hysterical about it. He couldn't have forced me into anything, really. It's just that he'd been so . . . I mean, when we stopped seeing one another, he'd acted so . . . barbarously, really.' She smiled ruefully. 'Said he was bored, and I was too old and fat and stodgy for him. He showed me pictures of his beautiful wife, and some of his other "ladies", as he called them. I hadn't even known he was married.'

She glanced at Anna appealingly. Anna sat staring at the window, head high, two bright spots of colour burning on her cheeks. Theresa sighed and lifted her hands, palms up. 'Honestly,' she said, to Birdie, 'I just, suddenly, went from thinking he was wonderful to thinking he was stupid and disgusting, and that I'd been a complete fool. Just like that.'

In his shadowy corner Toby felt a strange flutter in his middle-aged chest. This was something Theresa had never said before. He'd been thinking that it was quite on the cards that she still carried a torch for the fellow. Apparently not. What a fool the man must have been. Old, fat and stodgy, eh? That magnificent face would never be old. That serene, warm-hearted woman couldn't be stodgy if she tried.

'So when I found I was pregnant, a couple of months later,' Theresa went on, dropping her eyes and playing with the sheet, 'I don't know, I just shut his part in the whole thing out of my mind altogether. Nel was just my baby. Mine. Something I thought I'd never have.'

Her voice trailed off, and her face was full of memories. She looked up suddenly. 'It was such a shock to see him again. At Alice's, of all places, because Alice was the one person I'd actually told about the affair, hadn't I Alice? I realised suddenly that she must have known all along who the baby's father was.'

'And, the next day, when Damien was found dead, you thought Theresa had done it, didn't you, Alice?' said Birdie quietly.

'Yeah, well, it crossed me mind it might have happened that way,' said Alice. She hunched her shoulders. 'Oh, yes, I know, Theresa tells me she'd never've done it and I shouldn't have thought it. I like that. Why, I'd like to know, was she so scared and jumpy once she knew it was murder. By gum, because she thought *I'd* done it! For her. To get him out of her hair.' She grinned round triumphantly, showing uneven white teeth.

'Well, you put on a pretty good imitation of a batty murderer, Alice,' said Birdie, 'pretending you didn't know what you'd sprayed and then taking that back, and reviling the dear departed, and saying you didn't know he'd stayed around overnight when you must've done, and so on. Anyhow, I have to say that you and Theresa became my prime suspects. And then came the so-called suicide attempt. And in my book that wiped you both out. Alice because I didn't believe she'd harm a hair of Theresa's head, and Theresa because—well, I had this feeling, as Kate did, that Theresa wouldn't have suicided, leaving her baby unprotected like that, whatever she'd done or whatever she feared.' She lifted her pale, pointed face to receive Theresa's smile.

Toby cleared his throat in the corner. 'As a matter of fact,' he said. 'I found the suicide idea a bit hard to take myself. It was a surprise to find out that Mrs Sullivan had known the deceased before. We hadn't, as it happened, got round to checking that the prints and the negatives found in the wallet matched up.' He paused and ran his hand over his bald crown. 'But suicide didn't seem in character to me either, Miss Delaney.' He nodded to Kate, who beamed at him.

'For this reason,' Toby said, 'I took the precaution

of having the room where the gassing occurred checked for fingerprints, and taking possession of an empty milk bottle on the sink. The fingerprinting paid dividends, as most of you have by now heard. The bottle, and the mug that we also took, had unfortunately been too well washed for any trace of a drug that may have been there to remain. We have been unable to prove, therefore, whether the sleeping draught Miss Sullivan was given was in the milk, or in something she drank earlier—at the park, for example, where I understand she drank some coffee.' He paused. Everyone was still.

'How could anyone have got to the milk in Theresa's house?' asked Anna.

'In the same way that, presumably, they got to the gas heater later on. The key to Miss Sullivan's side door hangs permanently, as you know, Mrs Treloar—as everyone knows—by the telephone in Miss Allcott's kitchen. A very simple matter to take that and let oneself in, at any time.'

'Yes, of course, I see,' said Anna. She ran her fingers across her forehead in an abstracted way. 'I forgot everyone knew about that.'

'Birdie, let's get on,' said Kate restlessly. 'All this is leading nowhere. You've just raised a lot of people, and then dismissed them. Fortunately,' she added hastily.

'Exactly, Kate. That's exactly how I felt. I was going nowhere. I thought of Chris. He had no motive whatever that I could see. I thought of Sonsy. Again, she barely knew Damien Treloar. You and Jeremy I left out of my reckoning—unfair, perhaps, but there you are. I thought of Rodney and again there was the barest touch of a motive for killing Damien, but a very unconvincing one. He did see his mother's welfare as his responsibility to a certain extent, but I didn't think he'd commit murder on her behalf, and it crossed my mind also that he'd probably quite like the idea of Anna zipping off with Damien, leaving him an only child again, with all the attention for himself.'

'You really take the bun, Birdie,' said Jeremy, shaking his head. 'I don't think you've got a compassionate bone in your body.'

Birdie stared at him, and her glasses flashed. 'Be that as it may,' she went on, 'I felt at this point that I'd drawn blanks all round. I decided I had to take a fresh look at the whole thing. It was suggested early on that the murderer could be a stranger, with a motive, and movements, we knew nothing about. I was actually convinced it was a family affair. A friends-and-family affair, I should say.' She looked around with a small smile, but no one smiled back except Alice.

'But I thought, well, if it could be a stranger with a motive I knew nothing about, it could be someone in the house with a motive I knew nothing about. After all, no one had suspected that Theresa would have any reason to kill Damien Treloar. Perhaps someone else had a reason totally unknown to me, for wanting him out of the way.'

Birdie was now speaking with confidence and authority. Her wiry little figure, sitting forward in her chair, seemed filled with an awful energy. You could feel the fear and tension in the room as her voice went on and on, the voice of a relentlessly logical, untiring machine.

'So I did what I ought to have done at first, and just thought about the household I'd joined a couple of days before. I thought, if I had to pick a main theme in the day-to-day events and conversations of the last few days, it would be mothers and children. Maternal possessiveness and jealousy, infant dependence on mothers, and so on. There was Theresa and Nel, Kate and Zoe, Anna and resistance to being a mother, and, most obvious and overwhelming of all, Betsy's dominance of all her children, and their greater or lesser dependence on her. Kate said at one point that if it'd been Betsy, not Damien, killed, it'd be easy to point the finger at at least two people in the house. She was only half joking.'

Kate felt herself getting hot all over. Sonsy would know what that meant. She'd be really hurt that Kate had been gossiping about her to Birdie. There she was crouching in her corner, leaning on Chris. She was ashen. Oh, why on earth was Birdie dragging all this up?

Birdie was looking at her hands. 'I actually gave what Kate said a lot of thought,' she went on. 'She was right, of course. Of all the people in the house, including Damien Treloar, Betsy was the one who roused the most primitive emotion, the one who took the most risks in her personal relationships. Her treatment of her daughter-in-law, for example, was nothing short of mild but continuing torture.'

'What complete rubbish!' exclaimed Anna. 'What complete and utter . . .'

'It's true, Anna,' said Chris quietly.

'Oh, for goodness sake! All Sonsy had to do was stand up for herself! She didn't have to be such a little wimp!'

Kate closed her eyes for a minute, blocking out the too-bright light, trying to block out Anna's shrewish, spiteful voice. It's true, though, she thought. Sonsy should have taken Betsy on. Mind you, lately she'd been calm enough. It was Betsy who'd had the jitters. The biter bit, poor Betsy. She imagined them all back at the house this morning. Alice, Betsy, Zoe, Sonsy. Alice, in her best suit, looking at her trees, Betsy unpacking frozen food, Zoe, kneeling before the Ark, fitting on Mrs Noah's hat, playing some endless game. Sonsy, pinched and white, like Cinderella, sewing on the missing button from her red dressing gown . . .

Kate's eyes opened, but she didn't see the room in front of her. She saw Mrs Noah's hat, red and shiny, and knew where she'd seen it before. She heard Zoe's voice, '. . . found it . . . down the bottom of the orchard . . .', saw Sonsy's face, in the kitchen that first night, hating Betsy, wishing her dead.

And in a second, she saw it all. Saw Damien, sitting, waiting to die, that night in Betsy's favourite spot in the orchard. He wore a pale-blue parka, hood down, though the wind was tearing through the apple trees. He was thinking of Nel, and Theresa, and the new start he was going to make. The last of many self-deluding plans. He sat quietly, bent forward, his hair covered by its dark woollen cap, his white neck shining in the mist.

Kate saw his killer move down the corridor of the old house, filled with hate and loathing. Her eyes were pale and pink-rimmed. She carried a swab of cotton wool and a bottle. She stopped at the bedroom door, and listened. Her heart thudded. She looked inside and saw Wilf Tender alone in bed. Her quarry was not lying peacefully, vulnerably asleep, then, but was abroad. Well, so be it. She walked on, to the living room, and out the back door, while Betsy held her breath in the dark kitchen, afraid without knowing why, and soon to scuttle back to bed, and safety.

The killer crept down the stairs, looked out into the orchard. And saw what she wanted more than anything else to see—Betsy Tender sitting where she always sat, her pale-blue parka shining in the mist, her black head bent, her white neck glimmering like a target in the darkness.

Kate looked wildly at Birdie, and Birdie met her gaze unsmiling, willing her, it seemed, to say nothing. Kate gripped Jeremy's hand and felt him move beside her. Had he seen it yet? Had anyone? Birdie was speaking again, and Kate writhed in her chair. Sonsy's pale face, half masked by Chris's dark shadow, swam before her eyes on the other side of the room.

'I considered,' said Birdie, 'this question. What if, in fact, Betsy was the intended victim, not Damien at all.'

'What?' Anna's voice crackled in the silence.

'Damien was sitting in Betsy's favourite spot in the orchard, with his back to the house,' said Birdie quietly. 'He was wearing a parka the same colour as hers, he had on a cap which hid his hair. In the dark such a mistake would be possible. Furthermore, Sonsy went out, supposedly to the toilet, and was away, by the testimony of both Betsy and Jill, over fifteen minutes—quite a long time for a quick trip to the loo in the middle of the night.

'Sonsy's fright at meeting Betsy in the corridor on the way back, and her subsequent hysteria, seemed out of proportion. But it would be totally understandable if you postulate that she was meeting face to face someone she thought she had killed a few minutes before.'

'No . . . no, I didn't. You don't understand.' Sonsy's wail rose over Birdie's voice. Chris, his eyes blazing, crushed his wife against his chest.

'You . . . I don't know what you think you're doing, Birdie,' he warned, his voice trembling. 'But . . .'

Sonsy pushed him away. She was perfectly under control again now, and stared straight at Birdie. 'Go on,' she said, and set her lips. 'Finish it.'

'The next day,' continued Birdie, still in that quiet, calm voice, 'Sonsy was asked to check the body of the dead man. Betsy reacted to her statement that Damien was beyond help with what one couldn't help feeling was a rather egocentric complaint—"in my place", she said, meaning that her special place in the orchard had been tainted. She was under tremendous strain, and just said the first thing that came into her head. But Sonsy was very struck with the remark. She repeated it, and then began to laugh, uncontrollably. She in fact became hysterical again, and had to be taken inside. I wondered why she had reacted like this. Later, when I considered the possibility that she had actually killed Damien herself, by mistake, I could see that it might well have struck her as funny, in a grim sort of way. Because it would have been true that Damien had been killed "in Betsy's place", in more ways than one.'

She looked around seriously. Sonsy said nothing. She was pale as paper. Her hands, clasped before her, seemed so fragile as to be almost transparent.

'After that morning, Sonsy's manner changed. She seemed to have lost the tendency to hysteria, and she seemed far less shy and frightened. It was as though some crisis had been survived, and it had strengthened her. Paradoxically, however, she started showing signs of not being very well physically. She started refusing all but the plainest food, and avoiding alcohol, and was obviously very queasy in the stomach, suffering from bouts of vomiting. Perhaps the symptoms one might expect from someone who had had mild exposure to a contact poison. Then Zoe found a button from Sonsy's dressing gown at the bottom of the orchard.'

Chris stood up. 'I think we'd better stop here, Birdie,' he said. He was icily calm now. He put his hand in his pocket and played with his car keys. 'This is all rather irregular, I think. I'm sure you mean well, but I think it's time for Sonsy and I to pull out, and have a talk to our solicitor. I'm sure you'd agree, sir' he said, turning to Toby.

'If you think it necessary, Mr Tender, then naturally you should do so,' said Toby formally.

'No!'

With a shock, they saw Sonsy rise from her chair. She supported herself by holding its back. 'No,' she began again, more strongly. 'I'm not scared anymore, Chris. I've had it running away and hiding, and not facing things. It's in my interest that everything comes out. Everything.'

24

Revelations

'A lot of this has been my own, stupid fault,' said Sonsy. 'And I've got no proof at all of what I'm going to tell you. But I hope you'll see that my version of things is just as possible as the other.

'Birdie said that I went out to the loo in the middle of the night, and stayed away a long time. That's true. Actually it was because of the caterpillar.'

'The caterpillar—the caterpillar in the loo?' Kate looked wildly at Birdie, who raised her eyebrows.

'Yes,' said Sonsy, not quite comprehending, and smiling uncertainly. 'You said you'd seen it, Kate, when you were out there. Well, it's stupid and childish, but I honestly have a terrible *thing* about caterpillars. They give me the horrors. I went out to the toilet and there was this thing, this huge thing, crawling . . . oh,' she shuddered. 'Sorry . . . crawling on the cistern. I saw it there, and I just couldn't go in. I couldn't bare to touch it, even with a stick, and if I'd, you know, used the toilet, it might have fallen on me . . . ugh.'

Her disgust was so obvious, so silly, and so human that several people were surprised into laughing aloud.

She smiled ruefully. 'I know. Anyway, there the thing was, and I was simply *busting* to go to the toilet.

I'd been skulking away in my room almost half the night. I really had to do something. So I tramped down to the bottom of the orchard, out of sight, and went there. Leeches I couldn't see were infinitely preferable to a caterpillar that I could.'

'Oh, Sonsy!' Chris shook his head, and for the first time that night, smiled.

'I got cold down there, and wet from the grass, but I felt much better. I started back up the hill, and got my dressing gown tangled up in a branch of one of the trees. It took ages to get untangled again. I started to worry that Chris might come and look for me. I thought he'd think I was bonkers if he found me wandering around in the dark. I pulled at the branch and got free. That's when I must have lost the button off my dressing gown. I didn't think of that till much later, when I saw Zoe playing with it. I didn't say anything to her, because I wasn't keen for people to know that I was in the orchard at all, that night. By then, you see, everyone had been questioned about the murder. By the time I saw the button on Mrs Noah's head I was afraid to admit that I'd stirred out of the house. It would've looked so suspicious, because I hadn't admitted it at first.'

'But Sonsy, why didn't you? You've told us now. There's nothing so embarrassing about it!' exclaimed Kate. 'I mean, if I'd found that caterpillar on the cistern *I* would have done exactly the same.'

'Yes, well . . . it would have been all right for *you*, Kate. Everyone would've just laughed, and teased you, and you would've made a good story of it, and that would've been that. But I . . . it would've been different for me. Chris would've thought I was cowardly and silly and childish, and his mother would've either looked at me as though I wasn't right in the head, or as though I was some common little thing who'd as soon wee on the grass as look at you!'

'Oh, God,' Chris put his head in his hands.

Kate looked at Anna. She was shaking her head, lips pressed together, eyes closed.

'Anyway, I'm getting ahead of myself. There I was, having spent far too long away from the house, and thinking that any minute Chris or Betsy would come looking for me. And then I saw the garage, and re-membered that Damien Treloar was staying over-night. I'd completely forgotten. Betsy'd been teasing me about him, about having a crush on him. Well, a lot of you heard that, and it had really got under my skin, because it was just so . . . look, I'm sorry, Chris, she was your mother, but so spiteful of her, really. One of the reasons I was upset about it was that I'd thought you might have believed her, and it suddenly struck me, out there in the orchard, that anyone see-ing me there could have thought, could have thought . . . that I'd been creeping around trying to make a rendezvous with Damien. Or they could pretend to think it, and start teasing me and pecking me again, and Chris might really believe it, and . . .'

She put her hands over her face, and her shoulders began to shake. 'Oh, dear,' she wailed, and Kate real-ised with relief that she was half laughing. 'Oh, dear, what a fool I was!' She shook her head, and pulled herself together.

'So,' she went on, 'filled with terror by now that I'd be seen, I ran the rest of the way up to the house, got in the back door, and went to open the door into the hall, my heart in my mouth, because of my wet shoes and the hem of my dressing gown being all wet, and so on, and there was Betsy waiting for me. Oh, I've never had such a fright in my life. I screamed . . . well, you all know how I screamed.'

She looked around. 'But honestly,' she said. 'I never saw Damien. I didn't kill him. I'm really telling the truth now. Do you understand? Do you believe me?'

'Sonsy, how could anyone not?' said Jeremy. 'If I've ever heard a story that rang with silly truth, that's it!'

'I can see exactly how you'd feel,' said Kate eagerly.

'Exactly. Birdie,' she confronted her friend, 'you didn't really think Sonsy was guilty. I can tell. Why did you let me . . . us, think, even for a moment that she was? If you knew it all, why . . .'

'Well, for one thing, because I *didn't* really know it all,' said Birdie. 'I only had a theory. I had to get Sonsy to tell the whole thing, exactly as it happened, once and for all. It was only a matter of time before someone remembered Mrs Noah's funny hat, and put two and two together to make five. See, although I'd played with the idea that Sonsy had done the murder, I really couldn't believe that she'd go on with all that poisoned apple core business and so on. A trained nurse couldn't possibly believe that the police doctor and everyone else would trust that sort of evidence, and not do a proper post-mortem.'

'Of course not,' said Sonsy with dignity. She raised her chin. 'I really hope you'll all give me the benefit of the doubt. What Chris thought, or thinks, I still don't know. But I think he's been scared to death.'

'Sonsy, darling . . .'

Toby cleared his throat. 'Ah, perhaps, Birdie, we'd better leave it there, for tonight. It's getting late, and . . .' *And where is Martin?* 'and . . . it's not as though . . .' *not as though we've got a shred of evidence, yet my girl. Good Lord, you've just shown how one convincing case based on circumstantial evidence can be knocked down like a pack of cards. You'll do me out of my stripes, if you're not bloody careful.*

Birdie took off her glasses and rubbed her eyes. 'Well, it's up to you, Simon,' she said flatly. Her face looked vulnerable and small without the strong lenses and tortoiseshell frames that were so much part of it. She stared short-sightedly into Simon's shadowed corner, her glasses held loosely in her lap. She looked tired, pale and very alone.

'Wait a minute,' said Jeremy firmly. 'I want to hear the rest of what Birdie has to say.'

'I agree,' said Jill, shaking off Nick's restraining

hand. 'I've got to hear the end. Come on! We can't stop now.'

Oh, Jill, think! Kate silently pleaded. Just like Birdie said to me once, this isn't a game. She's cleared some of us, yes, but don't you see, *someone* must be guilty, and she knows who it is. She *knows*. Kate looked at Theresa, serene in her white-covered bed, Alice sitting grand and protective by her side. Then there was Jeremy, frowning and tense, and Anna, pale and looking very tired. Beside her Wilf looked half asleep, his eyes unfocused, his sparse grey hair ruffled. Jill was leaning forward, vivid and full of energy. Nick, by contrast, was sitting back, his small eyes watchful. Sonsy and Chris leaned together, safe for the moment on some private plateau. Kate looked closely at Sonsy, and suddenly another part of the jigsaw clicked in place. Of course, it had been there, all along, for her to see, and she'd never thought . . . she of all people. She'd taken the wrong tack entirely, and there was the answer to half her questions, as plain as the nose on your . . .

'Well, I suppose—I suppose if that's the general feeling,' Toby was saying, 'we'd best go on. I would like to say, however, that . . .'

'That what we are about to say is without prejudice,' said Birdie crisply.

'Ah, yerse,' growled Toby, and sank back in his chair. This little biddy was certainly a handful. His brother had thrown out a few hints in that direction, but he'd had no idea. Still, he might as well be hung for a sheep as a lamb. He noticed that Theresa Sullivan was smiling sympathetically at him, and for a moment basked in her fellow feeling, forgetting the troubles of office.

'I said earlier,' Birdie went on, looking around earnestly, 'that if I'd been asked to name a theme that's come up repeatedly over the last few days, it would have to be mothers and children. Well, that's so, and thinking about that took me a long way. All the way to Sonsy and back, you might say. I decided to think again about what had been done and said to see if another theme or pattern bobbed up. And it did.' She paused, for effect, thought Kate.

'Well?' exclaimed Jeremy impatiently.

'The other theme was old things—old houses, full of old things and old memories, old people, people who dealt in old things—bought them, sold them, wrote books about them, played with them.' She fell silent again, as if collecting her thoughts, and this time no one interrupted.

'Alice's house was lived in by her family for a very long time. Alice herself seemed overwhelmed by her property. Every drawer and cupboard was full to overflowing with things no longer in constant, or even occasional, use. She was always losing things.'

Kate looked at Alice. The old woman's eyes were sad. She was probably remembering that nothing of that old, cluttered house now remained. Eighty years of memories.

'There's nothing very strange about a person of Alice's age being a bit forgetful,' Birdie continued resolutely. 'But Alice seemed to me only to be vague when it suited her. She could lay her hand on anything of practical use, or anything she used frequently. Yet she'd give clear instructions on where to find other things, like books, or toys for Zoe, and sometimes they'd be there, and sometimes not. Why?

'Alice used to blame Betsy, saying she'd moved things around, but Betsy always said she didn't do this—just cleaned where she could on her monthly visits and left it at that. Certainly there was no sign anywhere of the kind of orderly packing up that I imagine would have been Betsy's style.'

'Poor Mum, poor old Mum.' Anna bent her head and the tears rolled down her cheeks. She got out her handkerchief but didn't use it, just twisted it in her fingers.

Kate noticed people moving uneasily and wished

Birdie would get this over. What was she driving at? *Someone knows.* The thought jumped out at her, and dug its claws in.

She forced herself to pay attention.

'. . . so I made a list of things that had, by Alice's account, gone missing just recently. A book called *Elves and Fairies,* full, Zoe said, of beautiful coloured pictures. An embroidered shawl, a set of fine crystal glasses, an ivory mah jong set, a wooden toy train and of course the Noah's Ark, which was subsequently found.

'Now, I don't know all that much about antiques, but I do know that quite everyday household objects a hundred or even fifty years old, can bring a good price in an antique shop. I actually bought Kate and Jeremy an old ivory mah jong set when they were married, and even then it was a tidy little sum. Very tidy, actually.'

Anna was looking at the small woman rather contemptuously. She thinks Birdie's view of a tidy sum would be very modest indeed, thought Kate. Birdie's camouflage is perfect.

'While you were shopping this morning I went to the library,' Birdie was saying. 'I also rang some second-hand book dealers in Sydney, and an antique restorer I once worked on a programme with. Small items like the ones I've mentioned turn out to be quite valuable. *Elves and Fairies* by Ida Rentoul Outhwaite, one of Australia's first illustrators of books for children, for example, is very sought after in its first edition. Collectors will pay a lot of money for a copy in very good condition.'

'Mine was in good condition,' said Alice. 'Blimey! And now it's a heap of ash!'

'I'm afraid so, Alice. I found a shawl like the one described in a book in the library. They're collector's items now. And a hand-carved Noah's Ark, intact, with Australian animals including koalas, kangaroos and a pair of platypuses—my antiques man nearly swallowed the phone when I told him about it. It was all I could do to stop him coming up here to sift the ashes of the house, Alice.'

'Blow me down!' said Alice. 'So. What are you driving at, lass? Spit it out!'

'Last night I didn't know how valuable the things were, but I strongly suspected they'd be worth a lot. And, except for the Noah's Ark, none of them had turned up despite pretty exhaustive searching. So, say they were gone. Perhaps other things had gone too, without your noticing. What if they'd been stolen?'

There was a heavy silence in the room 'By Damien, you mean?' said Kate at last.

'Well, maybe. But where did that leave me? Back with Alice and the problem of Theresa's "suicide". No. But what if the things had been stolen by someone else, and Damien found out about it somehow. How would he have reacted? He liked having power over people, and playing with them. It gave him a thrill. His conversation with Theresa in the garage, by Betsy's account, and as Theresa has now repeated it to me, also revealed just how bitter he felt about his treatment by the Tender family. What if he discovered that someone in that family had a guilty secret? He might well decide to threaten exposure.

'Right. Who then, in the Tender family, had the chance to take small items from Alice's place? Well, just about everyone. The whole family made regular visits to the house. Who, then, needed a regular extra money supply? Again, just about everyone, as far as I could see. Wilf's business, I gather, isn't prospering, and money is getting tighter. Anna earns reasonable money as a model, but she's not wildly successful, she's getting older, and her expenses are high. Her clothes, shoes, hands, hair have always got to be faultless, and if she wants to leave home and set up on her own, a little extra cash would be very useful. Rodney mixes with a lot of boys from very well-off families, and wants to keep up. Chris is a teacher, his wife is a nurse—not particularly well-paid professions, and Chris has always aimed high.'

'Now look here!' Anna's shrill protest rang through the room, making everyone jump. She sprang to her feet, shaking off her father's gently restraining hand. 'What are you accusing us of? How dare you.'

'Birdie, I hope you're going to explain your . . .' Chris was looking very grim.

Oh my Lord, thought Toby. Here we go.

'I'm sorry,' said Birdie. 'I know you won't want to hear what I've got to say. But it can't be helped. Stealing's not nice, I know.' She smiled grimly. 'But murder's worse, and it's a murder we're discussing. I'll tell you how I think it was.'

'I won't listen!' cried Anna helplessly, and Kate watched with sinking heart as she shrank back into her chair, staring at Birdie's tense face, the spectacles flashing in the strong light.

'I think someone in the Tender family saw in Alice's house the chance to make, on the quiet, the little extra that would help them keep up. After all, the things would come to the family one day, anyway. Alice wasn't using them, and didn't seem to care about them. Betsy had suggested to Alice, a year before, that she sell a few things to raise some cash, and Alice had refused. Damien had told you all that some of the items in the house were very valuable.'

'That doesn't prove anything, does it?' said Chris lightly.

'No, not really. But I'm sure that shortly after this someone decided to dispose of a few things on the quiet, using the list of outlets Damien had supplied. Just small things at first, then larger items of greater value. Finally, the thief was in rather deeply, but the extra money was very useful, and the pilfering went on.'

'Fantasy!' sneered Anna. But Birdie continued resolutely.

'Then a few things happened. The thief got a bit

reckless, and Alice started to notice that things were gone and complain about it, blaming Betsy for moving them. Theresa offered to sell a few bits and pieces for Alice, to help her out, and this time Alice agreed. Perhaps the extent of the losses would be discovered. The thief must have been under considerable strain by the time the party arrived at Atherton for the apple-picking.

'Then Damien turned up unexpectedly. At first things were as you'd expect. Damien had a drink, and left. He came back, with a tale about flat tyres, and asked if he could stay. Betsy at first refused. Then there was a strange exchange. He was elated and excitable. Remember, he'd just seen Theresa and the baby. He was determined to stay and had already made an appointment with Theresa for later that night in the garage. He began to argue persuasively. He said he couldn't sleep in his van because he'd bought a few things on his way up. He named the shops he'd bought them from, and then described them—really in much more detail than one would feel necessary—picture frames carved with gumnuts, a box of big old books, some embroidered tablecloths stinking of camphor. He even said he had receipts for them. It all seemed to me very strange and effusive, and I remembered it. But no one said anything, and Betsy eventually caved in, and let him stay on her own personal responsibility. She let him stay, but was fairly high-handed about it. That got under his skin, and he said that first thing in the morning he was going to have a talk with the whole family. Do you remember?'

Kate nodded, fascinated. The exchange Birdie was describing was vivid in her mind. The sudden shift in perspective was startling.

'Damien said,' she said slowly, 'that he'd been thinking and learning about quite a few things in the past few months . . . about selfishness, he said, and dishonesty, and manipulation. He said he thought it was about time to bring it all out into the open. I thought he was just . . .'

'Yes,' said Birdie, leaning forward a little, her glasses flashing. 'It was cleverly done. He could have been going in for a bit of neurotic role-playing, but I saw it even back then as a threat. A threat to cause some kind of trouble. I couldn't imagine what, but now I'm sure that Damien was telling the thief that he was on to them, and that, moreover, he actually had evidence against them in his van—some of the things that had been taken, and the receipts to show where he'd bought them. No doubt the owners of the shops would remember who had offered them to start with.'

'He talked about the dove and olive branch! He said the dove of peace was hovering meaningfully above his head. He meant he had the Noah's Ark! Of course!' Jill's eyebrows had disappeared into her hair, her face was full of colour. Nick, like Jeremy, was sitting back, looking grave. Both of them kept stealing looks at Chris and Wilf Tender. Chris's face was white, Wilf's was grey.

'But why,' continued Jill, oblivious, 'didn't he just spill the beans then and there?'

'I think he'd intended to. I don't think for a minute he'd tracked all those things down in one weekend. It'd probably taken months. Remember Jill, you said he'd been elated about getting evidence of something he'd been trying to prove for a long time? He wasn't talking about his book, but about the thefts he'd discovered. I think he made a little collection of things over the months, distinctive things that he recognised as Alice's, at the antique shops he'd recommended to the family all that time ago. He probably found one thing by accident, found out from the owner who'd sold it to him, and took it from there. Finally, when he felt he had enough evidence, he loaded the things into his van, and brought them up to tip the bucket on the thief at the worst possible moment—in Alice's house, with all the family and friends assembled. Then he was going to claim Anna, and take her off with him. His behaviour that night would fit in with all of this.

'But Theresa came in, and his plan changed. He put Anna out of it. Now he wanted to settle things with Theresa. He wanted to lay claim to his baby. So he needed a quiet meeting with her. He decided to put off his moment of revenge till morning, but, spurred by irritation at Betsy's rather contemptuous treatment of him, he gave out his threat, delighting in the belief that someone would spend a very unpleasant night. That was his fatal mistake. He miscalculated badly. He underestimated his adversary, who was from that moment planning to kill him.'

'This sounds like high melodrama to me, frankly,' said Chris, with a slight smile. 'I can't wait to hear the end.'

Birdie raised her golden eyes to him and moved a little in her chair.

In his dark corner Toby was sweating slightly. The rain beat down outside. He listened to it and wondered for the fiftieth time where Martin McGlinchy was hiding himself. He could need him badly very soon.

'The murderer had all the materials necessary to hand,' Birdie continued quietly. 'A supposedly batty old lady, poisonous spray theories all over the place, the apple trees. Everyone had been told where a very potent poison was, and the man who had to die was on the premises, and conveniently isolated. OK. The murderer acted, never, I would say, considering that Damien's death would be seen as anything other than an accident.

'This person, who, if you don't mind another touch of melodrama, I'll call X, met Damien Treloar in the orchard and put Parathion on the back of his neck.'

'But how could someone do that without getting

poisoned themselves?' interrupted Jill, leaning forward. 'If it got on their hands . . .'

'Oh, gloves would have stopped that. Rubber gloves, probably worn under ordinary ones, so as not to make Damien suspicious. One of the pairs of light rubber gloves from the pack of four in the kitchen seems to have disappeared. The police have looked everywhere, but can't find them, or any other discarded gloves.

'Anyway, the poison acts quickly. The murderer takes Damien's car keys, makes sure his parka hood is up, and then leaves him, throwing down a few old apple cores that have been dabbed with poison previously. Damien's a dead man already and there's no need to watch what's going to happen next. Besides, there's work to be done at the van.

'In the van the murderer finds the incriminating evidence, just as Damien said, among some other things he'd bought on the way up to the house. The Noah's Ark is particularly conspicuous, because of the rainbow and the dove, which stand up higher than anything else. At this moment, around 2 am, Theresa looks out her window and sees a figure in a pale-blue parka, dark pants, gumboots shining in the moonlight. Remember, Damien was wearing leather boots that were dull when wet, but Theresa saw the boots as shiny. This made me believe that someone in the house, not Damien, was at the van, even before we heard about the parka hood business.'

'Everyone in the house wore gumboots,' said Kate slowly.

'Everyone except Anna, who also wore leather ones,' replied Birdie composedly.

'Theresa goes back to bed, and the murderer, X, takes the Noah's Ark, the frames, the tablecloths and the copy of *Elves and Fairies* out of the van. It's too difficult and risky to take the heavy things back inside, so they're stuffed under the house, at the side near the door. This morning I went and looked in the place where the Noah's Ark was found. Alice had said other "good old stuff" was there. Sure enough, *Elves and Fairies* was stuck away behind a box, with the picture frames Damien described on top.

'I left them there, thinking I'd get Toby to come and see them, *in situ* this afternoon.' Birdie raised her hands, palms up, and dropped them again.

'Sorry, Alice,' she said, turning to the old lady. 'I'm afraid that was a mistake.'

'Ah well,' said Alice philosophically. 'You can't lose money you never knew you had, can you? I'd forgotten all about them frames. Sorry about the book, though.'

'The murderer has to get the receipts, now,' Birdie continued, 'and goes back to the van to look in the glove box, where the receipt books are usually kept. I would suspect there are two—one nearly full, and the other nearly empty. The second is the important one. Damien's kept a special book just for items from Alice's house. X pockets this, and for good measure looks through the wallet of photographs that's also in the glove box, perhaps thinking to remove the rather risque picture of Anna that the family knew Damien carried. It wouldn't do to have that getting into the hands of the police and being shown around to all and sundry. Not very salubrious.

'Possibly that picture is found and removed. As Anna told us, it wasn't in the collection when the police took possession of it the next day. But while looking for it, X discovers something else of interest. There's a photograph of Theresa Sullivan among all the others.'

Theresa stirred uncomfortably, and Alice muttered to her.

Birdie glanced at them briefly, and continued. 'No doubt the murderer is flabbergasted, but pockets both photographs, not really planning anything, probably, but just as a thrifty measure. The death mustn't be seen as anything but an accident, and the photo will complicate things.

'The keys are left in the van—it's all X can think of doing. It would be unwise to walk on the soft earth in front of the garage doorway, and unthinkable to go near Damien Treloar again, and see what was happening to him.'

'Oh, don't!' Anna was trembling now, her face in her hands. Wilf patted her awkwardly. He was starting to look more aware, as though the shock of what he was hearing was somehow galvanising him. He was at last paying close attention to what was being said, and beginning to react.

'So,' Birdie continued, 'X then slipped back to the house, and stowed the embroidered tablecloths in the sideboard, where we found them when we had drinks with Alice the next night. Somehow or other, the gloves, the receipt book and the photograph of Anna, and, of course, the poison bottle and swab, were disposed of.'

'You haven't found those.' Chris was looking thoughtful. Sonsy gripped his arm, but he didn't look at her.

'No, not yet,' said Birdie quietly. 'If we had, I wouldn't have to go into so much detail to convince you I was right.'

'Yes, I see . . . I guess.' He smiled grimly.

'In the morning, things went as planned at first. Then, catastrophe. A post-mortem is to be held. The police don't seem to believe in the accident theory. People in the house are being questioned. This isn't according to plan at all.

'X has been seen at the van by Theresa, and mistaken for Damien. X hears Toby ask Theresa to rack her brains about the person she saw, and about the van itself, and hears Theresa say that she just saw shapes inside the van, just shapes sticking up and showing through the windows. And X is in the room when Theresa sees the Noah's Ark silhouetted against the uncurtained window of Alice's living room.'

'What? What's that got to do with anything?' said Anna angrily. 'I've never heard such a . . .'

'No, wait Anna,' said Kate urgently. 'I remember that. I remember.'

'I wasn't wearing my glasses, you see,' said Theresa quietly. 'I was standing on the other side of the room from the Ark, and Chris, I think it was, went over and pulled back the curtains, so that for the first time I saw the Ark as a shape lit from behind—just a shape—a rough oblong, with the rainbow making an arch over it, and at the top of the arch the dove, with its wings stretched out.'

'So?'

'You see, Anna, I'd seen that shape before, through the windows of Damien's van, while he was talking to me, and telling me that I had to meet him later on. I saw the arch of the rainbow, standing up over all the other things. It was very distinctive. I picked it out again when I looked out the bedroom window later. I didn't know what it was then, of course, and I never connected Alice's Noah's Ark with the object I'd seen in the van until I saw it again in silhouette that afternoon. I was thunderstruck. I couldn't hide it. Surely you all must have noticed! I was sure you had.'

'I noticed,' said Birdie ruefully, 'but I thought you were upset because of Anna's description of Damien's photo collection. Everyone else, I think, just thought you were embarrassed by the rather nasty domestic scene you'd got mixed up in.'

'Honestly, I barely heard all the talk about the photos. It registered, but it was pretty obvious my picture wasn't in the collection Anna was talking about. Neither she nor Simon Toby had mentioned it to me, and anyway I really wasn't thinking about my position at all, just then. I was . . .'

'Thinking about mine, eh?' Alice grinned. 'There I

was, saying I'd found the Ark under me house, and
you'd seen it with your own eyes a few nights back in
a murdered bloke's car! I suppose that put the lid on
it, as far as you were concerned. You should be
ashamed of yourself, girl. Take me for an idiot?'

'Oh, Alice.'

Birdie cut in crisply. 'So, Theresa said nothing, because she thought she'd just seen definite proof that
Alice had indeed committed a murder for her sake. A
bit of a comedy of errors, but there you are. She went
to the park with the others, worrying away, and then
went home to feed Nel and have a sleep. Unfortunately, however, the murderer had seen what had
happened. X too had seen the Noah's Ark as a shape
in the back of the van. When the curtains were drawn
back X saw what Theresa saw, and knew that Theresa
had made the connection. X decided that Theresa was
a danger, and had to be disposed of.'

'Look, Birdie, I'm not exactly arguing with you,'
said Jeremy, glancing nervously at Chris and forestalling Anna's furious interjection, 'but you seem to be
assuming a lot. I don't see how anyone in particular
could be linked with the murder even if the Ark *was*
seen in the van before Treloar was killed. Theresa
jumped to the conclusion that Alice was involved.
Surely that's more likely? Why would any statement
Theresa might make point the finger in anyone else's
direction?'

'You're right. Except that there was another little
fact known by someone else, which, if it was joined
with Theresa's information, would put the murderer
in a very nasty position indeed.'

'What do you mean? What other fact?' Jeremy
looked at Kate, who raised her eyebrows and glanced
around the room. Everyone looked as bewildered as
she did.

'Well, come on,' said Jeremy impatiently. 'Who's
the someone else?'

'Your daughter.'

'Zoe?'

'Yes,' said Birdie quietly. 'You see, the murderer couldn't leave well enough alone. Alice was complaining about losing things, and that whole issue had to be dead and buried, for obvious reasons. The Noah's Ark was of particular interest to Alice, so X arranged for it to be found by telling Zoe where to look, not realising that Zoe had *already* looked under the house, in exactly that spot, among others.'

'But she *can't* have!' exclaimed Kate. 'I'd told her a dozen times not to go under there, because of the spiders. I'd told her, we'd all told her.'

'*Exactly*. Zoe couldn't admit she'd been under the house because she'd disobeyed, and she didn't want to get into trouble. When it was suggested she look there, taking Alice with her, she did as she was told, for the sake of peace. She knew she'd find nothing, but then, lo and behold, there the Ark was! Zoe couldn't understand it. She went back to X and explained her confusion. Her amazement and curiosity outweighed her fear of punishment by then, I imagine. X made the best of a bad job and told Zoe that the fairies had done it, that it was magic, and she mustn't say a word about it or they'd be cross.'

'And you know what?' said Jill. 'I can actually add something to this. Zoe had definitely been under the house before. I caught her crawling out the day we arrived. She said she'd been looking for something.'

'Oh, the little devil!' cried Kate. 'Honestly, kids! You never told me that, Jill!'

Jill looked hunted. 'Well, she was so guilty, and promised not to do it again. I said I wouldn't tell on her.'

'Dear, dear, dear . . .' Jeremy shook his head. 'What a mess.'

'Right.' Birdie looked pleased. 'Good . . . see, the murderer had to stop anyone from realising that, one, the Ark was in the van on the night of the murder; two, that two days later it was in a place where it certainly had not been before; and three, that X had known it was there. The vital pieces of information were held by two different people—Theresa and Zoe. Of the two, Theresa was the more dangerous because she was an adult, and also because Theresa had seen X at the van and might any minute think of something incriminating. Then of course there was the photograph, a magnificent clue for the police to find following a staged suicide.

'Theresa was invited to dinner that night. This set a timetable going. It provided a perfect opportunity for the body to be discovered at the earliest possible moment, because of the baby. Getting rid of a threatening person was one thing, but putting a harmless baby in danger was quite another, for X.'

'But Birdie, if it happened like this, why was gas used at all?' said Kate. 'If, as you say, someone got into Theresa's house, using Alice's key, and, say, put sleeping pills into the milk they knew Theresa would drink, why didn't they just triple the number of pills and leave it at that? People would think it was an overdose.'

'Yes,' said Birdie, 'but we'd had quite a discussion about pills, hadn't we, and Theresa made it clear that she never took them, and didn't have any in the house. To X, I think, that would've been a warning sign. After that discussion people might think it strange that Theresa would suicide in that way, and there might be an examination of the whole pill question. How much simpler, then, to just put Theresa to sleep, and come back later to start the gas.'

'But that's so risky! I mean, what if Theresa was still awake when the murderer got in?'

'Well, X was pretty sure that it would be OK,' said Birdie, looking at her hands. 'Because she'd sent Wilf over at two-thirty to check that Theresa was drowsy and about to go to sleep.'

25

Secrets

'What?'

'Birdie, what are you saying?'

People were standing, shouting, gesticulating. Only Wilf, Birdie, Alice and Sonsy sat pensively on, staring at one another across the room.

'Sent . . . but I went to get some parsley for Bet,' said Wilf slowly. 'There wasn't any by the tank, so I had to go over.'

'There was masses there,' protested Jill. 'I saw it there myself.'

'I think Betsy must have picked it all earlier,' said Birdie.

'Oh, come *on*!' cried Anna, flinging herself back in her chair.

'Well,' said Birdie, almost humbly, 'there was a massive bundle in a plastic bag in the fridge when I looked this morning. Two huge bunches.'

'We had tabouli for dinner last night,' said Kate, and shuddered.

'Yes. It was half parsley. Enough vitamin E for a week, and still a huge bag of parsley left this morning, tucked right at the back of the refrigerator.'

'Anyone could have done that, Birdie,' said Chris

slowly. 'Anyone could've picked the parsley. I mean, Dad could've, or I could've, or . . .'

Birdie smiled. 'Oh, of course, anyone could have picked that parsley, to give them an excuse to go over to Theresa's. But no one knew it would be needed except Betsy, and anyway there was only one person, of all the people in that house, who would have picked all of Alice's, to help set up a murder, and then carefully stored it away in the fridge for later use. Think about it. Betsy couldn't stand waste. She'd been a thrifty housekeeper for years. She just couldn't stand to do what anyone else would have done, and just thrown the stuff away. She kept it, and fed it to us, and would have gone on doing that until it was all gone.

'I told you—all three crimes—the poisoning, the gas and the fire, were obviously planned by someone who was daring, single-minded, quick thinking, and adept at using materials to hand. Who but Betsy fits this profile?'

'Birdie, Mum died in the fire,' said Chris stiffly.

'Chris, I'm sorry. Let me go on, it won't take long. Please.'

He nodded. Sonsy took his hand, and he turned to her gratefully as Birdie stuffed her hands into her pockets and began to speak again.

'When you think about it, Betsy was the only person in the house who really fitted all our requirements for X,' she said.

'Wilf's business wasn't prospering, and Betsy had no money of her own. Everyone was amazed at how well she managed, with Rodney at an expensive private school, the house needing redecorating and so on. And she still had enough left over to keep herself beautifully dressed, go to the hairdresser every few weeks, give generous presents to her children. Betsy mixed with people for whom the ability to pay for those little extras was an assumed fact of life. She needed to be one of them, and found that with prices going up and their income shrinking, it was getting harder and harder.

'On the night of Damien's murder, Betsy was clearly the one who had the power to make Damien go, or let him stay. She did allow him to stay, with no interference from anyone. Damien forced her into it by implicitly threatening exposure and then, fatally, let her know that he was going to expose her anyway. He didn't realise what an implacable enemy he was facing.

'Sometime, probably while she was giving him the hurricane lamp, Betsy organised a meeting with Damien. She'd made her plan. She was going to do what she'd always done. Improvise. Use materials to hand to cobble up holes and keep life going. Like covering a box with a rug, and calling it a dressing table, if a dressing table is needed, or lifting a few bits and pieces from an old relative's house to pay for little extras. She used what she had to hand to kill Damien Treloar.

'She didn't for a moment think that anyone would be suspected of murder, only that Alice's competence might be questioned, which would have suited her. She just saw what she had to do, and did it, blind to any complication.'

'I can't believe this is happening,' said Chris slowly. 'I . . . I can't seem to take it in.'

'Chris, wake up! There's not a scrap of evidence for any of this!' exploded Anna. 'She's shielding someone, and blaming poor Mum because she's not here to defend herself.'

'Anna, I assure you, that's exactly why I'm going through this so carefully. So that you and everyone else can see that every other possibility was considered, and no doubt can remain. I want everyone to be convinced.'

'I know you do. Well, you seem to be doing a pretty good job of convincing everyone else, but you haven't convinced me. 'And you haven't convinced my father either. Has she, Dad?'

Wilf looked at her with watery eyes. 'I . . . I'm a bit at sea, Anna,' he said helplessly. 'I need a bit of time to think . . . I . . .'

She gave him up as a hopeless case, and turned back to Birdie, who was looking at her warily. 'Well, I'm not convinced, anyhow,' she said. 'Let's hear, for example, how my mother could possibly have killed my husband in the way you've described.'

'Anna, I'd always wondered how the poisoning was managed,' said Birdie earnestly. 'I didn't really think that someone could successfully creep up on Damien and just splash the stuff on. Then, last night, I thought of a way it could be done.

'Damien loathed creepy-crawlies, and was completely paranoid about leeches. We know that. Now, we all saw what Betsy did when you had a leech. She called for salt, to remove the leech, and iodine to dab on the spot where it had been. She's always done that, hasn't she?

'Damien would be very familiar with that treatment too. Betsy had actually used it on him, last year. Right. Now. Betsy sits with Damien and they talk. Suddenly she tells him that he's got a leech on the back of his neck. He believes her, and gets the heebies. Don't worry, Betsy says, I've got all the doings here in my pocket, from earlier today. She pretends to remove the leech with salt. I'll give it a dab of iodine to be safe, she says, and paints his neck liberally with a big wad of cotton wool and her little bottle of nasty stuff, bold as brass. He'd expect that, and wouldn't think anything of it.'

Birdie gazed around impassively at the ring of white faces, aware of the strength of the picture she was painting. Anna was looking faint and ill.

'So Damien sits there, feeling a bit sick because of the leech that was never there, and suddenly he feels a lot sicker. He gets frightened. Betsy says, "Look, don't move, you must be having an allergic reaction"—remember Wilf talking about that? Damien was there then. "Put up your parka hood," Betsy says, "and sit tight. You must keep warm and for goodness sake, don't move, because that'll make it worse. Give me your car keys. I'll bring your car down here and take you to hospital." Damien is terrified. He's not going to argue, nor remember that the van's out of action.

'I've described what I think happened next. Betsy in her blue parka, blue ski pyjamas and gumboots, could be easily mistaken for Damien at the van.'

'But the next day, she was so upset about the whole thing,' said Chris urgently. His voice was trembling. 'She was really upset, I could tell. She wasn't pretending.'

'No,' said Birdie. 'She wasn't pretending. She'd realised, probably for the first time, that she'd destroyed something she'd really valued, by killing Damien in her special childhood place. She mentioned her regret to Kate afterwards. She was also sorry because Anna was now receiving a second shock, and perhaps some of the good done by the eavesdropping on Damien the night before would be lost. She'd had to choose between protecting herself and protecting her ascendancy over her daughter. Well, she'd chosen, and now she had to bear the consequences.'

Birdie looked around, glasses flashing. No one said a word.

'A couple of days later,' said Birdie, 'it's Theresa's turn. While Theresa is away from the house, Betsy puts some of her own sleeping pills in the milk she knows Theresa will drink just before two. At two-thirty she establishes that Theresa is very sleepy and is going to have her nap. Everyone except Zoe is out or asleep. Right. Betsy finishes making the casserole, and puts it on to cook. It's now about three o'clock. Theresa should be well asleep. She goes into the bathroom and turns on the shower. Zoe's playing with the

Noah's Ark. She'll have no sense of time. Kate hears the shower go on as she falls asleep. It runs on and on. Betsy slips through the storeroom, up the side verandah and out the front door. She gets into Theresa's house by the side door for the second time, does what she has to do, leaves the photograph, torn in half, on the table and gets back home again within, I'd say, ten or twelve minutes. Back in the bathroom she takes off her clothes, wets her head and face, turns off the shower and after a couple of minutes reappears in her dressing gown, to all appearances refreshed. She then changes, and carries on as normal.'

Birdie broke off and looked gravely at Kate.

'Kate, meanwhile, is still asleep. She's been having a weird dream. The dream starts with endless, flooding rain. A reaction, I'd say, to her unconscious realisation that the water in the bathroom ran for a very, very long time, far longer than normal.'

'Come off it, Birdie,' said Jeremy. 'This is all very ingenious, I'm sure, but you can't prove all that. The parsley thing's persuasive, but you've got no proof at all that Betsy didn't just have a harmless shower, like she always did at about that time.'

'Only three little hints, Jeremy. Two of them stemming from the one big mistake Betsy made—one so typical of her that once I saw it I started suspecting her at once. First, Betsy's hair usually springs into curls when it's washed. Those little perm curls, you know.'

'But that afternoon it wasn't springy at all,' said Kate slowly. 'It was limp and dull. I thought she was looking a bit seedy, and noticed her hair . . . but yes, it looked just like hair does if it's just been wet, not washed at all.'

'You saw it too!' said Birdie. 'Good.' She hesitated. 'But the other two things are even more persuasive, and you were a witness to them too, Kate. You didn't know what you were seeing, of course.'

'Of course,' said Kate drily.

'You see, Betsy just couldn't bring herself to run that shower using hot water, for all that time while she was out. It would seem such wicked waste, and anyway, she might have emptied the tank if she was away too long. So she used cold water. Kate went into the bathroom when she woke up, just before four. The door was shut. She opened it, went inside and through the window saw Zoe playing on the grass. She felt that something was wrong, but she couldn't put her finger on it. The room depressed her, she said. It smelt old and musty.'

'Nothing strange about that, Miss,' growled Alice.

'Ah, but Alice, if Betsy had really had her usual shower, and the door had been left shut as it was, the window would have been misted over, even an hour later—you all know that—you've seen it. Kate would've had to rub a clear space to see outside, and she didn't have to, did you Kate?'

'No,' said Kate. Her eyes widened. 'And . . .'

'And the bathroom wouldn't have smelt musty. It would have smelt of steam mixed with that soap and talc Betsy always used. Every afternoon I've noticed that smell in the bathroom, haven't you?'

'*Yes!*' exclaimed Jill. 'I have!'

'Yes,' echoed Kate. 'I *knew* there was something. That's right. No jasmine smell. Not a trace. And no misty window, or mirror.' She looked at Birdie and nodded her head. 'You're right, Birdie. Whatever else Betsy did she didn't have a shower.'

Birdie sat back a bit, a little more relaxed. 'If all had gone well, no one would have gone near Theresa's place till six-thirty that night, and it would have been all over by then.' She tightened her lips. 'As it was it was touch and go.

'I spent that night thinking a few things out. And in the morning I arranged to talk privately to the one person I hadn't talked to before. Zoe.

'In the car on the way into town we talked about Noah's Ark. She confided in me—you know how she does, Kate—about sneaking under the house the day before the murder. She said the Ark wasn't there then. Definitely. But the morning after next it was. Magic, she said. No such thing, I said. Auntie Betsy says there is, she said. And then she clammed up completely and wouldn't say another word. When we got to town I did my antique checking, and then went to see Theresa, who gave me the whole story about seeing the Ark in the van.'

'Once she knew I wasn't in the gun anymore,' put in Alice proudly.

'I thought . . .' Birdie stopped and ran her tongue over her lips. 'I thought Zoe was quite safe. Betsy thought Theresa was dying, so that even if Zoe did babble sooner or later, there'd be no evidence to link the Ark with Damien, so it wouldn't matter. I thought, as well, that she was going to lunch with you, Kate, and she'd be well out of Betsy's way, anyway. But then I found out that she'd gone back to Alice's and that by incredibly bad luck some blabber-mouth nurse had told Betsy at the shops that Theresa was better. Oh my God I was scared.'

'*You* were scared!' Jeremy growled.

'I found out that only Sonsy and Alice were with them and that scared me even more, because frankly they were both people Betsy could easily have lived without. Both of them were being very troublesome. I knew she'd single out Zoe if she could. But if she couldn't . . .'

'You're forgetting that it was only because of a broken tooth that Dad wasn't in the house,' said Anna, colour high on her cheeks.

'No,' said Birdie. 'I hadn't forgotten that.' She looked at her hands.

Again there was a rather unpleasant silence.

'Betsy made tea, and milk for Zoe, when we got home,' said Sonsy quietly. 'I only drank half my tea. I wasn't feeling well anyway, and I was worried about Betsy. I couldn't say so to Chris, but there was something about her. I've seen people strung up like that before, in nursing homes. Alice went into her room. Zoe was yawning and saying that she was going to read on the couch for a while. Betsy seemed calm and collected enough, so I relaxed and went and lay down myself, and I went to sleep.'

'I took me tea into me room,' said Alice. 'But thank the Lord I didn't drink it. Not that I had the faintest clue what was going to happen, but I didn't feel inclined, for once in my life. Someone up there must have been looking after us.'

Kate leaned forward. 'Oh, Alice, you don't know how grateful we . . .'

'Ah well.' The old woman looked embarrassed. 'Nothing very wonderful, love. I'm just glad I got to the little girl in time, like.' Her face darkened and the vision of that smoke-filled, smouldering room, so nearly ready to burst into flames, rose up before them. Kate's heart thudded and she gripped Jeremy's hand.

She groped in the pocket of her jacket. She pulled out a handkerchief and with it an envelope inscribed 'FOR THE FAIRIES' in decorative capitals. The tears fell.

'Come on, sweetie. Don't cry. She's OK. She can't even remember it,' murmured Jeremy.

'No. I know. She's fine.' Kate wiped her eyes. She fingered the envelope and opened it slowly.

'I woke up and heard the crackling and smelt the smoke,' said Sonsy. 'I was all confused and slow. I didn't really know what had woken me up, at first. And then I heard the screaming—next door, in Betsy's room.'

Chris put his hands over his eyes. Anna's tragic face was frozen. Sonsy's eyes were blank with remembered horror. 'The fire was . . . I got up and looked round and there were flames and smoke all down the front of the verandah. It started sort of roaring. And then the wall between our bed and Betsy's room started to burn. There were big black patches coming, and little tongues of flame. There was no more screaming. I ran to the window and tried to get out, but it'd only open a little way. I pushed and tried and then Birdie came and she helped me, and pulled me through onto the grass. She saved me. But Betsy . . .'

'She got caught,' said Birdie gravely, 'in a trap she'd made herself.'

'But how, Birdie?' Chris looked at her with anguish on his face. 'If . . . if it could possibly be true that my mother did all this, why on earth did she stay in the house? It doesn't make any sense!'

There was a sharp knock, and all eyes turned to see the wet, woolly head of Martin McGlinchy pop through the opening door.

'McGlinchy!' Toby's chair scraped on the floor as he struggled to get to his feet.

Martin edged into the room. He was wet and filthy. He clutched a dripping jacket and two grubby plastic bags, and the people nearest him shrank back so as not to be spattered with black mud.

He looked around in a hunted fashion. 'Ah, have you . . . ?'

'You've missed the entire thing, McGlinchy.' Toby's voice was cold.

Martin's nostrils flared slightly. 'I went back to the house—Miss Allcott's house—sir, because I had this idea.'

'You mean you've been crawling round that place in the teeming rain?'

Martin wordlessly thrust one of the plastic bags at him. Toby looked inside, and a curious expression came over his face. He pulled away the plastic slowly. The Noah's Ark lay in his arm, the rainbow arching, the dove exuberantly spreading its wings.

'Where was it?' he asked quietly.

'Under the rose bush, near the front gate. The idea was to go back and pick it up quietly, when all the hue and cry had died down, I suppose. There's a jumper in the bag, sir, too. For padding, I guess.'

Balancing the Ark carefully, Toby let the bag drop to the floor. A soft mass of mushroom pink was revealed.

'That's Mum's,' whispered Anna. 'Her cashmere. Her new cashmere.'

'Couldn't bear to leave either of them, see,' growled Alice softly. 'Waste not want not, that was Bet.'

Everyone stared.

'But still, I don't get it. If Betsy had her stuff outside, why on earth did she go back in?' Jeremy was sitting forward, trying to come to grips with it. Kate was watching Toby and Martin, and remembering words the three of them had heard some hours ago.

Toby looked up. 'She forgot something,' he said briefly.

He was looking in the second plastic bag. Martin stood watching, his hands hanging loose.

'This is what you went to find, boy,' said Toby, almost to himself, 'wasn't it?'

Martin nodded. 'The little girl put me onto it, earlier tonight. It was raining and I thought, the ashes will have cooled enough to look, so I . . .'

'So you took off, by yourself, because you weren't sure. And your hunch paid off.' Toby shook his head almost sadly. 'Once I would have done that,' he said. He faced the room, and lifted from the bag a blackened tin box. A koala's face stared blankly from one sooty corner.

'What is it?' said Jill impatiently.

Several voices began to answer her, but all gave way to Wilf's monotone.

'It's Bet's treasure box. I knew it would be. I knew.' He dropped his head.

Toby's blunt fingers opened the lid of the box. He tilted it, so they could see inside. 'A pair of driving gloves, some thin rubber gloves, a swab, a brown bottle, a receipt book and a photograph of Mrs Treloar,' he said formally. 'Where exactly did you find this, McGlinchy?'

'In the ash, under the frame of the bed, sir, just next to where the lady was found.'

'She must have got outside and suddenly remembered the box,' said Kate slowly. 'She'd done it all so quickly. She'd forgotten that the tin box mightn't burn with everything else. She waited till the house was well alight, so she could be seen to be "escaping" if anyone was watching. And then once she was outside, she thought of the box, and panicked. She had to go back for it. It'd be discovered after the fire for sure. But it was too late. The fire must have been too fast for her. It got to the bedroom just when she was reaching under the bed to get the box.'

'It would have been under the floorboards there, see,' said Alice gruffly. 'That was a favourite spot for her to hide things, in the old days. My Dad used to keep valuables there. Sovereigns. I should've thought of it.'

'Oh, Mum . . .' Anna covered her face with her hands, and this time Wilf leaned towards her, his arms outstretched.

'It follows the pattern so perfectly,' said Birdie almost dreamily. 'She was improvising the whole time, using whatever came to hand, seizing the moment. She used her treasure box to hide the evidence in a childhood hidey-hole. And remember she said once that she was afraid Alice'd burn the house down one day? She thought of that, and used it. She'd be destroying the source of her extra income, but I'd say all she cared about by then was preserving her safety, and that meant destroying Zoe, and the evidence that things had disappeared from the house. If her gamble had paid off, no one would ever have suspected her of anything, even if Theresa had recovered.'

'If only she'd known.' Kate held out the letter in her hand, and Birdie took it. She looked at Toby over her glasses, and began to read.

Dear Fairies

Thank you for bringing back the Noahs Ark. It must have been a heavy load. I have made you some decorations for your palace. I hope you like them. I know you brought the ark back, because Anty Betsy said. She told me to look under the house near the door, and I did even though I looked there before. Aunty Betsy says that I must not tell that the Ark came there suddenly or that she helped me find it because then you would be angry and take the Ark away. I will try to keep the secret.
Thank you

Love Zoe xxx

Ps Could you bring Aunty Betsys treasure box back too? She needs it for her cottons. When I found them all messy in her basket she was sad and said not to tell that you had her box. Aunty Betsy and I have lots of secrets now, don't we?

26

Winding Down

The sun was rising as they made their way down the mountain. In the back seat Zoe dozed.

Kate sighed. 'It's incredible, Betsy doing what she did. You know, Jeremy, it was only by accident that Wilf wasn't in the house. If he hadn't broken that tooth, do you think she'd have . . .'

'God knows. I think she would have been capable of anything. I think he'd have been a goner just like the others.'

'I think he thinks that, too. Poor Wilf. I think he knew it was Betsy all the time, you know.'

'Maybe he did.'

'Chris and Sonsy might have a chance now, anyway.'

'I guess so. They're a funny pair. She's still looking sick as a dog, Kate. She should see a doctor.'

Kate laughed. 'She saw one just before they came to the mountains. She's pregnant.'

'What?'

'Yes. That's where all the queasy stomach and sleepiness came from. And the hysterics, I guess.'

'Pregnant! How do you know?'

'She told me last night, but I'd worked it out already. I knew that her way of sitting with her hands over her middle was familiar. Lots of pregnant women do that, even early on. It's that protective feeling you get, I suppose. She hadn't told Chris till last night either, apparently.'

'*What!*'

'She didn't know what to do. She thought Betsy would take the baby over, and Chris would aid and abet her. She knew she couldn't bear that.'

'She's a case, that girl.'

'Well, she's very young, Jeremy. And Betsy had her bluffed. But she said the murder changed everything. She said she suddenly realised, looking at Damien dead in the orchard, and hearing Betsy carrying on, that *everyone* was mortal, and that Betsy wasn't some all-powerful wicked witch, just a selfish, determined woman. She decided that she had something of her own to protect now, and if she had to she'd just leave Chris standing, and take the baby with her.'

'Poor old Chris.'

'Well, he asked for it!'

Kate watched the mountain villages slip by. 'Birdie did a good job, didn't she?' she said at last. She glanced at her husband. 'Go on, admit it!'

Jeremy grinned. 'I don't mind admitting it. She had what the job required—a mind like a steep trap, and a heart to match!'

'Jeremy, honestly, you . . .'

Wrangling contentedly they leant together, as the mountains slipped away behind them.

Alice walked around her house—or what had been her house. Toby walked beside her.

'Bit of a mess, eh?' she said.

'Yes, I'm afraid so. I'm sorry, Miss . . .'

'Call me Alice,' she said automatically. 'Ah, that's life, isn't it? Least said, soonest mended, Dad used to say.'

He looked at her curiously. She looked back, and laughed.

'Did you think I'd fall in a heap, seeing the old house gone? S'pose that's why you came with me, eh? Look son, the old place didn't mean a lot to me. A few memories—a lot of memories—but I've still got them. I'll collect the insurance and I'll get a nice new little place built here that'll suit me fine. A place with a room for the children to come and stay. Chris and his girl, and the baby—if they make a go of it, and maybe young Rodney, if he wants to come. He might. Don't think Anna will. Oh yes, a new little place'll suit me down to the ground.'

'Look, that's fine,' said Toby heartily. 'It's fine you're seeing it that way, Alice. Theresa was afraid . . .'

'Ah, even Theresa doesn't understand. Look son, it wasn't the house, or the things in it. That's the tragedy. I'd have given Bet the lot if she'd told me she needed it. But that wasn't her way.' She sighed, and then turned her back on the house and grabbed his arm. 'See,' she said, 'it's the *place*.' She gestured towards the orchard, and the mountains beyond. 'It's the place, and it's me trees I care about. As long as I can be here, I don't care if I live in a tent.' She looked around with hungry eyes.

'The trees still want picking. I'll have to get some local lads in, and put me money down, for a change,' she said thoughtfully, then turned to him with a twinkle in her eyes. 'I'm going to stay with Theresa for a while, till the new place is built. Six months it might take, but she says she doesn't mind. I can look after the little one at night, if Theresa wants to go out, can't I? If someone wants to take her out, I mean, and get to know her better.'

Toby looked into the distance, and to his horror felt a flush rise to his middle-aged cheeks.

'As long as, if things go your way, you promise to stay on opposite instead of taking her off somewhere,' said Alice firmly.

In his confusion, Toby found himself fervently promising this weird old witch the comforts of Theresa's company for as long as she might live. Afterwards, with the memory of her chuckle ringing in his ears, he found it hard to imagine how he had let her trick him into revealing himself in such a callow fashion.

He left her there, sitting in a rickety garden chair, in the orchard.

'I'll be back in half an hour,' he said. 'Will you be OK?'

'Lovely,' she said, 'lovely.'

She settled back, to watch her trees grow.

If you enjoyed GRIM PICKINGS by Australia's answer to Agatha Christie, you'll enjoy Jennifer Rowe's next Bantam mystery, **MURDER BY THE BOOK**.

The following is an exciting preview of **MURDER BY THE BOOK**, coming from Bantam in January, 1992.

'Evie, they can't do this!' raged Kate. 'They can't just tell a man to get out of his own company like that! In one afternoon!'

'They've done it, haven't they?' said Evie Newell slowly. 'They own the thing now. They can do what they like.' She stood up and walked to her office window, leaning heavily on the wide sill. The windows buzzed slightly, picking up the vibrations of the peak hour traffic, rising on gusts of hot, humid air from the shimmering roadway below. But Evie was staring across the road, at the green park slipping away to the Harbour behind black iron railings.

'So,' she said softly, 'that's that.'

'We should all just leave. Just walk out,' insisted Kate, determined to get a response. 'How can you be so calm, Evie? You of all people?'

Evie turned to face her, stocky, tired and pale with anger. 'For God's sake, Kate, what's the good of going on like this? Brian knew when he fought the takeover what he was risking. He knew, I knew, you knew—everyone knew! Now the Gold Group's got Berry and Michaels, and they wouldn't want Brian Berry as mail boy, let alone managing director. That's it. The fight's over. Brian lost, and he's out.' She turned back to the window.

There was a knock on the door. Little Sylvia de Groot, the royalties manager, crept into the room. Her eyes were red and puffy under her heavy black fringe, and her nose was shiny pink under a thin film of powder.

'Brian's gone,' she whispered. 'Did you see him?'

Evie made no movement, but Kate nodded. Sylvia sniffed, and her eyes filled with tears.

'We waved him off,' she said. 'The girls from the order room, and accounts, and the computer room. He kissed everyone and just went. I couldn't believe it was happening.' She cast her eyes in Evie's direction and raised her eyebrows. 'How is she?' she mouthed. Kate shrugged, and shook her head.

'I've had authors on the phone all day,' Sylvia said aloud. 'They saw the piece in the paper. They say they'll leave Berry and Michaels if Brian goes.'

'They say that now,' said Evie, without turning around.

'Oh, they mean it, Evie, really!' said Sylvia earnestly. She brushed back her fringe. 'Some of them have been with us since his dad's time—and *his* dad's in the estates' cases. We keep saying what a crime Gerald Berry ever made Berry and Michaels into a public company. If he hadn't this could never have happened.'

'It probably seemed a good idea then,' replied Evie. She hunched her shoulders, turned away from the window and walked back to her desk. 'How was he to know a mob of greedy shareholders, and half his family, would sell his baby to the highest bidder one day—and that his son'd be tipped out on his ear.'

'An English company, too,' breathed Sylvia. 'Berry and Michaels being owned overseas. I mean, it's terrible! He'd turn in his grave. And this English man they're sending out to replace Brian—this Quentin Hale . . .'

'What about him?' said Evie through tight lips.

'Well, he won't know anything about us, or our authors or anything, will he? And someone said he was really awful.'

'He's a hatchet man,' snapped Evie. 'He's some marketing heavy who's been angling for the job. Brian met him in London. He says he'd sell his grandmother for sixpence if that was all that was offering.'

'How old is he?' asked Kate curiously.

'Early fifties. Aging *Wunderkind*, Brian said. He's spent most of his time in stationery, apparently. Great, eh?'

'Stationery!' Kate exploded.

Evie almost smiled. 'Thought the managing editor'd like that,' she said. 'Brian thought he'd get the job. The Gold Group's awfully old school tie these days, you know, and Hale's not quite quite, apparently. Not pukka enough, or something. Didn't go to the right school, doesn't talk proper. And there was some nasty domestic scandal he was involved in, about a year ago. Someone died, and it got into the papers. The

Gold Group people looked down their noses at that sort of thing. Puts them off their polo.'

She looked under her eyebrows at Sylvia's shocked face. 'Well, it wouldn't be the first time the poms have sent their embarrassments to the colonies to stop them lowering the tone at home, would it?' she said. 'You'd think the immigration laws'd stop them doing it.' She laughed bitterly. 'Great, isn't it? They make all these eager beavers wait years for residency, and they let Quentin Hale and his missus in just like that!'

Sylvia blinked, looked at Kate, sidled to the door and slipped out.

'What do you think's going to happen now?' asked Kate.

Evie shrugged, her eyes hard. She indicated a sheet of paper on her desk. 'I know exactly what will happen. They faxed me—or rather, they faxed "Miss Edie Newen, Publicity Manager", and we assume that's me. Anyway, Miss Edie Newen has her orders. The illustrious Mr Hale will be arriving on Monday, and will be in the office by lunchtime. He will be welcomed at a management lunch, which I am to organise. He will stay in a hotel, which I am to organise, until Brian's things have been removed from the apartment upstairs, which I am to organise, and then his wife, the illustrious *Mrs* Hale, will arrive, and they'll take up residence.'

'Then I would say the illustrious Mr Hale will begin to lay about him, sack a few people, appoint a few new ones, throw his weight around a bit and then settle down to charm everyone into submission—specially the press and the authors. His big job'll be to make everyone happy with the takeover, defuse the criticism, all that.'

'He'll want you to help,' said Kate quietly.

'I suppose he will. I always said public relations was the second oldest profession.'

'You're really not leaving? You always said that if Brian went you'd . . .'

Evie put her head in her hands. 'I don't know,' she said. 'Now that it comes to the crunch . . .' Then she looked up. 'The fact is,' she said fiercely, 'I've been thinking that I'll be damned if I'll just let them take his place over and have it all their own way. Push the authors around, muck everything up, break it all up because they don't know anything about our market, or the people, or any bloody thing! I care too much about it to just walk off. Twenty years, Kate. Twenty years I've given to this company. Even if I could find another job just like that, and I suppose I could get something . . .'

'Oh, Evie, don't be ridiculous! Anyone would want you!'

'Be that as it may, and I'm not as confident about that as you are, I just can't do it. The company's been good to me. I'll stick around. I'll wait and see what Hale's like. Then I'll decide what to do. He might be OK. He might, mightn't he?' For the first time her voice faltered. Her eyes strayed to the memo on her desk.

'He might,' said Kate doubtfully. 'Maybe he will, Evie. I'll wait too. We'll wait and see. We'll all wait and see.'

The meeting was not going well for Evie. She felt it, and so did everyone else, but typically, thought Kate, not a glimmer of uncertainty crossed her face. She just hunched her shoulders, stared at the smooth, polished surface of the conference table, and doggedly went on.

Kate stole a look at Quentin Hale at the head of the table. He was leaning back in his chair, his plump fingers carefully pressed together, his broad, pink face politely interested. He's hearing her out, she thought. He's the new boss being courteous to a long-serving staff member, showing that he's not just a savage new broom. But he's making her feel dusty just the same—dusty and old hat. The last thing a publicity manager should feel.

She looked back at Evie's familiar figure. She didn't have to listen to the proposals for the public relations campaign to 'celebrate' the company's takeover and 'promote its vigorous new image', as Quentin had put it on arrival. Evie had discussed them with her weeks ago—the party for Berry and Michaels authors and staff and the rest of the publishing community as the centrepiece, the children's competition, the advertising campaign with the new company slogan, the uni versity prize in the founder's name—a steady, sensible campaign which would involve not too much expense. Nothing there to set the world on fire, but after all what would? It would all work, anyway, and it would succeed however ordinary it sounded. Evie's campaigns always did succeed. She hadn't been with Berry and Michaels for twenty years for nothing. She knew the place inside out and knew how to promote its mixed image of sober literary merit and sound commercial judgement. Everyone knew that.

But Quentin doesn't, thought Kate suddenly. He only arrived a month ago, and he'd never heard of Evie Newall till then. With new eyes she looked at the Evie that Quentin Hale was seeing—not a familiar, eccentric figure, part of the office furniture, veteran of many an all-night work binge, many a marathon office party, closest advisor for years of the flamboyant Brian Berry whose shoes Quentin was now filling.

He was seeing a short, dumpy, middle-aged woman, with a toneless voice and slightly truculent manner. Not very impressive, no doubt, to someone like him. In fact, it was hard to imagine someone like Evie ever inhabiting Quentin's office world before. Amy Phibes, the intensely groomed, even glamorous, blonde secretary at his elbow was more his sort of thing—the sort of office furniture he would see as befitting a go-ahead publishing house. He'd hired her a week after his arrival. No doubt her cool English efficiency made him feel at home. It made everyone else extremely uncomfortable.

Evie glanced at her notes, folded them and began winding up. Beside her, angelic and attentive, a slight flush on his downy cheek, her new assistant Malcolm Pool moved slightly, with a suggestion of restlessness, and ran a hand over his close-cropped hair. Kate watched him catch Quentin's eye for the briefest of moments, watched his eyebrows rise ever so slightly, heard him take a deep breath that was almost a sigh.

Disloyal little go-getter, she thought. He's making the most of this. Evie'll regret she ever agreed to take him on, if she doesn't already. We were all taken in by those sweet little-boy looks, and the big blue eyes. Oh, what idiots! You can smell the ambition on him. For sure he's read one of those poisonous books on office strategy and Getting On. He's got Hale well and truly bluffed.

'Thank you, Evie.' The man at the head of the table sat forward and smiled briefly. 'Well done. We're not quite there yet, I don't think, but I'm sure everyone at this table would agree that you've given us plenty of food for thought.'

Evie blinked at him. 'I considered . . .' she began.

'Now,' Quentin interrupted smoothly, holding up his hand to silence her with the smile never leaving his face, 'perhaps we can hear some ideas from some of the other people here.' He looked around. 'Could you take some notes, Amy?' The woman beside him nodded and crossed her elegant legs. Her pen hovered over the shorthand notebook, her pale green eyes flickered up to regard the room with a cool stare. They waited together.

A small ripple of panic washed around the table. This had always been Evie's project. Anyone who'd had anything to say had said it to Evie weeks ago and those ideas, if they were good ones, were already incorporated in the carefully and fully worked-out plan that had just been dismissed as 'food for thought'.

Kate looked at the blank and fearful faces around her, realised her own must be just as revealing, and tried to pull herself together. Out of the corner of her eyes she noticed Sylvia de Groot leaning forward, small and eager, eyes intense under the black fringe. For sure she was going to put forward yet again that loppy plan of hers about the doves and her local church choir dressed up as book jackets. The man would think they were parochial idiots.

'I think, Quentin, that Evie has really summed up most of our thoughts,' she said quickly, to forestall the impending catastrophe.

'Ah, yes, I see. Well. Very good.' He looked neither disappointed nor pleased. Amy made a couple o squiggles on her pad, and studied a fingernail.

'As it happens, though, you're not quite right, Kate, Quentin went on casually. 'I believe the newest member of the team has a few points to make. He tells me he's been thinking about the project in his own time. He nodded and smiled briefly at Malcolm Pool.

'Well, for goodness . . .' Evie spun round to glar at her assistant.

The cynosure of all eyes, Malcolm blinked with a false modesty that deceived no-one. He opened the bright yellow folder in front of him, and cleared his throat. His perfectly clean fingernails rested lightly on the table top.

'I haven't been with you all long, I know that,' he said. 'A month is no time at all. And I wouldn't dream of saying that I could offer to this discussion anything like the knowledge or experience of an Evie, or a Kate, or anyone who's been with Berry and Michaels since I was a kid in short pants.' He smiled around beguilingly. 'But, just as an exercise, because I know I've got so much to learn, I thought I'd put together a few ideas. As a newcomer I'm seeing things fresh, you see.'

Quentin nodded. 'Exactly. The fresh view. One of the reasons I hired you, Malcolm. New blood's never a bad thing. As, I hope, you'll all decide in my case.' He looked around and smiled, showing all his teeth.

'Fair enough,' muttered Evie. 'Let's hear it, then.' She gave Malcolm a sharp, appraising stare and settled back to listen, arms folded.

Malcolm raised his clear blue eyes. He spoke directly to Quentin Hale. 'As a newcomer, it seemed to me that quite a few things here are taken for granted.

'This marvellous old building, for instance. It's one of the oldest in the city, isn't it? What a place for a publishing house to operate from. It's a landmark. I thought the whole promotion should be centred here.'

'It's much too small, Malcolm,' said Evie impatiently. 'The reception rooms don't hold more than a couple of hundred. The place I've booked has space for . . .'

'I'm not talking about the party you suggested, Evie,' said Malcolm softly, turning to her. 'If I can just go on?' Evie shrugged.

'The party Evie has suggested,' Malcolm went on, to Quentin, 'is basically a party to which our authors and staff and people like literary agents are to be invited. And I'm sure a good time would be had by all. The thing is, what benefit do we gain from it?' He looked around enquiringly, wide-eyed.

'Surely the benefits are obvious!' snapped Kate, very irritated by his self-possession. 'It's a PR exercise—a good-will event.'

'Will the press be invited?'

'Of course they will—the book reviewers and so on. Evie told us all that. Features and social page people too, of course, but nothing much will come from that.'

Malcolm leaned forward. 'Why not?'

'Because,' Evie said in a bored voice, 'it'll be a bun-rush, and not necessarily all that glamorous. They might come, but they won't write much about it.'

'Well, what a wasted opportunity,' said Malcolm coolly. He brushed a speck of dirt from his cuff.

'I disagree!' barked Evie, very red in the face. 'The purpose . . .'

'Evie, I'd like to hear what Malcolm has to suggest,' said Quentin Hale calmly. He glanced at his watch. 'And I have an appointment at three.' He nodded to Malcolm, whose mouth tightened slightly to conceal his pleasure as he turned a page before continuing.

'All our authors are very wonderful people, but of course as far as the press is concerned, most of them are of marginal interest,' he said. 'There are exceptions, however, and of these, four are notable exceptions. And I think here again I've stumbled on something that's been taken for granted. The Big Four.'

He held up a photograph neatly mounted on cardboard, and laid it on the table. A fragile-looking woman, holding a single daisy between her fingers, smiled enigmatically up at them from the polished mahogany.

'Tilly Lightly,' he said with a proprietorial air, as though introducing this household name to them for the first time. 'The author and illustrator of our all-time best-selling children's book, *The Adventures of Paddy Kangaroo*. A modern classic, constantly reprinted in multiple editions for nearly twenty years, and the first in a string of Paddy stories, every one a great success—for her and for us.'

He placed a second photograph, mounted as the first, on the table. A romantic studio portrait of a sensitive-looking man with a gaunt face, silvery hair and what used to be called 'soulful' eyes. If you looked at the photograph too closely, you could almost see the lips tremble.

'Saul Murdoch, our most famous and distinguished novelist. Again, there would be few who hadn't heard of him, studied him at school, or whatever. Winner of every award you can think of, published internationally. A great name.'

'His royalty cheques aren't so great anymore,' muttered Sylvia de Groot, still a little miffed because her publicity plan hadn't been aired.

Ignoring the interruption, Malcolm laid his third picture down. Jolly Jack Sprott, the gardener's friend, twinkled gnomishly through the branches of a camellia in glorious flower.

'Half a million copies of Jack Sprott's *Gardener's Almanac* sold, ten other gardening books in print. Newspaper and magazine columns, a named range of gardening tools, fertilisers, sprays. By far our most outstanding practical author,' said Malcolm briskly, already reaching for his fourth and final offering. Keeping the pace going, thought Kate. She glanced at Quentin. He was still leaning back in his chair, hands behind his head, but his expression was approving. He liked Malcolm's style, obviously, and of course, to him, this information about the company's leading authors was relatively fresh and therefore, possibly, interesting.

'Of course you all know who's next and last,' Malcolm was saying. And of course all of them did, but all looked nevertheless with unwilling fascination at the photograph of the redoubtable Barbara Bendix, all eyes, cleavage and exotic jewellery.

'Our lady of the knife jobs,' smiled Malcolm Pool, resuscitating the old office joke and offering it to them as newborn.

Quentin laughed heartily.

'A relatively recent arrival to our stable, Ms Bendix, but a very valuable one,' Malcolm continued, tapping Barbara Bendix's image with a pink finger. 'In barely eight years she's become one of the most frequently quoted women in the country, all on the strength of three books—biographies, warts and all, unofficial biographies, of prominent people. Every one's been a sensation—major newspaper serialisation, huge bookclub sale, and massive hardback distribution. According to records I saw, her last book reprinted in hardback *four* times, and the paperback, I know, is still on the bestseller lists. Her wit is famous . . .'

'Her malice, you mean,' said Kate drily. 'She always writes about people after they're dead, and those books are really the most scandal-mongering, scurrilous . . .'

'Sell for us though, don't they?' Malcolm cut in brightly. Barbara Bendix might have been his personal invention.

'We're quite aware of her value, thanks, Malcolm,' snapped Evie. 'We ought to be. There's a huge advance out on her next book. Which she's spent, I might add, and not a chapter of the new thing have we seen! We don't even know what it's about!'

'I think she's got interested in someone who's alive and kicking,' said Kate. 'And she's been spending all her time on that, and now she's stuck because of libel, and can't deliver. She's . . .'

'Sure. Yes, of course.' Malcolm glanced at Kate placatingly. You could see that busy, disciplined mind under the short-clipped hair giving itself a little slap—you must remember to be more tactful, Malcolm!

'Let's get on, shall we?' said Quentin, rather crossly.

'Yes, ah . . .' Malcolm flushed slightly, spread the photographs on the table into a neat fan, and began again.

'The Big Four, as I've called them, have good news value because they're famous, and their books are very widely read. Evie told me the presence of three of them at our celebration is in fact not expected, because they live in different parts of the country—Tilly Lightly in Western Australia, Saul Murdoch down south in Victoria, Barbara Bendix up north in Queensland. Only Jack Sprott lives here in Sydney. Evie didn't seem too worried.

'But think of what we have here—a children's author, a novelist, a practical writer, a best-selling writer of popular non-fiction. They represent the four great strengths of the Berry and Michaels list. Furthermore they represent the country's North, South, East and West. And—two men, two women. See? In these four people, *all* our authors are represented!'

'What if,' he drummed his fingers on the photographs before him and leaned forward, his eyes very bright, 'what if we abandon the idea of a huge "bun fight", as Evie called it, and instead spend the money on bringing our Big Four together. Flying them in for three or four days of group interviews, seminars, book signings. They can stay here, on the prem ises in the apartments upstairs. Now we've tipped out *News & Views* magazine, they'll be alone on that floor. The four together would be some package to offer, especially if we do the thing in style—first class travel, hire cars to drive them round. Really give them the star treatment for once.

'We'll get press features and profiles, radio and TV, everything! And all focused on this building. The ABC have already been onto us, wanting to do a story on the takeover. They want to send a researcher here to the office for a few days. We'll say, sure, we've got nothing to hide, be our guests! And we'll time the researcher's visit to coincide with the Big Four promotion, and let them do some filming at the party. Not a huge affair everyone and his dog gets invited to, but a really elegant affair downstairs, with the Big Four as guests of honour.' He pressed his fingers together and leaned forward.

'In my opinion, the idea can't fail. Except for Barbara Bendix, none of the Big Four, would you believe it, has made any personal public appearances for at least five years!' He spread his hands, palms up, and made a little moue of non-comprehension. 'Maybe they've been taken for granted. I frankly find it hard to understand why they haven't been pushed and pushed again. But this fortunately works to our advantage now—people will be so curious they'll fight for tickets to that party, and for interviews. And the whole project, most important of all, will make it clear to everyone that there's new management now at Berry and Michaels. An energetic, go-ahead management that's determined to do things in style and promote, promote, promote!' He closed his folder and waited.

'Malcolm . . .' Evie began slowly.

'That's more like it!' Quentin leaned forward, ignoring her completely. 'That's the thinking that's going to drag this company into the twenty-first century, Malcolm. Bold, and simple, and eyecatching. That's good promotion. Good work!'

Malcolm flushed with pleasure.

'It can't be done, Quentin,' Evie was shaking her head. 'It just isn't . . .'

'Evie dear, for God's sake, we're all on the same team here I hope,' Quentin interrupted firmly. 'You had your say, and Malcolm simply had a better idea. That's all there is to it.'

'It all sounds terrific in theory, Quentin,' said Kate, glancing at Evie who was determinedly drawing lines on the pad in front of her. 'But unfortunately . . .'

'Kate, please don't be negative about this,' said Quentin seriously. 'Any details can be taken care of. I'm sure, in fact, that Malcolm's already thought them through. He's put a great deal of work and clever thinking into this plan of his, that's obvious, and I think he deserves all our support. He certainly has mine. We mustn't ever fall into the trap of rejecting fresh ideas just because they're new and different, Kate.'

'Quentin!' Evie's voice was ominously quiet.

He shook his head at her decisively and put his hand on Amy's arm.

'Get this written up as a minute, Amy, please. Malcolm will give you any details you missed. Copies to everyone present. I'm putting Malcolm in personal charge of the implementation of his plan. Evie will give him what assistance he needs. Some aspects of her original plan can be retained—the children's competition for example, and the scholarship, as long as they're tied in with the central idea. You give that some thought, Malcolm. I'll leave it to you. You'll have to get a move on. Ideally I'd like you to plan for no more than a month from today. Fast work, but you'll manage.'

He smiled briefly, placed his fingers on the table and rose. 'I'm sorry to break this up but, as I said, I have an appointment. Thank you all.' It was a very firm dismissal.

As she left the beautiful old room, the scene of so many boisterous, jokey meetings in the past, Kate looked back once. Malcolm, head bowed, was listening as Quentin made some final remarks to him in an undertone. Ah, how times had changed.

Evie hadn't waited for the lift, but had bolted straight down the stairs to her office, an untidy cubby hole on the first floor of the building. She had complained for years about its size, but somehow always found a reason not to move when a change of office was suggested.

Kate found her looking out her window, leaning

against the deep sill. Perhaps that green view of the park was the magnet that had held her in this small room for all these years.

Berry and Michaels was—had been—the centre of Evie's life. For years she'd handled its publicity with confident aplomb. Mondays to Fridays she bristled with energy and activity, teasing, cajoling, and bullying her contacts and her authors; endlessly on the phone, endlessly running from one appointment to the next. On Saturdays she shopped, did housework, read. And on Sundays she slipped quietly back to town, let herself into the silent old building, and peacefully dealt with her paperwork, while the shadows lengthened under the trees she could see through her windows.

It had been a life she relished. She had seen no reason why it should not continue forever—or at least until she chose otherwise. But in a few short weeks, everything had changed. Kate, hesitated at the door, saw how much it had changed. Evie's bowed shoulders had a defenceless look.

'Evie.'

'What?'

'You know what. Evie, you've got to tell them.'

'Why should I?'

'Evie, if you won't, I will. Quentin's got to know.'

'I tried to tell him. He shut me up. You tried to tell him. He shut *you* up. That's it, as far as I'm concerned. He and that little swine Pool can stew in their own juice.'

'We'll stew too, Evie. The whole company'll stew.'

'The company'll be OK. It's lived through plenty of disasters in its time. One more won't kill it. But what will kill it is the sort of thing we saw just then—a total lack of respect for experience, snap decisions, shallow thinking, sneaky one-upping, all that.'

'Evie, it all sounded very convincing. You can understand Quentin . . .'

'You can understand Quentin Hale listening and being impressed. It sounded good. Of course it did. But can you understand him refusing to let us comment, and putting a little twirp who's twenty-two, if that, and who's been here *two weeks* in charge of such an important event, and asking *me* to assist *him*?'

'I know, Evie, it's awful, but . . .' Kate touched her friend on the shoulder.

Evie whirled round to face her. Her eyes were puffy and red, her face blotched with uneven pink patches.

'Kate, you know and I know. With Brian gone and just about all the other old hands moved on or given up the heave-ho, we're the only ones here now who do. So you keep quiet. This is my responsibility, not yours.'

'Maybe they won't come,' said Kate hopefully.

Evie snorted. 'Of course they'll come! Not one of them could resist the star treatment. They'll welcome the opportunity anyway. They've always wanted more personal promotion than I gave them. They'll love it!" She laughed a little hysterically.

'Let them try their wings for once outside the gilded cage I've kept them in. They might find I wasn't so silly and boring after all. And won't our pretty boy scout Pool have his hands full. Tilly Lightly, anorexic whimsy queen, vain as a cat and bored to tears with her blasted kangaroo, meets face to face, after twenty years of mutual hatred, her ex-lover Saul Murdoch, now, by all reports, heading for his third nervous breakdown. Lovely stuff. Jolly Jack Sprott, Jolly Jack Drink-like-a-fish, ghost-written for years because by lunchtime he can't hold his trowel straight, will add to the fun. He should come up well in group seminars. I hope Malcolm organises a literary lunch.'

'Evie!'

'And of course not forgetting Barbara Bendix. She'll have a field day! Material for half a dozen nasty little short pieces about the other three to tide her over while she finishes the book. Oh, and she's so charming, too. So sweet and endearing. So compassionate. So refined. And all of them tucked up in the flats upstairs together. Malcolm couldn't have chosen better. Kate, I'm looking forward to this. I really am!'

'Evie, it'll be appalling. It'll be murder!'

'I wouldn't be a bit surprised!'

BANTAM MYSTERY COLLECTION